By the same author
Kiss Tomorrow Goodbye

A GOOD TIME TO DIE

JAMES TATHAM

PAN
Pan Macmillan Australia

First published in 1996 by Pan Macmillan Australia Pty Limited
St Martins Tower, 31 Market Street, Sydney

National Library of Australia
cataloguing-in-publication data:
Tatham, James.
A good time to die.
ISBN 0 330 35734 4.
I. Title.
A823.3

Printed in Australia by McPherson's Printing Group

In memory of Coral

1

IT WAS THE DOG THAT ALERTED US THAT SOMETHING WAS not quite right, not normal. He stood there, looking towards the east, growling deep in his throat. Then from over the brow of the hill the Bell Jet Ranger came screaming in towards us like a mechanical dragonfly. Bright explosive lights, followed by geysers of dirt, erupted around the yard.

'Get inside fast!' I jumped up and yelled at Carmel. Then backing into the shed behind me, I reached up and took down the Winchester from the wall rack. The helicopter seemed to stand on its tail for an instant as it hovered, then turned in a lazy circle over the centre of the yard, looking for us. I stood against the wall of the shed, watching it through the window, jacked a round into the chamber of the .308 and started to take a bead on the hovering craft . . . but the chopper suddenly shot forward and hovered over the shed, as if the pilot knew he was in danger where he'd just been.

T'crack! a shot rang out from overhead, and with a yelp Diefer, our Doberman, was knocked onto his side. He tried to clamber back up onto his feet, got halfway up, then collapsed again. With a growl he tried to rise again but couldn't. He just lay there, gave a whimper and started to tremble, struggling for breath. Then he gave a spasm, his legs went out rigid, jerking before he suddenly went limp, gave another whimper and was still.

'You dirty fuckin' bastards!' I screamed up at the roof of the shed, and fired three rounds through the iron roof hoping to hit the chopper. But my words and the noise of the shots were washed away, drowned out by the sound from the helicopter as the pilot took up the collective. It quickly gathered momentum and swooshed away into the west. The glare of the late afternoon sun made it impossible for me to get off another shot in retribution.

I ran quickly over to Diefer, but he was finished, there was nothing that anyone could do. The bullet had hit him high on his right shoulder and exited in a massive wound below his left hip.

My thoughts were suddenly torn away from Diefer's death as Carmel screamed from the house . . .

'What the shit's going on, Jimmy?'

'Stay down, love, for Christ's sake stay down.'

My thoughts started racing . . . There must be someone on the ground . . . That's why they took out the dog . . . But where the fuck were they? The only decent cover was the low hill a good 500 yards from the house. There was a warm breeze coming from the east . . . Did Diefer hear the chopper or had he smelt something in the air? One thing was certain. We had to get out and away from here and we had to do it fast.

I sprinted over to the house and stood on the verandah, keeping the gun ready and my eye on the hill.

'Get some things together, Carmel, shove them in a bag, just basics. And for Christ's sake do it bloody fast, love.'

'Why? Was that you shooting? What's wrong with Diefer?'

'I don't know,' I yelled at her. 'But Diefer's been shot.'

She started to sob as she crammed some of our personal things into a small overnight bag.

'Poor Diefer. It's not going to start again is it, Jimmy?' she cried. 'Tell me it's not going to start again?'

'I can't tell you anything, love . . . all I know is that it wasn't fuckin' Santa Claus up there and we're running out of time, and bloody fast.'

I kept watching the hill. My senses told me that the danger, if it came, would come from there. But all was quiet. A cloud of flies had descended on the dog. Shit! I thought, we're going to miss him. Carmel came out and stood beside me.

'I've got a few things,' she sobbed.

'Did you grab the money out of the snooker?'

'No, I forgot.' A moment later it was stashed in the overnight bag.

'Let's go.' I said.

We quickly crossed the yard and as we passed Diefer the flies rose with an angry hum. Carmel started to sob again.

'Poor Diefer . . . what did he do to anyone? Bloody bastards.'

'Bye old mate,' I whispered, and swallowed a lump in my throat. And thought someone is going to pay for this shit.

With Carmel aboard the Landcruiser I ducked back into the shed, grabbed some extra cartridges for the .308, a knife, machete, and an old army duffel bag that I hadn't opened since I'd put it there on our arrival at this wonderful spot . . . nearly two years ago.

I chucked the gear into the back of the Toyota, climbed in behind the wheel, fired up the engine and floored the gas pedal.

A hundred yards out from the house it came again with a banshee howl overhead. Carmel screamed as three shots crashed out. One of them went through the right front mudguard and the other two sent up spurts of dust ahead of us. The chopper roared over and past us and banked into a turn. I slammed on the brakes and grabbed the .308. We had only one chance in a million but it was better to take it than let these bastards, whoever they were, use us for target practice.

'Get on the floor,' I said to Carmel, emphasising it with quick pressure on her shoulder. Then throwing open the door, and using the vehicle as cover, I sighted on the chopper as it headed back towards us. The .308 bellowed and bucked into my shoulder. I chambered another round and fired again. The Jet Ranger seemed to waver and veered off to the left. 'Got you, you bastards!' I screamed as hydraulic fluid spewed out from just below the upper engine cowling. The chopper was limping off towards the east again. I drilled another round after it, then vaulted back behind the wheel and started for the trees.

In the outback of Queensland and the Northern Territory distances are vast. If you stop your vehicle, to take a piss for instance, as you listen there is only an ear-ringing silence and the buzzing of flies. It's always hot and there's scarcely any rain. Then, almost without warning, the wet hits. You'll have rain hosing down for weeks at a time. Creeks that have been empty for months, and dry for years in some cases, will have a tidal wave of water racing through them, break their banks and cause massive flooding.

Because of the great distances between places, there were no telephones back then and the only way people could keep in touch was by two-way radio. Children raised in these parts had to receive their education from radio broadcasts, and medical treatment and emergency hospital attention could only be obtained through the Flying Doctor Service.

I had always loved the Top End, from the very first encounter. The jungle, the bush, and the sense of meaning they gave me. I loved to listen to the night creatures as they sang their nocturnal arias. How could you leave this? I used to think to myself. How could I ever have slept with the roar of traffic in my ears?

Our camp was in a natural clearing, situated near a lagoon fed by a tidal stream that was hardly more than a muddy creek in the dry season. Further over to the west, the red soil plains stretched to the foot of Mount Stuart. From here it was only a silhouette, but distinctive as ever with its sheer sides and its knobbly top. I'd always meant to climb it, to clamber through the lower light scrub at the base onto the candy-bright buttresses that changed their colour every hour of the day. But I never had. Perhaps it was enough just to look.

It was this very remoteness, this total isolation, that attracted Carmel and me to this lonely and vast area. Away from the city and the crowds and the crime. To escape from a life that, through the quirks of fate, we had been forced to lead. A life I thought was over . . . We were contented here, happy with our lot and didn't have a care in the world. We'd never expected that soon it would all come crashing down around us and drive us on a journey through the corridors of Hell.

The attack had come on a hot and dry Friday afternoon, just as Carmel was bringing in a load of washing. I'd been giving our four-wheel drive a bit of a tune-up and service as we intended going into Borraloola the next day for some supplies.

I was having a smoke and a breather, sitting in the meagre shadow of the Toyota and squinting into the shimmering distance. Sweat coursed down my face in little rivulets, mixing with the red dust I'd picked up and stinging my eyes. I wiped my face with a grimy handkerchief that was already sodden and took another puff on my cigarette. The flat drone of insects emphasised the heat of the late afternoon. It was the hottest day so far this month, without a cloud to be seen. Just eagles, circling, watching, sign-writing up in the sky. Not that they were ever too far away to notice when something moved or died. I shifted slightly and an ant panicked among the hairs on my leg, jabbing me with its sting. I scratched it and continued with my smoke. It was at this point that the dog had started growling. Then the helicopter had come over the hill, and now we were on the run.

We both knew this neck of the woods pretty well, we'd explored it enough and I knew just the place to go. It was about fifty miles away to the north-east. I reached over and patted Carmel on the leg to give her some assurance, though Christ knew what it was.

'Hang in there, love,' I said. 'We'll be right. Jesus! I'm busting for a smoke.'

Carmel opened the bag on the floor in front of her and produced a packet of tobacco.

'Want me to make you one?' she asked in a little girl voice that I knew was caused by her fear.

'Bloody oath I do!'

We were in amongst the first of the trees and I was thankful for the cover. But I had to slow down and weave my way through. It wouldn't be long now before it became dark. That was something that would be in our favour, even if driving was more difficult. It was nerve-racking as we made our way along the twisting bumpy track, forced to alternate the use of the headlamps with the intermittent appearances of the moon. Overlying this was the ever-present thought of pursuit.

By the time we reached the area, five hours later, we were both nearing the point of exhaustion. We'd been here many times before, and I knew this place like the back of my hand.

The Top End rainforest at night isn't something you forget in a hurry. There are huge cycads, palm-like trees whose stiff, evergreen leaves grow in a cluster at the top of the trunk. There are ferns that resemble something out of the Jurassic period. Snakes, including pythons as thick as a man's leg, grow to enormous

7

length. Parrots and their cousins the lorikeets as gaudy as fruit salad and ice-cream desserts. Flying foxes and bats that flap and glide effortlessly through and among the upper branches of the trees, black and brown furred, with clawed wings. The song of the cicadas rises and falls as if guided by some unseen conductor's baton. Then there's the ever-present sound of running and dripping water, and the smell, like sweet compost, as if the very earth was in ferment. Occasionally there's the sound of a swirl in the tidal-fed billabong as a crocodile makes a lunge at a barramundi. But much as this place would be uncomfortable for some, it was a haven and home to us.

I realised the Landcruiser would have left tracks but I had a feeling that whoever had come to hit us would have a hard job following us in here at night. And God help them if they tried it during the day.

Carmel climbed into the back of the Toyota and went to sleep on top of the camping gear we always kept there. I couldn't sleep and sat in the dark like some outpost sentry guarding the perimeter, and my girl. I became oblivious to the mosquitoes and let my thoughts try to solve the problem we now faced. The first thought that jumped to mind was that it couldn't be the police. Even they would use a more subtle approach than the one we'd just been through. It had to be something out of the past . . . but who would know where we were? This was the starting point. There would only be one person from that past, possibly two or three, with any idea of our location, and then only a general idea. But to those who knew how to hunt and find people, it might just be enough. Like a hunter quartering the track for spoor but on a larger scale. And whoever that hunter was I was going to find out one fucking way or another.

2

HIGH IN THE SKY, AN EAGLE HAD AN UNEQUALLED VIEW OF the ground below as it drifted lazily on the ebbing thermals of the mid-morning air. An endless crazily indented terrain of mangrove swamps, tidal creeks and the big lagoon was almost lost among the silvery veins of rivers and creeks that penetrated this part of the land. And away in the far distance above the horizon, vast tropical cloud shapes loomed which would turn to rain by the late afternoon.

My view was confined to the muddy creek which fed the billabong, smothered by the oozing shoals of mangroves and clouds of black saltwater mosquitoes that rose about me as I walked around the edge. Slapping and cursing at these biting parasites, I stopped and looked at a swirl as a barramundi chased a small green frog. The air was hot and heavy, with the faint breeze of the dawn now lost among the winding creeks and swamp.

As I threaded my way steadily through the tangled vegetation, my eyes were gritty, and red-rimmed with tiredness. I hadn't had much sleep these last few nights, forced as I was to stay alert and remain on guard.

I watched the eagle descending as it made a broad leisurely lower circuit of inspection, and as I turned a bend it dropped and settled somewhere out of sight. I walked onto a sand spit and edged forward a little, watching the shallows for signs of fish. Eyes taking in the water, I instinctively noted the details of the bush about me . . . including the signs of a crocodile slide on a mud bank just twenty feet away, where its broad slithering tracks crawled up to a shelf of salt hardened earth. And the patch leading down to the tidal creek on a further spit where I'd crashed the four-wheel drive through, just the other day, to make a new path.

I loved this place, and the one we'd just fled from. A vision of it flashed before my eyes. An old tropical green and white painted farmhouse, smoke drifting lazily from the chimney, and a garden with a patch of mango trees. Out the back, the shed, with everything in place, the Toyota in the lean-to, and the big lagoon sitting 500 yards away from the front porch.

Over the last few days I had dwelt practically alone in the prison of my own discipline. Driven by guilt and outrage, I had devoted nearly every moment to mind-conditioning and exercise. Repeatedly I had turned away Carmel's efforts to divert me from my narrow focus. I'd been intensely sullen and totally uncommunicative, repeatedly driving myself on in mind and body to the limits of my endurance . . . to equip myself for what I knew lay ahead.

We'd spent four days at this spot now, and even though I went scouting the whole perimeter, I could find no sign of anyone other than us. But the canned goods we'd kept in the back of the cruiser were depleted, so it was time to move on. I was ready now, ready to take on the hunt for our attackers. If I didn't, we'd never have peace of mind.

Another problem I had was to find a safe place for Carmel. A haven. Not only would it be far too dangerous for her to tag along, but she wasn't mentally equipped to handle this sort of shit. She'd only make the job more difficult than it already was.

Five days later, and travelling only at night, we arrived in Brisbane. Carmel had continued to correspond with Pamela Small, whom we'd met in Darwin at the time of Cyclone Tracey. She was the wife of a crazy preacher, a puritan ratbag Calvinist whom she'd now left, thank Christ.

It was around seven in the morning when we rang the bell at her Chermside house and after a tearful reunion between the two girls we were ushered in with a thousand bloody questions.

There was an old unused garage at the back and I stashed the Landcruiser in it. From the old duffel bag I took out a 9 mm Walther in a greased rag inside a plastic bag. I cleaned it off, ejected the magazine, worked the action and dry fired it. Satisfied that it was smooth, I removed the shells from the clip, replaced them from a box of ammo in the bag, then dropped a handful of loose rounds into the pocket of my jacket.

After a long private talk with Carmel and a farewell to Pamela, who assured me that Carmel could stay as long as she liked, I left.

I had a gut feeling that the problem I had must have started in Sydney. I can't explain why I felt this way but I did. But I also had an ace up my sleeve in Sydney.

There was a person there I knew I could trust. Not from my days with the *Famiglia*, but from my time in the army and Vietnam. This person was also in the know in the right places and if something was happening, or there was even just a whisper of it, then he could check it out.

It was 9 a.m. when the plane touched down at Mascot. I booked into a motel, had a couple of stiff drinks from the mini-bar and then rang my old friend Percy Grainger.

The phone rang for a while, then an answering machine cut in with . . .

'Hi! You've done all this before, so on the tone . . . just leave a number and I'll get right back to you as soon as possible. Have a nice day.'

'Jimmy D here. What fucks, winks and fights like a tiger?' I asked the machine. It was our old Special Operations Group code. 'Look I can't leave a number, mate, things are a bit shitty for that, but I'll be at the old haunt at Bondi at 1 p.m. and I'll wait an hour. See ya, son.' And hung up.

Then I rang a cab and had it head out to Bondi, so I could kill some time and check the place out.

Some Sydney suburbs wake up in the morning like a seventeen-year-old in a satin-sheeted bed, being caressed by the rosy red fingers of dawn.

In comparison, Bondi beach in the morning is a drunk, with a bottle clasped to his chest like a glass teddy bear . . . a wino who wakes up in a doorway with someone's boot in his ribs, usually a copper's, telling him to 'piss off'.

13

As I walked down Campbell Parade I found the Lamrock Cafe open and ordered cappuccino. The coffee was strong and fresh, so I had another. The night was over now and the nightmares were gone too. And the sun was shining over the ocean and beach with a light that most painters had never dreamed of . . . or even knew existed for that matter.

A garbage truck growled its way around the corner and pulled up out front, giving off a stench of the weekend's prawn shells, the carcases of lobsters and an assortment of rotten gasses.

Bondi would make a fascinating tapestry. Curving its way along the eastern suburban shores of Sydney, it is the nearest beach to the city, and the handiest. Every weekend a mass migration of humanity pours down to it by public transport, private car or on foot. Everything and everybody seems to pause for an instant at the top of the hill to take one famished, greedy look at the sugar-white sand that stretches for over a mile, the concrete esplanade, and the sloping lawns that sweep their way up to the main street and the shops that line it. Then like a pack of barracudas nosing into a reef at high tide, they charge down to quell their appetites, their fancies, and their lusts.

For the whole weekend, Bondi beach will teem with the well-dressed, the well-heeled, the well-tanned and the well-hung. The residents who live here retreat into their homes, taking with them frozen pizza and easy-to-prepare meals, a couple of cartons of their favourite booze. Behind locked doors they turn on their stereos and TVs, or jack a movie into the VCR, then sit back and await the sanity that Monday will return to them.

14

Of course, it wouldn't be entirely accurate to say that all the locals hide. The business community think the weekend's their best time. Summer clothes and suntan lotions are sold by the thousands, along with postcards, and fast foods of all descriptions. And all the cafes and coffee shops are full to overflowing.

But there is also a dark and seamy side to Bondi beach, where a different kind of economy prospers. In the labyrinth of narrow streets behind the main drag, purses and wallets are snatched and stolen, pockets of the unwary are plucked clean, drunks are rolled. Cars will have their stereos stolen and their glove boxes broken into for anything of value. In the lanes of the crumbling red-brick and white plaster blocks of apartment buildings and flats, heroin, Buddha sticks, grass, hash oil, coke, crack and ecstasy change hands, along with a varied assortment of pills.

Pick up anything or anybody at Bondi beach and you'll find a price tag stuck to it. Prostitutes, professional and amateur alike, male and female, are never short of work. Like mannequins in a shop window display, some even use the beach. By mid-morning the southernmost end is packed and customers are cruising through a giant supermarket of oiled and baking human flesh for sale.

It would appear that a day beneath the sun on Bondi beach turns everything and everyone on heat. You can introduce yourself to a sheila while setting up your deckchair or simply spreading your towel, strike up a conversation with the offer of a cold drink at ten, and by midday you're whispering bullshit over lunch.

But as the sun goes down, flesh starts to erect, with the aid of probing tongues, hot hands and sticky fingers. Then, as if by magic, salt- and sand-encrusted clothing peels away like skin from a banana. An hour later, as the moon begins to glow, the darker parts of the beach begin to move and swell. Silhouettes merge, then change shape and dimension, to finally separate back into their original forms with a groan or a sigh. Bondi beach, the place where anything goes . . . and everybody comes.

By the early hours of Monday this wave of humanity has reluctantly left the beach. The high rollers, who have had the best of the pickings, have left the earliest, leaving the dregs for the scavengers and the less fortunate, who browse on the debris that has been left behind, still hopeful for the promise of love. And the cafes all yawn open and empty with a lingering smell of cooking oil, fried onions and lost souls.

The sun was well up now as I sat drinking my coffee and gazing at the water, as it changed gradually from a bright blue to a uric and manure-tinted green. The yellow which changed the blue to a dirty green was mainly due to the first rich flow of effluent being pumped up half a mile offshore, where a line of pipes on the sea bed empties Sydney's bowels and bladders into the incoming tide.

Yes, this was the famous Bondi beach.

3

I HAD A FEW HOURS TO KILL, SO I CAUGHT A CAB TO THE junction and got a few more clothes. Then I went to the old haunt that Percy and I once used, the Hotel Bondi. It's a corner pub with some stucco on the outside walls. Inside, the carpets hadn't been changed for years and were worn and scorched in places. The bar smelt of beer and stale cigarette smoke. The shithouse smelt of urine and vomit and the mirrors had a greasy film on them. The towelling on the bar was threadbare in places and was already beer-soaked and ashy at midday. There were plenty of drinkers present, and even with the windows opened the air was heavy and kind of malty. The whole place had a surly and masculine smell to it.

I got a beer and steered myself into a corner where I could see everyone in the bar, and everyone who came in the door.

True to form, Percy arrived ten minutes early. He walked up to the bar, got a drink, then looking around he spotted me in the corner, lifted his glass in a lazy salute and ambled over.

When he was close enough he leant toward me.

'Long time no see, old son,' he said in a conspiratorial whisper, 'but what the fuck are ya doin' in Sydney?

17

You're worth big bucks, my man.'

'Listen, Perce, I'm here because I want to know what the fuck's goin' on.'

'You mean to say you don't know? Come off the grass, Jimmy, you're a bit smarter than that. Even the fuckin' coppers know about the contract.'

'What fuckin' contract, Percy? Cut all this shit out will ya? Just cut out all the melodramatics and fuckin' well enlighten me.'

'Jesus! You really don't know do you? It goes back to when you were thick with Paolo and you whacked Raffaele Vitelli. Remember? He became an embarrassment when he went to the *Famiglia* for help after he'd murdered his fiancee when she'd jilted him. Her old man was Agostini's godfather.'

I nodded my head in acknowledgement.

'Well, the problem is that Vitelli's brother is in the chair now. He's the fuckin' *capo di tutti* and he's lookin' for vendetta. It's *Famiglia*.'

'Where's Paolo? He wouldn't be puttin' up with this shit.'

'Up in Brisbane, Jimmy. Carlo had a fuckin' heart attack. He recovered but he's gone back home to Sicily to take it easy. Paolo hates Vitelli's guts, so the story goes, and two months ago there was nearly a Family war.'

'Jesus, Percy. How come you didn't get some word to me?'

'Christ almighty, mate, I didn't even know where you were, but I can tell you this now. It's gonna get a lot worse before it gets better. There's also this homicide jack in Brisbane who's got a thing about unsolved murders. He's got unsolved files three feet deep in his fuckin' office, he's clever like a fox, and he plays real hard and dirty. So watch your arse, boy.'

'Look, let's just tackle one thing at a time. Who do you know in the Vitelli camp that we could set up a meeting with?'

'Frangi,' Percy said with a whisper.

'What! Joey "Fingers" Frangiani? Christ almighty, Percy! He's a fuckin' loose cannon, he doesn't play with a full deck.'

'He's all we've got, old son, and he owes me a small favour that I have yet to call in. It's not like he's a *capo supremo*, all he's in charge of is the fuckin' escort and sex side of things. But he does spend a fair bit of time with Vitelli.'

'Look, try and set up a meet with him but don't mention my name. I'll just kind of run into you while you're with him. Can do?'

'Sure, I'll give it a go. Give me a bell tomorrow on this number,' he handed me a card, 'and I'll tell you where and when. That is, of course, if I can get the bastard to the table. Okay?'

'Make it daytime, Percy. That way I'll be able to see who's around.'

'Right, old son, hear from you tomorrow, and keep your fuckin' head down.'

We shook hands and he left. I picked up my shopping bags and hailed a cab to the city, then hired another to the motel, checking to see I wasn't followed.

I spent a good deal of the night thinking about Vitelli. And I remembered Paolo's words to me back

19

then . . . when Raffaele was causing trouble. 'This has to be taken care of real quick, *paisan*, I don't trust him. Every cop in the country is looking for him. And the cocksucker has insulted my family. Still, he comes to me for help. He was told to stay away and cool down. Does he do that? No, he's got to gun his fiancee down in broad daylight . . . with a hundred fucking witnesses. We don't make war on our womenfolk. He has to disappear, Jimmy, and fast. *Capisce?*'

My mind flashed to the evening when I picked him up from the rathole he was hiding in at Redfern. Knocking on the door and seeing his frightened nervous face as he opened it and let me in.

'Hi, Rafe,' I said. 'How's it goin'?'

'Heesa gonna helpa me?'

'Sure, mate, that's why I'm here. But we've got to get you out of the fuckin' city. The whole fuckin' police force is lookin' for you. I've got a car outside and when you get in it you get on the floor in the back. *Capisce?*'

'*Si. Grazie amico.*'

'*Prego*,' I said to him.

On the drive to Frenchs Forest, he wants to sit up and look at the fuckin' scenery. Me telling him to stay down. Into the park the look of surprise on his face when he finally gets out of the car and I give him the *beche de morte* (the kiss of death) . . . He's on his knees pleading with me. The gun in my hand fires, he falls to one side but I put two more rounds into his head to make good and certain. I seemed to dig all night. Sweat pouring off me. The body dropping into the hole with a meaty squelch. Taking the shovel and picking up the bloodied soil and grass and stuff where he's bled all over the fuckin' ground and throwing it in on top of him. Can't leave any sign . . . And the drive back after, the cool breeze blowing through the window and drying my sweat-soaked clothing and body. The sound of the car on the road as I drive gradually drowning out his pleas for clemency.

The night went slowly and I drank a good bit of the mini-bar. At three in the morning I finally got a bit of sleep.

I woke five hours later and settled for a cup of instant coffee compliments of the motel. Showered and dressed and read the morning paper. At nine I rang Percy. He was quick and to the point.

'Know Doyle's place on the wharf at Watsons Bay?'

'I'll find it.'

'I'm meeting with him there at midday.' And he hung up.

I memorised the number on the card he had given me, embossed with the federal coat of arms, then burnt it in the ashtray. Then I decided to get there a little early . . . get a good look at the lay of the place in case the worst came to the worst. I took the Walther out, field stripped and cleaned it on a motel towel, and removed the excess grease. Reassembled it and dry fired it. Wiped each round of ammunition before thumbing it into the magazine. Loaded up, I tried the gun in a couple of places but, being compact, it seemed to go best in the inside pocket of my leather jacket.

I advised the desk that I would be staying another night, then caught a cab into the city. Even though Percy had given me a warning about some hotshot bent copper, I wasn't really that concerned. The police didn't have a picture of me on record so I would be just one of a crowd of people on a day out.

I spent an hour or so prowling through the Museum, looking at things from the past. Thinking that each and every one of us carries his own personal museum of memories, some good, some bad, and some best forgotten.

It was just after eleven when I caught another cab. 'The wharf at Watsons Bay,' I said as I climbed in.

'Gotcha, mate.' He whipped the cab around in a screeching U-turn. 'Bit cool today, looks like more rain,' the driver said as he weaved his way through the traffic.

I had a rare breed here, as far as Sydney cabbies go. He could understand English, and he didn't have to ask me for directions.

4

I STROLLED ALONG THE PIER, TAKING IT ALL IN. WATSONS Bay is tucked away on the inside of the large southern headland that stands guard at the entrance to Sydney Harbour. There's a big park with huge pine trees and Moreton Bay figs that gradually slopes down to a small beach and jetty. Doyle's is on the wharf itself, and as I walked along I paid particular attention to the handful of amateur fishermen who were sitting there with dangling lines, hoping to land a catch. A cold drizzle started as I watched and one or two of the fishermen pulled in their lines hurriedly and headed for cover. Half a mile away, on the ocean side, huge waves smashed against the cliffs at South Head and the water in close was pewter coloured; it looked miserable, grey and cold.

I walked into the restaurant and took a table towards the back where the light wasn't so bright and ordered the day's special—rock lobster—and a carafe of the house wine. I was just finishing the last of the wine and enjoying a cigarette when Percy and Joey Fingers walked in. Percy didn't even look to see if I was there, he just steered Frangiani to a table alongside two old sheilas who were nibbling on a seafood platter.

Frangiani's back was towards me and he and Percy

appeared to be discussing what to eat. After they'd given their order to the waitress, Percy gave a casual glance around, caught my eye for a fraction of a second and gave me a look that said all was clear.

I waited till their meal had arrived and then casually strolled over. Standing behind Fingers, I put my hand on his shoulder and put a bit of pressure on.

'Well, well, look who's here,' I said. 'How's it goin', Joe? You still stickin' it up those cocksuckers you call female escorts?'

The two old sheilas at the next table stopped eating and looked up at me at the same time, their mouths agape in disbelief. One of them appeared to be on the verge of apoplexy. Joey looked up over his shoulder and a shocked look jumped into his eyes.

'You son of a bitch,' he hissed at me, 'What you do a here? Gino's a gonna to cut your heart out.'

'Bullshit, Joey, you and fuckin' Gino will be glad to suck my cock before I'm finished.'

'What!' cried Joey. His black eyebrows arched and his hand started to reach behind his jacket.

'You move one more inch Joey and you're fuckin' dead where you sit,' I said, lowering my head and talking coldly into his ear.

He put his hands back flat on the table and gave a sigh of resignation. 'Okay,' he said. 'What you want from me?'

'I want you to go to Vitelli and tell him I'm coming after him, you got it?'

'*Si. Capisce.*'

'And if you give me any more shit, Joey, I'll come after you.'

24

'Okay, okay, I tell him.'

'That's the stuff, Joey. Now just be a good boy and forget all about the knife under your coat and fuck off.'

Frangiani's eyes looked lovingly at the mound of king prawns, crab, lobster, calamari and oysters, but he stood up and started to walk away then stopped and said in a voice that the whole bloody place could hear . . .

'You'll stay out of my fucking life if you know what's good for you.'

One of the old sheilas at the next table dropped a fork with a clatter and gasped for air.

'I hope to stay as far away from you as possible, you fuckin' *mezzano*.'

'Don't call me a pimp,' he yelled.

'I'll call you any fuckin' thing I like, Joey, but as to what's good for me, I'll be the judge of that. Now *fila! Capisce*?'

I watched Frangiani reluctantly walk out and along the wharf in silent fury until he disappeared into the network of beach-front shops towards the hotel. Then I walked back to the table.

'Thanks, Percy, I'm on my way. Enjoy the meal.'

Percy just gave a nod and picked up a prawn.

As I left the wharf and caught a cab, I could well imagine what Joey Fingers would be doing, he'd be on the phone to Gino Vitelli. With these kind of bastards after me the last thing I wanted was to let them think that it was going to be all their own way. But there would still be those around who knew that if they wanted to fuck with me, they'd better kiss me first.

Two things concerned me now. The first was that I was going to need help if I was to take the war to Vitelli. The second thing was I was going to need money—and a lot of it—to get that help. Mobility was the thing. When you're hot, keep moving, and that takes money. I had one other contact in Sydney I knew I could rely on for what I had in mind, and he was another old army pal . . . Jack Coleman.

5

JACKO AND I HAD BEEN IN THE ARMY TOGETHER, AND ON his discharge I had thrown some easy and quick money his way when I worked for the Bellari Family in Brisbane. Jack could take care of himself in a tight spot and he was an absolute ace when it came to explosives and weaponry. I had no idea where he might be at the moment, but his mother lived in Petersham, her name was Violet, and Jack always kept in touch. Even in Vietnam he wrote constantly to her.

So I phoned Violet Coleman, told her I was an old friend of Jack's from Vietnam and I wondered if I could get in touch with him for old time's sake.

'Oh, yes,' she said, 'I think I've heard him mention you . . . But he doesn't live here, he's up at Kings Cross. I could let you have his number.'

'That'd be great, Mrs Coleman, thanks a lot.'

'Hang on, I've got it written here.' There was a pause while she put on her glasses and read it out to me.

'Thanks a lot,' I told her.

'Yes, well don't you two be getting into any mischief now,' she said with a chuckle.

'Okay. Bye, Mrs Coleman.'

Shit, maybe things would start to improve now. If I could get help from Jack we'd really begin to kick arse.

27

I rang his number and a woman's voice came on the line . . .

'Hello . . .?'

'I'd like to talk to Jack please.'

'Hang on.' I heard her calling out something.

'Jack Coleman,' a voice said after a while. It was Jack all right.

'Hi, Jacko. It's Jimmy Diamond.'

'Jesus Christ, Jimmy, how are ya son? Where the fuck have ya been?'

'I'd like to have a talk to you, but not over the phone, mate.'

'Sure old son . . . Look, what do you want to do?'

'How about if I meet you at the Rex in half an hour?'

'Sure, Jimmy. But I'm just about broke, mate.'

'Don't worry. I've got more than enough for what we'll need.'

'Righto old son, see ya in half an hour.'

The cab climbed up William Street to Kings Cross, the three lanes heading up the hill all thick with traffic. Most visitors to the Cross are older teenagers from the suburbs and they go there either to get drunk, try some new drug or get a brief sniff of vice. Not many have the guts, or the money for that matter, to get it off with one of the girls for sale or to take in a strip show. They just listen to the barkers and the spruikers and try to sneak a look past the curtained doorways. They check out one of the sex shops and indulge in a few expensive minutes of a porn peepshow movie. And one or two of the less faint-hearted get half-pissed then get a tattoo, so when they go back to their neighbourhoods they can boast about it. 'Yair, I got it done up the Cross.'

The place never changes.

At this time of the day there were not so many hookers on Bayswater Road. Most of them were gone with the night, but there were still a couple about and an ambitious one in a black spangled mini skirt made a move towards the cab as we were held up for a minute. A sheila with a heavy drug habit needs to turn ten tricks a day seven bloody days of the week just to feed that habit. The one in the spangles looked as though she was a couple short on her quota.

The cabbie dropped me in front of the Rex just as Jacko was walking towards it. I paid the cab and yelled out across the street.

'Hey! What fucks, winks, and fights like a tiger?'

Jacko's head snapped around. 'Well I'll be fucked,' he bellowed out. 'Jimmy, ya old cunt, how's it goin', son?'

He threw his head both ways, checking the traffic, then sprinted across the street and we embraced.

'Good to see ya, Jacko, feel like a cold one?'

'Thought you'd never ask, mate,' he said with a chuckle.

We made our way into the saloon bar, ordered a couple of schooners, then went over to a corner table.

'What are ya up to these days, Jacko? Working or anything?'

'Christ no, mate, I'm on the fuckin' dole, believe it or not. I'm sharin' a place with a couple of sheilas. I could go home to mum's but . . . well, I've got to be

29

where the action is. Why? Have you got somethin' in mind?'

Over the next twenty minutes I explained all to Jacko and in the end I said to him . . .

'Well what do you reckon . . . are you on board?'

'Fuckin' oath, mate, I'm in, but where's the money gonna come from?'

'We'll have to take a bank, Jacko . . . still in?'

'Listen, the way my life's been goin' over the last six months Long Bay couldn't be any worse. I'm in.' He shoved his hand across the table.

'From now on, Jacko, we'll have to run a pretty tight operation . . . you get the picture . . . we're going to have to watch each other's backs until this thing's finished.'

'Christ, Jimmy, compared to the Cong and the NVA these cunts are fuckin' pussycats.'

'Be that as it may, old son, they've got a lot of pull in some very high places, not to mention fuckin' bent coppers on the payroll.'

'Righto, well what do we do from here?'

'Here's fifty bucks,' I said, handing him some money. 'Get your things, just the basics, and come over to my motel. We're going to have to stick like glue. Okay?'

He downed his beer. 'Righto,' he said and stood up. 'I'm on my way.'

I shook his hand, looked him in the eye and said, 'There's no turning back now, mate, let's get it on.'

'I'll be there.'

Jacko left the pub and I strolled along the street on the opposite side, watching his back as he walked up the street. I stopped in front of one of the strip joints. The spruiker wore practically the same gear as the ones who'd done it in my time up here. He was stereotyped for the job, in his late twenties, with the hard tough face of an all-in brawler but trying hard to look sophisticated.

'Show's just about to start, mate, lots of lovely ladies.'

I took a look at my watch. 'They never used to be open at this time in my days up here.'

'Yeah?' He looked past me up the street, his eyes becoming more alert.

The club doormen are also the club cockatoos. In his eyes, I could be setting the place up for a raid by the vice squad, or about to have a go for the box office takings.

As I looked at him I suddenly realised how he got that face. He was not quite quick enough. He'd been suckered in with a low left feint to his rib area and as his eyes dropped . . . a big right hand out of nowhere had exploded like a bomb and put him away.

Behind him the steps to the club climbed up and faded into darkness, the carpet worn and threadbare from thousands of feet. The steady thump thump of a bass drum and the blare of supposedly exotic music drifted down from above.

'See ya later, mate,' I said.

Jacko was almost out of sight by this time, but no-one was even remotely interested in him. I walked back inside the pub to call a cab. When you're in the position that I was, you don't hang around the bloody streets to flag one down. And on the trip back to the motel I couldn't help but think that fuckin' Gino was in for one hell of a surprise. By the time Jacko and I got through with him he wasn't going to know if his arse was bored or sleeved.

6

JACKO MET ME AT THE MOTEL INSIDE THE HOUR. WE SAT down, had a drink and started planning. One thing we had to do was to keep moving until we could get something that we could defend. The next day we got a car. Cabs were no good for what we had in mind.

Over the next week we moved around from place to place and during the day we cased the bank we were going to knock off. It was a National at Burwood. There was a cafe across the street which we used as an observation post as we monitored deliveries, security, and police presence in the area.

The bank was a plate glass and aluminium affair with concrete besser blocks for the outside walls. Like all the new bank buildings there was only one front entrance, and that was a glass door. A night safe was built into the front wall, and venetian blinds covered the front windows to shield the place from the afternoon sun.

But it didn't look quite right for what I had in mind. To go charging in the front, maybe all right . . . but that'd only give us the cash from the tellers' cages and we needed more than that. Even once we were inside, and supposing we could get behind the counters, there was still no guarantee we could get to the strongroom or the safes. And it would take time and patience to get any sort of cooperation from a frightened and nervous staff. Someone might just panic and punch the alarm button. Not only that, but if the vault or the safes were on any sort of time-delay locks and someone locked them at the first sign of trouble, then we could kiss the job goodbye. It would all be over and for sweet fuck all.

It was on our third visit to the cafe that a thought struck me.

'You wait here and hold the fort, son, I've got to have a look inside that fuckin' bank.'

Jacko gave me a nod, sipped at his coffee and turned back to the magazine he was reading. I ambled across to the bank, walked in through the front door and looked around. There were about six customers. As I was waiting I casually moved until I got a glimpse of the strongroom, which was down a short wide hall. It had a pretty impressive locking system, including time locks. A corridor went down the side of the glassed-in offices towards the rear of the building, where there was another door. What the fuck was on the other side of that? When my time came I went up to one of the teller's windows, gave her a fifty dollar note and asked her to change it for me.

I left the bank, walked towards the corner of the building and down a side lane. A bus bellowed away from the stop just up the street, and I could smell something cooking . . . onions and meat . . . it must be coming from some upstairs flats. I let my eyes sweep up and over them for a moment.

There was not a single door or window in the side

wall of the bank. I walked down the lane, came to a small courtyard carpark and, lo and behold, there was my door! One look and I knew it would be steel-backed. There were also two small heavily barred windows with frosted glass panes and I presumed that they would be the staff toilets.

I ambled into the little parking area. One space was taken up by a big steel industrial rubbish container and there wasn't room for more than two other vehicles. But there was a car parked there and a stencilled sign on the wall in front of it. MANAGER ONLY. 'That's the money, honey,' I said under my breath and strolled back to the cafe.

'Come up with anything?' Jacko asked.

'Sure did, old son. I think that this is going to be a piece of piss. I think I've found the Achilles heel. Let's go.'

Over the next two days we timed the manager on his arrival. We knew his car and the number so there was no mistake. He arrived first and entered through the back door, then let the others in through the front when they arrived. We got balaclavas from two different places, then Jacko got hold of a sawn-off auto Mossburg shotgun and a .38 revolver that a mate of his was holding. We went over the plan a few times and did a sort of a dry run, to become familiar with the streets.

The next thing we needed was a getaway car. We got one of these easily enough from the long-term parking area at the airport. That night we tailed the manager back to his home, which was also in Burwood. We were now ready. It was all systems go for the morning.

That night Jacko and I had a bit of a celebration meal, as he called it.

'We'd better have a fuckin' good feed, mate, just in case something goes wrong.'

It was 7.45a.m. when we parked the car half a block from the manager's home. We walked down the street and turned into a lane that ran along his back fence. Scaling it quickly, we pulled on the balaclavas and walked up to the back door, which was open. Only a screen door stood between us and him and even this wasn't locked.

I quietly opened the flywire door, which led to a laundry. We went through quickly and found ourselves in the kitchen. And there he was, sitting at the table having tea and toast. He almost fell off the chair when he saw us.

'Who the hell are you?' he spluttered, half-rising from his chair, choking on a piece of toast. 'What the hell do you want?'

'Just sit down and shut up,' I said, pointing the .38 at him.

He sat down quickly, his eyes afraid and flicking back and forth between us.

'You on your own here?' I snapped.

'No, no my wife is in bed, she's not well, please don't hurt her.'

'Check it out,' I said to Jacko.

Jacko walked up a hall and a moment later a woman's short cry of alarm sounded.

'All under control, son,' Jacko called.

'What's your name?' I asked the manager.

'Harvey . . . John Harvey.'

36

'Right, John, let me tell you how this thing works. Nobody needs to get hurt unless you try some crazy fuckin' half-arsed hero shit. Get the message?'

He just gulped and nodded his head.

'You and I are going to your bank. In a few minutes you will take me there in your bloody car. You will let the staff in as you usually do and they will be secured. When that's done we'll wait for the time locks to open and I will then load up your car with the bank's money. My mate is going to stay here at the house. If he doesn't hear from me from the bank, your missus has had it. Now there's no reason in the fuckin' world why this operation shouldn't run smooth and easy. We don't want to hurt anybody . . . but if you force our hand some bastard is definitely going to get hurt and hurt bad. The bank carries insurance so there shouldn't be any fuckin' need for you or your staff to end up with your fuckin' heads blown off trying to be a hero . . . You got it so far?'

He nodded his head and I thought he was going to burst into tears, but he swallowed and said 'Yes.'

Jacko came back into the room with a roll of surgical tape in his hand.

'All safe and secure, son,' he said. 'She's not going anywhere.'

'Good. You got the number of the bank?'

'Sure have.'

'Just to let John here know that we're not playing silly cunts, tell him the number will you.'

'Sure, 448 1306, and I'll ring it fifteen minutes after you leave. If I don't hear from you at the other end . . . his old bird gets the treatment.'

37

'You get all that, John? Let me tell you one more time . . . no fuckin' heroics . . . and no one gets hurt. Got it?'

'Yes,' he stammered, 'just don't hurt my wife. I'll do what you want.'

The ride to the bank passed without incident. He was driving and I was on the floor in the back, with the .38 giving his ribs a tickle around the seat. It was a little after eight-twenty when we pulled into the small parking lot.

'Stay where you are for a minute,' I said to Harvey, and I slipped out of the car and had a peek around the corner of the big industrial bin. The shopkeepers across the road had lifted their shutters and were sweeping their doorways. There were kids hanging off poles and draped over the bench at the bus stop. The greengrocer was decorating a stand out the front, but apart from that all was clear. I went back to the car.

'Right, move,' I said.

Harvey quickly got out of the car and used his two keys to open the Chubb deadlocks. Inside, he moved to a wall panel with a key . . . I stuck the .38 in his ear.

'What the fuck are you doing?'

'I have to turn off the alarm. If I don't the security firm will come and investigate.'

He stuck a funny shaped key in the panel and turned it and the blinking light went out.

With the back door locked we went down the short hall into the main part of the bank. The venetian blinds were closed. We had no sooner got there when the phone began to ring. I motioned with the gun for him to answer it, but after hearing the voice he held out the hand set.

'For you . . .'

It was Jacko and I gave him the all clear. 'Ring again in fifteen,' I told him.

I told Harvey to sit down and wait for the staff, then glanced around the bank. It didn't look much different from behind the counter . . . the glass partitions, the glassed-off offices, the usual desks and filing cabinets, computers and photocopiers. And the short wide hall that led to the strongroom.

The first of the staff arrived at eight-fifty, the accountant. His mouth gaped open when he saw me, but Harvey begged him to comply. I threw a roll of tape to the manager and told him to bind the accountant's hands behind his back, which he did. I then told the accountant to sit on the floor with his back to the wall under the counter.

There were four more all-told, and one by one they were trussed up and told to get under the counter. One of the girl tellers started to cry and moan but the accountant soothed her.

'Now listen to me,' I said when they were all in. 'No-one is going to get hurt unless they do something fuckin' stupid. The time locks'll be open in a moment or two and then I'll take the money and go. Tell 'em, Harvey.'

'Just do like he says, please, we all know that it is company policy for no-one to interfere during a robbery. This man will be gone soon . . . well before the customers arrive . . . Just do whatever he says, please.'

'Right,' I said, 'Everyone on their feet and down to

the strongroom, and let's do like the man said. No fuckin' heroics.'

They moved down the hall like zombies and stood in front of the strongroom door. Some started to show discomfort with the way their hands were taped behind their backs.

A minute later came the sound of a soft buzzing, followed by a muted clunk of well-machined steel alloy, and oiled machinery. I waved the gun at Harvey . . .

'Open it.'

Harvey took hold of the massive door and it swung easily. A couple of the staff had to move back to allow the door to open wide enough.

'Right, everyone inside and sit on the floor against the wall.'

The inside walls had the sheen of high-grade polished steel. There were shelves with boxes and papers on them but the main item was a large safe fitted with a combination lock. With the staff trussed up and sitting against the far wall, I moved over to Harvey.

'Now the safe, open it, and no fuckin' bullshit.'

The manager moved to the safe and hesitated slightly. I thumbed back the hammer of the .38 and the noise seemed loud inside the strongroom. Harvey flinched, then leant forward and started twisting the big dial. He then stepped back and pulled open the door.

There were stacks of money with paper bands around them, bags of coins, and a box that the security people use to transport money.

'Pull the box out,' I told Harvey. He made hard

work of it but he finally had it out on the floor.

'Open it.' He undid the padlock on the latch and snapped the lid up. It was about three-quarters full of banknotes.

'Take that money off the shelves and put it with the rest.' Harvey obeyed my instructions. 'Now give me your keys.'

He reluctantly handed them over.

'Go and sit with the rest against the wall.'

I dragged the box out of the strongroom and came back to the door.

'Now listen to me, no-one has been hurt up to this point. I'm going to close this door, and I don't want to hear any bullshit about suffocation. This place is air-conditioned . . . there's the inlet up there . . . and an hour from now I will make a phone call and let the fuckin' coppers know where you are. So just sit and relax.'

'You will undo my wife, won't you, she's not well you know.'

'Listen, Harvey, you played the game right and so will we. No harm will come to your wife.'

One of the female bank staff started to sob again. I moved outside the vault and closed the door. It was surprisingly easy for such a huge door . . . it must have been beautifully balanced . . . then I spun the dial and heard a soft hum, followed by a clunk. I took off the balaclava, it was starting to make my face sweat and prickle, and hefted the box of money onto my shoulder. Shit it was heavy.

Making my way to the back door, I went outside and put the box on the back seat of Harvey's Falcon.

I ran back, locked the rear door of the bank, hopped behind the wheel of Harvey's car and reversed out without causing too much noise and drove away.

Jacko was waiting in the other car when I arrived. I pulled in behind him, took the box out of Harvey's Falcon and slung it on the back seat of the car we'd swiped from the airport.

'Let's go, son,' I said as I jumped into the back, and started transferring the money into a big overnight bag.

'No problems back there?'

'Nah,' I said, 'smooth as silk. How's Harvey's old woman?'

'Well, she wasn't in the best of moods, but the bloody tape'll keep her quiet and busy for an hour or so. What do you reckon we netted?'

'Haven't got a clue, but it's more than we need. I think you might have to toss the dole in, you've got too much money now . . . the fuckin' bastards'll means test ya.'

And we both laughed.

Fifteen minutes later we were in our own car, Jacko driving, and we decided to head out to Bondi beach, get lost in the crowds. We were leaving the city behind, winding our way uphill, past large, square sandstone mansions built for British Army officers when New South Wales was England's Devil's Island. Like anything made with convict labour, their stateliness was dismal and unfriendly. Balconies with wrought-iron lace had been stuck on in an attempt to ease the sharpness. They looked like the white paper frills restaurants used to put on lamb chops.

We swung into Old South Head Road. Below us, South Head Cemetery overflowed down the slope to the edge of the ocean, a massive Victorian boneyard with crypts like garden sheds constructed out of white marble. Angels and cherubs, Jesuses and Madonnas stuck out of it like so much wreckage in an avalanche. Old rugged crosses for the esteemed dead, broken and shattered pillars for those who died young. The signs on the tombs—'A Life Of Service', 'In Loving Memory'. I always found it strange how so many gravestones and tattoos look alike.

It started to rain before we got to the beach, and it was also getting cold. We booked into a good motel and after we'd stowed our stuff away we sat down and started to count the money. Two hundred and sixty-seven thousand dollars later, we stopped.

We had the radio on and the robbery was big news on every station. Apparently Harvey's wife had broken loose and raised the alarm. We couldn't have given a fuck. We'd worn gloves so there were no fingerprints. Nobody recognised us, no-one got hurt and the coppers couldn't track a fuckin' elephant through snow. Ninety per cent of their cases were solved by other bastards giving information.

The money problem was solved now, but I needed to clear my head and start thinking of other things. Drizzle or not, I was going for a walk. Jacko stayed behind to stand watch over our new-gained wealth.

It's the domino factor when autumn arrives in Sydney. It does so with a ricocheted gesture of sogginess, courtesy of the tropical wet. There's no Indian summers, no burning leaves, no New England reds and browns. We receive a sort of scaled-down version of what they have in Indonesia—grey skies, tattered gum trees, mildewy shoes and wet decay.

The glare of the summer sun turns Australia dry, dusty and hot. Colours fade and the radiation sizzles, burning the retinas like water on a hot barbecue. But the rain, when it comes, washes everything clean and sweeps the whole dusty surface away, revealing a cold damp grey undercoat. And in the autumn, it rains. A lot.

The beach looked as lifeless and colourless as *The Cruel Sea*. Cold grey shrouds of misty rain drifted across the water and the sand, as predictably as if it were coming from an automatic sprinkler system. I shivered in my jacket and cotton sweater on the steps of the old pavilion. From the changing rooms behind me, a draught carried the smell of dirty underpants, wet cement and piss.

The whole beach was dead. Even the Icebergers were keeping a low profile. Those tough old bastards who'd met here daily since their club was founded in 1929, to flounder in the gelid green water of the rock pool at the southern point, reassuring one another in strangled, gasping voices how great it made them feel. Today they were nowhere to be seen.

The only movement was a figure who came hobbling down the street towards me, hunched up in an old coat, carrying a bottle in a brown paper bag and waddling like a seagull with sore feet. Christ it was lousy weather. Stuff it! I thought. And dived back out into the drizzling rain, heading back down the Esplanade, away from the four-foot drainage pipe that was spilling untreated crap into the Pacific from the flooded and over-worked shithouses of Sydney. Jesus! I missed the Territory and North Queensland.

By the time that I got back to the motel I had a plan to start getting back at Vitelli. There would be no peace until I did something. War is war, no matter what the size, and I was a firm believer in Napoleon's philosophy . . . *When in doubt attack.*

7

I WENT TO A PHONE BOOTH AND RANG PERCY. HE CAME on the line after a bit of a delay.

'Who's Vitelli's best friend?' I asked him.

'Well, believe it or not, mate, he's a real weasel, a cunt called Pasquale Brocassi. He's a cock man, a real woman chaser, *and* a fuckin' shirtlifter. He'd fuck a brown dog, if you know what I mean. We've got a file on him. Thought he might have been connected but he's not. The dirty bastard operates a child-porno ring but he's a real Teflon man. Nothing sticks.'

'What's this cunt's favourite hang-out?'

'The Hampton Court . . . he's part of the fuckin' furniture.'

'And his connection to Vitelli?'

'If you can figure it out, Jimmy, you explain it to me. We think he supplies him with the occasional school-girl. Let me draw you a picture. Brocassi's a shoe repair man and bootmaker. He wears the best clothes, drives a brand new car, spends his evenings chasin' arse up the fuckin' Cross. So where does the money come from? He's a fuckin' cobbler for Christ's sake, they don't make that sort of money. Yet he's thick with Vitelli, he gambles like there's no tomorrow, and get this . . . he's not a winner. He's dropped some big money. He's a bigger fuckin' loser than Jack Davey was, and boy that's sayin' something. Vitelli might slip him a few bucks here or there for their nights out, but not the sort of bread this bastard throws around. Believe me he's dirty, a real fuckin' cockroach. But like I said, he's too cute for people to get anything on him. Hey, and by the way, we never had this conversation.'

'Come off the grass, Percy, your balls would be hangin' on a fuckin' meat-hook if it wasn't for me . . . You owe me.'

'Jesus, Jimmy, you know what I mean, mate.'

'Yeah, Percy, I know. But I don't go round blabbing about our conversations, we go back too far for that sort of shit.'

'Yeah, I'm sorry mate . . . keep in touch.'

Back at the motel it was time to seek Jacko's help.

'Listen, mate,' I asked him, 'do you know a real good sort that would do us a favour? Set someone up for the right money. She wouldn't have to be involved or anything, just be a decoy?'

'Katy'd be the bird you need, son, one of the sheilas I've been shacked up with. Ya wanna meet her?'

'I sure do, old son, I sure do.'

'Well hang on and I'll give her a ring.'

Jacko made the call and a meeting was set up at the Purple Parrot in Bayswater Road in an hour.

'You prepared to carry that .38 you've got?' I asked as we were about to leave.

'Yeah, sure.'

'Right, well go get it. And from now on we don't even go for a shit unless we're armed. I know these cunts, I know them real well, and they know that I know. When they come, it'll be quick and fast, so keep your eyes open and ya wits about you, mate.'

'Okay, Jimmy, I get the picture.'

We were sitting in the Purple Parrot drinking coffee when Jacko gave me a nudge, then gave a wave in the air.

I looked up and watched the girl coming towards us. She had nice dark hair, about eighteen, great tits, nice height and sexy. She wore fashionable green shoes, heels not too high, a pleated grey wool skirt, green silk blouse. Her hair hung at just the right length.

'How's it goin' love?' Jacko asked her. 'Katy Bowman, this is a mate of mine from way back, Jimmy Diamond.'

'Hi there,' I said. 'Sit yourself down . . . can we order you something?'

'Coffee will be just fine,' she said with a voice that would have melted the polar caps. I signalled the waiter and she ordered espresso.

'Shit, no wonder you didn't wanna go home to your mother's,' I said quietly to Jacko.

'Fair go, son. Me and Katy are just good mates, aren't we?'

Katy gave a nod. Her coffee arrived and she took a sip.

'I know the question's corny, Katy, but what's a nice girl like you doing in a place like this?'

'Trying to make enough money to move up to the Gold Coast. Start my own boutique.'

'How close are you to that?'

'I've got a bit put away but it's not near enough.'

'How'd you like to make some good money real quick?'

'Depends what it is . . . I might go to bed, but I don't go to gaol.'

'It's neither of those. I want you to be bait, a decoy . . . to put it bluntly I want you to give someone the big come-on so that I can get hold of him.'

'What happens to the guy then?'

'That doesn't concern you. All you've got to do is lure him.'

'What's in it for me? How much?'

'Five grand.'

'Shit! What's he done?'

'This will be the last question I answer, Katy. The mongrel runs a child-porno operation. There, now that's all I'm saying . . . do you want the fuckin' job or not?'

She looked across at Jacko.

'It's up to you,' he said. 'All you've got to do is lure the bastard and that's where your part stops.'

She looked back at me.

'When do I get paid?'

'If you say yes you can have half now.'

She thought for a moment.

'Okay. But let's get one thing straight. Once you've got him I'm out of it. I'm not into any of this heavy shit.'

'You've got our word. Do it right and you might get that boutique sooner than you think. Give her some money, Jacko.'

Jacko pulled out a wad that would have choked a fuckin' horse, peeled off $2,500 and gave it to her.

'Shit, Jacko, you've come good with a rush!' Katy said. 'What did you do, rob a bloody bank or something?'

'I'm only on the dole, love, you know that.'

Katy turned and looked at me in a different light, smiling. 'Do you look after all your friends like this?'

I changed the subject quickly and we turned to business.

'Right, here's what we do. Jacko and I'll rent a flat up here somewhere tomorrow, we'll let you know when we do. In the meantime you start frequenting the Hampton Court. The bloke I'm after is named Pasquale Brocassi. Now, this prick shouldn't be too hard to locate, he practically fuckin' lives there. He's a cockman, loves the ladies, and he's a fuckin' arse bandit. So don't get too close till we give you the nod. You got all that?'

'No problems.'

'Okay, well what are you doin' sittin' here? Get up to the Court and get a make on this prick. Start earning that dough.'

'Shit,' she said, 'you're a hard boss.'

'It could get worse, love. Let's do it.'

Katy gave me a look that said I wish you'd lighten up. Then she pushed back her chair, said bye to Jacko and left.

Back at the motel we went over the plan a few more times, looking for holes, and when we found one we'd start from the top until we got it right in the end.

'Well, it looks like it all hinges on Katy,' I said eventually. 'Whether or not she can pull this cunt.'

'She'll come through. She might act dumb, mate, but she's got brains that one.'

'Tell you what, if she comes through why don't we

50

give her a little bonus . . . you know, enough to piss off to Surfers. She'd be happy, and she wouldn't be around the fuckin' Cross any more. It'd be a good solution to her problems and she won't become one of ours if some cunt starts askin' questions.'

'It's fine by me, Jimmy. I don't mind setting her up. She's not a bad kid.'

So on that note we called it a night.

8

OVER THE NEXT TWO DAYS WE GOT HOLD OF A FURNISHED house at Potts Point. Rented it for a month in a bodgie name and gave Katy the address and phone number. Jacko and I made it our headquarters. On the fifth day Katy told us she knew which one was Brocassi and she really detested the prick. She even knew one of the girls who'd gone to bed with him.

'Brocassi makes me sick,' she told us, 'but the deal's still on.'

It was mid-afternoon two days later when we got a call from Katy telling us that she was having a drink with Brocassi but he didn't want to go to any house. He wanted to take her for a drive but there was no way she was going to the country with this creep. It wasn't part of the deal.

'Listen, Katy,' I said, 'give us five minutes and we'll be up there in the car. We'll tail you. I promise you, love, that no harm will come to you.'

She was silent for a moment or two.

'Righto,' she said finally, 'but if I don't see you two out the front I don't go, okay? There's no way known that this bastard is going to fuck me up the arse out in the bush. He's a real fuckin' weirdo.'

'We'll be there, love,' I reassured her. 'Just do your

stuff. But for Christ's sake don't keep lookin' over your shoulder or you'll give the game away. Trust us, we'll be there. Now let's get it together and get it on.'

'Okay. I'm trusting you now . . . I'll go with him.'

We were across the street and a little bit down from the main entrance of the Hampton Court when Katy and Brocassi walked out. She saw us and I've got to give her due credit, she didn't even give a sign. But I knew because her face seemed to brighten up and her step became a bit more relaxed. They climbed into Brocassi's Ford and drove off.

The traffic wasn't all that bad and we stayed well back, wondering where they were going. When we were out of Sydney we thought we were going to lose them. The traffic had started to thin out but Jacko spotted the car again.

'Ah, ah! He's turning in at that petrol station, Jimmy, we're goin' to lose em.'

'Pig's arse we are, mate. I'm pullin' in to take a piss. We know what this cocksucker gets up to and we're not gonna leave Katy with him. Okay?'

'Righto. I'm with you, son.'

Brocassi was just getting out of his car when Jacko and I pulled over on the side of the concrete apron. I hopped out, went over to the shithouse, and closed the door just enough so I could see through the crack. Brocassi was putting petrol into his car and Jacko walked over and started talking with him. I thought he'd lost his fuckin' marbles for a moment but they both laughed, something else was said and they laughed again. Then Jacko came walking towards the shithouse. Brocassi hung up the hose, gave some money to the attendant and hopped back into his car.

As Brocassi swung back out onto the highway, Jacko climbed aboard.

'There's no hurry, son,' he said. 'I know where they're goin'.'

'How the fuck did you manage that?'

'Well, while you were spying through the shithouse door I walked over and told him I was hitch-hikin'. Then I said I was a bit worried about you, that I thought you were a fuckin' poofter.'

'You rotten cunt.'

'Anyway,' he continued, 'he told me he and his girl-friend were just going up to have a look around the Lookout.'

'What fuckin' lookout?'

'The Governor Game Lookout, old son.'

'Where the fuck's that?'

'Royal National Park, old chap,' Jacko said, bung-ing on a pommy accent.

'How far from here?'

'Just down the road a piece, old boy. Not far now you know, tally ho, eh what.'

'Cut that shit out, Jacko.'

'Well there's one good thing about it. He won't be able to get out if we're behind him.'

Brocassi took the turn-off to the National Park and we slowed a little to let them get well ahead. Jacko said he'd been out here and the lookout was well signposted.

As soon as there were no more turn-offs I fed a bit more speed into the car and we came around the last corner just as Brocassi was climbing out. I pulled up close behind him so he had no chance of jumping in and reversing out.

I leapt out of the car with the Walther in my hand and aimed it at Brocassi.

'Just stay right there, bastard. Jacko, take Katy and get out of here now.'

'Jesus!' Katy said. She jumped out of Brocassi's car and ran back to ours.

Jacko slid over behind the wheel and started up. He reversed back the moment Katy climbed in, and did a turn.

'How far?' he yelled out.

'Down to the last turn and make sure no bastard comes up here while I'm having a chat to this cunt.'

'Gotcha,' he yelled and drove off.

Brocassi started backpedaling and moved around his car. I stopped on the passenger side.

'Get around here,' I snarled at him, with the gun levelled.

He slowly came around the front of his car.

'Why you do this?' he said in a wavering voice. 'What I do to you?'

'Get on the fuckin' ground,' I yelled.

He got down on his hands and knees. I walked behind him and pushed him down flat with my boot.

'So you like fuckin' and sellin' little kids?'

'Look . . . it is only business.'

'Who's running this stinking kids and sex outfit with you? And don't bullshit.'

'I don't know what you talk about.'

'Bullshit!' I yelled at him and fired a round into the ground alongside his head.

'All right, all right,' he screamed, 'is Gino and Joseph.'

'You mean Vitelli, and Joe Frangiani?'

'*Si, mi lasci in pace, favore.*'

'I'll leave you alone, all right, you piece of fuckin' dogshit.'

He rolled over onto his back and put his hands together, fingers entwined, and started to pray. But he wasn't praying for the kids he had preyed on and used, he was praying for protection.

'*Addio,*' I said.

And fired four rounds from the Walther. They all hit him in the side of the head. I kicked him over, belly-down, and put a final shot into the back of his head.

I sprinted down the road to our car and jumped in the back.

'Hit it, Jacko.'

No-one said a word until we were nearly back in the city. It was Katy who broke the silence.

'You . . . you shot him didn't you, Jimmy?'

'No, I gave the bastard a kiss goodnight,' I said. 'Of course I bloody shot him.'

She stared straight ahead through the windscreen and after a moment or two said 'Jesus!'

Back at Potts Point I left Katy and Jacko in the kitchen while I took a shower and changed. When I finished I made myself a good stiff drink. Katy and Jacko were in the lounge having a drink and had the wireless playing softly.

'Shit! I'm startin' to get a bit hungry,' Jacko said. 'Anyone want something to eat?'

'I think we all need something, mate. What did you have in mind?'

'I'll rip out and get us something. Okay?'

'Sounds good to me, bloke,' I said, 'but come up to the bedroom, I want a word before you go.'

We went up to the bedroom and I handed Jacko the Walther in a sock.

'While you're out get fuckin' rid of that. I've wiped it clean, so for Christ's sake don't go pullin' the bloody thing out.'

'Look, mate, I'm way ahead of you, don't say another word.'

Jacko took off and I sat on the lounge next to Katy. She was pensive.

'This thing got you a bit worried, love?' I asked her.

'Worried! That's a bloody understatement. I'm scared shitless. I left the hotel with him . . . remember?'

'Look, love, I know you're probably imagining all sorts of terrible things are going to happen to you. But Jacko and I, we don't work like that. I think we've got it worked out pretty well. So don't worry. You know you didn't shoot him. And do you think we're going to start spreading it around that we did? There's nothing in the world that can link you to him. Even if the coppers had a fuckin' picture of you with him, that still doesn't prove anything. You could say he dropped the hard word on you and you left him . . . that he was alive when you did.'

'What if they do start asking questions?'

'Look . . . at this point they won't even know that you exist.'

'I wouldn't know what to say if they did question me.'

'Yes you would. You'd tell them sure you had a drink

with him. Yes, he did take you for a drive. He put the hard word on you and you ran off and left him.'

'Where? How do I explain how I got back?'

'Hitch-hiked.'

'Wouldn't they ask me what sort of car, and what the driver looked like . . . you know, a description.'

'Yeah, they would.'

'Well, what would I say?'

'You'd give 'em mine and Jacko's, but for Christ's sake, it won't come to that. You won't be around for them to ask any fuckin' questions.'

She moved away about a foot and looked pretty scared, her eyes opened wide.

'Look, I'm sorry. I didn't mean it to sound that way. We had a talk about you the other night and decided to get you out of this fuckin' rat race. You want to start your own boutique in Surfers?'

She nodded her head.

'Well you're going to, not next month or next year, but tomorrow if you like.'

'What do you mean?'

'You've got another two and a half grand to come haven't you?'

'Suppose so.'

'Well you can forget all about that now, 'cause we're gonna give ya twenty-five grand.'

'You're joking, aren't you?'

'No, I'm fuckin' well not. You can have it right now if you want it.'

She gave a smile and a little squeal of joy, then put her head down and started to cry. I reached over and put my arm around her and pulled her to me.

'Nobody has ever done anything for me before,' she sobbed. 'All my life I've been a loser, it's not like I plan it, it just turns out that way. Oh, Jimmy, what can I say?'

'Say tah . . . that'll do.'

Just then Jacko came in and saw us cuddled up and the tears on Katy's face.

'Well, there's a pretty sight. What's all the water-works about, Katy?'

'Jimmy says that you and him are giving me twenty-five thousand.'

'Yeah, love, that's right, it was his idea but I'm all for it. Anyhow, I've got a heap of tucker out here. Let's have a feed before the bloody stuff goes cold.'

We had a great meal and washed it down with a couple of bottles of red. I was sitting on the couch with Katy and Jacko was lying back in the easy chair when he slowly got up.

'I'm absolutely stuffed, folks. I'm gonna take a shower and hit the sack. See yers in the morning.'

'Yeah, righto mate, take it easy. Good night.'

'Good night, Jacko,' Katy chimed in.

I had just put my empty glass down.

'Would you like another?' Katy asked. 'I know I do.'

'Why not?' I said.

She went into the kitchen and I heard the clink of glass on glass, then she was back. She took a pull on her drink and turned to me.

'I don't want to go back to my place tonight, Jimmy. You don't mind do you?'

''Course not, don't mind at all.'

'Where can I sleep?'

'You'll have to doss in with me.'

Over the years I'd come to have a pretty good idea of what I did and didn't like about a woman's body. As a rule I preferred brunettes, the dark triangle against the white of their skin excited me, and the more pronounced the mound on which that hair grew, the more unobscured the ultimate goal, the better I liked it. And I liked women with breasts, not like half the sheilas getting around today with big arses and built like a boy from the waist up.

'Would you like a coffee?' Katy asked.

'Yeah, it wouldn't go astray. Do you want to bring it into the bedroom?'

'Okay.'

Before she could get up I reached over and took her empty glass from her and put it on the coffee table. Then I took her in my arms and kissed her. Her lips opened under mine and our tongues probed deeply. I rubbed my hand across her boobs and she moaned into my mouth. I ran my mouth across her ear and whispered . . .

'Let's go to bed.'

'Can I take a shower first?' she asked softly.

'Sure.'

She just nodded her head and kissed me again.

Slowly I sat on the edge of the bed and leant forward to undo my shoelaces. I was very tired, buggered, and she was making, of all things, two mugs of coffee. Consciously, I remembered the last time that I had made love to someone other than Carmel. It was well over two years ago now, closer to three, a French girl that I'd found working in Oxford Street on a cosmetics counter. She had smelt divine, before, during, and after, but I hadn't pursued the matter after the first time. Little things about her had annoyed me, like the way she was always chewing gum. I had never been married, though I had thought I might at one stage, but the life I led and the demands it placed on whoever I was with made the proposition look pretty untenable. I'd been lucky with Carmel. She made no demands at all. But we had never discussed marriage. I would be the first to admit that as the years rolled by I was prepared to give less and less of myself. Pretty soon the only woman eligible for the position of Mrs Diamond would have to be a brainless idiot with her own views on nothing more controversial than the weather.

I took my shoes off and started to undo my shirt. It was a large bedroom, with an en suite, and finished in unassuming blues and greys. I heard the door in the bathroom close in the hall and felt my stomach tighten at the thought of a beautiful girl walking up the hall towards me carrying two mugs of coffee. Suddenly I felt a bit nervous, like a younger boy hoping to Christ she wasn't going to come in and just sleep. Nor was it a bad feeling. Too often in the past sex had been a *fait accompli* before it started, a mutual agreement between big boys and girls to blow the tubes through while they still worked.

Katy came in, silent in bare feet, and pushed the door to with her bottom. I sat on the edge of the bed and watched her as she placed the mugs of coffee on the bedside table. Then she came and stood in front of me. She had put her dress back on after taking the shower and I could see a little damp patch on the front of it where she'd missed a bit of herself with the towel. She turned and presented me with her back.

'Unzip me, Jimmy.'

I reached up and drew the zipper slowly down to the cleft of her buttocks. She watched my face in the dressing table mirror as I registered that she had nothing on underneath, and then turned to face me, letting the dress drop to the floor. Then she leaned forward and pulled my face in to her stomach. For a brief moment I noticed her breasts and the soft swell of her abdomen, and the fact that she was everything that I liked in a woman, then I buried my face in the warm fur between her legs while she leant over me and pulled my shirt off, first one arm, then the other. She felt my tongue probing hard and tried to make me stand to take my trousers off, but I wouldn't hear her. I could feel her legs beginning to tremble and grow weak, she was trying to say something to me, but all that came out was, 'Ah . . . oh, Jimmy.' Then I did stand, tossed my pants away and picked her up with one arm around her shoulders and one thrust between her legs, and placed her lightly in the middle of the bed. She reached forward and up and grasped me, trying to pull me down, but I crouched over and kissed her nipples, then her lips, then I stroked myself tantalisingly through her swollen pubes till I thought I could hold out no longer.

'Oh Jimmy, please stop, wait,'

Five minutes ago she had been a rational girl carrying two mugs of coffee, and now she was incapable of doing anything except feeling, breathing, drowning in a broken dam of sensation.

I slid my knees back and let myself sink into her

body. She exhaled in a long shuddering sigh and immediately I felt her pelvis pushing up towards me faster and faster, while her head turned from side to side on the blue bedspread. When she cried out, I could bear it no longer. Forcing my hands under her backside I slid deeper and deeper into her while her hands urged me on, forcing me to greater heights, reaching around and down and gently squeezing my balls while her inner muscles gripped me on each stroke and her breath came brokenly in my ear. I felt myself pass the point beyond which there would be no turning back. Deep inside me, a mechanism had triggered. Now what would follow was inevitable. I heard myself cry out like a man in agony, 'Now! Katy, now,' and then, with the final spasms of our bodies, I felt the hardness of her pelvis locked against me, and it was over.

Slowly I relaxed, and tried to take some of my weight off her, but she pulled me back and nuzzled against me. When I tried to speak, she laid a finger over my lips. For ten minutes we lay like the dead, and then she murmured . . .

'If you like we could have a shower together, and then drink that cold coffee.'

Her voice was warm and filled with the timbre of contentment.

I gave a chuckle, and then suddenly found myself laughing. Katy laughed too.

'I'm happy,' I said. 'Really. And it's all due to you.'

I lifted myself off her and felt, as always, annoyance that the aftermath of sex was so messy.

'It's not that good with stuff running out of me either,' she said. It was as if she was reading my mind.

With our new-found intimacy I cupped her vagina in my hand and felt the blood still pulsing there. She looked down between my legs.

'He's sleeping,' she said, and ran her finger along it.

I got to my feet and walked into the en suite. 'So would you be,' I told her. 'Christ, where's the bloody light?' After a shower and a cup of cold coffee we went back to bed, and we both agreed that it would be to sleep.

She lay in my arms and I kissed her softly. I moved her over onto her back and let my tongue slide down her chin over the centre of her throat, lightly, just touching the skin. I moved lower and lapped at her nipples which were standing erect and hard. I took one in my mouth and slowly and softly rolled the other one between my thumb and forefinger. Slowly, I moved lower and lower until the first of her pubic hairs touched my chin. I slipped my hand gently down between her legs and she responded and opened them. I moved down until my tongue found the soft wet entrance to her and gently licked and teased her as I let my finger just enter her a little, teasing and caressing. She was moving about and making soft mewing noises which got faster and louder until she could stand it no more and gave a cry. A shudder raced through her body and her hips arched up as if she was trying to swallow me.

She rolled on her side and pushed me over on my back and kissed me. Then she reached down and took hold of my swollen and hard penis and bent down and licked it for a time or two. Then she opened her mouth, wet and warm and soft as petals and took me in, trying to take it all in. After a while she straddled me and lifting up she guided the head of my penis into her and sank down on it and she was hot and slippery wet and demanding.

She reached for my hands and placed them on her lovely boobs and I slowly massaged them and rolled her nipples between my fingers. We could both sense it happening. We were a volcano on fire with pressures building and building until nothing could hold them back any longer and we exploded together, me in fluid spurting gushes and her in a shattering climax of feeling and emotion.

She collapsed down onto me and I put my arms around her, lifted her head and kissed her petal-soft lips and whispered to her, 'You're beautiful.'

She lay down beside me and I held her close. The light of dawn had already begun washing the outside of the curtains with early blues before Katy and I drifted off to sleep.

It was Jacko prowling around the kitchen that woke me. I slipped quietly out of bed and went to the bathroom and showered, slipped on a bathrobe and went out to the kitchen.

'Coffee?' Jacko asked. 'Did all right for yourself last night?'

'Arrr you know how it goes, son, I felt a bit sorry for her.'

'Bullshit, she's a top sort that one, mate. And I've got to tell you she doesn't just sleep around. I've tried but she wouldn't have a bar of me. I've done her girl-friend but not her.'

'Yep, you're right, Jacko, she is a bit of all right.'

'You are serious about the money aren't ya, Jimmy. You're gonna give it to her?'

'Bloody oath, mate, she deserves a break. And what the fuck, we've got plenty.'

'I'm glad you feel that way 'cause I counted it out this morning. That's it over there in the shopping bag,' he said, pointing in to the dining-room table.

'Good man.'

'They've found Brocassi. It was on the early news, some lovers discovered his body at 7.30 last night.'

'Fuck him.'

'My sentiments too, old son.'

'The cops reckon they have no clues, but say it looks like a Mafia execution.'

'Shit! I'd give my eye teeth to be a fuckin' fly on the wall at Vitelli's this morning.'

'He wouldn't be a happy man, Jimmy. That's for sure.'

'Listen, Jacko, before Katy comes out let me say this. You're a cool operator, son, and this thing isn't finished, not by a long shot, but we three have to split up for a while till this Brocassi thing cools a little. You and me could have been spotted at the service station. That doesn't put us in the most wanted list but the cops'll be lookin' for a fuckin' pattern. So, here's what we do. Katy gets her money and starts her shop. We'll split the rest of the dough and I'm heading up to Brisbane. I think I've still got an ace up my sleeve there. You take off somewhere but leave the number with your mum. Tell her to give it to no one but me. I'm assuming you're still in.'

'Jesus, mate, 'course I am.'

'Good then, it's settled. You get rid of the car. I'll get one up in Brissie.'

'No problems.'

'Now the last thing I want to ask is, did you get rid of that fuckin' Walther properly?'

'If you want it back you're gonna have to dive into Rushcutters for it. By this time it'll have six inches of fuckin' silt over it. And it hasn't been cleaned and oiled since it's been fired so the bore'll be fucked in a week. Rest easy, my man. It's history.'

By ten o'clock we'd all left the house. Katy asked me to keep in touch from time to time, which I promised I would. Jacko took the car and I caught a cab to the airport. By the time I'd had a couple of drinks and got interested in a magazine article, we were touching down at Eagle Farm.

Outside, the air was hot and humid. A cab driver picked up my two bags and dropped them in the boot.

'Where to, mate?' he asked.

'The Crest Hotel.'

As we travelled across the flat terrain near the airport I noticed that the grass that lined the highway was dry and dead. And the evidence of drought was illustrated further as we came closer to the city. There were patches of bare earth in the parks and private lawns. The sky was a light shade of yellow and you could smell the dust above the exhaust fumes of the heavy traffic. Somewhere out there in western Queensland, strong winds were scooping up the topsoil, stripping it away and lifting it up high so it could smother everything from there to the coast.

All of a sudden we were plunging through the deep

canyons of the city. It was all glass and aluminium, steel and concrete, brash and fast, and then the driver pulled into the undercover guest entrance of the Crest.

I booked a suite for a month and paid for it up front. Shit, did I get the treatment after that! They treated me like I was the fuckin' Premier.

Once I got settled in I rang Carmel and told her to stay where she was, that it wasn't safe yet. I thought she'd put up some resistance but Pamela and her, 'we're getting along just fine' she said. In fact she seemed quite cheerful.

I went down to the bar that overlooks Queen Street. With its big glass windows it's like sitting in a dry aquarium, and sipping on a scotch and soda I looked out into the street. Brisbane hadn't changed all that much. There were still pedestrians moving in formation like human ants, bunches of out of work kids, and bored police keeping an eye on nothing. And more and more fuckin' rice-burners everywhere. It looked as though Brisbane was becoming another Ho Chi Minh City. I had a bit of time to kill, so I decided to brave the dust and the Asians and go for a walk.

As I strolled down to the Mall I came across an open-air bistro called Jimmy's. I thought it must be a good omen so I sat down at an umbrella-shaded table set flush against the waist-high cement enclosure it separated the tables from the tourists and the shoppers. The cover was good and I could keep my eyes peeled for anything that might mean trouble should I be recognised. I didn't know how I stood with Paolo and the *Famiglia* up here, but I was as sure as shit going to find out. Rock 'n' roll music blasted out from an adjacent denim boutique and a guy with a guitar, trying to sound like Bob Dylan, was busking on the far side of the Mall. When the sounds met in the middle it sounded like a direct hit on a guitar factory. There was a raised dais and catwalk just down the way and a guy in an expensive dinner suit was spruiking into a microphone as girls paraded in beach and swimwear. I kept my eye on the spectators watching the fashion parade. Japanese tourists, three backpackers with peeling noses, students, shoppers, geriatrics and dropouts. Just about everyone wore shorts and sneakers, so I gave away looking for the kind of body language that said to the trained eye that someone was carrying a gun and knew how to use it. And wanted to use it on me.

9

IT WAS EXACTLY 7 P.M. WHEN I RANG LUIGI'S RISTORANTE.

'*Buona sera*,' a polite Italian accented voice said. 'Luigi's. Would you like to make a reservation?'

'I'd like to make a reservation for the whole family,' I replied.

Silence for a moment and then . . .

'What can we do for you?'

'*Posso lasciare un messaggio*?' [Will you take a message?]

'*Chi parla*? [Who's speaking]

'Jimmy Diamond. I want you to ring Paolo Agostini and ask him if you can give me his phone number. I'll ring back in ten minutes. *Capisce*?'

'*Si*, I will give him the message.'

'*Bene grazie*,' I said and hung up.

Fifteen minutes later I rang again.

'Ah yes, Mr Agostini would like you to ring him as soon as possible.' He gave me a phone number.

I jotted it down, thanked him and broke the connection.

Before I rang Paolo, I made myself a good stiff drink. I recognised the voice immediately.

'How's it been Paolo? . . . Jimmy here.'

'It's good to hear from you, Jimmy . . . Look, what can I say? We have heard about that thing up north and it has nothing to do with us here. I hope you can believe that.'

'I don't know what to believe, Paolo, but we've got to talk, *amico*, and pretty bloody pronto.'

'Yes, I agree. Where can we meet.'

'Are you at home?'

'Yes, I am.'

'Where's home now, Paolo?'

'I live at Carlo's place at St Lucia.'

'Good. How about meeting me in front of the Crest Hotel in one hour.'

'That will be fine, Jimmy.'

'No funny stuff, Paolo, I'll be watching. I'm not trusting anyone until we talk.'

'You don't have to worry, Jimmy. You have no problems up here.'

'Good mate, let's keep it that way. See you then.'

I hung up and thought about Paolo. We went back quite a ways and I had almost been like a brother to him. In fact we had shared confidences that ordinary brothers wouldn't share. I had laid my life on the line for him on several occasions and I thought that maybe I was doing it again. Well, I'd know one way or the other soon enough.

I waited in the bar so I could see the street and who came and went. That was the beauty of the Crest. It had one-way glass, you could see out but you couldn't see in.

Within the hour a taxi pulled up and Paolo climbed out. Shit, I thought, maybe he is on the level. He was

71

standing on the street looking up and down and across, but I wasn't too anxious and I let him wait. After about fifteen minutes he must have felt that I wasn't going to show. He walked towards the main entrance and stood on the taxi rank. The doorman walked over to him and Paolo nodded. I watched the doorman, but all was on the level. He walked to his taxi hotline phone and picked up the receiver.

I went quickly through the bar and the foyer, towards the big glass doors which opened automatically. Standing just inside I yelled out . . .

'Paolo!'

He turned around quickly. When he saw me he smiled and walked quickly up the steps to greet me.

We gave each other the usual embrace and I steered him straight for the bank of elevators.

Once we were up inside the suite I felt a bit more comfortable. I was booked in under a bodgie name so I wasn't worried about anyone finding out where we were. After I made us both a drink we sat down.

'What the fuck is going on, Paolo?' I asked. 'And listen, tell it like it is, not how you want me to hear it, the truth.'

'Okay, let me start from the beginning. Vitelli came out here about two and a half years ago. You were up here with Carlo and Sam. There was a lot of pressure put on us in Sydney to give Gino a break. Look I can tell you now, he and I didn't get on but we put him on. You know how these things work. He was always asking about his brother. It never stopped. We both know, Jimmy, that you don't break the oath . . . *omerta* . . . I never told him, and while I was down there no-one else did either. But old Carlo had a stroke, he's paralysed down the right side, he couldn't carry on so we bought into the action up here. I came up to look after things and Sonny Milano took over things down in Sydney. Don't ask me how or why, but Sonny disappeared. It was supposed to be a boating accident, but Sonny was too good a seaman for that to happen. Well, Gino took over and made Joey Frangiani his *capo*. Last year Vitelli's on the phone accusing me of having his brother hit. The only other person who knew, and also knew you, was Frangiani.'

Paolo sensed I was going to say something and held up his hand. He hadn't finished yet.

'You're going to ask me how they knew where you were. Well I can't answer that, *amico*, because I don't know. What I do know is that Vitelli has just come back from Cairns. He was game fishing. And we hear today that Brocassi got hit two days ago. You know who's going to have the finger pointed at them for that, don't you? Me. We just about went to war six months ago. You don't know Gino, he's a maniac. But I want to tell you this, while you are here, you're in my territory and I'll let it be known that you're under my umbrella. You know what that means, I don't have to explain that. So that's it, you have it.'

I looked at Paolo and smiled. Apart from a real blast he gave me some years ago for a cock-up that cost innocent lives, it was the longest speech I'd ever heard him make. I knew this man, I knew him real well, as well as I'd known his uncle. In fact I first met Paolo at his uncle's funeral, and that was a lot of years back. I made us another drink and said . . .

'Paolo, in all the years that we've known each other I've never told you a lie. And I think you've been honest with me. You've trusted me with your life, and I've trusted you with mine. So listen well, buddy, and remember *omerta* . . . nobody can point the finger at you for Brocassi because I hit him. And with or without approval, I'm going to whack Frangiani and Vitelli. All I want is peace, Paolo. Old Don Carlo gave me his blessing, as did Don Vincenzo. But fuckin' Vitelli has broken that peace. He shot my dog out of a fucking helicopter. And it's only by luck that Carmel and I are here. The bastard opened up on us as we were driving away from the house. We don't make war on each other's womenfolk . . . that's the unwritten law, women and kids are sacrosanct. I'm going to get him, Paolo, and I told that cocksucker Frangiani to tell him.'

'You've had a run-in with Frangiani? Where?'

'Don't worry about him, Paolo, I could take care of him on my worst day with one arm tied behind my back. And a fuckin' bag over my head. Fuck him.'

'Look, Jimmy, I hear what you say, but do me one thing. Don't do nothing till I make a few moves, promise me this, because if you wait we'll both finish off better in the end, promise me?'

I thought it strange that Paolo would want such an assurance, but I figured he knew best.

'Righto, Paolo, you've got my word, but if those bastards from Sydney try to fuck with me they better bring a good supply of fuckin' body bags with 'em.'

'Okay, you sit tight, eh? Now what have you been up to since I last saw you?'

74

We spoke to each other for hours. At two Paolo rang his wife and said he wouldn't be home till the morning. It felt great. No-one of Paolo's rank in the Family would do what he was doing now, and I knew he was doing it for me . . . knew that we were still brothers.

The first rays of sun were brushing colour into the east when Paolo finally left, promising to call me later. As dawn broke the sun lit up the far horizon and a bright shaft of day streaked through the window and lit up the room. It had been a long night with an old and trusted comrade. I needed companionship, I needed love. I picked up the phone and rang Carmel, asked her to catch a cab and come straight over.

Soft filtered hotel music drifted into the suite as I sat in an easy chair and stared out over the city. The door-bell chimed and I let Carmel in. She held me tightly and kissed me softly, then walked around the suite and said she'd like to take a bath. The suite seemed to fill with the beautiful fragrance of lavender as she emerged from the bathtub, towelled herself dry, powdered herself with a light scent and stood gazing out the window with her back to me. She was naked.

I walked up behind her and put my hands on her shoulders. Her skin felt smooth and warm. When I leant forward and kissed her between the shoulderblades, she gave a slight shudder and leant back. I closed my hands around her boobs and let my lips travel slowly the length of her spine. All the way down I travelled, breathing in the lavender perfume. I turned her around and I knelt between her legs and came up under the taut swell of her womanhood. I pushed my face up into her and probed with my tongue, tasting the inky bitterness. Suddenly I found myself swimming through a warm swamp with sodden weed.

Moisture ran down the inside of her leg. She took me by the hair and pulled me up. I stood and lifted her and supported her against the wall. I entered her and was drawn up into the surprising heat that pulled from deep inside her. She gave a tense cry and arched her body into mine, letting her head fall back against the glass. Her hands gripped the edges of the window frame.

Bucking, she pushed hard against me with a flurry of rapid thrusts that made a flat hollow sound like waves slapping against a jetty. Rocking, legs and arms intertwined, tongues duelling, jabbing sideways in a crazed froth of saliva. With my hands under her buttocks I started to slowly knead and squeeze. The curtains were moving around us, and the sun was bathing us in a warm glow.

She fell to the floor, dragging me with her. We rolled apart and lay panting, facing each other across the carpet. She was shivering uncontrollably. Little moans escaped her, little grunts and cries. She got up on all fours and began to circle around me. Nosing and nipping and licking me all over. I pulled her towards me and she straddled me and I pushed hard up into her, thrusting.

She gave a moan that started somewhere in the back of her throat and rose to a shrill wail as she was transported by the first spasms. The sound went right through me. My head seemed to blow open, and suddenly I was with her. I let out a deep, bellowing cry that joined hers,

76

wavering between unison and an eerie harmony, then soared like a bird through the window out into the bright new light of day.

'Can't I stay with you?' she whispered.

'You'd only be in the way. It's too dangerous yet.'

'I love you, Jimmy, I really do.'

'I know you do.'

She kissed me tenderly, showered, dressed, then she was gone, back to Pamela's place, and I was alone again with my thoughts and my nightmares.

I awoke with a start, in a cold sweat. I'd drifted off to sleep after Carmel had gone, dreaming that a man in a camouflage mask was chasing me with a noisy chainsaw. His mouth slit was twisted in a satanic grin, and he was gaining on me.

Joints aching, I got up off the lounge with an effort. Muscles protesting. Mind groping. My dreams were always followed by the need to wake up. And Christ knew I had plenty of bad dreams. This morning I didn't know what was worse. It would just be as easy to lie back down and sleep and let the crazies win. Shit, with the fuckin' life that I was living the law of averages said they were going to win anyhow. If not today, then tomorrow, next week, or next year. What fuckin' difference did it make? One look at the papers or the TV told the bloody story. The whole fuckin' world was in intensive care and nobody gives a shit. The terrorists, the sadists and drug dealers, the scum with twisted minds were all multiplying like cockroaches in sewers all over the world, oozing out of every crack and crevice. They were hidden behind masks, and police, and political protection. Even in the Family, it seemed, there was no respect or honour any more. A different breed. Their victory was inevitable.

I walked into the bathroom and stared into the mirror. The face that gazed back at me was getting older, its eyes were red-rimmed. I opened my mouth and looked for the parrot that had shat in there. I ran my tongue over the coating on my teeth and spat into the toilet. I ran my hand over the stubble on my chin. Even the damn whiskers were turning a lighter shade. I was getting older, losing my youth. I splashed water over my face and swished some through my mouth, and was about to turn the shower on when the phone rang.

True to his word, it was Paolo.

'Jimmy, you remember the club down the Valley. Be there in an hour.'

The cab dropped me at the Club Italiano (which according to the police does not exist). There had been some renovations since I'd been here but, over all, it was pretty much the same. As I walked in a strange feeling of peace swept over me. The foyer had been redecorated with maroon drapes and black leather furniture, and the left-hand wall was covered with mirror tiles, making the place look bigger than it actually was.

The reception desk was still where it used to be, only a little more lavish, and behind it was a nice looking receptionist.

'May I help you?' she asked, eyeing me up and down, wondering if I was a copper on the take.

'I'd like to see Paolo Agostini please.'

'Does Mr Agostini know you? Is he expecting you?' she said in a cold voice.

I'd had enough of this bullshit.

'No. I'm from the fuckin' planet Mars. 'Course he's bloody well expecting me, just ring.'

The receptionist was staring at me now with some concern in her eyes. Then she reached behind her and, without taking her eyes off me, pressed the buzzer I knew was there.

Thirty seconds later Paolo came through the curtained doorway, accompanied by a guy who looked like Son of Kong. Paolo saw me and threw his arms out . . .

'Jimmy, you made it.' And he gave me the embrace. Then he turned to the sheila behind the desk. Her mouth was gaping open.

'This is Jimmy Diamond,' Paolo said. 'He is a very special personal friend of my family. Anytime he comes in you are to look after him with respect.'

The receptionist turned on a dazzling smile for my benefit and for a moment I thought she was going to curtsy.

'Jimmy, this is Rocco.' Paolo turned me towards the gorilla.

'Hi Rocco,' I said and gave him my hand. I thought it would be mangled but his grip was warm and friendly.

'Come on in. There's someone here I want you to meet.'

We walked through the club, then down the old familiar hall to the back offices. As we walked into the main one a figure sitting in a Jason recliner stood up.

He was thin, at least six feet in height, with a well-cut lightweight suit and white shirt. As he adjusted a dark grey tie, I took in his broad forehead, deep-set eyes and high-boned cheeks. Not an unpleasant face, I thought, yet somehow it was a face that would be elusive in memory.

Rocco didn't accompany us into the office, but just closed the door when Paolo and I were inside.

'Jimmy, I would like to introduce you to a friend. This is Alonzo Rissi.'

'Nice to know ya, 'I said and gave him my hand.

'I've heard quite a bit about you from Paolo,' Rissi said. 'I'm impressed.' He had a strong American accent.

'Shit,' I said, 'I hope he only told you the good bits.'

It seemed to break the ice because everyone laughed.

Paolo walked over to his desk and pressed an intercom button.

'Mandy,' he said, 'let's have some drinks in here would you.'

The drinks arrived and we sat chatting for a while, then Paolo got down to business.

'Jimmy, Al has a business deal he'd like to speak to you about, but before he does I'd like to tell you that the conversation we had last night depends on the outcome of your decision. You may not like the deal . . . then so be it. Nobody will hold you to anything, but if you decide to take it on then the world is not enough. So just hear what Al has to say, eh? Just hear him out.'

'This isn't really that complicated,' said Rissi. He took out a pen and began doodling, drawing two circles on the back of an envelope he'd pulled from his pocket.

'Let's start at the top with these two circles. See the "A" with the Rissi under it in the middle of the circle?'

I nodded.

'That's me.'

'Doesn't look like you,' I wisecracked. Paolo shot me a look, but it didn't phase Rissi.

'The circle next to it we'll call "B", Giovanni Gabrialdi. This black arrow pointing to the left and meeting the A means that I want Gabrialdi executed. That is the only relationship I have with B. Now let's draw a circle underneath and call it "C" with your name on it and draw an arrow from C to B. It means I want you to execute Gabrialdi.'

'Couldn't we have done this without all the bloody drawings?' I asked Rissi.

'Yes, but I want you to understand that this is the only conversation we are going to have concerning this matter. After this meeting you and I will not meet again, and I wanted you to be certain of the facts. This is not going to be easy. Gabrialdi is well guarded, and he's alert, he knows he's a marked man. And the people he has with him are good at what they do.'

'Well, why me? Couldn't you use somebody connected?'

'That's the very point. This is a delicate political matter and it cannot be done by anyone "connected". You have arrived at a very opportune moment. You've done work for us, so to speak, and Paolo has spoken of certain qualifications you possess. Putting it simply, you look the best man for the job.'

'Why do you want to make it so fuckin' complicated?'

'Because apart from the three of us in this room, no one else is to know about it, or better still who's behind it.'

'Come off the grass,' I said. 'Anyone in the know with half a fuckin' brain will be able to make the connection and figure out who wanted Gabrialdi hit.'

'That's the point. I am only the contact here. Although I am endeavouring to engage your services, I do not know Gabrialdi personally. And for that matter have no connection with anyone in the *Cosa Nostra*.'

'What's this Gabrialdi done?'

'That need not concern you. However, I will say this. Gabrialdi is a threat to the national security of the United States of America.'

'Jesus, Paolo! Where is this guy from—the fuckin' CIA?'

'It really doesn't matter where I come from,' Rissi said calmly. 'What does matter is that we terminate Gabrialdi with extreme prejudice.'

'Okay,' I said, 'let me put another question to you and I want a straight answer. Is this Gabrialdi connected to the Mob in the USA?'

'He has had dealings with them, said Rissi, 'but I am at liberty to say that he is not a member of any of the known families in the States. Gabrialdi is a Colombian.'

'Christ, Paolo! This is starting to look kinda shitty. Okay, what's in it for me, what's the bottom line?'

'Al will explain,' said Paolo.

I turned to Rissi. 'Well, what's the deal?'

'Right, anyone you use to assist you, you will have to recruit yourself. They are your responsibility. Any expenses in setting up the operation will be met by us. You will personally receive $50,000 on the successful completion of the contract.'

'What guarantee do I have? You said we won't meet again after today.'

'Mr Agostini will guarantee payment. Is that not so, Paolo?'

'Yes, that's true,'

'How much scope do I get on the expenses? This could be a costly operation.'

'There is no limit on the expenses, but an account of them must be kept.'

'Whereabouts is this fuckin' Gabrialdi?'

'He has set himself up quite cosily at an abandoned goldmine in the area between Port Douglas and Mossman in the far north. Are you familiar with it?'

'Yes, very familiar.'

'There is another matter that you must take into consideration before accepting the contract. Gabrialdi has competent people with him—four of them, in fact. They must not remain alive. However, there are also two women with Gabrialdi, and they are not to be hurt.'

'What is he, a cockman? Are they both girlfriends?'

'Emphatically no.'

'Are you trying to tell me that this bastard is holding hostages?'

'Let's call it security,' said Rissi.

'This sounds like a job for the fuckin' SAS to me.'

'Yes, it does, doesn't it? However, the circumstances surrounding this matter forbid any sort of official intervention.'

'Is there a time factor on this thing?'

'As expediently as possible,' said Rissi.

'What happens if we fail?'

'Then we will have to try harder, won't we?' Rissi replied.

I turned to Paolo. 'And Vitelli and Frangiani?'

'Tidy this up, Jimmy, and they're yours with my blessing and assistance.'

I stood up and made myself a drink and paced about a bit. One thing was for sure, there was a lot at stake here. There were big irons in the fire. Something must be causing a lot of embarrassment to someone. Now that I was assured Rissi wasn't connected to the Mob, the more I looked at the bastard the more he smelt like CIA. Maybe NSC. And there was an intriguing factor here, too. It was not unusual for the CIA or ASIO to recruit outsiders on a contract basis, but what was fuckin' Gabrialdi doing in Australia?

I let the thoughts I'd had earlier in the day run through my mind again. Then I turned to Rissi.

'Right I'm in . . . but I don't want any interference from anyone once I put this thing in motion. I want $20,000 up front, I want a clean car in Cairns that can't be traced to anyone. And a fuckin' lot more. I'll let Paolo know once I've got this thing sussed out.'

Rissi stood and offered his hand, which I shook.

'Remember, no harm must come to the women.'

'Okay,' I said, 'we've got a deal. I've got a few things to do to get this rolling. The money by tonight and, Paolo, I want a clean gun in the meantime. Just for insurance. You know what I mean?'

'Rocco will deliver both to you tonight.'

'Right, I'm off.'

I had a few things to do all right and one was to make a long-distance phone call to Sydney.

10

BACK AT THE HOTEL I SHOWERED AND SHAVED AND LET my thoughts work for me. I poured a good shot of whisky into a tumbler and lit a cigarette. Then I rang Percy's direct number at his office. Thank Christ he was in. The information I wanted I needed pretty damn quick. After we had exchanged pleasantries I said 'What do you know about a guy from Colombia . . . Giovanni Gabrialdi?'

'What do I know about him? Christ, where have you been . . . fuckin' Siberia? He's real bad news, boy. He was the *segundo* for one of the big cartels down there, but he ripped them off for Christ knows how much. There was a rumour of someone in the CIA or close to it having a finger in the pie, but nothing could be substantiated. Gabrialdi went to the States and threatened to blow the whole thing sky high with information he had from just about the Secretary of State down, then he dropped out of sight. There was some talk that he had some hobnob's daughter with him that was hooked and another shiela who's related to a fuckin' Congressman would you believe. None of this is that sensitive, Jimmy, why do you ask?'

'Does the name Al Rissi ring a bell?'

85

'If it's the Al Rissi I'm thinking about, he was once a covert operations adviser to the CIA.'

'Have you ever seen him?'

'Sure, twice when I was liaison officer . . . if my memory serves me right.'

'Describe him for me, Perce.'

'A bit over six feet, about forty-five with a large forehead and deep-set dark eyes. Dresses well. And speaks with a bit of a plum in his mouth.'

'Yeah, that sounds like him.'

'What do you mean that sounds like him? For Christ's sake, Jimmy, what the fuck are you on about?'

'I'll get back to you Percy.'

'Hey!' he yelled into the phone. 'Where are you ringing from?'

'The Russian Embassy Perce,' and I hung up.

On a piece of hotel stationery I wrote down a list of the things that would be needed for an operation like this. And I thought of poor old Percy in Sydney. He'd be having a fuckin' coronary by now trying to fathom what the questions were about.

An hour later the door chimes sounded and Rocco was there. He had a Qantas flight bag with him.

'The boss said to give you this.'

I took it from him and handed him an envelope with my list in it.

'Give Paolo that, Rocco, and tell him I'll need that with the car. He'll understand.'

'Okay,' he said. 'I'd better get going. Have to pick him up in half an hour.'

When Rocco left I opened the bag. The money was there and so was the gun, a Browning GP.13 with a detachable silencer, wrapped up in an oily rag, with three full thirteen-round magazines of 9 mm hollow points and a box of shells. I wiped it off, checked the action and loaded it. One thing about Paolo, he didn't do things by half measure.

The next thing I did was ring Jacko's mother to get his number. He'd gone to Tasmania to have a look at the Casino. I rang the number but he wasn't in his room, so I left a message for him to contact me.

It was eleven-thirty that night when I received his call.

'Hi mate, what's the problem?' he asked.

'None old son, just get your arse on a plane and get up to Brisbane as quick as you can. I've got something right up our alley. I'm at the Crest, suite 1204.'

'Right, you're on, I was starting to get bored shitless here anyway. The place is like the fuckin' North Pole. Can you say anything about it?'

'No mate, just trust me. See you tomorrow.'

After I hung up, I switched out the light and decided to get some sleep. I had a feeling I wasn't going to get much from now on.

I woke up in a lather of perspiration from another horror show. The clock alongside the bed said it was 4 a.m., the time when old people die and babies are born. City night-glow still seeped through the window, bathing the suite in a light that reminded me of night in the Gibson Desert. And my thoughts began to roam.

The desert here in Australia isn't all sand dunes like the Sahara. It has a rugged, and sometimes lethal, beauty like nothing else on Earth. It's a flat wilderness of hard red earth, flinty gravel and rock that seems to

87

be always clean as a table, thanks to a wind that seldom stops.

But as hostile and barren as it looks, you could set a family from the Pitjantjara tribe down in it stark bollocky naked, and within no time they'd erect a shelter of some description and manage to get a fire going. Make a kind of bread out of ground-up grass seeds, catch a couple of goannas, and have the whole lot baking in the coals for their evening meal.

But will the do-gooders and the missionaries leave them at peace like that? No fuckin' way. As far as they're concerned the parents can stay out there and rot and live off the land as their forebears have done for thousands of years, but the children . . . Hell no, they have to be educated and indoctrinated into 'our way'. Take the kids, shove shoes on their fuckin' feet and dress them in 'civilised apparel', all standing around nervous and fidgeting in their new and uncomfortable attire. And for the first time in their lives have them crapping in bathrooms and eating off a plate with a knife, fork and spoon. Then people wonder why all of a sudden we've got Abo activists.

I lay there thinking about that beautiful and lonely emptiness . . . the peace that the quiet brings . . . the infinity of the star-filled night sky. Once you've been out there for a while you see it just as the Abos do . . . a gigantic inhabited space, where every tree, rock, pool and plant has a face and a name and a personality. And a place of its own.

Fuck it! I thought to myself, when this shit is cleaned up I'm going back to the bush. I rang room service and told the sleepy voice on the other end to bring up some fresh ground coffee.

It was eight in the morning when I received a call from Paolo telling me that the stuff on the list would be waiting for me in Cairns, and giving me a phone number to ring when I arrived there.

At nine that night Jacko arrived, all smiles and questions. I told him what I knew and laid out the deal I'd been given. It was pretty heavy shit and smelt like one of those covert operations that were pulled with no paperwork when we were in Vietnam. They just 'never happened'. And that was what was happening here. If we came unstuck, we were on our own, nobody would know us. In fact nobody would want to know us. There wouldn't be a single person we could name. If we got in the shit, so what? Everybody else would be squeaky clean. The only consolations were that we were getting paid well, and the equipment would be the best. We went over the pros and cons of the thing. Spoke about the logistics that we would need to penetrate whatever perimeter they had set up. And the fact that we had to extract two females who weren't hostile. It wasn't going to be a piece of piss.

'So what do you reckon, Jacko, are you in or out?'

'Yeah, I'm there, son. What the hell difference does it make? You can't live forever. Have a look at us, Jimmy, two warriors without a war. Well the bastards, whoever they are, have given us one, so let's get it on.'

Cairns was hot and humid and sticky. We booked into the Trade Winds, paid cash up front so we could leave at a moment's notice, and decided to keep a very low profile.

It would have been great to go out and paint the town, but to be out and about was to be noticed, and that was the last thing we needed. For all we knew Gabrialdi could have lookouts in town for just that purpose.

I rang the number Paolo had given me, gave the pre-arranged code, and arranged for the car and all the gear to be left in the motel car park.

'Right, Jacko,' I said, 'I'm going out to cover the delivery. You stay here and be ready to bring our bags when I give you the toot. I want to have a fuckin' good look at whoever's delivering this car, and I want to see him leave and how he does it, right?'

'Loud and clear.'

There was a good observation spot in a latticed and vine-covered beer garden. I'd be able to see them, but they wouldn't see me. Five minutes later a dark blue Falcon pulled into the car park. A figure got out, locked the door, had a look around, then slipped the keys on top of the tyre while pretending to examine the right front wheel. He stood up and walked to the foot-path. A minute later a brown Commodore pulled up beside him and he got in. I had a beer coaster in my hand and I wrote the number of the Commodore down. And the number of the Falcon.

I scanned the street and the buildings opposite for lookouts for a good ten minutes, but there was nothing out of the usual. Then I walked across to the Falcon, drove over to the unit and gave a short honk on the horn. Jacko came out, threw the bags on the back seat, climbed in the front and we headed north.

As we drove my thoughts wandered back over the years, trying to fathom why I had finished up the way

I was. God knows, I'd never really planned any of the things I had done. It was as if some force I had no control over had been there from the moment of my birth. I had been denied the love and attention of my natural mother and father. Been abused and mistreated as a child by a couple of monsters who spoke like angels on Sundays and played cards with the devil for the rest of the week.

I had absconded from their grasp to find peace, love and happiness, and when I did find them they were ripped away from me. Without any action from me. When I lost the greatest love I had known I had wreaked vengeance on those responsible. But in so doing I had come under the scrutiny of those who could use this unnatural human coldness. I became anti-social, hard to reach, a machine that was activated out of hate.

In an attempt to break this pattern, I had joined the army and shone head and shoulders over the others because I had already received special training from an ex-commando. I did training then in the special operations group, and when I did this job too well I was removed and sent to an infantry battalion, in which I had served my country with dignity and pride, and been decorated in the field. But on my return home I'd been abused and spat at and accused of atrocities by the man in the street, thanks to mass hysteria whipped up by Jim Cairns and the Moratorium. I was finally discharged on medical grounds after a run-in with an officer—we'd been on a collision course from our very first encounter. The old school tie ganged up on me. 'Not cricket, old boy, can't have our officers treated like that, you know.'

So I had returned to the only people I could trust, who understood me, and showed me kindness and loyalty. I committed some terrible deeds while hanging on to this family. But the enemies of this fraternity are just as bad and corrupt: police, bent politicians, perverted men in power who hide behind a veil of false decency. Their hands are held out, snatching at a blizzard of bribes. A moral wrong and a civil right are one and the same thing to these fuckin' hypocrites.

Every day new laws are legislated to stop someone from doing something. We are all born free but are everywhere in chains.

Not quite two years ago I decided I had had enough, and with the blessing of the *Famiglia*, I had made a clean break, gone away from the fast city life, which reminded me of a street lamp on a summer's evening with myriads of bugs busily bashing their fucking brains out getting nowhere. I took my girl and left. We made a new home and life for ourselves. Then out of the blue a maniac invaded our peace, trying for a square up . . . And here I was again, back doing the very thing I was trying to get away from. I was between a rock and a hard place, fucked if I did and fucked if I didn't. But this time was a little different. I had no choice but to clean up this mess, but if I survived it I was going to put the fear of Christ into the right people so that I would never be bothered again.

I pulled the car into a side road that led to one of the many isolated beaches between Cairns and Port Douglas. We got out and checked over the gear in the boot. Everything was new, very new, and not one item was missing. It took us an hour to check and double check what we had.

'What do you reckon?' I asked Jacko.

'I'd say this stuff has come from someone with a fuckin' lot of pull . . . Christ, look at these? You just can't pick up night vision gear from a fuckin' disposal store. Or hypo-darts with curaeium . . . just about instant paralysis. Shit, this stuff is restricted. Bloody special ops coveralls. Yep, whoever set this up has a lot of wallop in the right places.'

'Come on, bloke, let's get this show on the road,' I said.

We set ourselves up in a house just outside the northern outskirts of Port Douglas. It was private, very quiet, and cost a fortune in rent and bond, but we took it for a month. We unloaded the gear and stashed it away from the prying eyes of anyone who might drop in. Then we went into town and bought a heap of fishing gear—rods, reels, you name it, which we left on the front verandah. It would be a good cover.

Later on I rang Percy. He wanted to know the answers to a lot of questions, but I managed to calm him down. Then I gave him the numbers of the two vehicles and asked him to run a make on them for me. He wasn't that keen, and tried to get me to answer all sorts of questions, but on the promise I would fill him in later he asked me to call him back at four o'clock.

For the rest of the afternoon we sat down and planned. The first thing we did was hook the scrambler, one of the pieces of equipment we'd asked for, up to the phone; it also had a seek prohibitor. Then we got the aerial up for the base station. We were going to need that. It was no good two of us going out there tramping all over the place, the set-up had to be sussed out and I was going in tonight to do just that. I hopped in the car, taking with me one of the hand-held pocket-sized radios, and drove thirty miles north of Port Douglas.

'One to Base . . . do you read me, Sunray!'

'Sunray to One . . . turn your squelch up a notch.'

'Complying Sunray . . . how do you read me now?'

'Five by five, One. Sunray out.'

That took care of the radio bit. We had that tuned and we wanted to keep our messages short and coded. I made out like I was a rubbernecked tourist and located the turn-off to the old Uralla mine where the quarry was staying. Bloody wild country. Now and again the odd prospector has scrub-bashed his way in, to try and find a nugget or two, but the place was closed down fifty years ago and the jungle and scrub had taken over. The old mine and the small settlement that used to be there were three miles off the highway. I was going to have to do it on foot. Hard, and very quiet.

My mind wandered once more as I drove back to Port Douglas. How strange, I thought, how strange that the drops of malice and revenge that started with Vitelli shooting at Carmel and me had evaporated as the details of the job at hand began to crowd in. The exercise had become just that, an exercise, existing for its own sake, not for spite or to satisfy my vanity that I could still do it . . . but just for itself, like a junkie's fix. Nothing except the exercise was of consequence. If completed satisfactorily it would give me access to the peace I was looking for. Only the job mattered. This philosophy had been drummed into me many, many moons ago during Special Operations Training. *Just do the job. Don't think of anything else. Remember, thinking is perfection's greatest enemy.*

I rang Percy at 4 p.m. and I wasn't really stunned with the information he gave me.

'Listen, Jimmy, just what the fuck are you into, my man? Those two vehicles are American consular attache cars, or that's where they're supposed to be. You know what that means don't you? They belong to the CI-fuck-ing-A. I'm starting to get a bad taste in my mouth.'

'Don't get excited, Perce, you're supposed to know how to act under duress. You've had enough training at it.'

'Don't get excited! Christ almighty, Jimmy, I'm gonna be up front with you, mate. After our conversation the other day I've been waiting for your call and I've had a tracer unit going from the moment this call started, and do you know what I'm getting? I'm getting shit. Sweet fuck all. Now this can only mean one of two things. You're on an untraceable hook up, which I know you just can't have, or you're using a sophisticated scrambler. Now fuckin' come clean.'

'Can't fool you, Percy, you've got me with my pants down, son. Yeah I'm using a scrambler.'

He seemed to quieten down a bit.

'You're not going to tell me where you are, are ya, mate?'

'You don't want to know, Percy. I'll keep in touch. See ya.'

'Did he jerry to the scrambler?' Jacko asked.

'Sure did. I knew that he'd try to get a line on us. He's no mug you know. He spent seven years in the SAS before he became a spook, and he'd be trying to work the angles out right now.'

I wasn't telling him anything he didn't know already.

'Right,' I added. 'Now it's time to call a cab, go into town and rent a car. I'm putting this bastard in the garage. You can bet your balls that there'll be a national alert, and if this Falcon is spotted we'll have Special Branch and ASIO breathin' up our arses.'

11

IT WAS 8 P.M. WHEN JACKO STOPPED THE RENTAL CAR near the turn-off to the old mine. I left the road and moved into the bush. There is a brief time when you first move into bush or jungle in the night when you feel that you're lost, and you are sure you'll be lost forever. Your heart gives little flutters as the adrenalin pumps, you become winded with very little walking and everything you know or thought you knew about the jungle and scrub is forgotten . . . or you think to yourself, maybe I didn't know enough from the beginning. The fuckin' compass reads an impossible direction. The view from the tree you climb with a great deal of effort reveals only the tops of more bloody trees. If you've followed a creek or river you know you've walked at least three times further than necessary because of the way it twists and turns. The ground is swampy underfoot and there are swarms of mosquitoes clouding around your head. It is first of all embarrassment, mixed up with a little bit of panic. When the frantic pumping ceases and you start to regain your breath again, it's easy enough to turn around and retrace the path you've made. The deaths that too often occur in the bush and jungle are simply a matter of the lost waiting far too bloody long before they turn around.

I lay along a log fallen across a narrow creek and I rested for a while as I inspected the rifle I was carrying. Then I moved on to a large outcrop of rocks. Thank Christ for the Litton night-vision scope. I was about a mile from the settlement but I wanted to move further upstream. There was higher ground up there and I might be able to pick up a bit of breeze, get a little relief from the bugs that were attacking and biting the fuckin' arse off me.

'One to Sunray . . . One to Sunray . . .'

'Sunray receiving five by five, come back.'

'One is about two clicks into target area out,' I said quietly.

I made it to the high ground, set up the hootchie tent and camouflaged it. Then I got the entrenching tool and dug a shallow ditch around the tent as quietly as I could, scooping most of the soft composty soil out with my hands. By the time I had finished, my skin and the black special operations overall I was wearing were soaked in sweat. I'm getting too old for this shit I thought as I crawled into the hootchie which was to be my base, and unloaded the gear from the webbing harness. I stripped naked so I would cool off quicker. Out of nowhere, there was a cloudburst with rain pissing down and wind breaking small branches and scattering leaves and twigs. I dozed off, exhausted after crawling half the night, stepping and carting the gear through the dense scrub.

I awoke, shivering, about two hours later and reported in to Jacko. Headquarters were set up and no good would come of going any further at the moment, so I checked the gear on the floor of the tent. I had an

98

AK-47, 300 rounds of 7.62 ammo for it. A Ruger B3000 gas-operated hypodart pistol and a dozen darts in a plastic protector case. A cube of C4 plastique. Three self-priming detonators. Knife. A pair of 100 power binoculars and a Litton M-845 night scope. I opened the flap of the hootchie and peered out. The area in front of me lit up like day.

As the early morning noises associated with the scrub were just starting, I moved carefully up the creek, taking advantage of the natural cover. Ten minutes later I crossed the creek on some rocks, but the last step was too great and, rather than make a sound, I had to get one boot wet. The position I was in, a half stoop and sometimes a crawl wasn't very comfortable. A noise came to me that was foreign and I moved quietly under one of the broad-leafed ferns that grew in abundance. As long as I stayed down I could move but couldn't be seen. Shit, I thought, I hope the snakes stay away, and pushed myself another foot closer. A mosquito entered my ear and I mashed it with my little finger. That's why we have wax in our ears I was once informed, it's to keep the fuckin' bugs out.

When I finally left the low ferns it was almost 4 p.m., the sun was getting lower and everything under the higher canopy was bathed in an emerald green light. As I sat with my back against a tree and smoked an imaginary cigarette, I gave Jacko two Mike Mike clicks on the radio. I heard his return hiss but it would not have been audible for any more than a few feet because I'd turned the volume right down. He knew his job well, Jacko.

The timber and trees were starting to thin out now, though the ground cover was good. I crawled up a slight rise and smelt it before I saw it . . . smoke. My heart gave an extra thump, I was practically on top of them. I sent a short and two longs to Jacko, which meant 'contact', and heard the soft ffft of his acknowledgment. As I moved, my mind was racing. Where is he? I wet my finger but there was no real wind. He had to be close . . . fuckin' real close. In a regular war, killing this outpost without risk would be easy. A lobbed grenade into his position, a burst of fire from the Kalishnakov, there were many ways, all noisy and bloody obvious. Anything like that here and all hell would break loose and the hostages would die. No, whatever I did had to be quiet, and whoever else was here couldn't know it had happened. I was hoping whoever it was would move . . . I'd be able to see him then. I lifted myself up an inch and snaked forward two inches. Jesus! He was practically beside me. Automatic reflexes took over . . .

In two strides I was beside him. His face turned in total disbelief, his mouth gaping frozen, the yell of alarm jammed in his throat. At close range and with full force I smashed the butt of the AK-47 into the uplifted face . . . Stunned, nose and teeth shattered, he crashed backwards off the small termite mound he'd been sitting on. I dropped the Kalashnikov and leapt on him. Knee going into the solar plexus, blood spraying as the air gushed out of him, left hand around his throat reaching for the jugular, finding it and squeezing hard with thumb and fingers. My right hand flew to my upper webbing and removed a dart from its

100

sheath. I held the dart poised, ready to plunge it into his chest, but it was over. He was unconscious. The dart went back into its sheath as I wanted this bastard alive. I tied his hands behind him and his ankles, found a dirty handkerchief in his pocket and rammed it into his mouth, then took out some tape and wound it around his head and mouth.

He wasn't that heavy but it was awkward on the uneven ground and it was starting to get dark. The trees were waving in the wind and casting eerie, dancing shadows on the ground. Moonlight started to reflect off rocks and shiny dwarf palm fronds. I'd had a little bit to do back there before I could get my prisoner and myself away. I disposed of his weapons: a rifle and a knife. He had a canteen and food, I got rid of the cigarette butts. And I swept the area with a dead branch till there was no sign where he'd been.

The moment I gave Jacko the 'contact' code was his signal to join me. I was far enough away from the mine for me to use the radio now, and I put my prisoner down.

'One to Sunray. Do you have my 1020 come back?'

'Sunray is inside outer killzone. Talk me in.'

I looked at the compass on my wrist.

'Heading Sunray.'

'Nor-west 130.'

'Heading needs to be affected 15 degrees east, I'm out.'

An hour later I was back at the hootchie. I threw a rope over a low branch and attached it to my victim's wrists, then pulled the rope up tight. He was still pretty groggy and the rope pulled him up into a sitting position, with his chin being pushed onto his chest and his arms back at ninety degrees to his back. Not a very comfortable position. But comfort was not what I'd planned for this mongrel. I grabbed a flashlight and shone it in his face. He was breathing with a rasping noise through his smashed nose and one of his eyes was closed, but the other one, though puffed, was showing an evil glint.

Ravenous, I grabbed an emergency food ration pack and tore into it, washing it down with some water. I put the Litton night scope on and, keeping my eye on the perimeter, I grabbed the radio. With me out front there was no need for stealth from the back-up and he would make good time.

'One to Sunray 1020.'

'I'd estimate less than five. Message near blew transistors . . . out.'

He wasn't far wrong and I picked him up in the night scope coming up the rise. I gave a low whistle, well-known from days gone by. He had his scope on and when he saw me he doubled his step.

Jacko stripped the gear he was carrying and, putting my mouth close to his ear, I said 'We have company, a captive audience.'

Jacko was a hard man, he was good in Vietnam, and he had a cold side to him that let him get the job done. I let him have his way and he soon extracted the information we were after: there were three more guards, plus Gabrialdi and the girls. But our friend did not survive the interrogation.

'Get some rest,' I told Jacko, 'I'll take first watch, but if we hit these cunts before first light I think it's

going to be a cakewalk, old son. They'll be wonderin'
what's happened to the dear departed but there's
nothin' up there to indicate foul play. With a bit of
luck they'll think the poor prick got lost. It'd be easy
enough. But if they think he's been taken they'll really
be on their toes, so we move before first light. They'll
be anything but sharp then. Go get some rest, old son.'

Jacko's in the hootchie asleep, I'm out here keeping
watch, I think to stay alert. I think of my early child-
hood with the hypocritical Bible-bashers that had me
for my first eleven years. When I was young there was
the exciting breathlessness of looking up the word
'sin' in the big dictionary after a morning spent in
Sunday school. Jezebel, Mary Magdalene, Ruth at my
feet, Lot's daughters, Solomon's concubines. They
caused one hell of a frenzy at Gadara when the mad-
man who broke his bindings over and over was healed
and the spirits went into a herd of pigs, three thousand
of the bastards, and they cast themselves into the sea
and drowned. Froth and huge waves from pigs drowning. I remember when I went to a farm and saw the
pigs in a pen and tried to multiply them into three
thousand. There were only twelve and it was difficult
to imagine them having the spirit of an evil woman in
them . . . take heed there all you men, when you have
changed your ways and cleansed your bodies of all
vileness of the dozen or so quickies, or one night
stands that you have had around the country. Yes,
these women that you have mistreated will know this
and cast themselves into the ocean or into a fuckin'
pigpen. Underpants down, me and the next door

neighbour's daughter behind the chook coop. She said at twelve, see my arse. In front of your eyes and not a soul to confess it to. The old dead sheila who used to play piano at the mid-weekly prayer meetings is in heaven now and can see what you do to yourself at night and what you do to others at school at home or work or play. Nothing can be hidden from the dead, and the poor buggers can't really help us at all, though they must weep for us when they see what we do. You could hear the chooks squawking and clucking, scratching at the bare ground. You have no hair on yours, I've got some on mine. I'll get mine after my next birthday, I was told. Uncle Fred's in Korea, Mum says he could get killed. You touched her thing. At the Nazarene Scripture Night the preacher trumpeting out . . . the young couple's little daughter fell into the pig-pen and she was devoured by the swine in punish-ment. He turned to drink, and women. She turned to drink and other men. Then they heard a real nice hymn on the radio and everybody had prayed really hard for them, especially their mothers, and they all wept by the bloody wireless and asked for forgiveness. Soon they had a brand new baby. God works in many wondrous ways, you know. I'll go to Africa and be a missionary and save all the heathen niggers, they're savages you know, Jesus will save me from the dan-gerous lions and snakes. Her arse is bare, the chooks running around in circles, they think we're gonna feed them. The missionary in the church played us a hymn on the organ and sang it in an African language and showed us some picture slides of the Dark Continent. And the poor leper with a great big giant jaw and one ear missing who had been brought to Jesus at the mission. All the girls over there are forced to get married when they're ten, they'd only be in the fourth grade at school. I found a book about Flash Gordon in my mate's desk where in the rocket ship, Flash Gordon put his thing all the way through the woman and out the other side and a bloke had it in his mouth. And it had Joe Palooka, too, with boxing gloves on and his trunks were down around his knees before the fight with all the famous people lookin' at him. A friend of mine gave an Abo sheila two bob to pull her dress way up. What did it look like? Don't know, he wouldn't tell me.

My mind flies to poor Diefer. When a dog barks or growls his warning in the night, I try to fathom from the sound whether it will be a fuckin' stray cat, a possum, an innocent pedestrian, a killer or a ghost. It occurs to me that people don't talk about death because even to the simplest of them death isn't very interesting. This of course will all change when it draws near to the individual, but until then death has the probability of zero. There must be a reason why I parcel funerals, weddings and love affairs together. Christ, look at the time. Got to wake Jacko. I haven't slept, doesn't matter, couldn't have slept anyway.

We moved out with the aid of the Litton night scopes. It's an eerie feeling. You think that because you can see them that they can spot you. But the feeling passes if you turn it off for a second. We stopped for a breather and set a fire flash charge. Jacko set the code on the detonator and handed me the control box.

'Just pull the aerial and push. It's all set.'

Then on an invisible signal we moved out again. Just like lookin' for Charlie in the DMZ. All of a sudden the rain starts slashing down. We're wet. Then we're there. I gave Jacko a tap on the shoulder and he doesn't even hesitate, he knows the drill. Hit from two sides. I'm peering through the night-scope. They're there all right, two of them crouching against the building trying to escape the rain. Tsssh tsssh on the radio . . . Jacko has flashed me that he sees them also. A-ha, there's the third bastard! Standing in a kind of lobby, out of the rain. I flash three to Jacko and he sends back the acknowledgement. There seems to be some sort of an entrance on this end of the building. There's a chimney coming out the roof with a wisp of smoke, probably a kitchen. But I've never been in there so shouldn't guess. Read it as you see it. I don't know the layout.

I send the signal to Jacko. One long push on the radio button. Come to me. I see him coming in the night scope. We are squatting just fifty feet from the building now, the rain is hosing down, drumming on the corrugated iron of the roof. I place my mouth against his ear.

'Do you reckon you can get to that door at the end of the building?'

'In this shit. Not a problem.'

'I'll set the flash charge off when you're in position. Then I'll take these three out. They're too close together. You'd better get through that door awful fast, but don't hit the women for Christ's sake.'

'Gotcha.'

106

Jacko pats me on the shoulder and I watch him move away, slithering along the wet ground like a snake. The one inside the door lights a cigarette . . . Shit! Fuckin' near blinded me with the Litton on. Jacko's getting close to the door, with the building between him and the three sentries. Then he's up, back hard against the wall beside the door. He waves his arm, he's set. Moving the rapid fire lever of the Kalashnikov forward, I take the detonator-radio-control out of my pocket, pull the aerial out, put it in my left hand. AK by the pistol grip in my right. Thumb on the button. I'm facing the target, the flash won't affect me. 1 . . . 2 . . . 3.

Woooomph! The incenderary goes off in a blast and a sheet of flame.

The three targets are caught completely unawares. The Kalashnikov is dancing in my hands and the targets are punched back. Doing crazy dances like marionettes on strings. One's right down, one's hit bad, the other hit but moving. I pick him up and gut him with two quick bursts. Roll, move, come up, new mag in place. I'm moving in on the zigzag, only slight movement from the one on the right. Quick burst and he shudders as the 7.62s tear into him.

I stay put. Then the signal from Jacko. All clear. I run up to the building and step over the guy who was in the door.

'Jacko . . .?'

'Move in, all clear and secure.'

I'm inside.

'Let's get some fuckin' light in here.'

I can hear whimpering from the end room. I move to the door, kick it open. Two girls sitting on the bed with their arms around their knees. I close the door. All of a sudden Jacko's got a light going. The body on the floor must be Gabrialdi. We strip the Littons off.

'Nice work, son,' Jacko said. Then pointing to the body on the floor with his weapon. 'Fuckin' nearly got me. He was standing in the corner behind the fuckin' door. His bloody shadow saved me, just got a glimpse from the last light coming through the window from the incendiary. What's the next move?'

'Clean this mess up. We can't leave it like this.'

'Got any ideas?'

'It's starting to get light. There's an old mine shaft over to the right. You can still see the gantry. How much plastique have we got?'

'Three blocks, including yours.'

'Shit, that'll entomb the whole fuckin joint.'

We got Gabrialdi and the other three down the shaft. It must have been deep because we didn't hear them hit the bottom. Jacko made up a charge with the three blocks of plastique and lowered it down on a coil of rope he'd found. We couldn't just drop it in because there'd have been enough water at the bottom to short-circuit the detonator.

'How long before that lot goes up?'

'About fifty-five minutes,' Jacko said, looking at his watch.

'Right, we burn this joint to the fuckin' ground. There's two drums of fuel out there, and we'll spread it over those bloodstains out the front as well.'

'Righto, you get the sheilas out. There's a four-wheel drive in the shed. Get 'em into that and I'll fix this lot.'

'We're gonna have to blindfold these birds, you know, Jacko. They can't see our faces, mate.'

'You organise that too.'

I pulled the balaclava out of the overall and put it on. Jacko saw me and followed suit. Then I walked into the back room. When the girls saw me they gave a whimper.

'Look,' I said, 'we're not here to hurt you but we're going to have to blindfold you. But no-one is going to hurt you.' I walked over, took the pillows from the bed and ripped the cases off them, talking quietly to the girls while I placed them over their heads. They were too scared to resist.

An hour later we were back at the house. When the girls were secure in one of the bedrooms, I rang Paolo.

'Job done. We want a private plane out of this joint right now, Paolo.'

'That is not a problem, Jimmy, but what about the other parcels.'

'They're both here. Grab a pen and I'll give you directions. We've had to blindfold and tape them. Couldn't let them take a look at us.'

'I hope you're on the scrambler.'

'That's affirmative.'

I gave him the location of the house. 'What about all this other stuff?' I asked. 'We can't be carting that around.'

'Leave it. You get to the airport now.'

The only thing I kept out of the whole shebang was the Browning and the scrambler. I gave half the money to Jacko and told him there was more to come.

As usual, Paolo was good as his word. We had to touch down once at Mackay for fuel but all in all it wasn't too bad.

The pilot banked the Cessna steeply as he came in over Archerfield, then levelled and touched down. There was no cross wind and the airsock drooped like an empty condom. He taxied around to a forgotten corner of the airfield and pulled up near an old hangar. The next thing I saw was big Rocco driving over towards us. The Fairlane was listing badly to one side with his weight. I didn't introduce Jacko to Rocco and Rocco didn't say a word.

We pulled up in front of the Crest and Rocco spoke for the first time as I was climbing out.

'Boss said he'll see you later.'

'Fine, Rocco, just fine. Thanks for the ride.'

Jacko wanted to return to Sydney. I told him I'd be there any day, too, and arranged to meet him through his mother.

Up in the suite I poured myself half a tumbler of Scotch, kicked off my shoes and scuffed my feet as I walked around on the carpet. It is strange the emotions I go through after the job is over. I have a hard job of keeping down the feeling of hate that has a habit of stealing its way into my consciousness, and it is a feeling I have had far too often. It was the one barrier, or defence, which kept out, momentarily at least, the more shameful emotion of fear. But for someone like me, whose career, for want of a better name, had been made from other people's fear and hate, it was no solution. Hate was slowly consuming me, an acid that etched its traces onto heart and soul. The world I lived in was one where no person entirely trusts another, which was reflected in the way I treated others who were not within this dark world that I operated in. My world was a madness which brought death and turmoil to others, some of them innocent, and put money, bloody though it was, into the pockets of people like me, and not just here but all over the fucking world. But all this does is foster more hate. I detested some of the people I had associated with, who lived off the misery of others. Compared to them I was a mere tool, a means to their ends. But, worst of all, I felt trapped. There was no honourable way out for my conscience. But in some twisted way I hung onto my sanity by believing that I was at least attacking that which I knew was bad, and didn't deserve to live.

But I had too much experience in the underworld scene not to be a realist, and I was plagued with the feeling that a climber must get when he takes two steps upwards on a shale-covered mountainside, then the rocky soil slides out from under him and he is carried one step backwards. I was, I knew, a sensitive man, a man who wanted to believe, but this ability I had to feel, to sympathise, to fear, and even to understand my enemies made me dangerous . . . more dangerous by far than a thug or a mere adventure seeker. I had been doing this sort of thing now for fifteen years. In the beginning I had believed, but there had been too many casualties to maintain those early beliefs. It was now a case of survival, but I too was becoming a casualty . . . I had to live a life full of suspicion that turned to fear, and then hate took over. As a child I had learned how to hate before I learned there was love. I used hate because I understood it. But I knew there must be something better for me. I was becoming sick with the glib discussions of expendables in the big picture. I have known many other men of character who had lost their lives for a cause. I served with them in that shitty hole called Vietnam. They were not expendable. There are never enough of those kinds of people to go around. And now, I'm about to call in another . . . for a cause, my cause.

I walked over and made myself another drink. I wanted a lot of drinks, wanted to get drunk. I took the phone off the hook. Fuck the lot of 'em.

When I woke up I was lying across the bed, damp and naked, in my tenth floor room. The hotel had a thousand identical fucking rooms, the same bed lamps, the same drapes with big white flowers on them, the same bathrooms and shower stalls with sliding glass doors . . . when you took a shower you felt like a bloody fish in an aquarium. I was sweating like a pig. It was crazy when you thought about it, really crazy. This bloody great enormous hive I was staying in, and the insignificant little people moving around in each cell for one brief moment in their lives before they died, each in his own little niche, needing sleep, insomnia, love, money. What in Christ's name did it all mean . . . Shit! what a farce. I lay heavily on the bed, hungover and sweaty. What a prick I am, I thought. After two showers I felt better for about five

minutes, but I was still sweating. Nerves are jangling
. . . can't breathe. But the cool air from the air-conditioner was landing on my face. I got up and turned it
off, then went over and tried to open a window. Fuck
it, they didn't open. There was no choice—cold air, or
suffocate. Totally stuffed, I threw myself back on the
bed, exhausted, all my nerves quivering, gut all tense
and tight. A terrible head pain tried to spread down
my neck. I dug my fingers into the back of my neck
and tried to massage the pain away. I was so lonely. I
wanted to pick up the phone and call Carmel. Bloody
ridiculous . . . What would we say to each other under
these circumstances? A few smiles, a few words, a lot
of silence. We don't even have any kids yet. God, I love
her big boobs. I reached over, put the phone back on
the hook and then took another shower.

12

BRISBANE IS A TOWN IN WHICH YOU CAN GET MOST things, including hurt if you tread on official toes or put official noses out of joint. I let the shower pound down onto the back of my neck to try to relieve the pain and when I couldn't stand it any more I turned it off. It was only then that I heard the knocking. Thinking it was Paolo, I wrapped a towel around my middle and went and opened the door.

There were two of them, one tall and lean, the other one shorter and stocky. Both dressed in business suits, both wearing sunglasses. I saw myself reflected in the dark glass. A shrunken figure with a drooping towel, twisted by the curve in the glass like an imp in a bottle.

'What's the problem?' I asked.

The taller one cleared his throat, looked up and down the corridor.

'We'd like to have a quiet talk,' he said. 'We're from the Mormon Church.'

Religious spiritual guidance in the Crest? I should have woken up immediately, it was fuckin' ridiculous, but I was crook and hungover and not thinking straight.

'Look, if you've . . .'

That's when the taller one shoved me hard.

I landed flat on my back halfway across the suite. They both came in quickly, the tall one produced a short-barrelled .38 and aimed it in my direction. The stocky one placed the 'Do Not Disturb' sign on the knob and slammed the door.

'Now, you just take it easy and we'll get along just fine,' said the tall one.

I stood up, but they never gave me a chance. The stocky guy walked behind me, locked an arm around my neck and dragged me back, ramming me down into a straight-backed chair. His offsider kept me covered with the gun. My arms were pulled back behind the chair and secured with electrical plastic lock ties. Then they fastened my ankles to the front legs of the chair with another pair.

'Look, what the fuck do you want?'

The tall one lit up one of those smelly Russian Sobranie cigarettes. The pungent smell of the smoke stank the room up as surely as if he'd pissed in the corner.

'He wants to know what we want?' said the stocky one to his mate.

The taller one didn't answer straight away, but started prowling around behind me. It made the hairs on the back of my neck start prickling.

'Don't be in a hurry, we'll get around to it in a minute, and when we do you'll tell us what we want to know. Have no fear about that.'

'Well, why don't you start asking right away?'

The stocky one just grinned at me. Some dentist had done a lousy job on capping his teeth. Probably after someone had done just as good a job of knocking the bastards out.

I tested the lock ties that secured my arms.

'Don't waste your time,' said the tall one. 'My mate's pretty good with those ties.'

'Fuck you,' I said.

A hand grabbed a fistful of hair from behind, dragging my head over the back of the chair. It felt like my whole fuckin' scalp was being torn off.

'Righto,' the tall one waved his Sobranie and the hand holding my hair let go. My head fell forward and I blinked away the tears.

'You don't want to upset Ralph like that. He's real mean when he gets upset.'

From over on the other side of the room I heard bottles rattling in the mini-bar.

'What the fuck are you up to over there?' the tall one yelled.

The bottles stopped jingling.

'You're not going to get stuck into the piss, are ya? You know what happens when you do that.' The tall guy turned his look back to me. 'Doesn't mix with the tablets he's on,' he said conversationally.

'I didn't think they had pills for fuckin' stupidity. I thought it was incur . . .'

He kicked me hard in the side of the shin. The pain was agonising as it speared up my leg into my groin. My heart gave a stumble . . . and started pumping again.

'Now don't let's have any more fuckin' crap,' he said to me.

A jack-hammer started up somewhere on some new

116

construction. The sun lanced into the room through the gap in the curtains, and down in Queen Street people would be going to work. But here in the room I was tied up and naked and at the mercy of a couple of guys who worked for the Marquis de Sade.

'Okay,' said the tall one, 'let's get down to business, and let's have the right answers . . . When did you have a meeting with Al Rissi?'

'Never had a meeting with anyone. Who's Al Rissi?'

He gave a deep sigh and walked over and slapped me hard across the face.

'Let's start again. How did you get to know the name Al Rissi?'

I started to put two and two together now. Fuckin' Percy had sent this pair of Neanderthals to find out what was going on.

'Go and tell Percy to get well and truly fucked.'

The hand wasn't open this time, and I just managed to turn my head before the punch landed. Instead of flattening my nose, it hit my cheekbone and I felt the skin split. Then I felt a trickle down my cheek.

'A real tough guy, eh?' said the stocky one. 'We've got just the thing for that. That's a nasty cut you've got there, we better do something for it, to stop the bleeding.'

He had a miniature bottle of vodka in his hand and leaning forward he grabbed my head by the hair, turned it and poured the vodka into the cut. Shit, it stung. It ran down my neck and onto my chest, and with the hangover I was suffering, the smell of it nearly made me throw up. He got another miniature of vodka, screwed the lid off and tipped some in my hair. Then he took out a disposable lighter and flicked it alight. The flame burnt unwaveringly in the still air. Even when he pushed it toward my chest.

He grinned maliciously at me.

'This stuff is pretty volatile,' he said. 'It burns real good, you know, you'll have burns all over your body.'

He tipped a bit of the vodka down over my cock.

'That'll burn real good, too.'

There was a knock on the door . . . The stocky guy flicked the lighter off and put his finger to his lips to indicate I was to be quiet. I knew I didn't stand much of a chance whichever way it went. There was a louder knock and Paolo yelled out . . .

'Jimmy, open the door.'

'I'm fuckin' tied up, Paolo, break the bloody . . .' and the stocky one shoved his hand over my mouth.

There was one unholy crash and the door flew back, tearing the striker plate out of the frame and big Rocco stood there with a gun in his hand.

'What fuckin' gives here?' Rocco asked. 'Who are you cunts?'

They both stood back and looked at Rocco. Paolo came over to me.

'You okay, Jimmy?'

'Not fuckin' really, mate. Get me out of this shit.'

Paolo pulled a short folding knife out of his pocket and cut the lock ties. I got up out of the chair and walked over to the stocky guy and hit him flush in the mouth. When his head went back I kicked him as hard as I could in the balls.

The tall one was starting to say something but I

never gave him a show. I king hit him flush on the nose and felt the bone and cartilage fracture under my knuckles. He collapsed to the floor and I leant down and took the gun out of his coat. Thumbing back the hammer I stuck it in the stocky guy's ear.

'How's it feel now, smartarse?' I asked.

'Who are they, mate?' Paolo asked.

'I'll tell you who the cunts are, Paolo. They're a couple of spooks from bloody ASIO that I'm going to have a word about with a certain Percy fuckin' Grainger.'

'ASIO!' he said in a sharp whisper. 'What's all this about?'

'Just get this pair of cunts out of here and I'll tell you all about it.'

I walked into the bedroom and got a bathrobe and put it on and when I walked back into the lounge the floor manager and a maid were standing in the doorway.

'Ah . . . we've had a report of a disturbance.' He eyed the situation, looked at my cut cheek and the other two bleeding. 'I think I should call the police.'

I went and got my wallet.

'There's been a bit of a misunderstanding,' I said, handing him fifty dollars, 'but everything's cool right now.'

'Well . . . you're sure you don't want the police?' Then he pointed to the two bleeders. 'Who are these gentlemen?'

'Look, everything's all right. I don't want to make a complaint to the house or the police and these bastards are just leaving.'

Thirty minutes later I was in another suite and running over the events of the last few days with Paolo. He made quite a deal about the run-in I had had with Percy's heavies. And I could see that it troubled him that ASIO had somehow become interested in me. But he calmed down when I explained that Percy had no idea what the operation was about, but that he had been used to check out a couple of things and had become suspicious.

'There's one thing that's got me baffled, and I think we've known each other long enough for the truth. What is Rissi's connection to all this?'

Paolo looked hard at me for a moment.

'I wish I knew, Jimmy, and that's the truth. He came highly recommended from an overseas source. We had the option to either assist him or flag it away. I decided to help because of the source who asked.'

'When you say overseas, do you mean the States?'

He nodded his head.

'Family . . .?'

'No, but closely associated.'

It would have been unwise to push the matter any further, but I knew from the look on Paolo's face that he was lying to me. So I let it rest, storing away what he'd told me. As he was leaving he stressed that I was to keep my finger on Percy's involvement. And after he'd gone I wondered why he'd come in the first place.

I rang Percy in Sydney and the moment he answered I gave him the treatment.

'What sort of a fuckin' cocksucker have you turned out to be, Percy, you rotten bastard? I'm going to do you good when I see you, you cunt.'

'Listen, mate, I have already been informed of the fuckin' fiasco that took place up there, but let me get one thing straight. They exceeded their authority. They were told no rough stuff, but decided to free-lance and I can tell you they're in deep shit. Now I want you to listen to me, Jimmy. You've got every right to be pissed off, and if there's any way that I can make it up to you I will, but we've got to have a very serious talk down here. You and I go way back, and have I ever let you down? Now get on a fuckin' plane because let me tell you, mate, friendship or not, if you don't the fuckin' Special Branch will be notified and I'll have you fuckin' well arrested. It's that fuckin' serious.'

I knew Percy well enough to know when he was for real.

'Right, Perce, I hear you. But if you're having a lend of me by Christ I'll . . .'

'It's very fuckin' serious,' he cut in. 'Call me when you hit Mascot and I'll send a car.' He hung up.

I wasn't able to get a plane till the next morning and, to tell the truth, after the workout I'd had from Percy's two sadists I didn't fuckin' care.

I was driven into the city by a guy that had ex-Special Branch oozing out of the pores of his skin. He didn't say one word during the journey. The strange thing was we didn't go to an office. I felt better when we pulled up in Oxford Street and the driver pointed across the road to where Percy was sitting at a table outside a cafe.

It was about 9 a.m. and the footpath was crowded

just about shoulder to shoulder. People were converging on Taylor Square for croissants and coffee, or cruising home after a hard night out. Some of them still wore evening dresses, and some had five o'clock shadow and bloodshot eyes.

The Darlinghurst Courthouse was just across the way, a red sandstone monstrosity, and people stood about all around the place. Lawyers in wigs and gowns appeared to be doing most of the talking. Their clients, dressed in anything from suits to jeans, looked like a bunch of kids on their first day at school.

As I sat down at the table Percy gave a signal to a waitress and she put a cup of coffee in front of me, smiled and drifted back inside.

'I assume your summons is official?' I asked him.

He had a mouthful of his coffee and looked at me. 'Sort of . . .'

'What do you mean fuckin' sort of . . . Have you had me bloody well fly all . . .'

'Shut up.'

'What?'

'Shut the fuck up, Jimmy, and listen . . . Let's cut the crap and talk this out. Now that thing at the old diggings up north, that was you and a partner wasn't it?'

'You're tellin' the story, Percy, but keep going.'

'Right then, you are contracted out to a guy who calls himself Al Rissi. You whacked four guys up at the mine. Christ knows where they are now. And you got two birds out of the place and out of the hands of a cunt named Gabrialdi.'

'Where's all this heading, Percy?'

'I'll tell you where it's all fucking heading, mate. We've all been conned. You, me and that Mafia *capo di tutti capo* you call friend up in fuckin' Brisbane. We were led to believe that it was a joint overseas operation to eliminate Gabrialdi. But those two girls, Jimmy, have turned up dead . . . DEAD, do you hear? In the back of that fuckin' Falcon you left in the garage at Port Douglas.'

'You're fuckin' kiddin' me?'

'I bloody wish I was. Christ, Jimmy, we set up the deal that supplied the fuckin' vehicles for Rissi. From the fuckin' US Consulate for Christ sake.'

'And you think I did it. You think I killed those two girls. Jesus, Percy.'

'Look, I've got to ask you . . .'

'You know that's not my style, Percy.'

'Yes, but I still had to ask.'

'Are the police involved with this yet?'

'What! Are you fuckin' crazy? Christ, it'd start an international incident.'

'How come you didn't know I was involved until it was over?'

'Rissi was given the green light to do his own recruiting. We really didn't want to know. I put two and two together when you rang. It wasn't that difficult. And we wouldn't be having this talk now apart from the fact that we've got two very dead females chopped up in plastic garbage bags in the back of a fuckin' vehicle on loan, for Christ's sake, from our friends at the Consulate. Fuck me, what a mess.'

'So you and whoever have been doing a covert operation . . . Jesus, Percy, those poor bloody girls. What sort of an animal is this fuckin' Rissi.'

'Never mind about that for the moment, what part did that *Cosa Nostra capo* Agostini play in this? God almighty, Jimmy, what a fuckin' mess, but I'll tell you one thing. We might be known as the four-letter agency, but we clean up our own mess.'

'Well what the fuck am I doing here then? Why bring me all the way down here when we could have had this conversation in a phone booth?'

'You were part of this thing, Jimmy, and it's payback time. You're gonna help clean it up. You let me down now . . . and so help me I'll have a contract on you before you can say fuckin' Jet Jackson. You're comin' with me right now. We've got to meet somebody.'

At Percy's signal the car that had brought me from the airport did a U-turn and pulled into the curb in front of us. We climbed in and drove off. And it started to rain again.

From the top floor of the State Block Building I could see most of downtown Sydney, even through the rain. The Regent Hotel. The stump of some new development going up. The topmost sail of the Opera House seemed to be cutting through the lush and dark vegetation of the Botanic Gardens like the fin of a great white shark.

We walked into Percy's office and he told me to take a seat, then went to a filing cabinet which he unlocked. He pressed a button on his desk and a girl I assumed to be his secretary walked in.

'Let's have some refreshments in here, Pam, if you wouldn't mind.'

The girl looked at me and smiled.

'Tea or coffee?' she asked.

'Coffee'll do just fine.'

'Regular or espresso?'

Shit, I thought, the fuckin' civil service has the lot.

'Just black will do, thanks.'

I dropped into one of those instruments of torture made out of black vinyl and chrome that someone had the gall to call a chair. It was as quiet as a doctor's surgery, the only sound was the hum of an air-conditioner somewhere and the rustle of papers as Percy turned a page on the file he was studying.

Pam brought me back my coffee and poured some milk into Percy's. He stood up, put the file back in the cabinet and locked it.

'After John McCreedy gets here, Pam, no calls please.'

She nodded her head and left the room, closing the door behind her.

'Must be nice up here on a fine day, mate.' I said.

'Yes, it is as a matter of fact, real nice. It'd even be good today if I didn't have this fuckin' mess on my plate.'

I turned my attention back to Percy.

'Well, I'm waiting, mate,' I said. 'Where do we go from here?'

'If you don't mind me asking, how do you get rid of four bodies in the middle of nowhere without trace?'

'Five, Percy. Gabrialdi died too . . . The earth just swallows them up without trace. Why do you ask? You want to notify the next of kin?'

125

'Just drop it, Jimmy. Look, I'm a risk-taker, that's my job, but this Rissi thing is sticking me right up the arse. And it's got some friends of ours pissed off, too. Rissi's not getting away with this one and you' . . . he jabbed his finger at me . . . 'are going to do the dirty work, fuckin' like it or not.'

John McCreedy entered the room shortly afterwards and we were introduced. 'He's our liaison man from the States.'

One hour later the meeting was over. It had been carefully, calculatedly vague. We might have been discussing the imminent and violent overthrow of the nation. Equally, we could have been planning a surprise party for an old mate. Towards the end I started to wonder, had I become *we*? And just who the hell *were* we? Percy had asked me to wait for him down in the foyer after the meeting.

The lobby of the State Office Block is lined with grey-veined marble and black glass windows, so you can see out but not in. And a couple of security men with faces that said one false move and you're dead. The weather outside was getting worse and I watched people being blown along Macquarie Street. A mini gale suddenly battered at the glass walls of the foyer with all the momentum it had picked up on the way from Antarctica. The hole in the fuckin' ozone layer is widening and creeping closer to New Zealand, I remember reading. Today it felt as though some bastard had climbed out and forgotten to close the fuckin' trapdoor.

13

THE PA SYSTEM ON THE QANTAS 747 AMPLIFIED THE
captain's husky voice. It made him sound like a cross
between Gough Whitlam and Bob Hawke. I'd had a
bloody gutful of it between Sydney and Los Angeles.

'If you'd care to take a look out the port-side windows, ladies and gentlemen,' he intoned, shattering the
peaceful doze I was having—brought on from a pint or
so of scotch out of miniature bottles—'you'll be able to
see one of most talked-about features of Los Angeles.'

The plane tipped, and as I slowly opened my eyes I
pushed myself into an upright position. I was looking
straight down a two-mile shaft at mountains that
looked like giant teeth that had been designed by the
devil himself. Crawling and creeping towards the
range was a sulphurous dirty fog.

'That's San Bernadino down there, ladies and gentlemen. And the yellow stuff you can see is LA's most
unpopular export. Smog.'

The plane levelled again, then seemed to slouch in
the air with a sort of weightlessness. It was a sensation
I hated. I reached up, pushed the buzzer for the flight
attendant, and held up my empty miniature of scotch.

'Let's have another one of these, love.'

She gave me a dirty look.

127

'We'll be touching down shortly, sir.'

That's exactly why I needed it. I hate flying.

Twenty minutes later I was standing in front of an Immigration and Customs officer at Los Angeles International.

'How much money are you bringing into the United States, Mr James?' he asked, looking at my immigration form and the passport that Percy and McCreedy had organised for me.

'Close to five thousand dollars.'

'Could you be a little more specific?' he drawled.

'Four thousand three hundred dollars.'

'Do you have a credit card?'

'Yes, American Express.' Hoping this might make him friendlier.

'May I see it please?'

I took out the little wallet that held my tool kit and took out the green plastic card.

His eyes jumped to the open wallet with the funny keys and the three lock picks that had become visible. Sweat started to prickle like ants on the cheeks of my arse.

He reached over and took the small wallet and began examining the picks and things. Then he looked straight into my eyes.

'Just some tools of trade,' I said to him.

He slowly pulled out a tickler pick and twirled it between his finger and thumb.

'And what trade would that be, sir?'

I was getting pissed off with this officious nosy bastard, and in so doing made a mistake.

'I'm a fuckin' locksmith, what's the problem?'

128

Whatever button or lever it was he pushed, I never saw him do it. But it took less than ten seconds for a response and they were on either side of me. They were big, and in uniforms.

They took me, my luggage, and my little tool kit away down a long corridor and a couple of flights of stairs and then locked me in a small room with a high barred window. Half an hour later, and after a thousand questions I said I wouldn't answer unless I had a lawyer present, I was allowed to make a phone call.

I rang a number that McCreedy had given me and was told to stay put.

Twenty minutes later a guy called Evan Munro came and squared things away.

'Thanks a lot,' I said as he signed for my release from the holding cells under the airport departure lounge.

'Yeah, well shit happens all the time.'

It was clear to me that I was just part of the shit as far as Munro was concerned.

'Here, put these away,' he said, tossing me the little wallet with the keys and picks.

Munro's clothes were ten years too young for his forty years, his hair was cut in a college boy's style, and the folds of flesh under his chin and a beer gut suggested too much of a good thing too often.

Having been locked up from the moment I stepped into the country hadn't been a good experience or a nice welcome to America. My temper was on hair trigger.

'It's a good thing you know your way around out here,' I said to him. 'I might still be in there.'

He gave me a dirty look which said: I've got more

to do than being fucked around out here.

I suppose I was expecting a real Hollywood scene at the famous LA International—Jesus, they even made a song about it—but it wasn't anything like I expected. No millionaires with their entourages, no models with Gucci luggage, no film stars in white linen suits, and no palms silhouetted against a sky of bright blue.

The reality was absolute fuckin' chaos and noise and hot air. Gobs of flattened chewing gum spotted the floors and, behind a ceiling of some sort of frosted acrylic, half the lights were dead. Passengers mobbed the check-ins, dragging wheeled plastic suitcases on leads, like big oblong dogs. Anything larger was usually packed in cardboard cartons, held together with sticky tape or coloured string. The Gucci bags were Taiwanese copies, the linen suits were crumpled terylene-wool with ugly creases around the crotch and all the palms had choked to death. Whatever filtered down from above the smog gave off heat, not warmth; glare, not light. It was like a chemical facsimile of sunshine.

At the main door, a small dark man looked at my one bag and carefully compared the label number with the claim docket that was stapled to my ticket.

'Come on, come on,' Munro said impatiently. The guy just ignored him. He was good at it, he'd had plenty of practice.

Outside the air was hot, even under the concrete overhang, and thick with fumes. Cars stacked up three deep as passengers wrestled with long squashy suit bags.

A midnight-coloured Lincoln glided up and stopped opposite us, blocking the whole outside lane. The paint was shiny and the windows were black.

The driver climbed out, walked slowly around to our side, adjusted his dark glasses and opened the passenger door.

'We've been waiting here a fuckin' hour,' Munro lied to the driver.

'Sorry about that, Evan, but the traffic's bad today.'

I climbed into the back seat and sat down with a lot of care. A full body search leaves you pretty tender. It felt like they'd left a couple of socket wrenches up my arse.

The grey carpeted floor of the Lincoln was plush and smooth, and nearly big enough to dance on. Opposite, and further than my legs could reach, was a small bar and a stereo deck.

Munro slid in next to me, mumbling about drivers being fuckin' lunatics. The guy in front must of heard this but he remained silent . . . and just glided out into the traffic.

Munro thumbed a button in the armrest and a glass screen rose silently, cutting us off from the driver.

After about half an hour we were coasting north up Route 405, the San Diego Freeway, among the towers of Westwood. I looked in at fifth-floor level on vast open-plan offices, everyone busy, everyone clean and neat. Shows what ants can do when they have money.

All of a sudden we were part of the jam on the Santa Monica Boulevard, once described by Bob Hope as not a road just an elongated parking lot. Then we were back up Wiltshire, and the driver took Veteran north to Sunset. On one side of the street, uniform white tombstones marched over hectares of green lawns. Rows of gum trees screened this bad advertisement for government-funded medical care from the surviving patients in the Veterans' Administration Hospital just over the hill.

Opposite, girls jogged on the track that skirted the brick walls of UCLA, a picture of brown legs, firm tits, short skirts, white shorts and rubber-soled joggers. They ran as if all those dead soldiers' bones didn't matter a bit. At their age, to be fair, I hadn't cared much either.

We drove through a set of high gates into Bel Air. Two uniformed guards were on each side of the entrance.

A narrow hillside road wound through the walled estates of Los Angeles's most exclusive private suburb. There was no footpath, or sidewalk. If you didn't have a car, you had no right to be here in the first place.

The car finally pulled up outside the gate of a walled and guarded building of huge proportions. We had arrived.

'Now, I've been informed that you don't need any briefing at all,' Munro said.

'According to McCreedy, I'm to be given assistance only, and only if I want it. I know the whos, the whys and wherefores already; that you'll take care of transport expenses and weaponry to a certain point. If I come undone . . . I'm on my own and you, naturally, will deny all involvement, or that you even know me.'

'Sounds to me like you know the score.'

In the background you could see the famous Hollywood Hills. There was no sign that the weather was about to change. You could see the vegetation and the rocky outcrop that lined the slopes and what grew on them. The people of LA love to moan about the smog but, in comparison, Parramatta Road in Sydney on a Friday afternoon in summer made Beverly Hills look like an Alpine ski resort.

On top of the gate, a remote TV camera swivelled around to stare at us. Our driver powered his window down and mumbled something into a phone that stood in a box on his side of the road.

I climbed out of the car and breathed the warm aromatic air of Beverly Hills. Playground of the rich and famous and, it appeared, the infamous.

'You want me to hang around while you get settled?' Munro asked.

'I'm expected, aren't I?'

'Sure, it's all been arranged.'

'Then you don't have to worry.'

'Good, there's just a couple of things. The car's at your disposal whenever you need it. Just call Ben here, on the number McCreedy gave you.' He spoke to me patiently. Like a missionary's wife explaining to a wild bush Abo how to flush a shithouse for the very first time. 'Ben can have the car here within thirty minutes —depending on traffic that is,' he stressed sarcastically in Ben's direction. 'If you have to go into LA city and you want to stay the night, we keep a suite available at the Hyatt, 904. If you get any problems, ring me.' I felt like jumping to attention and saluting. He handed me a card out the window . . . 'That's the office, and my unlisted home number, you can call me day or night till this thing's finished. Everything else you might need is in the house. Just ask Penny, or Joe. This is a safe house, it's practically got diplomatic immunity, but don't push it.'

'Percy Grainger and McCreedy must swing a lot of weight over here,' I said.

'We're happy to assist when it's needed,' said Munro.

Ben was around the back of the car lifting my bag out of a boot that was the size of a fuckin' Commodore. In this light and surroundings my vinyl flight bag looked like a discarded giant condom. I carefully took it from him before he got the chance to throw it down at my feet.

'Good luck,' Munro said, and powered the window back up.

The gate to the safe house swung open without a squeak. Ben looked at it, then looked at me ...

'You have a nice day, you hear?' He smiled, and drove the car away.

As I walked up the drive I heard the gate clack shut behind me and started to wonder about the big smile Ben had given me. It was the first one I'd seen since my arrival, and in this part of the world they didn't give them away for nothing.

There was no uniformed chauffeur in shiny black boots polishing cars. It was quiet and silent. I thought that with all the money exhibited in this suburb, cars wouldn't need to be polished. If they got dirty people probably just threw the bastards away, and went out and bought another one.

The guy who opened the door was big, well-muscled and had a face that looked like something out of the FBI's ten most wanted. But he smiled too, and offered his hand.

'Jimmy? . . . Hi! . . . I'm Joe.'

I stepped into a large vestibule. Joe took me up a wide staircase and steered me into a room about the size of a football field.

'I'll get back to you later, I've got a couple of things to do,' Joe said, closing the door.

I'd just dropped my bag on the bed when the door opened again and a sheila walked in. She was the best thing I'd seen since I'd arrived. Her skin had a lovely dark honey tan. She was about five foot seven, with a long, soft, muscled look and beautiful breasts. Her face was something you saw in a fashion magazine. Now I knew why Ben had smiled.

'Hi,' she said, 'I'm Penny, would you like to come down and have some coffee?'

'Yeah that would be real nice,' I said to her.

She led me back downstairs and into another room the size of a supermarket. A soft, soot-black leather couch was its primary furnishing; the rest was all brass and marble. There was a pair of abstract paintings on the wall that were so black they looked like a couple of holes in the wall until you got up close and checked out the brushwork.

Penny saw me looking about.

'Not what you expected?'

'You can say that again,' I replied. 'Safe house I was told. Is that all this joint's used for?'

'Not really . . . Jimmy, isn't it? . . . do you mind if I call you Jimmy?'

'Feel free,' I told her.

'Well, among other things, it's a house for high-paying clientele. Most people expect a brothel to be straight from Toulouse-Lautrec,' she said, 'you know, the flock wallpaper, girls in red see-throughs draped on velvet couches.'

'Yeah,' I said, 'and a black guy in a bowler hat and sleeve garters playing an old upright piano.'

'I should know better than to talk about whorehouses to an Australian,' she said.

'Well, we like the ones in the suburban terrace houses,' I said, 'with a girl at the front desk who looks like a secretary.'

'With free beer and cheap champagne? And a waiting room with big loose-leaf albums of dirty polaroids? Oh, we've got plenty of those too.' She looked towards the high wall that surrounded the joint and beyond it. 'Over there in the valley.'

She made the other suburbs sound as remote as Timbuktu.

'But here in Bel Air we have a far more generous and demanding clientele.'

I glanced through the door and saw a man and a girl who had just come down the staircase. He was tall, fat, grey and balding, and she was pretty and not a day over sixteen.

At the foot of the stairs, they stopped and embraced. And she let him give her a peck on the cheek. Like a daddy saying goodbye after visiting his daughter at college. Then the dirty old bastard ran his hand over her heavy boobs. She smiled and glanced at me over his shoulder with a look of amusement on her face.

I looked away again at Penny. Yeah, I sure as hell

knew now why Ben had grinned.

Penny poured herself some more coffee, then leant over and refilled my cup. Her elegant dark hair flowed halfway down her back, and there was a shiny black whip to it as she moved, her clothes were Oriental, sort of loose, and had a modern kind of look, and the colour could only be described as matt black. I wondered what she looked like without them.

'It looks like they like 'em young around here,' I said, pointing out through the door with my thumb.

'Why so censorious, Jimmy? Don't you secretly lust for . . . oh . . .' She looked me over and up and down, like a tailor sizing up a client for a new outfit. And then for just a moment the hardness in her poked out through her elegance and charm like an inch of artificial arm below the sleeve of a laced and starched cuff '. . . two beautiful sixteen-year-olds, for instance?'

'What do we fuckin' talk about afterwards? Our favourite pop star, cabbage patch dolls? Come off the bloody grass, I'm not into kids.'

'No tastes? No tendencies? No secret desires? Whatever they are, Jimmy, I promise you we can satisfy them here for you.'

I felt guilt at her words. I had a young girl once in Vietnam. At Bein Hoa. I was propositioned by an old man who offered me his daughter, who could only have been about thirteen or fourteen.

'You want me to fuck your daughter for money, you filthy bastard,' I said.

But I ended up paying him. The other guys around me were geeing me on, telling me some of their exploits. What the hell, I thought, and the girl fol-

137

lowed me as if it was the most natural thing in the world.

It was, I knew, the most bizarre act of my life at the time. And it offended every moral bone in my body. In many ways, it was an offence against myself.

'I won't hurt you,' I told her but she didn't understand the language. I wanted to be kind to her but she showed no emotion whatsoever, her eyes steadily watching me. I tried to make myself feel right by telling myself, why not? All the other guys are doing it.

By the time I got back to where I was staying during my leave, I felt exhausted, my energy sapped. I wasn't sure of her and was genuinely worried that she might run away and tell someone. Then I realised that this thing was going on every day. I brought her into the bedroom and I pointed to the bed and she walked towards it. Then she dropped to the floor and stretched out at the foot.

'No, not there,' I said. I bent over and lifted her onto the bed. She lay there, flat, her arms folded like a corpse. I smiled down at her gently, bent over and kissed her on the mouth. I stretched out on the bed beside her but I was so exhausted my mind felt drained. Plunging into a vacuum, I felt my body slip into a deep, dreamless sleep.

When I awoke I felt a panic of strangeness and it took me a few moments to regain my sense of place. Remembering the girl, I felt the pores of my body open. What had I done? I felt the enormity of the crime against myself, and against her. I had bought her as if she were a commodity. Or by buying her off her father, was I delivering her from the everyday drudgery and despair that she was accustomed to? Would the money help her?

And, after all, I had not yet touched the girl, not invaded her body or her soul. It was a cleansing thought. Enough to provide the courage to turn over and face her.

She was still there beside me where I had placed her, looking darker against the sheets than I remembered her last night. Her eyes were open and, as before, totally expressionless.

'Hi there,' I said to her pleasantly. At the sound of my voice, she got off the bed and stood before me, a small perfectly proportioned doll.

'Come here,' I said gently, moving my hands in a beckoning pantomime. She drew closer to me, standing barely inches away, and I could smell her body odour, rancid like that of an animal. Then it occurred to me that she hadn't had a piss or anything since last night. I took her arm and guided her towards the toilet, then realised that she had probably never seen a plumbing appliance of any nature, let alone a shithouse. Even the old folk used the outdoors, as the animals did, so I gently led her through the side door to the overgrown garden that was out there. A sort of miniature forest. She understood immediately and squatted behind a bush.

There was some takeaway food in the small fridge and I got it out and put it on the table. But she didn't begin to eat until I sat down. I watched her as she ate, nibbling away with her front teeth, looking blankly ahead of her.

When she had finished everything on her plate, she

looked down, contemplating its emptiness. The smell of her filled the room, running out of her pores, a gaseous presence. Leaving her at the table, I got up, went to the bathroom and filled the ancient tub with warm water.

When the tub was filled, I brought the girl to the bathroom and undressed her. At the sight of her perfectly formed body, my penis rose up hard. Her breasts were small but high, the nipples protruding from large, dark puddles. I felt them, kissed them, watched them harden. I deliberately averted my eyes from her face, wondering if she felt anything. She had worn nothing under the grey dress, and although the scent of her disgusted me, it also excited me. She had a tiny thatch of wispy hair on her pubes and I couldn't resist kissing that as well. Lifting her, I put her in the tub and soaping my hands, moved them over her body until her skin was slick to the touch. My fingers gently probed and cleaned every part of her body. I couldn't understand my passion to suddenly cleanse her. Perhaps it was my own heart, my mind, or my soul that I wanted to cleanse. What am I trying to wash away? I wondered. The girl was completely docile under my touch. I wondered again what she felt. I also knew that to take her back without doing anything would result in the loss of her life. Her father would think she hadn't pleased me. With a great loss of face. I washed her hair and soaped her again, titillated the tight, small crevice between her legs, massaged her nipples until they stood.

So there is something inside, some feeling, I thought joyously, lifting her from the tub. She was light, hardly an effort, and I wrapped her in a towel and patted her dry, watching her eyes. They just looked at me blankly.

'You are my little doll,' I said, drawing her to me, enveloping her in my arms, wondering if she had ever received such love, such warmth.

Carrying her to the bed, I unwrapped the towel and put her on it. The old smell of her was still on the sheets and soon her body was immersed in it again. Undressing, I stood before the edge of the bed. Her eyes watched my erect penis.

Sensing the madness of it. I looked around the room. Was someone watching? I walked to the window and pulled the blinds. The light in the room became muted.

Standing beside her again, I lifted her fragile hand and put it on my penis, and she began to stroke me.

Then I disengaged her hand and spread her legs, putting my tongue in the little crevice. I couldn't distinguish whether she was wet from me or herself.

I squeezed one of her erected nipples. But her expression did not change.

I lifted her to a sitting position and put my penis between her breasts, pressing them around it. I moved her arms around me so that her hands held my buttocks, and leaned her head against my belly, caressing her hair.

Then I moved her back till she was laying flat on the bed and I kneeled over her, directing my swollen penis against the tiny pink mouth of her vagina.

I moved toward her, the weight of my body plunging my penis forward, slowly penetrating, feeling the pain of it.

I continued to move forward, her tissue yielding, beginning to lubricate the passage. I felt her heartbeat speed up, the pumping of her blood. Or was it my own? Then her body began to twitch, her lips parted slightly as she gasped for breath. She was fully penetrated now, her body opened like a flower, moving on its own power. Her eyes had closed. I couldn't tell if it was pleasure or pain, or both. Was I feeling the power of her race now, I wondered, the brutality of the unconquered dominating by their submission. I moved my body ruthlessly, feeling her squirm beneath me.

I felt my pleasure begin, a suffusion of energy at the base of my spine, focusing its centre in my loins, my penis moving without mercy in the fragile form below me, vanquishing, self-contained in its power. Then she screamed, a long wail of anger, like an animal being quartered while still alive. It was impossible to believe the sound could come from such a tiny figure, but it continued, both frightening and exciting me, urging my energy. Then I felt the pleasure come, an ejaculation that shook me as if my blood had become a gusher, pumping through my veins with an intensity that I had never felt before. Only then did her screams stop and I lay on top of her, my pores dripping with the liquids of myself, our odours mingling.

I couldn't tell how long I lay over her, still penetrated. When I opened my eyes she was watching me. Then she smiled and started working herself up and down under me. But I stopped her.

'Have I been unjust to you?' I asked her.

142

'Exploited you for my own pleasure?' But she didn't understand.

Yes, I admit that. I am just as vulnerable as the next man. Who cares for the world's conventions when passion swings the lash?

I took her back to her father in the village. He examined her and came out nodding and smiling. Two days later, on the last few hours of my leave, I found her squatting in my doorway, a fragile lump of flesh. Her feet were raw and bleeding and I carried her inside the house, washed and bandaged them. Then gave her some money and kissed her goodbye . . .

'Hey! a penny for your thoughts,' Penny said. 'You must have some secret desire,' she repeated.

'How about the love of a good and generous woman?' I said angrily, feeling the guilt of my previous thoughts. 'How about peace of mind? Or is that too fuckin' kinky?'

'There's not much of a market for that sort of thing around here. And the talent's mostly amateur. Anyway, for that sort of thing don't most people make their own arrangements?'

The doorbell chimed, and Joe yelled loud enough to be heard all through the bloody house.

Before Penny or I could stand up a guy stood in the doorway.

'Who's this?' I asked.

'Oh, he's one of your crowd,' Penny said, 'but the women adore him.'

You could see why. He had the casual power of a young bull, and that go-to-hell look. He'd drink all day, and fuck all night, and be ready to do the same again by morning. One look at him and I knew we were on a collision course.

'I wanna go upstairs,' he snarled in a drunken way.

Penny put down her cup.

'I think you should leave, Danny,' she said. 'It's for the best.'

'I'm going up.'

'I'm afraid that's impossible,' Penny stressed firmly.

'Who's going to stop me?' He looked at me like I was a dead dog lying in a gutter. 'Him?'

'If necessary,' I said and stood up. Except for five years and twenty pounds, we were evenly matched. I knew this type of shit, I'd seen it before.

He headed for Penny, mumbling under his breath. I grabbed his shoulder and pulled him around. Shit, it was like handling a bloody fork-lift. When he turned it was really in his own time, he was very strong. The look on his face was unpleasant and his eyes were wild.

'Get your fucking hands off me.'

'Only when you're out of this fuckin' joint, like the lady wants.'

'Fuck you,' he spat.

The one lesson I learnt from unarmed combat was to never lose your cool. He telegraphed the round-house right so bloody early I could have sent out for a pizza while I waited. Ducking inside the punch, I slid my hand up over his chin, rammed two fingers deep into his nostrils and hooked them there.

For a moment he was too astonished to move. It was like he was suddenly paralysed. Then he tried to pull his head back . . . and stopped, wincing with the agony. I yanked him in close so we were face to face, and stared into his alarmed eyes, brimming with tears of pain . . .

'You move again and I'll rip your fuckin' nose wide open. Now, are you going to behave and piss off, or what?'

He froze for a moment and then nodded meekly.

As he was walking across to the door, holding his bleeding nose, a young bird who must have been just sixteen took hold of his arm, comforting him. She glared at me through mascara-painted eyes.

'You fuckin' bully,' she said.

Penny moved over close beside me on the huge couch and placed a hand on my leg. The heat from it travelled through the cloth of my pants.

'Thanks for that but you really didn't need to get involved. That's what Joe's for.'

'I can't stand fuckin' pricks,' I said to her.

14

AN HOUR LATER WE WERE STILL SITTING IN THE BIG lounge room. Penny had changed into an outfit that was split up the side and showed off her arse and her long brown legs. And they really were worth putting on display.

I had another mouthful of Chivas Regal and was starting to unwind. But I had to start this thing and get it over with sooner or later.

'I should be getting out of here,' I said at last.

'Forget about that for the moment, Jimmy. Tell me about this lover of yours?'

I felt a chill start to build inside me.

'What lover's that?'

'You said you believed in true love. Someone must have made you believe.'

A flash of Margo's beautiful face came from the past.

'I'm not sure that that's the way it really goes,' I said. 'First you must love, then you attach it to the one you believe in.'

Christ, I thought to myself, you're starting to sound like a fuckin' philosopher. The whisky started to take on a greasy taste and I thought that if I don't shut up the next thing we'll be on about will be sin and bloody redemption. So I closed my mouth.

Placing her hand on my arm, Penny raised her head and said. 'Can you smell it?'

'Smell what?' I sniffed the air, grateful for the change of subject. But she was right. Beyond her perfume there was something else . . . like dust and sandalwood. She walked to the window and slid it open . . .

'It's the Santa Ana,' and she turned her face to the east.

I'd read about the Santa Ana. Hot air piled up over Las Vegas during the day and then moved down, through the El Cajon and San Gorgonio passes, carrying the dust and the smell of the desert into Los Angeles. Then I remembered the yellow smog I'd seen from the plane over San Bernadino. It looked as though mother nature was stepping in and helping the desert. And now it was getting its own back.

'I love that smell,' Penny said. 'It really excites me.'

The thought of all that red dust sifting down over us and the rest of the city made my throat feel dry. My skin started to feel prickly and sticky. I thought hard about where I had read about the Santa Ana and remembered that it had been in Raymond Chandler. He also said that it had the ability to make women start fingering the sharp edges of knives and then look at their lovers' and husbands' throats.

'I feel like taking a dip,' Penny said. 'Want to join me?'

'I don't want to sound like a party pooper,' I replied, 'but I didn't bring any togs with me.'

She took hold of the lower hem of her dress and pulled it straight up over her head. She wore no underwear. Her body was beautifully proportioned and smooth right down to the crease between her thighs, as hairless as a young girl's.

'And I don't want to sound corny, Jimmy, but you don't need any.'

We swam around for about ten minutes in the heated pool. Steam drifted lazily from the surface and climbed towards the glass ceiling. The pools around here had to be covered, otherwise the smog would fill them full of shit. Penny climbed out of the water and lay on her back along the diving board, one beautifully shaped leg draped over the edge. I surfaced alongside her, pulled her foot down lower and slowly licked the length of her sole. Then I took her toes in my mouth and used my tongue on them. She gave a mmmmmm sound and shivered.

'Well, I suppose that will have to do for dinner,' I said.

She gazed down at me, and draped her other leg over the other side of the board. The stretching effect made her labia open widely and I looked into the wet pink softness of her.

'You've forgotten that we've got dessert,' she said huskily.

An hour later I climbed out from between the silk sheets of Penny's bed. She knew her stuff, all right. My cock had had so much treatment it felt like I'd need a handful of cotton wool just to lift it up to take a piss. Shit, it was tender.

After a shower I got dressed and asked Penny for the keys to her car.

'All you've got to do is ring Ben and he'll come and pick you up.'

'That's why I want to use your car,' I said, 'I don't want fuckin' Ben to pick me up.'

'There'll be hell to pay if they find out, Jimmy. This place does not belong to me, we're just so much cover.'

'Tell them that you didn't know until too late,' I said. 'You don't think I'm going to tell them, do you? Listen, I'm not sure if you're aware of what's going on here, but there's some things I do better alone. I don't need a fuckin' great black limo to advertise the fact that I'm around. Do you get the message?'

'I don't know and I don't want to. All I've been told is that we're to look after you while you're here, and assist you if possible.'

'Good, then bloody well assist me. Let's have the keys.'

'I'll have to ring after you leave.'

'Make it two hours and you've got yourself a deal.'

'That's all you've got—two hours. And try to avoid Joe on the way out. If he sees you leaving he'll let them know straight away.'

The windows on the front of the house gave a good view of the parking area, and there were three cars down there in view. One was Penny's BMW.

The BMW fired up on the first turn of the key and so did the clock on the dashboard. It was 11.30 p.m. in Los Angeles. Brisbane, the Cross and Bondi felt a very long way away. I put the car in drive and fumbled amongst the switches on the dashboard for the lights. That was a mistake.

149

BMWs are filled to overflowing with all those gadgets that car cranks just love. Press the wrong thing and you get an LCD display of the speed, revs, distance you've travelled, miles you've done to the gallon, how much gas you've got left in the tank . . . there's probably something there too to take your pulse, temperature, and fuckin' blood pressure.

Everything went on at once including the bloody stereo, with Rod Stewart blaring 'Tonight's the Night' at about 120 decibels. The bass was so heavy it made the seat tremble.

There was no time to try to correct anything, so before Joe could come down and intervene I accelerated down the drive straight at the big double gates. They swung open for me just when I was about to hit the brakes.

I raced out of Bel Air but it wasn't until I hit the Santa Monica Freeway and saw I didn't have anyone following that I started to relax.

It is strange driving in a strange area for the first time. You've got some idea of the direction you're travelling in but there are no familiar landmarks and you don't know how long it will take to get anywhere. And that is how I found myself. I knew where I had to get to, but had no familiar landmarks to rely on or to give me a sense of distance.

The exits flicked past under the lights but they were all unfamiliar. And I felt like I was driving on the wrong side of the road, and on the wrong side of the car. La Brea. Arlington. Western. The Downtown Towers, Hill and Main.

As I hit the big knot of the interchange south-west of the business district, the signs above the road became more complicated. Harbour Freeway. Santa Ana. This lane only. Arrows dividing, and directing. I stayed on 10. All of a sudden it changed to 60 and seemed to swing north, along the outskirts of the city. Then it changed again and became the San Bernardino Freeway, heading due east.

My eyes started to feel heavy. The strain of driving on a strange road in a foreign country was starting to take its toll. I shook my head and blinked a couple of times to get my mind back on the job. As I drove through a flat area that said Alhambra and San Gabriel, the hills on my left seemed to be petering out. When I'd climbed the last of them into a place that said El Monte I was out of Greater Los Angeles, and nobody had caught me. I relaxed a little more, and shook my head to clear it again. Suddenly I was hungry. Apart from coffee and scotch I hadn't eaten all day.

I pulled into an all-night diner and ordered steak and everything that went with it. The waitress slid a coffee on the table without me even asking for it.

I was halfway through the meal when I felt another flutter of apprehension. From what I had seen on my short stay so far, all American police cars look the same. This one was reversing into a parking spot just outside the glass wall for a quick take-off. On the door of the car was the LAPD badge with their motto emblazoned on it . . . 'To Protect and To Serve'. There were two horizontal bars of tubular steel bolted onto the front, covering the radiator and grille. Just like the cockies have in the outback, in case they happen to hit a kangaroo at speed. But I didn't think that these were designed for that.

One of the cops stayed behind the wheel while his partner ambled into the cafe. He was about mid-thirties, tall, and had a swagger that was probably caused by the amount of ordnance he was carrying around his middle. I looked it over and this cop was carrying a Smith and Wesson Model 13 .357 Military and Police Heavy Barrel revolver, extra shells in quick loaders, Mace spray, riot baton, handcuffs, a five-battery torch, walkie-talkie, a traffic violation book and a couple of other things I couldn't hazard a guess at.

He glanced over in my direction and let his eyes run over me without taking any interest. I ate a bit more of the steak and ignored him too. He chatted with the waitress and laughed.

She went into the kitchen and came back with two cups of coffee in takeaway containers and an open cardboard tray of doughnuts. He strolled back to the patrol car and it drove away. But I noticed that he hadn't paid. I guess some things don't change no matter what country you're in. After the meal I went back and sat in the car and closed my eyes to rest them.

When I opened them again the sun was coming up. Shit, I thought, I dozed off. I went round the side of the building to the toilets, took a piss and then swooshed water onto my face and dried it on a paper towel. For breakfast I had a bottle of Coke.

After El Monte, 110 got really ugly. And the early morning did nothing to flatter the long, straight free-

way. It was lined on both sides with factories, shopping malls and hospitals.

After a few fumbles I managed to get the radio
working. It was on a station calling itself KLON, the
Long Beach all-jazz-and-news radio. There were riots
in Tel Aviv, and a UDA man had blown himself and
twelve others to smithereens in Belfast. But nothing
about anyone looking for a BMW.

At the end of the national bulletin, the news reader
said . . .

'In Foreign News, Australians go to the polls today
to elect a new prime minister. If elected the opposition
candidate has promised to strengthen relations with
the USA.'

Well, they won't be worried about my vote, I
thought.

As the factories faded out and the gaps between the
developments grew wider, the empty ground separating them looked increasingly unwelcome. Wasteland
turning into wilderness.

It's at the edges and fringes of the desert, not the
centre, that the weirdness shakes out, the way that
specks of gold suddenly appear at the edge of the pan.
I passed a large stone building that said 'VACANT
FOR SALE' and a mile further on was a life-size
replica of a dinosaur that stared east, as if hoping the
morning sun would turn the cold cement into living
flesh and bone. Through a big round window in its
belly children's faces looked out.

The sky was hard, blue and empty. The vapour trail
of a jet scribbled a white line high up, inbound I
supposed for LAX. But all this seemed to do was make

the sky look even emptier. Dark brown cliffs and abutments began to crowd the road, coming straight up out of the earth. And the canyons between them were polished and abraded right down to bedrock from the abrasive droning wind you only find in deserts.

On the crest of a large sweeping hill was a line of pylons, as skeletal as crucifixes. As I got closer they resolved themselves into windmills, their metal propellers turning lazily. Further on they became as dense as a forest. It was like something out of *Mad Max* or *Star Wars*. Some of them completely motionless. Others whirling, and trickling power into the national grid. What price power?

I opened the car window . . . and shut it quickly again. The desert air was so dry it sucked out moisture like blotting paper. My skin felt withered where it had hit me in the face. I reached forward and turned up the air-conditioner full bore.

Then all of a sudden the road divided and a sign said 'PALM SPRINGS EXIT 1 MILE.' I slowed the car down and took the exit. If my briefing was correct, I was getting closer to my quarry.

15

I PULLED UP AT A PHONE BOOTH IN PALM SPRINGS AND dialled a number for Rissi's place at a joint called the El Cabana.

'We don't have anyone registered by that name at the moment sir,' the operator said. 'Would you like to try later?' I said I would and hung up. From now on it would be the waiting game. Rissi was staying there all right, I now felt sure of that.

Two hours later I saw Rissi walking in through the glass front doors of the El Cabana. How would I ever forget the lying bastard? I waited for ten minutes and then walked across the road.

The girl at reception looked at me, then at a video screen just below eye level, then back again.

'I was told to meet a friend here, his name is Rissi. Could you check? I believe he's a guest here.'

She tapped some keys in front of her.

'There's no-one by that name registered here I'm afraid.' I'd been given the phone number of the place and the extension to Rissi's suite, but someone forgot to tell me what name he was registered under. I thanked her and walked back towards the main doors, where I stood behind a fake palm tree.

The foyer of the El Cabana was like something out

of ancient Rome. A fountain frothed white under the centre dome. Whoever had designed the place must have thought he was going to make an historical statement about the time when Palm Springs offered the first drinkable water after 600 miles of desert. Instead, he had created a lavish and very expensive oasis.

I couldn't let Rissi slip away again and I couldn't very well go knocking on every door in the place. Christ knew what name he had registered under. The hotel's coffee shop gave me a good view of the lobby and the lift bays, so I went in and ordered espresso black.

Fifteen minutes later I spotted Rissi heading into the dining room. I gave him ten minutes to make his order and start on his meal, then I headed in after him.

'May I find a seat for you, sir?' asked the pretty girl at the entrance.

'Don't worry, love,' I told her, 'I'm with a friend.'

I wove my way among the tables and took a seat opposite the man sitting alone against the far glass wall. He was chewing slowly and staring through the glass, as if he didn't have a worry in the world.

'What's the food like here, mate?'

Rissi swung around as if he'd been slapped. The look of shock on his face said it all.

'What are you doing here?' he hissed.

'Now that's a fuckin' good question, Al. I was hoping you could give me some answers.'

He looked around with alarm in his eyes, wondering if we could be overheard.

'Keep your damn voice down,' he grated between his teeth.

'Fuck you,' I said to him. 'You conned me you cunt

and you'd better have a fuckin' good reason. You and that toad from Colombia were as thick as thieves. It was the girls who had the information, wasn't it, Al? Not Gabrialdi at all. Oh, he might have been able to do you a bit of damage, but getting rid of him was a bonus. How many other women have you butchered, you bastard, to keep a lid on your activities?'

'Look, will you keep this until we can talk some place that's quiet.'

'Yeah, sure, Al,' I said. 'But just one other thing. I haven't been fixed up with the money I was promised. Where's the fifty grand you owe me, you fuckin' weasel.'

'Just calm down. I can get it at a moment's notice if that's all that's bothering you.'

'Good, you do that, Al, because I'll be right behind you all the fuckin' way.'

He signalled a waitress and asked for the bill. With that out of the way he went to the foyer and presented a plastic card. A moment later a security guard handed him a briefcase. We walked over towards the fountain.

'Look, it's too dangerous to talk around here,' Rissi said. 'I've got a car down in the basement. We could go for a drive and talk.'

'Sure, Al,' I said. 'Why not?'

The leather upholstery in Rissi's big black unmarked Trans Am looked so soft I reached down with my hand to feel it. As I did I noticed an odd shape out of the corner of my eye. Racked out of sight below the dashboard was an Ithaca pump-action shotgun with a pistol grip.

When Rissi looked around the basement parking

lot it seemed casual enough, but I knew he was checking to see that we weren't observed getting into the car.

'The desert is beautiful on nights like this, and there'd be no chance of eavesdroppers out there.'

'You're the driver, Al,' I said.

An occasional car drifted by as we drove along Palm Canyon out of town. Everybody seemed to be driving well below the 55 mph limit. Probably careful drunks, I thought, hoping to make it home without being pulled over by the cops. I saw a few city police vehicles, and one state trooper in a tan patrol car.

We passed miles of white coloured houses with well-manicured front lawns, then the country clubs, with their long bricked walls and guarded gates.

Suddenly there were houses on only one side of the road. Opposite them were fields of sand, spiky vegetation and broken trees that looked like they'd been dead for some time.

Then Palm Springs suddenly endēd. The street lights just disappeared. There was only the desert and the night.

For fifteen minutes we swept over a two-lane country road, racing between stands of tall palm trees and past citrus orchards. Occasionally the lights of the car brushed a farmhouse with blank windows. Then we made a turn-off and bumped along a track dead slow. I was trying to make out the road in the starlight.

'I need to take a piss,' I said to Rissi. 'Pull up.'

'Sure,' he said.

As I took a half step from the car, I heard the noise of the shotgun being unclipped.

'This is as far as you go, my friend,' Rissi said.

Before he could pump a round into the chamber I leant quickly back into the car, put the .22 to his forehead and shot once. The impact of me hitting him and the shot drove him back away from me. I got out quickly, ran around and opened the driver's door and let Rissi fall to the ground. I wiped the .22 Woodsman clean and placed it in his right hand, closing his fingers around the butt and placing his index finger on the trigger, then let his arm fall. There was no pulse. Rissi wouldn't be cutting up any more young women.

I lifted the briefcase out of the back. It was full of money all right. Probably more than he had promised. It was time to drive back to Palm Springs.

I left the Trans Am in a public parking lot, took the elevator down and caught a cab back to the El Cabana. The BMW was still where I had left it.

It seemed to take forever to get back to LA and I got lost twice, but finally made it.

I was lying up in bed in Penny's room. She came out of the bathroom naked, with her hair tied back in a ponytail. As she lay down beside me I rested on an elbow and gazed down at her.

'Your legs are beautiful.'

'Yes they're not too bad.' She put her feet together and then said, 'So tell me, Jimmy, who are you after?'

'What makes you think I'm after someone?'

'Don't try to kid a kidder, pal. After you took off I started thinking, and this morning I rang a friend who has a friend who looked through some files and something very interesting came up. Applications for immediate entry to the USA have to be accompanied by a passport-size photograph.'

'So?'

'Well, not only is there no photograph but there's not even an application. You don't even exist.'

'Don't let it bother you, Penny. It'll only get you burnt.'

The sun was sinking into the desert like a nuclear fireball. Penny hopped up and yanked the heavy drapes together. The room turned from crimson glare to dead black.

Men have a definite sexual advantage over women in that they can do everything women can do and a lot more besides. For half an hour we did it all, and it was very, very, pleasant. It was also very mechanical.

Trying to make it a bit more interesting for her, I tried something different on Penny. She didn't like me making her lie face-down, and even less when I lubricated my thumb and started sliding it up her arse. But as I caressed her from below with the forefinger of the same hand . . . slowly and persistently, tormentingly . . . she became submerged in pure sensation. When, twenty minutes later, I allowed her to have the long-delayed orgasm, it wasn't so much multiple as a sustained crescendo of pleasure. The pillow barely muffled her screams.

'No more, Jimmy, no more, no more, no more, Jesus, no more!' she panted.

She rolled clear of me. 'Jesus fucking Christ, where did you learn that?'

My fingers were numb and the sheets were soaked with sweat.

'A Chinese sheila showed me how to do it in Bangkok, when I was on R&R there from Vietnam.'

Penny scrambled back and wrapped her arms around me as if she was afraid I would disappear. 'Nobody,' she said rapturously, 'nobody's ever taken so long to please me before. Must you go away?'

'That's the way it goes swheetheart,' I said, trying to sound vaguely like Humphrey Bogart.

16

EVAN MUNRO DROPPED ME BACK AT LAX, WITH BEN behind the wheel. He got me through the VIP departure lounge out into the waiting area and said that Sydney would be expecting me. The fuckin' air in the place hadn't improved in the last forty-eight hours.

'Look, thanks a lot,' I said. 'What happens now that I'm in here?'

'Nothing, this is no man's land. You're a tourist going back to Australia. Then again I wouldn't walk down too many dark alleys. People can change their minds. But Percy will meet you in Sydney. Have a good flight.'

The couple behind me boarding the Qantas flight were from Brisbane. They'd had a 'wonderful time', they kept telling me, 'especially when we went to Disneyland. And everyone was so helpful and polite.' The boarding officer finally saved me from more of this shit when he waved me through into the plane.

Not long after I was looking at night-time Sydney from the twenty-first floor of the Electricity Company Building. Lightning was flashing along the midnight-blue horizon.

A mile or so away, on the opposite hill and almost at eye level, was the Cross. William Street climbed up

162

to it like an artery of glittering light, feeding people and power to the clubs, bars, brothels and hotels.

And far below me the neat and manicured greenery of Hyde Park with its fountains and memorials was silent, like a demilitarised zone, separating us from that blue and pink neon den of iniquity up on the hill.

Trust the United States Consulate to have the best view in town.

Our driver was a young attache of some sort in a neat pearl grey suit, a spotless white shirt and the personality of a plastic shopping bag.

He brought us through the underground car park. It had a couple of large metal barriers, at the second of which we picked up a Marine guard with an old Colt .45 in a worn leather holster. From what I could see of the gun, it had more nicks and dings than a Los Angeles taxi. No terrorist suicide squads, to my knowledge, had ever attacked the Sydney US Consulate and paralysed the issue of visas for Disneyland. So the guard probably figured he didn't need a hotter piece of weaponry.

The reception area was sealed behind double layers of armoured glass, just like a bank, and all visitors had to pass through airport-style metal detectors. Above us, a TV monitor watched everything.

Our escort flipped on a light in an empty office. There were framed posters of New York and Boston on the walls, and a painting of the Arizona desert, bleached and dead under a moon as white as a bone. It reminded me a lot of Palm Springs.

'Would you mind waiting in here please, Mr Diamond.'

163

'Wait for what?' I asked. Percy nudged me, and the junior consul, attache, or whatever he was just ignored the question.

'You'll find some magazines. And I think the TV works.' Then he looked at the desk. 'I'm afraid the phones are off, they're not switched through at this time of night.'

I dropped into an armchair in the corner and grabbed a magazine. And thought to myself, now we play I fuckin' spy.

I tried reading but I just couldn't concentrate. The magazine had nothing to keep my interest, so I stood up and went to the window and meditated on Hyde Park and Kings Cross, dead people and a lot of lies.

After about half an hour it was my turn to go in.

The door opened to a large office lit with strange indirect neons cunningly concealed in the ceiling somewhere. Behind the desk was a picture of the President.

'Take a seat, Mr Diamond.'

The man behind the desk looked a bit like Gene Hackman. He had the same twang to his voice.

'My name is Sullivan.'

'Where's Percy?' I asked him.

'He'll be joining us in a minute or two.'

I looked up at the fancy lighting.

'Isn't it a fact,' I said, 'that fluorescent lighting interferes with radio and video recording.'

'We're not recording this, Mr Diamond. You have my solemn word on that.'

The door swung open and John McCreedy strolled in and pulled up a chair.

'Mind if I take over for a minute or two, Walter?' he asked.

'Not at all,' said Sullivan and left the room quietly.

'Jimmy . . . a night of surprises, huh?'

'Look McCreedy, we had a deal. I had a score to settle, Percy had a score to settle, and you wanted to be rid of an arsehole who, let me remind you, you used in smelly covert operations as a freelance. You hired this fuckin' Rissi, and he turned, he fuckin' used you lot as a backdrop to set himself up in the fuckin' drug business. You lot brought Gabrialdi out here, under Rissi's recommendation. And you lot ended up with shit all over your faces. I clean up a nasty mess for you and fuckin' Percy, and I feel like a piece of arse paper. Now let's drop the crap. Percy's in bloody ASIO and has been since he left the army in 1968. How long have you been playing James Bond?'

'With the Agency?'

'Yeah.'

'Nineteen sixty-two, I think . . .'

'You've been here all that time?'

'I guess so. Australia was my first big break. I never went back to the States, well not in any official capacity. I was the Deputy Station Chief, then all that altered when they rearranged things and we came under the wing of the South East Asia desk. Then they started running things out of Saigon. I suffered a slight stroke and went inactive. But with this crowd you never really leave.'

'Well now that we've cleared that up, where does all this leave me?'

'That's up to you, pal.'

'Do you want to tell me more about Gabrialdi and Rissi?'

'No I don't want to tell you about that, or anything else.'

'Why not? I know a lot about it already. You've been working hand in glove with Percy, you've even involved people in Brisbane that you lot like to call *Cosa Nostra*.'

'That's not something I'd go around advertising if I were you. There are people around here who think it'd be the best for all concerned if we dropped you into a big deep hole and forgot the fuckin' map reference.'

I was starting to get pissed off . . . 'You and who else, McCreedy?'

'Look, Jimmy. Let's be frank. People die. Don't think they don't.'

'What are you going to do, get one of these fuckin' marines to do the job? Or is it rifle and silencer? Maybe something more subtle. Like my car just fuckin' explodes one day, for the hell of it?'

'Take it easy will you, you're not making it easy with a hardline approach. There are some dumb things get done, sure. But has it ever occurred to you that, even so, maybe there's a real percentage in it for us? So when someone does just . . .' He opened his fingers quickly and made a fffft sound. 'You figure that it wasn't all part of a plan. Look be realistic for Christ's sake. Just like the book says, the perfect hit has already been committed a hundred times over. It just happens to look so natural that nobody ever suspects foul play. *Capisce?*'

166

'Yeah, well take a look at this last fuckin' mess I've just had to tidy up. It's not too bad about the cockroaches getting whacked, McCreedy, there were two innocent girls who the bloke you contracted butchered. Christ there's more bodies on this one than the last act in fuckin' *Hamlet*. I was involved in six of them myself.'

'Well they wanted me to take care of it but, Jesus, I'm too old to be dodging in and out of the fuckin' cactus with a blazing Peacemaker. And your army buddy said he knew just the guy, so we listened to Percy.'

'So you mental giants . . . Station chiefs use me and guys like me to do it for you, then all of a sudden you say hey! we've got another problem . . . this guy knows too much. Great planning. Christ, compared to you guys, the fuckin' Keystone Cops were a model of bloody efficiency. When did all this contract stuff start, and they decided to go outside for the dirty work? When they asked the *Famigilia* to 'hit' Castro, or was it Kennedy's funeral? Where have you got Harold Holt . . . managing a motel in Colombia?'

'No, he's running a marina in the Bahamas. Loves scuba diving . . . Now let's get real will we . . . Listen we're prepared to make a deal if you cooperate. It's as simple as that so don't make it harder than it really is.' He suddenly stood up and looked out the window. The storm that had been gathering on the horizon was almost on top of us now.

'Christ,' said McCreedy. 'It's got me fucked why they call Australia a tropical paradise . . . it never stops goddamn raining.'

'Why don't you ask for a fuckin' transfer to Palm Springs? That would be an end to your problems, they get no fuckin' rain there at all.'

He looked over at me.

'Just listen to the man, Jimmy . . . Listen to the man.' And he turned and left the room.

Walter Sullivan came back in. He sat down and looked at me for a moment.

'You have been involved in a most sensitive matter,' he said thoughtfully. 'Our concern is the security of our nation and your continued silence. What we would like you to do is to sign a document that will leave everybody sleeping a little easier at night.'

'What have you got in mind—a signed confession?'

He looked at me like a blocked toilet.

'No, Mr Grainger and the Second Secretary are preparing a paper for your signature. You are aware of the *Official Secrets Act*, and the penalty it carries should you abuse it?'

'And what does that get me? Am I signing my life away to ASIO or is it more contracts for the CIA?'

'Neither. You will be free to go. However, you will not be at liberty to discuss events of the last four days with anyone, and that includes me. And you will never again be permitted to enter the United States without a special visa endorsed by this office.'

'Yeah, well that bit doesn't worry me too much.'

'Nevertheless, do we have your assurance?'

'And say I won't sign, what happens then?'

'In the event of that, Mr Diamond, I'm afraid you wouldn't be permitted to leave the building. Am I making myself perfectly clear?'

'Real clear.'

'Good, then what's it to be?'

'I don't really have much choice, do I?'

'I'm afraid not.'

'Bring in the bloody paper.'

He pressed a bell on the table and Percy and the Second Secretary came in. I signed, three copies. Percy signed, everybody fuckin' well signed.

'Am I free to go now?'

There were nods and yeses all round.

I suppose in the movies a clap of thunder would have underlined my exit. Instead I had to wait until the Second Secretary used his key card and punched some buttons.

After I had collected my luggage from the consular car and been given an assurance from Percy that everything was fine, I booked into the Regent and fell exhausted on the bed.

However, I was too buggered to even sleep and my mind kept wandering. After this last episode I felt everything was going to come unstuck again. All my life it's been fuckin' questions, as long as I can remember. Why do you do this, or do that? Or why do you feel like this or that? Always the questions, loaded with implications and advice, bearing down like a ten-ton truck on a flower bed, flattening any feelings I might have, skidding across them, uprooting them as though they were unimportant weeds . . . these road-hog truck drivers who are so sure they've got the right of way.

You get immune to good advice. Sometimes I resent it, other times it bores me. Margo was the only person

169

I've ever thought it was worth the effort of trying to answer properly . . . that I ever felt I could entrust my feelings to. I felt she really wanted to know me, that she wasn't trying to get back at me with how right she was and how wrong I was. With most people there's usually been an axe in it somewhere—either to be ground or to be held over my head.

This last deal was a prime example of that. I had another axe hanging over me, and I wondered how long it would be before the bastards threatened to drop it.

The next day I flew back to Brisbane and the Crest. When I rang Carmel she came over like a shot out of a gun.

I took her shopping and let her have whatever her heart desired. Then we went back to the hotel so she could go through her 'presents', as she called them.

The remainder of the day we spent in enforced idleness. We swam in the pool, read newspapers and had lunch. Then we went upstairs and made love and fell asleep for an hour or so. The rest of the afternoon was spent by the pool where Carmel sunbathed in a bikini she had bought in the morning. We had a great dinner that night and after a good night's love romp and eight hours of sleep she caught a cab and went back to Pamela's place.

17

IT WAS JUST AFTER 10.30 IN THE MORNING AND THE phone started to buzz. It was Jacko.

'Where the hell have you been, Jimmy? I've been ringing all over the fuckin' country.'

'Well Christ, Jacko, I'm a big boy now, and there must be someone else you can share a drink with.'

'Look mate, this is bloody serious. Katy's in trouble.'

'Where is she?'

'Shacked up with me. She's too scared to put her nose out the fuckin' door.'

'Look this phone isn't what you'd call exactly safe, old son. Where are you ringing from?'

'Phone box.'

'Give me the number and I'll call you back. Got it?'

'On the button.'

I walked along Queen Street till I found a public phone, then rang the number Jacko had given me.

'What's all this about?' I asked him.

'Well two coppers came and saw Katy at her new shop. They said that they had information that she was seen with Brocassi the day he was gunned down. And get this mate, they know your name. One of the coppers is Jack Murphy. He left a card with her and asked her to tell you to contact him.'

'How long ago was this?'

'Three days. Where the fuck have you been?'

'Away. Now listen, have the Jacks been back to see Katy again?'

'She hasn't been back to the shop. There's a girl working with her and she's been looking after things.'

'Well have the fuckin' coppers been back to the shop and asked this . . . whoever she fuckin' is anything?'

'No. But the other cunts have.'

Jacko had the ability to drive me crazy sometimes. He was a good soldier, he did exactly what he was told but nothing more, like giving you the whole picture. You had to extract it from him like a bad tooth.

'What other cunts, Jacko?'

'A couple of Mediterranean lookin' bastards. Jesus, Jimmy, you're the guy who knows them, not me. They've been back to the shop three or four times, and they're keepin' a watch on the place too.'

'Righto, fuckin' calm down. Where are you staying?'

'We're in a motel at Broadbeach, the Sundowner. In number nine.'

'What name are you booked under?'

'Jackson. You're comin' down, aren't ya? Katy won't listen to me.'

'Nobody's been to the motel to talk to you?'

'Nobody knows we're here, if that's what you're askin' me.'

'Right, keep it like that and stay inside. I'll be down later today. And listen, stay loose will ya?'

'Yeah okay, mate. See ya the sarvo.'

After Jacko had hung up I rang Percy. It was a bit

early to start calling in favours, but I had to be able to move and I couldn't do it if half the fuckin' police force was after my arse. I put him in the picture, or some of it, and he asked me to give him half an hour, then to call him back.

I had some coffee and read a paper while I waited.

'Right,' Percy said when I got back to him. 'Listen, go to Roma Street and see Murphy.'

'What, at fuckin' Police Headquarters?'

'Yes at fuckin' Police Headquarters. Murphy doesn't know you're coming in but by the time you get there he will, so just go and do it. If you don't then it's up to you, Jimmy. But if you report in everything will be hunky dory. Now I've done my bit from this end so go and do yours.'

I caught a cab to Roma Street Police Building. Most people think police stations are all alike, but as cop shops go, Roma Street can only be described as elaborate. And big. They cleared a whole bloody city block just to build it. They filled the areas around the front with lawn, but it's still pretty bleak looking. It shimmers in the Brisbane heat and it looks like the Saigon Hilton. You can take it from me only someone squeaky clean and of consummate innocence could feel at ease here. When I walked up the big stairs and into the foyer I felt like Daniel in the lions' den, but kept going up to the main desk.

Once you're inside the hotel image evaporates before your eyes. The floors are hard and covered with vinyl, the lighting is all fluorescent and everyone on the job walks around or sits at desks with .357 Magnums on their hips.

173

'Yes, what's the problem?' I was asked by one of the blueys. A twenty-year sergeant.

'I'd like to speak to Detective Senior Sergeant Jack Murphy.' I said.

'Does he want to talk to you?'

'I presume so,' I said, 'That's why I'm here.'

He studied something in front of him that I couldn't see, picked up a phone and mumbled into it, then wrote on a card and handed it to me.

'Room 501,' he said and then watched me all the way to the elevators.

The fifth floor was a mass of corridors with narrow doors and petitioned offices. Some of the doors had names on them but the majority just had numbers.

When I finally found 501 the door was open. There was a small outer office with an unoccupied desk. As I looked in the inner office I saw an overweight beefy faced guy who was on the phone.

'Hang on a tick,' he said and placed a big beefy hand over the phone. 'Are you Diamond?'

I nodded and he pointed to a chair, then went back to his conversation. Something about they'd need a lot more than that before they could hope to take it to court.

After he'd hung up Murphy looked at me and smiled unexpectedly.

'I appreciate you coming in like this.'

'Yeah,' I said looking past him out the window, 'well anything to help the police.'

'Yes.' His eyes were looking right into me in a flat unemotional way. The silence between us lengthened and it started to get on my nerves.

'You did want to see me?' I said, breaking the silence.

He just sat there staring at me in an unnerving way.

'Are you a keen hunter, Mr Diamond?' he suddenly asked.

'I can take it or leave it.'

Murphy's hooded eyes were fixed on my face. A muscle in the corner of one of them jumped, then he leant forward slightly.

'But you do like guns, don't you?'

'Why?' I said inquiringly, 'Are you interested in guns?'

'Not really.' Murphy puckered his lips and leant back in the chair, placing his hands behind his head. 'I'm more interested in your experiences. You know, the thrill of the hunt. What do you really like about guns, Mr Diamond?'

'It's very simple,' I said.

'How's that?' he asked cunningly.

'Well a gun is like a woman, you place a cartridge in the breach between her thighs, so to speak.' Murphy sat upright in his chair. 'And then with the bolt you push it home and squeeze the trigger. The short straight firing pin, hard and commanding, strikes the soft nub of the percussion cap, which gives way. Heat is engendered . . . a fierce, rending heat. There is pinkness and redness. There is an explosion. And the lips of the cartridge part in the ferocity of the orgasm and the bullet is ejaculated.'

'I've never heard it put . . . quite that way.'

Murphy picked up a glass of water on his desk and took a gulp, his glance still locked on my face.

175

'Death is always dramatic when it is fired from a gun,' I said, and stared back at Murphy. 'Yet I could kill you with my bare hands just as easily.'

Murphy squirmed in his chair and changed the subject.

'Do you know somebody, Mr Diamond?'

'Who did you have in mind?'

'Do you have any relatives on the police force?'

'Not to my knowledge I don't.'

'Technically,' he said, opening a file on his desk, 'the only thing we've got at the moment is suspicion. But I suspect that the suspicion is well-founded and, if investigated . . . at first glance . . . conspiracy to commit a crime, suspicion of murder. Not bad for starters.'

He kept studying the top sheet for a while, then shut the file with a pat of his hand.

'Unfortunately, I have been denied the privilege of investigation. You're free to go whenever you like.'

'You're serious, that's it, no more questions?'

'Well I was serious up till a few minutes ago when I was directed to stop all investigations regarding you. That's why I wondered if there was a police officer in your family. Possibly the Commissioner?'

Jesus! Percy had really pulled some strings this time.

'Okay, I'll be off.'

At the outer door I looked back. Murphy picked up the file and threw it into a wastepaper container marked shredder.

Back at the Crest I packed my things and asked the desk to get me a Renta-Car. In fifteen minutes they rang me back and said the vehicle was downstairs.

176

Just over an hour later I pulled up in front of the Sundowner and knocked softly on the door of number nine. A curtain was pulled aside from a big glass window and Jacko's mug appeared.

'Christ!' he said as he opened the door, 'I never thought you were ever gonna get here.'

Katy came scrambling out of one of the bedrooms and locked me in an embrace, with her head on my shoulders.

'What are we going to do?' she asked through her tears.

'Well the first fuckin' thing we're going to do is take it easy. As of now you can forget about the coppers charging in, that's been taken care of.'

'What do you mean?' Jacko asked.

'Someone has had a whisper in their little pink ears. Look, it's cool, I've just come from fuckin' Roma Street, so loosen up a bit, Jacko for Christ's sake.'

'What about me? I can't even go to the shop.' Katy wailed.

'Just relax a little bit too, love, you'll be back before you know it.'

'So what's the next move?' Jacko asked.

'I want to check a few things out, old son. You go out and enjoy yourself or put ya feet up here, I'll be in touch. In the meantime I'm going to get some place to shack up.'

'Well I'm coming with you,' cried Katy. 'I'm not staying here. I'm scared.'

I looked at Jacko, who shrugged.

'She'd be better off around you, mate. She's just about got me up the wall.'

'Yeah well it's not you they're after,' Katy wailed.

'Righto, righto,' I said, 'just go and get your things.'

She took off like a scalded cat and came back in record time with a plastic shopping bag and her purse.

'That all you've got?' I asked her.

'He wouldn't go and get my things,' Katy said, pointing an angry finger at Jacko.

'And you want to thank Christ that he didn't. You'd have every bastard around here by now if he'd done that. Catch ya later, bloke.'

'I'll stick around here for awhile in case you need me,' Jacko said.

'Good man,' I said. And Katy and I took off.

We booked into the Sands, right on Marine Parade at Surfers. The whole building was a maze of security, from the basement garage to the penthouse. Katy seemed to settle down once we were in the suite and looking out from the balcony fifteen floors up.

I was hanging some of my things in a closet when Katy walked in and put her arms around me. She turned her face upwards, pulled my head down and kissed me softly, yet with passion.

She spoke into my mouth and at the same time her arm slipped down and her hand started rubbing my crotch.

'Make love to me please, oh please,' she said through her kisses.

I could feel a tension in her that needed to be released. She was looking for assurance and some sort of comfort in her fear.

'Sure, Katy, sure,' I whispered back to her.

I undressed her slowly and when I unclipped her bra and let it drop I put my mouth over one of her

178

nipples and teased it with a sucking motion. She gave a little moan and it seemed to accelerate the urgency she felt.

When we were naked and on the bed Katy virtually took over. She held my penis in her hand, then took it into her mouth and slowly and rhythmically went up and down. At the same time she reached down between her legs and started rubbing at her clitoris with the middle finger of her free hand. Every now and then she'd insert her finger in herself to make it slipperier. She moved her head down and started to lick my testicles and at the same time slowly masturbated me with her hand. I tried to take over and do something to her but she just said 'Mm, mm' and pushed me back.

She went back to sucking me once again, slowly, with the same rhythm. It was as though she didn't want it to end. She seemed to know just when to stop and take her mouth away.

When she finally started to climax she threw herself back on the bed and pulled me over on top of her. She raised her knees and lifted her hips and I pushed into her.

'Harder, Jimmy, harder!' She was spurring me on, and pushed herself up to meet me. Her moans grew louder and she dragged my head to hers and kissed me deeply. When the tips of our tongues touched, it was as if something inside us switched on at the same moment.

We exploded together and Katy's head went back. Her eyes were closed and her mouth was open and she let out a wail and a scream that she controlled by clenching her teeth.

The look on her face said it all . . . it was bittersweet, like the agony and the ecstasy at the same moment.

We lay there for a while and she clung to me like a frightened little girl who's woken in the night and is afraid of the dark. I held her to give her reassurance. It was a responsibility I owed to her. It had been me who had steered her life into dangerous waters and I felt it was up to me to help her.

Later, I sat down with Katy and we talked about her shop and the plans she had. And then the crunch line came. 'I'm going to get some gear for you.' She became all concerned about them following me.

'That's the general idea, love,' I said to her. 'I want them to.'

I rang Jacko to tell him where we were, then put him to work.

'Right, old son, get in your car and get up here. We'll give you twenty minutes. You should be able to shit it in in that time. Then you put a tail on me, but be real careful with this one. When I pull up at Katy's put yourself in a position where you can see me and whoever follows. Don't get too close. After you pick up the tail you stick to them like fleas on a fuckin' dog. But from a distance.'

'Yeah right, Jimmy, good as done.'

'When they finally leave me, find out where they go and I mean everywhere, Jacko. If they pull up for a piss I want to know about it . . . Clear?'

'Loud as a bell, Jimmy.'

'Right, well let's do it. You leave now and wait for me to come out of the basement.'

I went to Katy's place and told her offsider that I

180

was going to pick up some gear. Katy had already rung.

There was a two-room and bathroom addition to the back of the shop that was screened from view by a frosted glass door.

I emptied drawers and whatnot and left the boutique loaded up with two cases. As I walked out and down to the car I paid no attention to the street. I just dumped the bags in the back, climbed in and drove off.

I drove south out of Surfers and down through Broadbeach until I came to the turn-off for the island. Once I'd crossed the narrow bridge I put the foot down. I'd kept an eye in the rear-view mirror but I wasn't quite sure if I was followed, so I did a circuit of the island and then headed back towards Surfers. I travelled along Elkhorn until I hit Lennon's. I knew the guy that ran the car park alongside and I zoomed in there, giving him the 'Hi' sign as I went by his guard box and up the back, parking out of sight. Nobody followed me in and it was impossible to park, or stop for that matter, in Elkhorn day or night.

A cigarette later, I glided out of the parking lot, gave the old digger who ran it ten dollars for the trouble and glided back out into the one-way street.

I passed three turn-offs where I could have gone back but I waited and took the last. I checked and double checked every vehicle behind me but no-one was on to me, so I drove back to the Sands and pressed the little black box that came with the keys. The barred barrier went up and I drove down into the basement garage.

I rolled to a stop in my designated parking spot and ran quickly back to the entrance. Quiet as a church. Not a car in sight. I retrieved Katy's things from the car and went up to our apartment.

Forty-five minutes later Jacko was on the phone.

'They were onto you all right. Two of them in a light brown Toyota Crown, but you gave 'em the slip on the island. I lost the cunts there myself but I picked them up again.

'Good on ya, son. Where are the pricks now?'

'You know that Garter Club just down from the Pelican, where all the poofters hang out? They went up the stairs there. The club does strip shows all fuckin' day and night and the bastards are still there. I'm in a phone box just up the street and their Toyota's still out front.'

'You got that .38 of yours handy?'

'Yeah it's in the boot with the sawn-off.'

'Well get it out and wait for me.'

Katy was looking apprehensive, but I gave her a kiss on the cheek and a pat on the arse and told her I was only going to check things out. But before leaving I went into the bedroom and got the thirteen-shot Browning Paolo had given me.

18

THERE WERE RED PLUSH CURTAINS AT THE TOP OF THE stairs. All the sleazy clubs around the world had them. I guess they were to stop anyone from looking up from below. Just outside the curtains a couple of boxed speakers relayed the music so those coming in off the street would be programmed before they got inside.

I stood with my back to the curtain for a couple of minutes, then slipped inside and let my eyes become adjusted to the darkness.

These joints never changed. The same smells of stale piss and spirits, cigarette smoke and cheap perfume filled the low-ceilinged room, which was painted in a matt black. The same sort of tired white legs and droopy tits moved mechanically to the music under lights that changed colour about every ten seconds, red, yellow, green, then blue. And the same lifeless eyes stared out over the heads of the watchers, or voyeurs, sitting huddled in the dark, drinking and pulling on cigarettes that were not all made under government approval. The smell of lantana on fire was enough to let you know there had been plenty of joints blown.

They were playing the same monotonous music these joints were into . . . played on a tape as worn and faded as the sheilas who were grinding away to it. The 'Peter Gun' theme and 'Hey Big Spender'.

The girl on stage at the moment gyrated awkwardly and was trying to undo the catch on her red bra. She was a faded blonde with stretch marks and tits as small and flat as fried eggs. She was probably doing her fourth or fifth show of the day and it was starting to show.

I took my eyes off the stage to get my night vision back.

Jacko was suddenly beside me.

'That's them' he whispered, 'those two cunts up the front there.'

I got a reasonable look every time the light went yellow, but I hadn't seen them before. They weren't any of Paolo's boys.

'Let's sit this out,' I said.

We went to a table by ourselves at the very back. The only other light in the place was a red one over the bar, where for ten bucks you could have anything from a watered down scotch to a Bloody Mary.

Jacko came back with a couple of vodka and orange juices. We sipped on them and as we watched our out-of-towners, I couldn't help dragging my mind back to another time and another place when Jacko and I were together in Vietnam . . .

We were looking for some action and came across this club that we'd been told was crash hot, The Typhoon. So we climbed out of the rickshaw and checked it out.

Inside, the air was heavy with smoke and the smell of alcohol. Sailors and soldiers shuffled with the

184

whores on a tiny beer-soaked floor. The band was a brass and drums only combo from the Philippines who were openly smoking dope and had left the threshold of pain far behind. On the benches in the recesses of the room sat girls from twelve to forty, waiting for the soft touch. They all had some English, the word fuck. Jacko and I pulled a table round and sat with our backs to the wall, a couple of yards from the curtain. A topless girl appeared to our left, a small towel tucked into her waistband.

'What you like to drink?'

'Couple of beers.'

'Okay.' Then she leant over the table and wiped it with a few circular motions, her nicely rounded tits swinging two inches from my face.

A girl, no more than thirteen, stopped at the table. She wore a shiny green dress and high heels. Smiling at me, she worked the dress up over her thighs revealing minute white panties, brilliant against her skin. In a second she bent at the knees and lowered herself onto my lap. Then she leaned back and slipped an arm around my neck. I could feel the muscles in her arse twitching provocatively against my cock, and perversely I felt myself start to react. I lifted her roughly and plonked her protesting form on the chair next to me. Jacko smiled.

There was a tinny screech as the band played a fanfare, then a mauve light hit the dance floor. The band leader gave a spiel in broken English, and then the drummer broke into a syncopated rhythm on a set of tuned bongos. And on came Meli, in naked time to the drums. I gave a low whistle, caught my breath, and the chatter in the smoke-filled room died away. The girl was perfect, even, in an Asian way, beautiful. Her pubes were shaved, her nude body glistened with oil. High, full breasts moved to a rhythm of their own with an elasticity that revealed she had yet to bear a child.

She might not have come from anywhere near Arabia, but she certainly moved in that type of way as she twisted and writhed, bent and spread, with a controlled abandon that had me and every other bastard in the room spellbound. Then she picked up a beer can in one hand, shaking it up and down suggestively. She hooked a finger through the ring and eased it open. Froth under pressure hosed up her belly and over her breasts. With one hand she smoothed it over her skin, teasing the pinkness of her nipples until they stood erect with fine white beer spray frothing around them. A soldier in the front row started out of his chair but his mates held him back. Then the drummer went into a limbo and the girl slithered over the floor like a serpent, legs wide under a stick resting on two beer bottles. The drum beat slowed as first one breast, then the other, cleared the stick by a hair's breadth. The audience started to applaud but the girl rose effortlessly and picked up one of the bottles that was supporting the stick. Without preamble she licked its neck and inserted it between her legs. The drummer's hands were a blur as she leapt into the air. When she landed the neck of the bottle had disappeared. Legs wide, she crouched on the floor and little by little absorbed the bottle with her body. Ripples of muscle flowed over her abdomen and she kept gasping in pain, whether real or part of the act it was impossible for me to say. Then she threw back her head and went into a crab. The rhythm slowed, her body opened, the bottle slid from her vagina and clanked to the floor. The lights went out.

There was pandemonium of shouts in various languages and I found myself yelling and clapping with the rest, wanting more.

My train of thought was broken when Jacko gave me a nudge, 'Here they are, mate.'

By the time they left the joint it was starting to get dark. They must have been a couple of sex-starved maniacs to have put up with that shit for two fuckin' hours. Jacko and I had been sitting outside in his Falcon because we couldn't stand any more of the crap inside. They drove off, headed south, and we just ambled along behind them. The beauty of the thing we had here was I didn't know them, so they wouldn't know Jacko and me.

As we came into Palm Beach my mind flashed back to the night Sam and Angelo and Jacqui had died. Jacqui had burnt to death, the others were shot, and I was lucky that I didn't finish up with them. A shudder ran through me as the memories flooded back. It was a treacherous hired shit that had caused that, just like this double we were following. Hyenas preying on the ones that can't defend themselves.

Katy wasn't going to finish up like Jacqui, Sam and Angelo. This time I'd be there first.

'Hey, they're turning off.'

'Follow em, Jacko, and just drive by when they pull up.'

Two minutes later they had turned into a driveway and parked the car. The tail-lights went off and they both got out. We went further down the street, did a three-point turn and parked a house away on the other side.

For ten minutes we sat and smoked, both of us with our eyes glued to the house. I thought it strange that these two guys should drive all the way from Surfers to land here.

There was a phone box up towards the end of the street, and it gave me an idea.

'Keep your eyes peeled, Jacko. I'm going up there to the phone.'

'I'll be watchin'.'

I rang the club from the pay phone. Paolo wasn't in but Rocco was.

'Yeah, Jimmy, how you doin?'

'Not bad, Rocco. Listen, the Family got any property in 21st Avenue at Palm Beach?'

'No we don't have nothin' there.'

'Do you know anyone that does business who has?'

'Blacky Morrison and Tony Woodland have a house down there somewhere, you know a cat house, they runnin' an escort agency or somthin'.'

'Hey Rocco . . .'

'Yeah,'

'I owe ya a beer. See ya.'

I knew who Blacky Morrison and Tony Woodland were. A bigger pair of cunts you'd never meet. They'd sell their mothers if they could get away with it.

Back in the car I aired my suspicions to Jacko. We ducked our heads as a car came down the street and

188

turned into the drive behind the Toyota. A couple of birds came out in short black evening dresses and hopped in the car.

'You see what I see, Jacko?'

'Yeah, that must be the agency driver.'

'Smart boy.'

'How'd you like to go and recce the house from around the back?'

'No worries.'

Jacko was out of the car and in no time he'd dissolved into the shadows alongside the house. Twenty minutes later he was back.

'Heckle and Jeckle are sittin' in the lounge watchin' TV.' The names he'd given them were perfect. 'The only other person is the sheila answering the phone. Do we go in and take em out now?'

'It'd be nice if we could, bloke, but what about the receptionist? Once in Sydney I was involved in a thing that had innocent parties hurt. I vowed then that it would never happen again.'

While I was speaking, a car on the main drag had its blinker on and was about to turn down 21st.

'Down!' I said to Jacko.

We both slid down below the door level and the interior of our car lit up from the approaching headlamps. The car was a late model Falcon, with a small whip aerial on the roof, and it parked right outside the house we were watching. Car doors opened and closed. There was the sound of voices, and a low chuckle.

I raised my head and had a peek . . . Two guys climbed up a couple of steps that led on to the small front verandah. They were dressed in dark slacks and short-sleeved business shirts.

They gave a knock on the front door and it was opened by a sheila in short shorts and a boob tube. As light spilled out from inside the house it illuminated the two visitors. One of them was holding something that looked like a hand-held two-way radio.

A minute later these suspicions were reinforced when I heard a police dispatcher's voice coming from the Falcon. Cops!

'Let's haul arse out of here, Jacko, nice and easy.'

We drove up 21st Avenue to take the highway back to Surfers. As we were waiting for a break in the traffic to make a right-hand turn, a car pulled in behind us.

'Shit!' Jacko said, 'you ain't gonna believe this. The Toyota's right up our arse.'

'Just take it easy and let 'em pass us when we get out on the main road. Couldn't be better.'

We drove in silence for ten minutes. The Toyota had passed us and we stayed back and played follow the leader. When the Toyota signalled a right turn we followed suit, behind a Holden panel van with a couple of surfboards on the roof. There was an all-night pizza place on the far side of the highway and the cockroaches pulled over into an empty parking spot alongside the takeaway. The surfies accelerated and looked like they were heading up the street towards the Esplanade to catch a wave.

We parked half a dozen cars from the Toyota, facing in the same direction.

'Don't these cunts ever go to bed?' Jacko asked.

'Well, while ever they're up so are we, mate.'

It was fifteen minutes before they came out, loaded down with a pizza. The Toyota drove past us and headed east towards the Esplanade. They were going to eat their pizza while they watched the ocean.

We spotted them up on the right, parked under some big pines. A few hundred yards up to the left a bunch of surfies were all parked up for the night in their shaggin' wagons.

'I don't think we're gonna get a better chance than this, Jacko. Go and park beside the bastards, and put me on their driver's side.'

We pulled in quickly and as soon as the car had stopped I leapt out and stuck the Browning in the ear of the driver.

'You even twitch, you shit, and I'll blow your fuckin' head clean off.'

Jacko had raced around the back of the Toyota and was giving the offsider in the passenger seat the same treatment.

'What the fuck do you guys want?' The passenger's voice was muffled from a mouthful of pizza.

'We want you to meet somebody,' I said to him.

'Who you talkin' about?' asked the driver.

I pulled the gun back a fraction and then punched it hard into his ear. He gave a yelp of pain and dropped his slice of pizza.

'Give me the fuckin' keys . . . now! Use the left hand.'

He reached forward and took the keys out of the ignition, then handed them across his body to me.

I opened the driver's door and wrenched him out. He fell down on his arse with his legs still in the car. I kicked him as hard as I could in the side of the neck and he collapsed like a rag doll with a loud sigh.

I aimed the Browning through the car at his off-sider.

'Now you, cunt! Slide on over here and do it real slow.'

Jacko touched the back of his head with the .38 to let him know he was still there. When he was sitting under the wheel, I stood back a little.

'Come on around here, Jacko.'

I went to the back of the Toyota and opened the boot with the keys, then went back alongside Jacko.

'Right bastard, out! Pick this piece of shit up and put him in here.'

The guy was so scared he was trembling, but he got his unconscious partner off the ground and into the boot.

'Go and open the boot of the Falcon, Jacko.'

Jacko went over and opened up.

'Now you, cockroach, get over and get in.'

'Can't we talk about this?'

'Yeah we will when we get to where we're goin'. Move!'

'Look . . . I won't give you any trouble.'

'Get in that fuckin' boot or I'll fuckin' shoot you right in the balls, here and now.'

He went up on his toes and slid his arse over the edge of the boot and then with a shove from Jacko he was in and curled up. Jacko slammed the lid down. I wasn't feeling sorry for this bastard. If the roles were reversed I knew what he planned to do with Katy. I'd seen a ton of this shit.

We walked over into the centre of the road and Jacko asked me what I had in mind.

'Ya need to ask?'

'S'pose not.'

'You want out?'

'Come on, Jimmy, you know me better than that.'

'Righto. Follow me.'

'Can ya give us some idea where we're goin'. It just makes it easier to follow.'

'Down the other side of Tweed Heads, mate.'

'Gotcha.'

We were at the spot an hour later. Once we had hit Tweed Heads I had taken the road that follows the coast. There's a lot of scrub and places that people never go. We left the road and bumped over the uneven ground till we were out of sight of any late-night travellers.

I opened the boot of the Toyota and the guy in there was still inert. We got the other bastard out of the Falcon. And I told him to get shit for brains out.

He struggled but got him out and as his back came clear you could see by the way he was hanging that he wasn't alive.

'Jesus!' his offsider wailed. 'I think he's dead.'

'Good,' I said. 'Now if you don't want to join him, who the fuck sent you up here to come lookin' for Katy Bowman? And listen, cunt, it better be the fuckin' truth.'

'Look we're only up here havin' a look around and enjoyin' ourselves, you know.'

'You lyin' fuckin' bastard,' Jacko yelled at him

and smashed him down the side of the head with the .38.

The guy dropped to the ground and Jacko put the boot in. 'Listen you greasy bastard,' Jacko hissed, 'that's a load of shit. I followed you fuckin' pair this afternoon and we've been right onta ya all fuckin' night.' And kicked him hard again.

'Joey sent us.'

'What?' Jacko screamed. 'Who's fuckin' Joey?'

'Joey Fingers.'

'What's this cunt talkin' about?' Jacko asked.

'Joseph Fingers Frangiani,' I told him.

'Who the fuck's he?'

'Vitelli's whorehound. That's who he is. And a real nasty sonofabitch at that.'

'What did Joey tell ya to do up here?' I asked cockroach.

'He said she knew who got Pasquale. We were to get her back down to Sydney, or make her talk up here, and then get rid of her.'

'Where's Frangiani live?'

'He's got a big place in Lowery Street, you know, it runs off Oxford Street.' I didn't know it but I sure as hell was going to.

I walked over to the bloke on the ground at the back of the Toyota and felt his carotid artery. There was no sign of life. The moon was shining bright, almost full, and the guy's eyes were open and lifeless.

'He's dead all right,' I said to one and all.

'Well what about this cunt here?' Jacko asked, toeing the guy on the ground.

'He can't tell us more than he already has.'

194

'Good,' Jacko said, and shot him straight through the forehead. Before the body stopped twitching he put another round into the side of the head.

There was a small tidal creek about ten yards away, and we decided to get rid of the bodies in that.

In the back of the Toyota we found a tow rope and some jumper leads. We took the trousers off both the bodies and tied the bottoms of the legs up and filled them with stones from the side of the creek. Then we pulled their belts up tight, like a big marble bag, and lashed them to the bodies with the tow rope and jumper leads. We hefted them one at a time to the edge of the stream, and using the old one . . . two . . . three and let go method, had them sailing out towards the middle. They landed in the water with a ka-ploosh.

'What are we going to do with their car, mate?' Jacko asked.

'Drive it back a couple of miles and burn it. That'll give the impression of joy-riding vandals.'

'Do you think they'll find those cunts?'

'Well I know this area, mate, and that creek is pretty deep. It's also full of marine life. Small fish, shrimps, and mud-crabs. If anyone is lookin' for them they'd better be real quick.'

It was 3.15 a.m. when I got in. Katy had fallen asleep on the settee in the lounge. I suppose she was waiting for me and worried, too. I picked her up and she gave me a tired smile as I carried her in and put her in the double bed. She went back to sleep almost before I had her head on a pillow.

Looking down at her I saw that she possessed a kind of special alertness. Even as she lay there asleep, there was an energy that stayed in her face. It showed in the set of her mouth, the way her chin was poised, and it stayed there no matter how relaxed she was. It's the kind of energy that sculptors can see—a coiled spring that makes the stone they have fashioned seem alive.

There were still a few matters I had to take care of before I went down to Sydney. One of them was something that I never thought would ever happen to me again. A feeling that I thought was lost. That feeling was love. I don't mean a 'love' for someone that was better than 'like', I mean a love that was like a fire, filling me with a happiness I wanted to hold on to and not let go.

I had been with Carmel for a few years now and we had done a lot together. We had come together under unusual circumstances, through cruelty. I had known cruelty too as a youngster, understood what it was all about, and I suppose this was what brought us together. Yes I loved Carmel and wouldn't want to hurt her. But it wasn't the love that I felt now. This was different. It was a feeling I had only had once before in my life. The same love that I'd had for Margo.

It was strange how I came to realise how I felt. It was 10 a.m. the same morning I had carried her into bed after coming back from the Tweed.

I woke up and stretched and Katy came in and gave me a kiss and handed me a cup of coffee. Then she walked over to the dressing table and rolled a joint, using one of the Camel cigarettes I liked, and tipped some hash into it.

She came and sat on the bed beside me and lit it. Took a drag and then gave it to me.

'You have it, love,' she said. 'I blew one a minute ago while you were asleep.'

Drawing the smoke deep into my lungs, I held onto it as long as I could, almost choking. I let the air out and took another toke on it and so on until I'd finished.

It was pretty good stuff, with nothing sneaky about it. Wham! I was way up there. I got up and had a piss. Then I went over and washed a distant face that didn't seem to belong to me. As I looked into my red-rimmed eyes in the mirror, my face seemed to change shape. My tits were another pair of eyes looking at me out of my chest. I walked back to the bed and drank some coffee.

I could see it going down the pipes into my stomach and making a black puddle. Katy came back into the room and kissed me.

'Come on into the shower,' she said. 'I want to wash you.'

She leads me in holding onto me with one hand, reaches with the other and turns the water on, feathering the taps till it's just right. Then she takes off her clothes and pulls me into the shower. Katy is rubbing me all over with the soap but I don't seem to feel it. The shower feels like I'm under steaming rain, and I hear the drumming noise it makes on a tin roof. I nearly fall asleep. She kisses me again, then gets a towel and dries me off. I don't remember her turning the shower off.

When I look down my belly button looks like one long hole that goes right through me.

She leads me back into the bedroom and I drink more of the coffee. She turns my face up towards her

197

and she smiles at me. I'm sitting on the side of the bed and my eyes are level with her stomach. And I think how lovely it is and I reach out and run my hand down it. She pushes me down on the bed and lifts my legs up off the floor. They don't feel like they're mine. It takes me forever to turn on my side. Katy stretches out alongside me and we kiss. I hold my hands against her breasts. My hands seem to be on fire and I wonder if they're burning her too. Then all of a sudden I feel this strange sensation that seems to come out of nowhere. I feel it start in my heart and burst through my body in a rush. Like circles racing away from a stone that's been tossed into still water. I am completely overwhelmed with love for her. I am not standing out there looking at the rest of the world. I have someone I can confide in and let out all my secrets knowing they'll be safe.

She sits up and looks down at me and lets her hand run down my face, leans down and kisses me.

'I love you, Jimmy,' she says.

It's as if the circles have left my body and reached out and enfolded her, wrapping us up together. She lies down beside me again and we wrap our arms around each other. And before we fall asleep I kiss her softly and our lips tingle with a warmth I could taste and I turn my head until my mouth is against her ear.

'I love you, too, Katy.'

She squeezes me.

We woke up practically at the same time. The clock on the bedside dresser said 1.40 p.m.

I kissed her and knew that the things I had felt earlier were still the same. We made love to each other that was so beautiful it would be hard to describe. It was as if the clock had been turned back and I was being allowed to capture that magic moment I had lost all those years back.

But there was a difference. There was no part of her that I didn't want to taste and kiss. Her sex tasted delicious. I just kissed and licked her, every bit of her, and for how long I don't know. She had taken on a new aroma. All the different scents of her body made me want more of them.

Sometime later I rang Jacko and told him we were heading up to Brisbane on business, and then we were going to take a break. He told me to contact him through his mother again.

KATY AND I WERE STAYING AT THE CREST. WE HAD discussed a lot over the last couple of days, but the one thing we were sure of was that we were in love. She let me know that what I did might have been wrong in the eyes of others, but she didn't care. That if something was going to happen to me then let it happen to her too.

On the second night back in Brisbane we went down to the Italian Club for dinner.

Rocco came lumbering over to us.

'Where you been?' he asked me. 'The boss has been wantin' to talk to you. You better come and see him.'

I got Katy a table, said I wouldn't be long and followed Rocco out the back.

Paolo was sitting at his desk.

'What's this about the meeting you had with the cops at Roma Street?' he asked.

'Don't you trust me, Paolo?'

'Of course I do. The reason I'm asking is to be of assistance if I can.'

'Well it's all taken care of. I rang that mate of mine in Sydney and he pulled some strings—ropes would be a better word. He told me to go and see Jack Murphy and I did. He'd got the message before I'd even arrived and wanted to know if the fuckin' Commissioner and I were related. I wonder what Frank would say if he heard that.'

'What was the call to Rocco for, about Blacky Morrison's place?'

I looked over my shoulder at Rocco standing there, but Paolo had said you can trust him with your life.

'We had a couple of visitors from Vitelli.'

'What sort of visitors?'

'Jesus, Paolo, what sort do you reckon? Nasty ones.'

'Look, Jimmy, I gave you my word nothing like this would happen in my district. You're sure they were Joey Fingers' guys?'

'Bloody oath I am. I had quite a good talk to them.'

'Well, come on. What did they want?'

'They wanted to take my girl back to Sydney so that cockroach Frangiani could get his hands on her. And if that wasn't possible they were to get the story on Brocassi out of her, then get rid of her.'

'Who? Carmel?'

'No, Katy.'

'She could be dangerous, Jimmy.'

I felt a fire start deep within me, and I wanted to reach over and smash the face of the man who had been my friend.

'Listen, Paolo,' I said in a voice I scarcely recognised. 'If one hair of her head is hurt . . . Do you remember the stuff that took place after Margo?' He looked down at the floor and then up at Rocco, then waved him out of the room. When Rocco had gone, he stood up, went over and made us a couple of drinks.

'Jimmy, I don't want to get mixed up in your love life, but have you talked this over with Carmel?'

'No I haven't, Paolo, but when the time's right I will.'

'You trust this . . . ?'

'Katy.' I answered for him. 'Katy Bowman. Yes I do. I can't explain it to you. I can't explain it to myself. But I love her, Paolo, just like I loved Margo. Christ, I ought to know, don't you think?'

He sat down again and shook his head.

'How do you think Carmel is going to take this? You don't think she'll just let you walk away do you? She knows an awful lot . . . Hell hath no fury like a woman scorned.'

'I know Carmel better than anybody and I'll guarantee her.'

'Okay, let's drop it. It's your decision and she's your responsibility.'

'No, it's not that simple, Paolo. I want your blessing and your protection for Katy. And that's something I've never asked for with Carmel, or anyone else for that matter.'

Paolo became pensive and seemed to weigh up my loyalty over the years. He kept looking at me then up at the ceiling, as if going to a higher plane for guidance. Then he walked over and held out his arms and we embraced.

'You've got my blessing,' he said, and kissed me on the lips.

I knew that he'd given it because the kiss on the lips is a seal that can only be broken by the death of the one who gives it. Katy was safe.

'What about these people Frangiani sent up here?' he asked.

'They've gone away for good.'

'I see,' he said with a nod. 'Much chance of them turning up again?'

'Not in this life, Paolo.'

'All neat and tidy then.'

'Yeah, I suppose you could put it that way.'

He then pointed to the briefcase I had brought along with me.

'What's with that?'

'That's the money I got from Rissi, but it's all US dollars. Can you get it changed for me?'

A change came over Paolo's face. I had never seen the look before, and he turned and looked out the window when he saw me watching him. When he turned back he had regained his composure.

'You've actually seen Al Rissi?'

'No,' I lied. 'Let's just say I had arrangements made and the money delivered.'

That look reappeared on Paolo's face.

'There'll be an exchange fee,' he said quickly. 'I can't get it done for nothing.'

'Take it out of that.' I pointed to the briefcase.

'Is it as much as he promised you?' he asked, 'before he left for the States?' watching my reaction.

'Is that where he is?' I tried to sound casual. 'No it's more than that, but he won't miss it.'

Paolo actually gave a little jump. 'What do you mean he won't miss it?' His voice hardened.

'Christ, Paolo,' I lied again. 'All I meant was that he looks like he's got plenty.' Then I decided to take the bull by the horns. 'Look that job up north was a pack of fuckin' lies. You know it, I know it, and everybody concerned knows it. It was drugs and politics, engineered by that animal Rissi. How he got you to play ball I'll never know. But did you think that I'd just walk into something and not check it out? Two innocent girls were butchered after we left them at Port Douglas, Paolo, and that didn't sit real well with me. So I did a little probing and found out the truth. Let's not try to con each other, we've been around too long now for that.'

He watched me, locking his eyes on my face. There was something amiss here and it made me feel uneasy.

'What are you going to do now then?' he finally asked. His tone was curt.

'I'm going to see Carmel. And then I'm going to do what I should have done right from the very beginning. Piss off outta this scene. Katy and I will go away.'

'What about the thing with Vitelli and Frangiani?'

'Fuck 'em both. If they start any rough stuff again I'll take care of it in my own way. I've got a long memory.'

'Yes, I suppose you have. Right, I'll take care of this.' He tapped the briefcase. 'You'll have the money within the hour. Go order, and order something for me too. I must meet this lady that has captured your heart.'

We wined and dined well that evening, with Paolo turning on the charm and champagne for us, and it was in the small hours of the morning when Katy and I got to bed.

I couldn't sleep, so I got up without disturbing Katy and made a cup of coffee. Then I carried it out to the lounge and looked through the big glass window at the approaching dawn.

Some cigarette smoke caught in my windpipe and I had a coughing fit which left my throat feeling raw and dry. I lubricated it with some more coffee. Down below in the street a cat crossed the road. Then took off with fur bristling as the street sweeper approached. The high-pressure water sent a mist that bounced off the bitumen to float out and under the wheels of a parked car. I lit another cigarette and wondered why I was standing at the window looking out over the empty city. It was because I had to go and see Carmel.

Katy kissed me at the door as I left to catch a cab. Even when I knocked on the door I was still searching for the right words to say. When Carmel came out, I suppose she could tell from the look on my face that something was wrong.

She just stood there looking at me, then took my hand.

'Do you want to talk about it?' she asked.

I nodded, still searching my brain for the way to tell her the truth. How could I tell this lovely person, who had been my companion, my lover and my friend, that I loved another woman more than her? She led me into her room and I sat on the bed. She sat beside me.

When I tried to speak, the words wouldn't come out. I put my head in my hands. My eyes filled with tears and sobs of anguish tore through me. I couldn't control them.

She put her arms around me.

'Let it out, let it go.' She sensed that I was ashamed. 'Everyone needs to cry sometime.'

Then out of the blue she said, 'There's somebody else, isn't there?'

All I could do was nod.

I was waiting for the explosion, but she looked at me with a soft smile and squeezed my hand gently.

'We've been together quite a while now, but I always knew that somewhere, one day, you'd find the love you were looking for. I've slept beside you, Jimmy, I've heard your dreams and nightmares. I know more about you than you realise.'

I looked at her and held her close.

'What can I say, Carmel? I'm not too good at apologising.'

'Don't say anything. Just let's remember that we met and shared a bit of each other.'

'You really deserve someone better than me,' I said. 'I can't even look you in the eye and tell you how I've let you down. But I have. I've never planned any of my life, it seems to have made the plans already, and I just jump through the hoops.'

I stood up and she kissed me on the cheek.

'Be happy, Jimmy, just be happy. I'm happy here with Pamela. I feel secure and safe. So you be happy too.'

I reached inside my jacket and took out an envelope that I'd prepared before coming out.

'There's enough in there, love, to get you started in something you like.'

She tried to push it back to me.

'Please take it,' I said. 'I'll feel a lot better if you do. And I want you to have the Landcruiser. I won't be needing it.'

I pressed the envelope into her hand, held her once more and squeezed her tight.

'If ever you need a hand, or you're in trouble, ring Percy Grainger. His number's in the envelope.'

I kissed her cheek and quickly walked out, before she could speak.

I let myself back into the suite and walked into the bedroom. Katy was still there, propped up, with all the pillows behind her, with a sheet that draped across the lower half of her body. Her skin was a honey colour and the little tattoo of a red and blue heart looked like a bruise on her left shoulder.

She turned off the radio and smiled at me.

'Are you all right, sweetheart, how did it go?'

'She understands, I didn't think she would, but she really understands, and wishes us well.'

I walked over and looked out through the bedroom window. Queen Street was awash with sunlight. It was so bright it made me squint.

I went over and sat on the bed and was about to say something when Katy piped up.

'Let's have a smoke.'

She reached over, dragged her purse to her and pulled out a rolled joint. The room filled with the sweet pungent odour of marijuana. I walked into the bathroom and had a glass of water, then picked up an ashtray and took it in to her.

'Ta,' she said, and put it on the stand beside her. She

passed me the joint and I took a long haul at it, held it, exhaled and took another. We finished the joint off and she lifted up the sheet.

'Come back to bed and let me do nice things to you?'

I stripped off and lay beside her. We kissed and held each other. Then she threw the covers back, and rolled on her face, turned round a bit, then lazily raised her hips off the bed and presented her rear end to me. The hair around her vagina was dark and soft and wispy, you could see skin between the hairs, and the pink lips were moist and loose and inviting. She tossed her head back, looked around and down at me and gave a smile.

'Oh darling, look at that. I've made it angry haven't I?'

She spun around further and caressed my penis, then she bent her head over it and her dark hair cascaded down and around, like a screen shielding my view. I felt her lovely warm mouth close around me and her tongue working.

She stopped and turned around again and straddled, reaching down between her legs as she guided me to her opening. She sat down a little and worked herself up and down over the head of my penis. Then gave a little moan and sat all the way down on it.

At the end of the bed there were two walk-in robes with big mirrored doors on them. As she worked herself up and down she kept looking over her shoulder, totally unembarrassed, watching the reflections of our lovemaking.

She kept up a slow rocking movement until we could stand it no longer, and with an 'oh oh oooooh,' she collapsed down onto my chest at the moment of our orgasm. It left me with my heart pounding and a weak feeling in my knees. Then she lay back down and doodled with her finger in the puddle of semen that had leaked onto my pubic hair.

'Was that nice, Jimmy? It was for me.'

'No it wasn't nice, Katy, it was beautiful,' and I rolled over and kissed her.

Katy placed an ad in the paper for the sale of her boutique, and three days later a lady had bought it. She told me she had no real regrets. She just wanted us to be together and happy. I knew she loved me all right. She showed it in everything she did for me and every word she said.

She would have bared her arse and slept on a dirt floor with me if I had asked her to do it.

20

KATY AND I MOVED DOWN TO TWEED HEADS AND rented a house on the river. Life took on a new meaning for me. I tried to change my lifestyle and become domesticated. We started a garden in the backyard growing tomatoes and cucumbers, the whole works. I even got a regular job, driving a taxi.

Katy became the real little housewife. No longer did I have to rely on myself to do anything in the house. That was her domain.

It went like that for practically a year. Sometimes I'd ring Jacko and we'd have a yarn. If we went up to Brisbane we'd stay away from the club and the old crowd and the rest of the team I knew. We'd just do our own thing. I kept in touch with Carmel and with Pamela on a friendly basis. Katy and Carmel met, and became friends in a sort of way. I sensed the odd bit of possessiveness if Carmel brought up something we had done in the past, but there was no open hostility. Carmel still lived with Pamela and had got herself a job. And she got me to sign the transfer papers for the Landcruiser, which she traded in on a small car for herself.

Life was uncomplicated, without a worry in the world. That was until the phone rang one morning at 2.20 a.m.

It was Pamela on the line, weeping and nearly hysterical.

'Poor little Carmel,' she kept crying, over and over. 'Oh my God.'

I knew something was wrong but it took a while to get Pamela to talk.

'The police have been here. They found Carmel in her car at Mango Hill, on the side of the road.'

'What!' I said, stunned. 'A traffic accident?'

'No, the police say she'd given herself a massive overdose.'

'What did she take? For God's sake Pamela, speak up.'

'They say she injected something, I don't know.'

I knew at once that this was dirty and started to boil inside. The feelings of hate that I thought were lost behind me bubbled to the surface and I wanted to hurt somebody or something.

'What are you fuckin' on about, Pamela? Carmel wasn't into drugs. She didn't even smoke dope.'

'I know, Jimmy, I know. Please don't get angry with me. I'm too upset as it is. And there's more, too.' She started crying again. 'I got a nasty call. Somebody rang and told me to tell you that the other bitch was next. Are they going to get me too? What have I done? All I was was a friend to her. I'm scared, Jimmy.'

'Have you told the police about the second call?'

'No. I'm too scared. I've only rung you.'

'Don't mention it to anyone, Pamela. You stay put and we'll be up there in an hour or so, okay?'

'Please hurry, I don't know what to do. Oh God, poor Carmel.'

'Just hang in, love, we won't be long.'

I put the phone down and the whole thing hit me at once. I was seething, bitter. When I saw my face in the mirror it was terrible to look at. There was death written in my eyes . . . and vengeance. Carmel would never take drugs, she hated the things. This was a payback, I knew it. I wouldn't rest till I'd wreaked havoc and destruction on those who'd done this. And may God have mercy on the souls of those responsible, because I was going to have none.

Katy came out to the lounge.

'What's going on Jimmy? Please tell me.'

I sat down and told her.

'Katy whoever's responsible for this . . . the world's not a big enough place to hide the fuckin' bastards.'

Katy opened her mouth and I thought she was going to try to talk me out of doing anything. 'Don't say one fuckin' word Katy,' I broke in. 'Not one. You hear me? Nobody in this world will fuckin' talk me out of this. Do you know what they said? Do you know what the dirty bastards have threatened? They've threatened you're next. So don't say one fuckin' word.'

She came over and stood beside me and put a hand up on my shoulder.

'I suppose I should be scared,' she said. 'But for some reason I'm not, I know you'll do your best to protect me. It's not me I'm scared for, I'm scared for you.'

Then she broke down and cried. And so did I. In shame and bitterness. I had been responsible for what had happened to Carmel. And it looked as if the same fate could befall Katy too.

No fuckin' way, something screamed inside me. No fuckin' way! I became cold all of a sudden, with cold flames licking around inside me, chilling me into a cold rage. I felt like a wounded animal in the bush, circling around to ambush and kill the parties responsible for my hurt.

We arrived at Pamela's place and quietened her down. I took her and Katy to Paolo's place and told him the story.

'What sort of animals are we dealing with?' he yelled.

'I know what sort, Paolo. They have no honour, no creed. But I'm gonna fix who ever did this. And properly. You gave me your blessing, you gave me a solemn promise, now the fuckin' bastards have got at me through Carmel. She's dead, gone, do you hear me? And you gave me your blessing.'

'Do you want me to go and shoot myself?' he yelled. 'Do you think you're the only one who's feeling pain? Look at you. You want revenge, so be it, and so do I, but we're not going to do anything until we've calmed down and stopped fighting each other. Do you hear me?'

He was right. I was wild with rage, but that wouldn't solve the situation. It would only make it worse.

It was three days before the coroner would release Carmel's body to the undertakers. I had been in touch with them and agreed to take care of the funeral costs.

When the day came, all was solemn and quiet in the funeral parlour chapel. When I saw the lonely coffin in front of a small altar, I walked over to it. The top half of the lid was lifted up.

I gazed down at Carmel. She was white and had a strange look on her face, as if she was trying to say something. I bent over and kissed her lifeless cheek.

'So long sweetheart,' I whispered. 'I never meant for this to happen. Please forgive me. I swear to you that I will get who did this, if it takes me the rest of my life.'

I kissed her again and then stood up, lowered the top half of the coffin lid and walked away.

There was an old lady being taken through the back, by one of the morticians. She was not in a very good state, I presumed that she had either lost her husband or a loved one.

Waiting for her was a minister who had watched me walk away from Carmel's coffin. 'Can I help you my son?' he said. 'Would you like me to pray? She has gone to a better place.'

I felt like grabbing him by the throat.

I've never really trusted the church or its officials. Ever since I was a little boy I had distrusted the church and clergy. I'd seen how the hypocritical bastards who were my foster parents conducted themselves. And I remembered how at Sunday school one of the curates had tried to choke me when I said 'Jesus Christ', other than in a prayer. None of the experiences had endeared me towards religion, and as I became older my experiences took on a broader and wider awareness. I developed a contempt for the church and the clergy. They all trot around telling people what joy there is in the Lord, being jovial and smiling sweetly, and it's all a show, a fiction, a fake. It is all so unreal and forced that it makes me want to cringe. And at times throw up.

So many of the clergy remind me of the type you see in movies and plays, the ones who come breezing into the centre of things, dressed in a blazer and white flannels and say 'Who's for tennis?' The clergy go around in the same manner, but they're saying 'Who's for Jesus?'

Then there was the time I was locked up in the cells at Broadbeach. I was down and out and worried. I had been there three days when a court chaplain came in to see me. There was no glass in the windows, just bars. There had been a storm the night before and water had come through onto the cement floor, intensifying the stench that was already there of vomit and piss.

I was lying on the damp cot that was no more than a solid frame bolted to the wall. He came in breezily, saying, 'Hello there. God bless' all over the place. I could see from his frown that he expected me to stand up when he walked in, instead of just lying there buggered and miserable.

'Well now, how are you getting on?' he said with one of those beatific smiles I hate.

'Simply fuckin' marvellous,' I said, looking at the water on the floor.

'Good, good, that's the spirit. Have you prayed for forgiveness yet?'

'No, no I haven't.'

He looked down at me. 'Well you should. It will make you feel a lot better.'

'Pig's arse.'

'I think you're a bit of a trouble-maker aren't you?'

'Listen, I'm not making any trouble, I'm just lying here, locked up for something I know nothing about, keeping quiet and making no complaints, even with the state that this joint is in, so where's the trouble?'

Shit, he didn't like that one little bit. They never do, and off he went into a long tirade about mending my ways and repenting to the Lord, and not to think myself better than anyone else all the time.

It was okay for him. Five minutes later he'd have his arse in a chair, drinking a cuppa with the coppers up in the station, shaking his head over what a hard time he had trying to get all the bad people locked up in these places to see the light.

'Go fuck yourself,' I told him. 'Preach to your bloody converted. Leave the rest of the world alone.'

If it hadn't been for Percy, Jacko and Pamela's people, there wouldn't have been many at the funeral. But we laid Carmel to rest at the lawn cemetery at Lawnton, and may God have pity on the people responsible for her demise. I certainly wasn't going to have any.

We held a sort of a private wake at Pamela's place and lifted our glasses and said so-long to a sweet and gentle lady who had been a part of my life. And who had brought sweet memories to all those who knew her.

Katy and I returned to Tweed Heads. We hadn't said a lot over the last few days. She walked in ahead of me when I opened the door and when I turned around after locking the security door she was standing right behind me, so close we were practically touching.

'You're acting so strange, Jimmy.'

'Yeah, I guess I am acting a little crazy. Why don't you go and sit down?'

'Because,' she said slowly, 'I prefer to stand.' She paused and looked into my eyes. 'And because I want you to kiss me. You want to, I know you do . . . And you need to . . . Please!'

I took her into my arms. Her lips felt unbelievably soft and willing as she put her arms around my neck and returned the hug. We stood close and kissed each other over and over again. She kissed my eyes, the corners of my mouth and my neck. Neither of us said a word. But the moment was broken when Mrs Godfrey from next-door walked up to the door and saw us.

'Oh look,' she said, 'I'm terribly sorry, but there's been a couple of strange men here the last couple of days asking about you and Katy. I didn't know what to tell them.'

'Have you ever seen them before?' I asked.

'No. And I didn't like the look of one of them. He scared the living daylights out of me when I answered the door.'

She tried to give me a description of the two, but it was pretty vague and could have fitted a million guys. But I had a pretty fair idea what was going on.

'Thanks, Mrs Godfrey. If you see them again and we're not here, don't open your door. Tell them you're calling the police. We don't know them either.'

'Well I certainly will. The hide of them.'

She was a sweet and caring old thing who'd come and talk over the fence when I was out in the garden and tell me how much she missed her late husband.

After Mrs Godfrey had left I was desperate for a drink, and I made one for Katy too. We sat in silence for a while and then she broke the ice.

'You're going down to Sydney, aren't you? Going down there to get them?'

I nodded my head.

'Jimmy, I won't try to talk you out of it. But I'm coming with you. You're not going to leave me stuck in some place, worrying if you're all right.'

I knew by her tone that she meant it. And I didn't want to leave her either.

'You can come with me. But you've got to do as I say without one fuckin' argument. Is that clear?'

'I'll do whatever you want, sweetheart, just don't leave me here.'

'Good. Now that we've got that settled, go and get some of your wacky backy. I want to get shit-faced.'

'Yes sir!' she said as she jumped to her feet. 'What a bloody good idea, sir!'

And that's what we did, got shit-faced, and when I was high I dared the Devil himself to come near us.

21

WE MOVED DOWN TO SYDNEY AND AFTER TWO DAYS OF hunting around we got a furnished apartment in Potts Point. It cost an arm and a leg but I was happy with the security.

I bought a short-barrelled auto shotgun and showed Katy how to use it. She assured me that she wouldn't hesitate, if someone tried to lift her from the place.

Then I roughly explained to her what I had to do. She took it all in her stride.

'Be careful,' was all she said when I went out on the beginning of my vendetta.

In a rented car, I cruised slowly into Lowery Street. The developers or the council had created a cul-de-sac with an urban surgical amputation. Three big coloured steel posts embedded into the asphalt at the far end of the street prevented drivers from using what must have been a very handy short cut onto Oxford Street, and to the city.

I drove on slowly, turned around, came back and parked. And looked the place over from the outside.

Like most of the surviving Edwardian mansions around Sydney, this one had been renovated into expensive flats and apartments. Looking between the buildings I could see slices of the harbour. The distant rumble of the traffic on the Harbour Bridge drifted up, but the street itself was silent and empty. Nothing moved.

I checked out the Browning, loaded a round into the chamber and thumbed the hammer down so it would be ready to fire with a flick of the thumb, then hopped out of the car and slowly walked over to twenty-one. The address that the cockroach had supplied before he left the planet south of Tweed Heads.

Number twenty-one was named The Croyden. A large sandstone mansion with lush grounds that had been copied from a sub-tropical botanical garden. Huge Moreton Bay figs towered above the oleanders and the numerous shrubs. The dark green vegetation was penned behind the tall marlin-spiked railings of a perimeter fence and enhanced the mansion's arrogance. Frangiani could do whatever he liked here, camouflaged behind an expensive screen of prestige and discreetness.

There were electronic car gates in the spiked security fence and beside them was a smaller pedestrian gate. A closed-circuit surveillance TV camera kept an eye on both entrances.

As I crossed the street I heard a buzzing sound, like a blowfly trapped on a window pane. The smaller gate wasn't properly closed. It was being held ajar by a small stone that had wedged underneath it.

As I stepped into the courtyard, I left the small stone in place so I'd have an easy exit. I walked over cautiously and stood under the trees. It was cool beneath the lush greenery, but an odour of damp filled my nostrils, like the stink of grave dirt.

220

An old gardener's cottage had been converted to a security office. A cobblestone path led up to an open door that was painted dark green to match the surroundings. Inside, three TV monitors mounted above a desk showed empty paths and foyers in three shades of grey. Why it was ever called black and white, I'll never know. There was a vinyl copy leather jacket hanging over the chair behind the desk, with badges of a security company I'd never heard of stitched on the shoulders. They could have easily been mistaken for the state police emblem. A walkie-talkie lay on the desk.

I stepped back outside, even more alert now. Nothing felt right. Sometimes a trap can be used to an advantage, but my reflexes tensed, waiting for the hit of a bullet from an ambush.

In front of the mansion was a wide cobbled parking area, but even this was vacant and empty. I moved along the front of the building and eased my way up the wide front steps. And after another quick look around, I pushed open the frosted glass main entrance door. Four apartments led off a large mirrored and marble foyer. Number two was on the right.

There was a deadlock on the door but I made quick work of it with the aid of my little tool kit. I stood back around the wall and reached across and pushed the door open. No hail of gunshots followed. Everything was quiet.

I stepped quickly inside and to the left in one movement.

The renovators had kept the high ceilings, along with the old fireplaces and big windows. And the floor was covered in thick pile carpet.

221

Frangiani hadn't gone all out on decorating the place. There was an L-shaped lounge covered in soft cream fabric, an over-size coffee table and some expensive padded chairs. A big colonial dresser had been turned into a bookshelf and bar, which had no books but one empty bottle of Chianti decorating it. And there was an oblong mark on the wall over the fireplace where a painting had once been.

My heart chilled. This was starting to look to me as if they knew I would come looking.

Gun in hand, and ice in my heart, I went through the whole place, but the apartment had been emptied. Even the fridge was clean and empty.

Nothing, not a sign of anybody or anything. I walked quickly out of the entrance and down to the small gate, and as I stepped outside I kicked the stone away so the gate closed behind me with a clack. The buzzing stopped.

As I let the car drift slowly down the street and turned out of it, a built-in sixth sense warned me that I was being watched. Well, I thought, the best way to find out just who and why is to keep on driving.

I drove down into Centennial Park, which takes up 400 acres on the eastern edge of central Sydney. It is decorated with trees, lawns, swamps and ponds, with riding tracks and enough avenues of palms to make you wonder if you are in the right country.

The four miles of spiked iron fences that surround the park don't make it formal. There's a feeling of country casualness about the place. Ducks squawk in the reed-filled ponds. And even though vandals periodically smash the pricks and balls of the male statues that line the paths, more virginities have been lost under the lantanas and rhododendrons of Centennial Park than in all the hotels of Kings Cross and Bondi beach.

As I drove along, girls who looked as if they came from the posh suburbs like Woollahra and Bellevue Hill cantered and trotted along the bridle path on their horses. Occasionally, a big thoroughbred proudly paced by, working away from prying eyes at Randwick racecourse, which lay a stone's throw away. As the horses cantered they raised little clouds of dust and the smell of horseshit floated in to me through the open window of the car.

I cruised along the narrow perimeter road trying to get my thoughts and plans straightened out. In front of me a Datsun Bluebird displaying L-plates was crawling along. The solitude of the park and its one-way road system made it a popular place for driving instructors to bring their students.

As I pulled in behind the Bluebird the middle-aged lady learner sort of flinched and shot me a scared look through the rear-vision mirror. I smiled at her to try to give her some reassurance, but she inched closer to the edge of the road and slowed down so much that even the horses were passing us. I could almost hear the instructor. 'That's fine. Nothing to worry about. He'll pass you in a moment. You're doing fine . . .'

I glanced up at one of the girls, with fawn riding breeches tightening rhythmically over her narrow hips. She returned my look with an insolent pout and stuck her nose in the air.

When I looked up into my rear-vision mirror I got that chill and iced-water treatment in the heart again.

A dusty black Fairlane had fallen in a few lengths behind me. No L-plates on this one. And the two guys sitting in the front seat weren't watching the girl riders, their attention was riveted on me. I was getting too old for this shit, I wasn't doing my homework. How could I be so fuckin' stupid? I had to settle down real fast and get my act together.

The Bluebird signalled a right-hand turn. The learner pulled out gingerly onto the crown of the road, feeding the wheel through her hands, just as the instructor had taught her. But I'd had a gutful and wanted to get out of here fast.

I slammed my foot to the floor, gave a loud blast on the horn and darted around her on the inside. My back wheels spun on the edge of the riding track and dirt sprayed back under the startled noses of the horses. One of them reared up, almost throwing the girl who'd just given me the uppity look. She was using language at me that wasn't taught at June Dally Watkins.

As I shot past the Bluebird I caught a glimpse of the astonished instructor's face. He should have been keeping an eye on his pupil. Gripping the wheel in a death grip like a life preserver, she stared in frozen horror at the bole of a date palm floating towards her at thirty kilometres an hour.

I didn't see it hit but I heard the crunch. When I looked back, the Bluebird had blocked the intersection, with the Fairlane on the other side and a horse rearing hysterically in the middle of it all. Then I was accelerating down the long straight stretch that takes you towards the main gates, with the blaring of a jammed horn fading away behind me.

It gave me a minute or two on them, but they picked me up and hauled me in as I was gunning the car down Ocean Street. Maybe there was somewhere I could pull in and give them the slip, but the Fairlane was closing the gap, growing larger in my rear-vision mirror as I accelerated through a yellow light at the corner of New South Head Road and roared off down the hill to Rushcutters Bay. Then without any real plan or conscious thought, other than to lose them, I began to follow the signs indicating the Harbour Bridge. Maybe they'd be easier to shake in the maze of streets in the hillside northern suburbs.

I hurtled down William Street like a banshee, hung a right into Woolloomooloo and picked up the Expressway just outside the Conservatorium of Music, with its strange false battlements.

Cars gave angry horn blasts as I shot through a red light and dropped into the outside lane of the Cahill Expressway. The windows of the Imperial Hotel flashed by. My pursuers were still back there and I hadn't gained that much since they had picked me up in the park. I was back where I'd started . . . and not much better off.

At one hundred kilometres an hour, it doesn't take long to cross over the Harbour Bridge. Switching lanes and diving in and out of the traffic, I used the Fairmont's power steering for all it was worth and managed to keep the big Fairlane at least one change of lights behind me.

The wide and spacey eight concrete lanes of the Warringah Expressway climbed up and over the hill on the other side of the bridge. It was tempting and very inviting, but I remembered in the nick of time that the freeway narrows just over the hill as it crawls its way into Castlecrag. A single car ahead of me could trap me.

So I dived into the cloverleaf roundabout at the foot of the bridge and sped out of the first exit into the narrow harbourside roads of Kirribilli. Big apartment blocks crammed the foreshore here, tall and dense as a giant cedar forest. With some luck on my side I could disappear somewhere among them, like a rabbit into a burrow, and hide.

But when you've been away from Sydney for some time, you lose some of your direction and road-sense. The turns and the one-ways really began to confuse me.

Relentlessly, they forced me to go uphill, towards Military Road. Once I got jammed in that arsehole of a place with its creeping traffic, they'd have me, and I'd be dead meat. And worst of all, the Fairlane stuck, never more than a bloody block behind, its two occupants motionless silhouettes framed by a dirty windscreen.

It appears that the smarter and the trendier Sydney suburbs get, the more greenery they have on display. I dropped off the higher slopes and headed at speed for the thickest and greenest part I could see. Dodging down and through narrow and twisting streets, I hurtled by steep-sided parks and reserves that carried the names of long and best forgotten politicians and statesmen.

Then, there were fewer houses, and only on one side of the street. Opposite them, the road sloped steeply towards the harbour. I could see the water sparkling through the thick stands of gum and undergrowth.

I turned and spun onto a narrow dirt side road. Unsignposted, it was just a track, heavily wooded on both sides and with no sign of houses. It looked perfect.

Suddenly I was out of suburbia and into thick bush. But just as suddenly the Fairlane was there, right up my arse, and the guy on the passenger side was levelling a gun in my direction out the window. Shit! I thought I'd given them the slip.

One part of my mind told me that these bushland roads never really led anywhere . . . but I thought fuck it! Sydney or the bush, and floored the accelerator.

I caught glimpses of blue water glinting through the trees. Lantana brushed and scratched at the side of the car. Then, suddenly, the road stopped. There was nothing. I put the car into a sliding dust-billowing turn and I was off the road. Branches swatted the windscreen, scratching and tearing down the side of the car and the windows, crashing and bouncing through the bush till I spun sideways down a slope and slid into the trunk of a big gum and stopped.

The driver of the Fairlane hadn't had the front view that I had, and unable to anticipate my move, he and went straight past me. The car ploughed straight ahead, flattening some small saplings, and suddenly it was airborne. The engine note rose to a scream as the tyres spun in the air. They were flying. Diving towards a blinding shield of sun, silver water, and oblivion.

When I got out of the car my legs felt rubbery. If I hadn't spun the wheel when I did . . .? I looked at the tree that the car was jammed against. It was only a yard away from the drop-off.

I scrambled my way back up through the scrub to the track and followed it to the sealed road. Then I trudged along this for a couple of miles till I finally found a phone booth. Rang a cab, and waited around smoking to calm my nerves until it arrived.

It took three double scotches before the shaking stopped, and even then I gave a shudder when I thought how bloody lucky I'd been.

'You're shaking all over, Jimmy.'

Katy put her arm around my neck and pushed up very close to me. As I smelt her hair and felt the warmth of her body we could have been any young couple who had just discovered that they were in love. We should have been able to dance all night, to confess our love, to drink a toast to one another over a candle-lit dinner. We should have been able to escape from the type of life I was leading again, just pack up and go away and live in peace. We should have been able to, but we were not just any young couple, and in the present circumstances we couldn't act as others would. We would always be looking over our shoulders. But the love was there all the same for anyone not totally blind to see.

When this thing is over we're going to have our happiness, I thought to myself. No more looking over our shoulders. We could be just like any other couple. And we were going to get some practice right now . . .

It was lunch time and I was ravenous.

'Katy,' I said, 'You and me are going out to have something to eat. So go put on something gorgeous.'

We were sitting in the open-air part of the restaurant, wearing dark glasses, enjoying a delicious salad and a mixture of cold meats. We ordered the most expensive wine on the list. Le Montrachet . . . a Burgundy. And the wine waiter made a thing about the way I pronounced it 'You mean the mon'rachay, sir?' He said it without pronouncing either 't'.

It was a beautiful wine, and it brought back something I had read where some connoisseur said a superb wine should be drunk kneeling. It was a good wine all right, and after the second bottle I thought I'd like to try it lying down.

'I can't understand,' Katy said, 'why you don't want to tell me everything that happened this morning?' She held up her hand as I started to speak . . . 'I don't mean that you refuse to tell me, but you never unburden yourself. You go out and tell me that you'll be all right, then you come home shaking all over but say bloody nothing. Don't you think I deserve something better than just guessing what's up?'

She was right of course. So I apologised and told her exactly what had happened. Leaving out nothing. And the strange thing was I did feel better. She was quite a girl.

When I'd told her the whole story she didn't berate me, but just asked how Percy and I had met.

I drew deeply on my cigarette.

'It was in Vietnam in 1967,' I said. 'Six of us had been through Special Operations Group training. We'd been yanked out of our units and banded together to operate with the Montagnards, a pretty fierce tribe of bastards that hated Charlie. The Viet Cong had us

229

pinned down in some heavy jungle.' I deliberately left my voice coldly factual. 'Two gunships came in to lift us out. One rode top cover while the other set down in a small clearing. Three of us made it to the ship, and before we could do or say anything, the pilot lifted off. It was then that I saw Percy run out from under the cover of the trees. He was wounded, and hobbling. I yelled at the pilot to take it down and pick him up, but he pointed to the VC coming. I lifted my gun and told him to take it down or we'd all go down. He did. Hovering about three feet off the ground with the top cover chopper and the one we were in opening up with the mini-guns. I reached down and grabbed Percy's hand and yanked him up on board.'

We spent the rest of the afternoon doing things that normal people do and round about five we went back to the apartment. It was an expensive place but it was worth it.

We were in the bedroom and it was beautiful . . . a mixture of soft pastel and mellow wood panelling, a large bed with a high carved headboard and matching footboard. Cream coloured wall-to-wall carpet covered the floor. The desk, wardrobe and chest of drawers matched the bed. At the end of the room was a giant glass door which framed the balcony and the view beyond.

Hand in hand we walked out onto the balcony. We just stood there looking, saying nothing, watching as the sinking sun painted greys and blacks in the streets and buildings down below. And watching as the golds and yellow of the trees turned to amber and charcoal with the setting sun. I became conscious of my arm around Katy, and turned my head to find that she was watching me. Her eyes were shining happily, her lips parted, and her hair joined the symphony of colours in the sunset. I kissed her and felt her respond. I picked her up, carried her into the bedroom and laid her on the bed and kissed her again as I undressed her. We made love slowly and with tenderness, then we lay in each other's arms and allowed our thoughts to drift.

My thoughts went back to the morning we first moved in here. We had brought up a huge pile of groceries, and beer and spirits. We both had a beer and I was walking around looking at this and that, Katy was sitting at the dining table finishing her beer. I asked her if she wanted another. 'In a minute, love,' she said. Then she got up and walked into the bathroom.

'There's dead bugs in the sink,' she called out.

I went in and we stood looking down at the cold whiteness of the sink and the two dead beetles lying along side the chrome plug hole. We both looked up at the same instant . . . the mirror looked back at us with a startling clarity . . . her face looked less tanned in the fluorescent light, her smooth brow, her long hair falling down to one side. I stood behind her with a look that was so obviously absurd that she started to laugh. At that moment I felt that I attained a new consciousness of her. It was as if her beauty had previously been only a dream to me . . . a dream that had suddenly become reality. She slipped off her blouse and then let her skirt drop to the floor. I felt light and electrically alive, as if I was watching the scene from a distance. She turned to me and put her lovely face against the side of my neck. I kissed her briefly and looked into the mirror. The cheeks of her bum were pressed tightly against the sink, her back was smooth and nicely muscled, and my hands looked dark against her skin. Then I saw my faced poised over her shoulder and I smiled, then stuck my tongue out. It is strange how certain memories have the quality of a trance. They float into a place in your brain where they sit, and stand out like a golden temple in a grove of beautiful palms . . .

22

I RANG PAOLO IN BRISBANE, GAVE HIM THE PHONE number and also told him that Frangiani had moved out, that I had checked his place. He said he would make some enquires from someone in Sydney who was one of the old school and detested this new-generation style of Vitelli and Co.

Later that evening I received a call from him inviting me to go to a phone booth and ring him at a number he supplied.

I made the call.

'I haven't been able to get a make on Frangiani, but I did get something on the guys who put the arm on Carmel. They weren't regulars . . . They came up from Melbourne and they've gone to ground in a farm outside a place called Oak Flats. Do you know where that is?'

'Yeah, just a bit south of Wollongong.'

'Right, well the farm's about three miles south and there's a big wooden gate with a sign, W. McDonald. You got that?'

'Sure have.'

'I'll keep trying for the others. Good luck.' And he hung up.

Back at the unit I told Katy that I was going to Oak Flats. I explained that she would be better off waiting for me right here but she said she'd drive the car for me.

We hummed and harred for a while and in the end I gave in to her.

'Okay,' I said, 'but that's all you do.'

We made it into Oak Flats at 8.30 that night. It was a small sleepy place with a couple of shops, a post office and a pub that was more of a roadhouse than a hotel. We drove through town heading south and slowed down a bit so we wouldn't miss the gate.

The headlights picked it up as we came around a curve in the road. I drove past, noticing as I did that I couldn't see any lights from a building. We drove for about another half mile, then I turned and went back. What was of some interest to me were the cattle sale yards we'd just passed.

In a few minutes we were back at the yards and took the turn-off into them. We bumped our way over the deep ruts that trucks had made when the ground was wet and soft, but had now dried as solid as concrete, into the delivery area. There was also a cattle dip for tick treatment, and the stench of it wafted through the night air.

I went around to the boot, got the Browning out and screwed on the silencer, checked the clip, cocked it and stuck it in the belt of my trousers. Got out the Litton night glasses and let them hang around my neck by the strap. Then I picked up the shotgun and took it around to Katy . . .

'Here, take this. Now lock the doors and stay in the car till I get back. Okay?'

'How long will you be?'

'As long as it takes. Now wait here.'

I moved out into the night and soon had to scale the barbwire perimeter fence of the farm.

Moving up a slope I heard barking. I moved back down and skirted around to change my approach, so the light wind was blowing into my face. The barking stopped.

Reaching the top of the rise I finally had the house in view. Light was coming out of two windows. Lying on the ground I focused the glasses on the house. I looked for, and located, the dog. It was on a chain sitting under a tank stand near the door. Anyone going up the steps would have to pass it. Training the Littons on the house I saw a guy watching television. My movements or scent had definitely aroused the dog. He was sitting there looking out in the direction of my initial approach.

I moved in a hundred yards closer, still downwind from the dog, which was now lying down, its head resting on its paws.

I inched my way forward about another ten yards and the dog got to its feet, looked over in my direction and gave three deep barks. As I was trying to work closer to silence the dog the door at the top of the stairs opened, spilling light out into the yard. A guy threw something out to the dog and told it to lie down.

The guy walked back inside without closing the door, leaving the dog in a pool of light, as it paid full attention to the food it had been given. I wormed my way forward till I was in range.

Taking out the Browning I checked to make sure that the silencer was securely in place. When I'd worked my way a little closer and the dog lifted its head. I took careful aim and fired.

The dog fell, its back legs jerked twice and lay still.

A sense of remorse came over me as I looked at the dead dog. In other circumstances I would more than likely have patted it. But it stood between me and those bastards in the house, and I was going to kill them as sure as this was night.

It was a pleasure that I wanted for myself. I could taste it. I had been savouring this moment from the time I'd looked into the coffin and saw Carmel's pale and cold face. I would enjoy every moment of my revenge.

Slowly and carefully, I made my approach to the house, measuring each step. As I rounded the porch towards the back door I could hear the television blaring. With the dog dead I had no need to worry about them being warned.

But my heart gave a flutter and started to pump adrenalin. A muffled cough came from outside the house. I glanced around and heard the sound of tearing paper from the outhouse. A country thunderbox. And one of them was inside taking a shit.

I moved over and stood to the side of the door. A moment later the door opened and before the guy could take a pace out I moved across and shot him twice in the face. He collapsed back onto the box and slid sideways off it onto the dirt floor.

Then I climbed onto the porch, moved to the back door and inched my way through the house, hugging the wall until I got to the living room. The door was open and the second guy sat with his back to it, his eyes glued on the television screen. A revolver lay on top of a newspaper on the floor at the right of his chair.

'If you move a fuckin' muscle, or make a move for that gun, I'll blow the fuckin' back of your head off.'

The guy jumped a foot in the air and he whirled around, his eyes glazed. Automatically, he reached for the gun.

I fired a shot down into his hand.

A howl of pain erupted from him and his face twisted in pain.

'Yes, you're going to squeal all right,' I said. 'I'm your worst ever nightmare you piece of shit.'

He was bent over in the chair with his wounded hand in his lap, the other hand covering it, and moaning. I circled around the chair till I was facing him.

'Do you remember going to Brisbane, you cunt?' I snarled at him. 'And do you remember taking a pretty girl and shoving an overdose of shit into her veins? Do you?' I screamed at him.

He looked up at me and nodded his head. His fingers and legs were twitching and he was finding it difficult to control himself. He kept glancing down at the hand gun and back up at me. I realised there would be no room for talk, and he knew it too.

Reacting like a trapped animal, he couldn't seem to make up his mind which direction to move in and jerked, first, toward his gun, then toward me, and back again to his gun, leaning down and trying to pick it up with his injured hand.

I just lifted the gun and shot him twice in the chest.

The body slumped back into the chair. I moved forward and shot him again through the forehead. What was left of his brain deposited itself all over the back of the chair.

Back at the saleyards, Katy was sitting behind the wheel. I slipped into the passenger side of the car and let my head rest back against the seat. Katy reached out and put her hand on my arm.

'You all right, sweetheart?' she asked.

'Yeah love,' I said tiredly, 'I'm just fine. Let's go home.'

Katy fired up the car and drove us back to Sydney.

23

WE GOT ON A PLANE AND SPENT TWO WEEKS UP ON Green Island. Just lazing around soaking up the sun, relishing the fact that we had each other. The tropical nights were beautiful and I found myself reminiscing.

I told Katy about the beautiful place that Carmel and I had found. About the lush beauty and the tranquillity of the spot.

'Would you ever go back there?' she asked me.

'I don't know how I'd react to the memories, even though they're good ones. But I'd certainly go back and find out.'

'Jimmy, let's do it. Why can't we just up and go? You don't need money. Who'd know where we were?'

'Look, nothing would give me more pleasure. But how long would it last for—a week, a year? I thought Carmel and I were out of it too, but look what happened. We could run, sweetie, but we couldn't hide. You can't hide from Australia in Australia. One day they'd come and we'd be right back where we began. While ever those bastards are around we'd never have any peace.'

Why can't we just be here, like this, forever, I wondered, watching Katy's beautiful face. I sensed a growing paranoia in myself. The future loomed, and filled my mind. A future without her seemed sterile, a living death. Could I cope with that, I asked myself.

I turned my face away from Katy and watched the sun moving toward the horizon, the big fluffy clouds orange in the sky, the coconut palms along the beach nodding in the freshening breeze. I wanted to be able to see the sunset and the dawn in peace. But before I could find peace there would have to be war. It was the story of my life.

I drew Katy's attention to the sunset and shared the sight with her, knowing she was enjoying it. Both of us believed that every sunset held the promise of a new dream.

But the new dreams would have to wait until those responsible for Carmel's terrible end got their just desserts.

Back in Sydney and getting nowhere fast on the where-abouts of Frangiani, I was watching TV when the phone rang. It had to be Percy or Paolo or Pamela, or a wrong number. They were the only three people we had given it out to. It was Paolo.

'Do you have a pen handy?'

'Yeah, ready when you are.'

'He's in a place out near Frenchs Forest.' He gave me the address. 'Now listen, Jimmy, I want to tell you something. This information is spot-on. Not only is he there but he's got plenty of help with him, you under-stand what I'm trying to tell you.'

'Yeah, loud and clear, Paolo.'

'Right, well that's all I can give you.'

'Thanks,' I said. And we broke the connection.

I knew what he was trying to tell me all right—that Joey Frangiani had a bunch of fuckin' *Famiglia* soldiers with him and they wanted me to show my ugly dial. But I have always believed in that theory of Napoleon's—*When in doubt attack*.

We took a drive out past the place in a hired Falcon and did a recce on the place. With hats and sun glasses on, we looked like a pair of fuckin' gigs. The place was walled, right around, and looked like it might have been an old convent. Paolo had been spot-on, right down to the two guards at the entrance, but I couldn't see any gates.

When I told Katy my plans she wanted to be the driver again. I had no qualms about that. She had become a pretty gutsy lady of late, and I was proud of her.

We prepared ourselves for the job. I put on some dark clothing, checked the Browning and took two spare clips. Katy, on the other hand, I practically didn't recognise. She was wearing the shortest skirt that I had ever seen her in, and her blouse was cut so low that you could just about see her navel. She had paid a lot of attention to her hair, which was piled up on top of her head, and to her make-up. She looked ravishing, and I told her so.

Half an hour later we drew up noiselessly a couple of properties away from the old building and switched off the lights. We waited for about five minutes just to be satisfied that we hadn't attracted attention before I got out and shut the door quietly. The front of Frangiani's place was floodlit but the nearest street lamp was more than a hundred yards away, so I was able to cross to the other side of the street and walk past in semi-darkness without the risk of being seen. I then recrossed and moved back towards the guarded entrance, just outside the zone of comparative light, and moved in close under the wall. I'd already judged it would be impossible to scale in a hurry without a ladder. The only practical way in was through the front entrance, and that was what it was going to have to be.

I had a quick look at my watch but couldn't see the time. As I held my wrist up and tried to see it in the light that was coming through one of the slotted cavities that were built about every ten feet into the wall, I heard the unmistakable sound of the Falcon's V8 engine and watched as Katy drove to within twenty yards of the entrance before pulling into the side of the road and switching the engine off.

I watched her get out and look down at the tyres one by one, before stopping by the nearside rear wheel and uttering an oath.

'Shit, shit, shit, shit.'

The two guards stood at the entrance and moved no further while they watched her open the boot and get the jack out. But then she came round into the light so they could see her better . . . even more when she bent down, without bending her knees, to poke feebly at the hubcap with a screwdriver. It became more than flesh and blood could stand. After glancing over his shoulder at the house, the more susceptible of the two walked towards her, smiling, and spoke to her in Italian.

Katy straightened up and gave him one of her most devastating smiles. The effect was immediate and shattering.

'I'm terribly sorry,' she gushed. 'I don't understand what you're saying. Do you speak English?'

The guard grinned at her sheepishly.

'A little,' he admitted. 'Are you have a trouble?'

'Yes I've been visiting friends and then just back there I felt something was a bit funny, and when I got out found I had a bloody flat tyre.'

She had let the air out of it while I was moving into position.

I doubted that the guy understood a tenth of what she was saying, but his course was obvious.

'Would you like a some help?'

Katy beamed at the guy and rested her hand on his arm for a moment.

'Gee, would you really? That's really very sweet of you to offer.'

The guy shrugged, half-embarrassed, half-delighted, then he set to work with Katy bending down close to him, hindering his movements, but he wouldn't have asked her to move away for all the tea in China. And all the time she's chatting away, with the guy nodding his head as if he understands.

Unable to bear it any longer, the second guard kept looking over his shoulder at his mate, then came to join him. He glanced quickly back at the house again, then hurried to help Katy.

As the two of them bent down to help unscrew the wheel nuts, I slipped out of the darkness and through the entrance, then plunged into some shrubbery for cover. I paused for a moment, and almost immediately one of the guards raised his voice.

I froze, expecting them to come running back inside, but a moment later I heard one of them tell Katy that the jack wasn't in the right place.

There was no concern for Katy, she was doing well, and I could still hear her voice piping over the rest. And the guards' attention was focused in a way I couldn't have possibly imagined. I moved carefully round to the side of the house and out of the lights, where I found a sort of semi-basement window half-open.

As I rolled over the sill inside, I heard the Falcon fire up and drive off.

Once my feet were firmly on the floor I turned and stuck my head out the window, listening to the sound of the Falcon's engine fading into the distance. I didn't hear shots being fired or a crash as a badly tightened wheel came off, so I pulled my head back in and drew several deep breaths to try and stop the thumping in my heart.

Somewhere above me was the sound of music, but it was barely audible, and not loud enough to mask anyone moving around, as was borne out a few seconds later when I heard a door open and the sound of voices. Then another door opened and closed and all was quiet once more.

My eyes had grown accustomed to the dark and I could see I was in a pantry or storeroom that led onto the kitchen, which had a back door and a staircase leading up to the rear of the house. It also had one of those old dumb waiters which probably meant that the dining room was directly above.

I stuck my head into it and looked up the shaft between the runners. All was in darkness above. I then went to the back door and unlocked it, leaving it slightly ajar, and moved over to the bottom of the stairs. There was a bend halfway up, which prevented me seeing to the top. Around the corner a light was burning, but there seemed to be no one around. I began to make my way slowly to where I could see round the corner.

A loose board in the fifth or sixth stair creaked like a rusty hinge. Convinced that everyone as far away as Bondi must have heard it, I froze, but nothing happened and I rounded the corner, checked to see no one was in sight, then went up the rest of the stairs. I found myself almost opposite another door and at the end of the passageway which led through to the front of the house and a well-lit carpeted hallway.

I opened the nearby door, only to shut it again hurriedly when a door somewhere else slammed, giving me a few more uneasy seconds. Then I moved quickly towards the well-lit hallway, stopping when I found myself at the foot of another and much wider flight of stairs.

My thoughts wandered momentarily to Katy and I wondered what she'd be doing at this moment. Probably checking to see that the bastards had tightened the wheel properly before coming back for me ... if she hadn't lost her nerve. But I discarded this thought as my rating of Katy's nerve was much higher now, and growing all the time. Even so, the chances were she wouldn't be back for another ten minutes or so. Then I pushed the thoughts aside and started to concentrate on my own position.

If that kitchen lift was anything to go by, the door to the left led to the dining room. But the place was far too big for that to be the only room unless it was of ballroom dimensions. The door probably opened into yet another corridor.

I opened the right-hand door instead and moved into a large office, in darkness, with a desk, and several chairs and a bookcase. At the far end was another door which was open.

On the wall was a clock with luminous hands which read 11.50.

I inched my way across the office and poked my head around the door. It let to a storage area with extra chairs, a lampstand and other bric à brac.

There was yet another door, leading towards the rear of the building. The place was like a fuckin' rabbit warren. I carefully opened that door and went in. There was a large filing cabinet. The drawers were locked and I reasoned that breaking them open was hardly worth the risk of the noise. But my guess was that they wouldn't contain just business papers. There was the unmistakable odour of hash-oil.

I moved quickly back across the two rooms and stood once more in the hallway, listening before I slowly mounted the stairs. The layout of this floor was entirely different. A corridor ran the full length of the house with doors on both sides. Doors and more doors! These numerous rooms had probably once been the nuns' bedrooms, and it was from one of these that the music was coming.

I stood outside the nearest door for a long time before turning the handle . . . at about the same speed as the second hand of a clock . . .

This was a kind of sitting room. The air held the stale smell of cigar smoke and there was a crack of light under the door to the right of the fireplace.

This must be Joey's sitting room, I thought. Pity the bastard wasn't in it at the moment. As I looked around I noticed an electric radiator standing in the hearth, but the fireplace didn't seem to have been used for quite some time. Suddenly the far door opened and a woman wearing a dressing gown stood in the doorway, light streaming past her.

She said something in rapid Italian as she looked out into the darkened room. It was too quick for me to pick up, but it sounded like, 'Is anyone there?' Then she noticed the half-open door leading into the corridor and went across to close it. The minute she turned she was bound to see me against the white walls.

I ducked down behind the nearest chair and crouched there, fingering the butt of the Browning that I had slung in a shoulder rig. She still couldn't help seeing me if she looked directly at me. But perhaps she won't, I thought.

I heard a key turn. What the fuck was she doing that for? Then it sounded like she had removed the key altogether, but I wasn't game to take a look.

As she came back I held my breath. But there was no sudden challenge or cry for help. She walked back to within a few feet of me, through the doorway . . . back into the room she'd come out of . . . and closed the door behind her.

I started to take a deep breath, and then I held it again. The sound of a key in a lock. How the fuck was I going to get out? All other thoughts vanished.

I went to the bedroom door and listened. My heart was thumping so much that I had to hold my breath to hear any bloody thing. I heard her pick up a telephone and dial. She spoke in low urgent tones.

A few seconds later I heard feet pounding up the stairs. The bloody woman had seen me all right. She'd just made sure I couldn't get away first! More feet on the stairs.

Trapped, I looked around desperately. I contemplated bursting into the bedroom door and taking the woman as hostage. But the chances were she'd already got a gun trained on the doorway, just waiting for me to try. Then there was a crash noise from the corridor and the door flew open. I turned my head from the noise and saw, immediately behind me, the dumb waiter.

I tore the hatch open with my left hand, at the same time taking out the Browning with my right. A guard jumped into the room and I belted him over with a shot to the chest. The ones who were about to follow him turned and fell over themselves, diving back into the corridor as they saw the first guy go down.

I had already turned. Beyond the hatchway was empty space . . . and two thin ropes.

I'd slid halfway down and was just passing the dining room when I heard a shot. The ropes parted suddenly and I fell the remaining fifteen feet to the kitchen.

I realised afterwards it had been a blessing in disguise, for in doing so I had shattered the wooden bottom of the lift and was able then to scramble out into the kitchen. Otherwise, I might have been trapped.

Three shots fired down the shaft blasted the already shattered contraption behind me.

There was a fuse box above the kitchen door and in a moment I was on a chair, flinging the fuses over my shoulder like salt. It took longer than throwing the main switch, but that could be reversed just as quickly.

Section by section the lights went out upstairs and around me until the kitchen itself was in total darkness. Then I flung the main switch off and felt for the remaining fuses by hand.

Upstairs I could hear shouting and cursing and the sound of people colliding. Then I saw a light from the stairway, and I realised a couple of the guards were coming down with a torch, cautiously.

With just enough light to avoid crashing into the kitchen, I ran for the door. I removed the key quietly as I closed it behind me.

A flight of stone steps led up from the back door, and I reached the top at the same time as one of the outside guards. My eyes were more accustomed to the dark and I gave him an unarmed combat punch in the groin. He screamed in pain and dropped the revolver he was carrying.

As he doubled up I stepped to one side, reached out with my other hand and pulled him past me and down the stairs. Then I bent down and felt for the gun before setting off for the outside wall. The guy I'd hurled down the stairs was making no sound.

Halfway across the lawn I ran straight into another guard, we collided heavily and both of us fell to the ground. I was pretty badly winded and lost the gun I was carrying in all the confusion. But I picked myself up and started off again. Before I'd limped more than a couple of steps my right ankle seized and I toppled over again. The guy on the ground started to yell for help.

I lashed out with my good foot and, despite the softness of the shoe, I connected with something that gave and turned the shouts into a shuddering gasp. However, the damage had been done already, and there were others running in my direction.

I hauled out the Browning, and just as I did I was caught in the beam of a torch. I ducked and fired at the light, which dropped to the ground, and I rolled aside quickly. A moment later a burst of gunfire missed me by inches but hit the guy I'd tripped over.

Hauling myself to my feet I started to run through the darkness. Lights came on just as I reached some shrubbery, but they must have been expecting me to make a dash for the entrance. A few seconds' grace enabled me to disappear from view and begin a frantic search for a tree close enough to the wall to help me to scramble over.

There was fuckin' none. I reached a corner of the wall where it backed onto a neighbouring property and was about to follow it in desperation when I registered that it was two feet lower and was without any broken glass on top. The bushes too were closer together here, which was an advantage in one sense, but they also got in the way.

Holstering the Browning, I flung myself at the top of

the wall. My elbows, face, and then the rest of my body hit hard and painfully against the rough brickwork as my fingers felt for the top edge, but my leap was too low and I fell back again. Shit!

There were more lights behind me now, and I could hear a car being started. Any moment now the bushes around me would be raked with a hail of gunfire.

Flinging myself up again with all my might I felt the edge of the brickwork cutting into my fingers . . . but they held. I strengthened my grip on the top and then pulled myself up. A second later my foot was over the edge and I was lying on top of the wall, panting like a fish out of water.

I heard a yell followed by three shots, which sent bullets smashing into the wall below me and showered me with brick chippings. I scrambled up past the broken glass on the front wall, dropped to the footpath and hobbled across to the comparative darkness of the far side of the road.

The guards at the gate had been waiting for me, but no sooner had they sent a couple of shots in my direction when a car crossed their line of fire and they had to stop.

The car slowed down just past the main entrance and came to a halt, with engine revving, close to where I was crouched. I looked in amazement as the rear door was flung open.

'Get in . . . quick!' Katy yelled.

I flung myself in and Katy accelerated away, with the door swinging wildly on its hinges before it slammed shut of its own accord.

'Stay down, Jimmy!'

The words were unnecessary and had scarcely left her mouth when the guards started firing, but we had already passed the lonely street lamp and disappeared into the darkness beyond.

I looked out the rear window. Just before a bend cut off my view I saw a car fling itself out of the entrance and execute a tyre-torturing left-hand turn.

'Shit, we're being followed!' Katy shouted.

'I'd be bloody well surprised if we weren't,' I replied.

Katy flung the wheel round when we reached a road junction. By the time I'd picked myself back up off the floor we had almost doubled back on ourselves and Katy was accelerating down the hill towards the main road. There was no sign of the following car . . . yet.

I glanced at Katy for the first time, with feelings of love, gratitude and pride. Not to mention relief.

'Thanks.'

'That's all right.'

'You've saved my life.'

'Think nothing of it.'

'Why did you do it?'

'Just happened to be passing, darling.'

'You might have been killed.'

'Never really thought about it, sweetheart.'

The exchange showed me another part of this woman I loved. She was incredibly brave.

'Time for plan number two, Katy.'

A moment later we pulled up beside the second car we'd rented, just in case, and climbed into it.

I brought the car back out onto the road carefully, it was no time to break an axle or draw attention to ourselves with a smoking wheelie.

In the driving mirror I saw the lights of a car sweeping towards us, but I drove forward without speeding up and turned right.

'Where are we going?' Katy asked.

'Back home.'

'It's the other way.'

'I know. We'll turn later. I didn't want to have to wait to cross over.'

As we slipped into a gap in the traffic, I saw the car behind us pull up momentarily at a STOP sign. It was a Monaro, with three guys sitting in it staring straight ahead. I drove a fair way down the road before doubling back just in time to see three police cars heading out in the direction of Frangiani's place. Their lights were flashing and sirens howling.

I gave Katy as coherent a picture as I could of what had taken place. She lifted my left hand off the wheel and kissed my fingers.

'Don't take any more risks like that again, Jimmy.'

'I'm going to get him, Katy.'

'You're not going back?'

'Don't worry, I'm not that crazy. I'll just have to figure out another way.'

Katy was silent for a while and then she said 'God I feel horny!'

She placed her hand in my lap and started to fondle me through my trousers. In a matter of moments she had me so hard I couldn't get home quick enough.

I knew deep down that if I kept taking the play up to Frangiani and Vitelli that I would end up making a fatal mistake. I'd almost done that already. So I decided the only way to get the desired results was to lull them into a false sense of security.

On the other hand, they weren't so soft as to leave me and Katy alone while I waited. But there is an old saying in the underworld—*When you're hot, keep moving*—and that's what we decided on. We would keep travelling, and enjoy ourselves at the same time.

We moved out of Potts Point, bought a four-wheel drive and took off.

24

ALICE SPRINGS NESTLES AMONG THE MACDONNELL
Ranges. Windswept rocky hills rear in folds around the
town. Cliffs, smoothed humps of granite, canyons,
with a pool of water glinting here and there from some
deep, silent cleft . . . a harsh landscape where lightly
timbered cattle country can change utterly in a
mile to a surface red as rusted metal and bare as a
desert. The Centre is said to be one of the oldest parts
of the Earth's crust. And, as is customary with great
age, its arteries have hardened and dried up. When the
rains do come, the ancient eroded rivers, the Finke and
the Todd and all the others that scar the Centre's surface with their spidery pattern, fill, burst their banks
and spread through the country. After a brief rampage
they peter out in the desert sands south of Alice. Pools
of moisture quickly disappear, leaving only marks on
the plain which will soon be baked hard. For most of
the time the creek beds are arid, dead, mere ghosts of
what rivers should be. The nearest permanent water to
the Alice are the Katherine and the Roper Rivers, more
than 700 miles to the north. Because of this, water is
always a problem in the Centre.

The inland is harsh country. Even today you could
perish only half an hour by car from the Alice itself.

The sun, generating temperatures of forty-five degrees plus, and the dry, arid atmosphere, can dehydrate a lost man, leaving a blackened corpse within forty-eight hours.

The red sandhill tracks are usually covered with spinifex grass and studded with stately green desert oaks.

The vast inland plains are like a distant waveless sea, grey with the foliage of huge mulga expanses. There are the rugged peaks of ancient ranges—blue, purple, orange and red, according to their distance from your eyes. The grandeur and peace of eternity pervade the scene, you seem to feel the pulse-beat of the most ancient continent in the world as it slumbers, tranquil in its old age. And then some little accident happens and you are left alone in the desert suddenly awakened from its sleep and ready to pounce upon you.

We stepped out of the vehicle into the heat and dust of Todd Street.

The face of Alice Springs had changed over recent years. The tumbledown buildings, hitching posts and pot-holed streets had succumbed to the twentieth century. And the completeness of the transformation was staggering.

Buildings and houses in the Alice were more modern than those we had seen in Darwin. In the northern capital government-built houses stood in their hundreds, most of them built since Cyclone Tracy, row upon row of them in a barrack-like uniformity. And there was still the odd shanty or two, a common eyesore.

By contrast, the 5,000 residents of the Alice lived in

a beautiful town of wide streets, leafy trees, and colourful shrubs and gardens. And despite a chronic water shortage there was greenery everywhere. Several of the homes and the motel where we stayed had their own swimming pools fed by private bores.

We watched as the Abo stockmen clustered around the station outfitters, saddlery stores and the pubs. We mingled with other tourists and sightseers in the new arcades, where Namatjira prints were offered side by side with native weapons, including boomerangs labelled 'Made in Switzerland', and other tourist curios.

Tourism in the Alice was booming. Planes, trains, cars and buses unload thirty to forty thousand people a year, six times the normal population. This mass invasion of a once sleepy town has provided a new and specialised market and a whole new range of firms had opened up to cater for it. The arcades and shops had reached a standard that you would expect in the sub-urbs of Sydney or Melbourne. Restaurants featured continental cooking. Goulash and wiener schnitzel had toppled the traditional steak and eggs. Hot dogs, ham-burgers, and tacos were munched by the ton.

Teenagers gathered in espresso bars. And juke-boxes were blaring everywhere.

Perhaps the greatest transformation was the Stuart Arms. Now a hotel of international standard, the old-est pub in the Alice was once regarded as the 'stock-man's pub', with constant arguments and frequent brawls. It was once a low, rambling, wooden building. And on the footpath outside was the seat of wisdom where the legendary bushman Bob Buck and his mates sat and yarned for hours.

Katy and I went to visit a place called Pitchi-Ritchi, set in spacious grounds just outside Heavitree Gap which featured a huge cement house on many levels, including underground.

It was a strange building with a large sunroom and a swimming pool on top. If it weren't for a few windows the interior rooms gave the impression that you were in subterranean passages. Apparently the person who built the place did so on a small scale. Then, when additions were needed, he reacted like the miner he was, sinking a shaft here, making a drive there . . . and all in solid concrete.

Pitchi-Ritchi was also a bird sanctuary. It had its own water bore producing 6,000 gallons of water an hour and birds flock there in their thousands—parrots and finches, and beautiful spinifex doves, so tame that we had to be careful not to tread on them.

We left the Alice refreshed and Katy wanted to see Ayers Rock. As we approached it there were terra-cotta red sandhills, relieved by the grey of saltbush and dead wood. Then stretching out before us was a wide sandy flat, spotted with dark-leaved desert oaks and so much spinifex in seed it resembled a wheat field ready for harvest. Ten miles away, resting on the waterless billows of sand, was the great, red leviathan of a rock.

Rising out of the desert more than 200 miles south-west of Alice Springs, Ayers Rock must truly be one of the wonders of the world. We rested through the heat of the day and as the evening arrived we decided to climb the path to the top.

The great humped expanse of rock was topped by a

cairn that was almost completely covered with scribbled names and initials. Bits of dried orange peel, rubbish and empty bottles failed to mar the brooding majesty of the monolith. We looked out over the desert to where the Olgas, a collection of huge, rounded boulders, showed on the skyline. The tallest, Mount Olga, was more than 1,700 feet high, but lacked the bulk and majesty of the Rock.

During the descent, busy talking, we started to wander away from the normal route, but quickly got back on the path. It was not a difficult climb on the path, but once off it you can easily strike trouble.

Once the Loritjas venerated it as Oolera, a sacred dreaming place. But now the ragged remnants of this tribe, riding their camels far to the west where even the nomadic Pintubis seldom venture and trailed by their retinue of dogs, give the Rock a wide berth. It is Oolera no more. The white man has taken over, roaring to and fro in his planes, cars and buses, clicking camera shutters by the thousand and littering this weird humped crest with picnic debris and scrawled initials.

We left the Rock with the feeling that we had left a little of ourselves there somewhere.

Soon we had crossed the gnarled and twisted MacDonnell Ranges . . . said to be one of the oldest geological formations on Earth. We trudged through the Simpson and Honeymoon Gaps, Stanley Chasm, the Serpentine and Ormiston Gorges . . . great canyons appeared below, with a pool of water glinting here and there at the bottom of some secret rock cleft. At Hermannsburg, the Lutheran mission, nearly a century old, we saw our first sign of life since leaving the Rock. A few Aboriginal children waved listlessly at us as we went by, and half a dozen horses stood out on the baked plain, tails and heads drooping in the heat.

We drove through a winding gully scoring its way through the desert, then there was Palm Valley with its patches of shady greenery and a string of clear rock pools surrounded by nodding cycads and livistona palms. The tallest of these graceful trees waved more than a hundred feet above ground level. And scattered amongst the palms were ghost gums, in bold contrast with the deep brown of the cliff walls. It is like a mirage when you first see it, but it is real enough. We set up camp and stayed for three days in this beautiful wilderness in the middle of the desert.

The Centre has a beauty and an attraction different from any other part of Australia. Its silence, its colour, the shape of the hills and the sheer immensity of the landscape boggle the mind and make you realise, as individuals, just how small you really are.

As we pushed on the terrain was varied and interesting. We were once more out in the open country with mulga scrub, gidgee trees and witchetty bushes (home of the famous grub). There were varieties of wattle, patches of saltbush and scattered whitewoods and ironwoods. And on the limestone slopes falling away from the flat-topped ranges there were stunted gums, while the red-soiled plains had the odd graceful desert oaks and the huge pincushion-shaped spinifex clumps. The lines of the waterways were marked by eucalyptus trees, including some huge ghost gums. And the game was plentiful. Kangaroos, emus, euros and wild bush turkeys abounded, with plenty of lizards, snakes and smaller animals.

We made our way down to Lake Eyre, in the driest part of the continent, yet this is not the true desert. There was still some herbage around, and evidence of old properties where, years ago, someone had tried to make a go at raising stock. We could still see the remnants of fence lines—old posts and bits of wire trailing forlornly across the desolate plain. To the east lay the sandy wastes of the Tirari Desert, stretching away to the horizon. To the north the parallel dunes of the Simpson imposed an effective barrier.

Nitrebush, spinifex and canegrass were sparsely dotted around the dry lake. And the air was so dry that it swallowed up moisture like a roll of kleenex.

East of 'The Track' and north almost to the Gulf of Carpentaria stretched the Barkly Tableland, a huge savannah of Mitchell and Flinders grasses. The fascination of its vast expanses hadn't left me. You can travel for miles over the black soil plains of the Barkly without seeing a hill or a tree. There is nothing at all to break the flat line of the horizon. In fact it's hardly a tableland at all, for the rise above the surrounding countryside is almost imperceptible.

We pushed on northward and visited Mary Kathleen, known as Uranium City, in the rugged, weather-sculptured ranges between the Isa and Cloncurry.

Mary Kathleen had all the modern amenities; a company store which stocked just about everything at reasonable prices, a school, a picture theatre, a large cafeteria which was also used as the local hall, a six-bed hospital and a brothel. Katy and I got pissed as rats there, and finished up with hangovers so bad it took two days to recover.

But once we recovered we made our way out of there, left Mount Isa behind and headed down the 400 miles of bitumen along the Barkly Highway to the Stuart Highway. Some of the stretches are as straight as a gun barrel and one of them went for fifty miles without the slightest deviation. Another two travelled for about thirty miles each without a single bend. The ridge that the highway followed was mostly poor country with gibbers, spinifex and stunted mulgas.

Camooweal, on the upper reaches of the Georgina River, was just a small huddle of buildings in the middle of a vast plain. Eight miles west of the town we crossed the lonely fence which is the border between Queensland and the Northern Territory. These long straight stretches of bitumen, fading into the haze of a shimmering mirage, left us feeling hypnotised. Yet as desolate as it is, the Stuart Highway is a bitumen artery that pumps lifeblood through the outback and central Australia.

At a place called Wycliffe Bore we were told that the owner had just upped and left, that he'd had a gutful and was returning to prospecting.

Greeted by a riot of moisture and greenery, we climbed down and walked around the place. The bore was overflowing, running in rivulets down to a dry creek bed where it gathered in little pools around which scores of birds were squawking and drinking. On the far side of the track stood an old galvanised-iron building flanked by ploughed fields, and a citrus orchard whose greenery was starting to wither from the hot sun and a lack of water.

The place was totally deserted, but the owner couldn't have left the area more than a week or two earlier. Everything was in a perfect state of repair. The house was furnished with beds, tables, chairs and even a kerosene-run refrigerator still standing in the kitchen.

Beside the house was that rarest of all sights in the inland . . . a swimming pool about twenty yards long. Katy and I stripped off and jumped in. The water was warm and made us feel sleepy.

Wycliffe Bore also boasted a shower building made of galvanised-iron, with a sign that read: ALL PER-SONS MUST SHOWER BEFORE ENTERING POOL. And near the pool was a large plunge bath made of cement . . . Empty.

Katy followed me, snatching up our clothes as I walked naked towards the house.

'Where are we going?' she asked with a laugh, knowing her question needed no answer.

Once inside I took her in my arms, kissing her neck, then I drew her face up to mine, pressed my lips lightly on hers and then I kissed her with more pressure. Her lips were soft yet strong, and demanding, and her tongue darted into my mouth. She had no illusions about my demands and the urgency of her sexuality made me tremble with pleasure. Her hands were just extensions of her nerve endings, transmitting electrical thrills as they ran over my body, feeling it, caressing it. Her touch had a mysterious invisible pull, as if her body had some magnetic field that reacted to the unseen forces that dragged me helplessly inwards.

She knelt down on the floor before me, taking my

erection in her hands like a supplicant before a shrine.

'You are beautiful, Katy,' I heard myself say. Her eyes looked greedy as she kissed me and took me into her soft warm mouth. I ran my hands through her hair and could feel she was growing shivery with pleasure, her orgasmic urgency beginning, the sensation making her cry out with pleasure.

Unable to stand it any longer, I lifted her up onto the bed. She lay back, watching my body loom over her while I watched the flecks of passion in her lovely blue eyes, the wonderful smile. A gift. Then she drew me inside her as I plunged, gently at first, sliding inward, filling her up with the largeness that she longed for, wanted. The power of it, the pleasure of it made her gasp as I lingered for a moment and she moved her body to meet mine, waited, drew back, returned again until I was moving into her with a hardness. She began to tremble and shake, waves of pleasure unfolding inside her like some vast surf responding to the pull of the moon. I could feel myself throbbing inside her, the beat of my blood as it gained strength, then hesitated, like a predatory bird who glided, then moved downward toward its prey, an explosion of energy. She made some inchoate sound, I felt her shudder and the receding surf . . .

'I'm going to come!' she cried.

And I could sense the pleasure coming from deep inside her as I increased my urgency with swift jerking motions.

'Jimmy I need you!' she cried as her orgasm washed over her with the heat of an explosive force, the joy of it captured on her beautiful face. She cried out in a long wail and I felt the release in me start and I let go

264

and Katy cried out again and wrapped her arms and legs around me, holding me to her as she gasped for breath and my heart was pumping. 'I love you,' I said to her.

When our trembling had stopped we went back to the pool and swam for a while, then hand in hand we walked back inside to escape the heat of the sun.

It was only then that I began to take an interest in the room. It was sparsely furnished. The double bed on which Katy was lying was a mattress on a homemade frame. There was an old card table, its felt top worn through in spots and piled high with magazines. Books lay everywhere and a forest of old bottles, some with odd shapes, sat on a long packing case. There were bookshelves along one wall, held up with home-made brackets that were nailed in place. The shelving was painted the same dull white as the walls, which were barren of pictures. Beside the bed was a night table of unplaned timber, made from a wooden box, with a hurricane lantern siting on top as a reading lamp, and along the windowed wall three piles of old newspapers nearly reached the ledge. The blinds were split and broken. I found it hard to envisage the man who had lived in this cell. On one of the old chairs was a grease-stained pizza box, all that was left of a trip to town. There were no means of communication, no radio, no phone. Katy had her eyes closed, dozing.

'The den of an exile,' I said.

My voice startled her, and in an act of modesty she stood up, pulled her light cotton dress over her head and let it fall around her.

'It needs a woman's touch,' she commented and in a

stray moment of embarrassment she suddenly bent down and picked up her panties that lay in a crumpled heap with the rest of our clothes. Gathering the rest up quickly, she put them on the bed. We walked into the room that had been used as a bathroom. There was an old rusty tub with the enamel worn off the bottom, and hanging over it a bush shower made from a kerosene tin. A ring of greasy dirt circled the cracked porcelain washbasin bolted to the wall. On top of it was a thin sliver of soap, perhaps from some motel. A single toothbrush, the bristles worn and dirty, lay inside the washbasin. The mirror was filmy and the back was peeling away, leaving patches of plain glass. I walked back out into the other room, gazing out the window at the dry red plain. Dust devils danced and the heat shimmered out of the ground like steam. Katy moved beside me and, tilting her face up, she kissed my earlobe. I put my arm around her, staring into nothing, trying again to picture the man who had lived here.

There were about a dozen or so wood and iron buildings, including a garage full of machinery and spare parts for cars and trucks. A hut made out of wattle boughs had a wooden door painted green and inscribed 'THE GREEN DOOR . . . COOL MAN COOL'. There were slogans everywhere, painted on walls, boards, tanks and oil drums . . . 'OUT JACKAL!', 'Please do not walk in garden', 'Bird Sanctuary . . . Leave your guns at home, Bill'.

The vegetable gardens were bare. The orchard, deprived of water, was still green but gradually withering under the relentless sun. The seats outside the fence, in the shade of the parkinsonia trees, were eaten through by whiteants and termites. A hundred yards from the house stood the inevitable grave, with an iron fence and a white cross made of tin. It bore no epitaph. Like the unknown soldier. And over everything hung a deep silence, broken only by the chirping of hundreds of tiny finches which had gathered to drink from the untenanted bore.

This place, with its greenery, its swimming pool, its slogans and its silence, was symbolic of man's determination to better his surroundings. Now it was in the process of mouldering back into the arid mulga plain which gave it birth. Once more, I wondered who built this garden in the middle of nowhere, and where was he now. Katy and I stayed there for nearly a week.

All the questions we had been asking ourselves about the place were answered when we arrived at a town called Wauchope. Wycliffe Bore had belonged to Fred Vandenburg. He'd built up the garden and the swimming pool and used to offer vegetables and citrus fruits for sale by the roadside and in Wauchope. He told people that many years before he had struck gold deep in Arnhem Land Aboriginal reserve. Since then he had returned several times to search for it, but without success. Now Vandenburg was back in Arnhem Land, hunting for his 'lost reef' while his garden at Wycliffe Bore withered slowly away . . . That's how the story went, anyway.

We arrived at Tennant Creek, a place that has been called the ugliest town in the world. The houses were made mainly of weatherboard or iron and, apart from the two hotels, most of the business premises had a temporary look to them. We got the feeling that

Tennant Creek will simply disappear when its gold and copper wealth runs out, as other mining towns have done before it. But that time still seems a long way off.

A hundred miles up the track we drove into Renner Springs. It was just another one of those roadside inns which you know you are approaching when you see a huge sign with a cold glass of beer, with condensation on it, advertising 2 MILES SWAN.

At Larrimah we took a break for a couple of days and spent most of the time either asleep or soaking up moisture in the local bar.

Further north, as we entered Mataranka, pandanus and thicker scrub beside the road told us we were back in the Top End. Darwin now lay just 278 miles away.

We arrived in the leisurely little town of Katherine and decided to stay for a while and look around. About twenty miles out of town we visited the Katherine Gorge, where the river flowed, clear and swift, between towering canyon walls. There were native paintings done in ochre high up on the rocks. The fishing was great and we caught barramundi, dining on it almost every night. There were crocodiles in abundance but none of them bothered us. We spent hours in the many limestone caves which honeycomb the district.

Closer to Darwin, civilisation has just about wiped out the emus and the plains turkeys that once teemed there, but there seemed to be an increase in the numbers of kangaroos, wild horses and pigs. You never knew when one was going to dart out in front of the headlights, so we took it easy when driving after dusk. Generally the cattle shied clear of the traffic, but kangaroos would jump straight at the vehicle. The buffaloes were the most unpredictable. Since the hide-hunting eased off the buffaloes have become tamer, but it is not uncommon for one to lower its head and charge at headlights. And they are solid enough to cause damage and shake the heaviest truck.

Soon the lights of Darwin were before us. Behind us lay the bitumen, 946 miles of it stretching back to Alice Springs, and hundreds more that we had travelled off the beaten track.

25

IT WAS AFTERNOON AS KATY AND I STROLLED TOGETHER along the streets of Darwin. The heat was intense, with a humid thundery sky threatening to break into showers at any moment.

This part of the world always seemed strange to me, it was so full of contradictions. There was wealth here as well as poverty. All types . . . lawyers, speculators, alternative lifestyles, battlers . . . all up here to try to make a dollar and get away from something. What was this word, lifestyle, I wondered and smiled wryly to myself. When I thought about the number of drunken fights, wife beatings, car accidents, robberies and so forth that happened up here, I didn't see how lifestyle helped anything. People take their problems with them.

Katy stopped suddenly and turned to me.

'Jimmy, why won't you let me see where you and Carmel stayed? Is it really that painful?'

I thought for a minute.

'Is it that important to you?'

'Well you must have really liked it, otherwise you wouldn't have gone back twice. All I'm saying is that I'd like to see it. Wouldn't you like to?'

There was an ache in me to go and check the place

out, just to see what had become of it, so I agreed. She jumped up and down like an excited little girl.

'When can we go?' she asked.

'Would tomorrow be soon enough?'

Katy gave a squeal and hugged me as her answer.

For the rest of the day we went shopping. Stacking the Landcruiser with enough provisions to last us a month of Sundays.

That night we ate really well, since we'd be travelling hard again and only eating cold provisions or what we knocked up on the side of the track.

In the morning we left Darwin behind us and headed south. We travelled all day, making several stops, and as the red sun finally started sinking we decided to make camp for the night. I made a fire and told Katy to knock us up a meal . . . that she'd better get in practice because where we were going there was no such things as electricity or gas.

She did really well coming up with bacon and eggs, and toast made in the hot coals of the fire using a wire fork she'd fashioned from a coat-hanger.

We started off again soon after dawn, driving between the grey-green patches of spinifex, over the red earth that showed between them, and past the gnarled and stunted trees that gave us no protection from the sun. We stopped after two hours and had a drink out of the Esky. Then, taking my bearings off the map and a compass, we pushed on again.

It was three in the afternoon and we were getting closer to our destination, weaving and winding our way through bush, the Landcruiser singing in third gear, the vegetation getting thicker all the time as we headed east. One minute we'd be in the green light of the bush, the next bursting out into clear sunshine. When I finally saw the sign that I was looking for, I told Katy we'd stop and stretch our legs.

We both stood in the silence, listening to the ticking metal noises coming from the Landcruiser. Then I pointed out to Katy the sagging broken gate. It had rusted a dark red and grass rose around it like hair above a dirty collar.

Walking over to the gate, I lifted and heaved. It creaked in the knees, then let go and came open. Time for the final leg of a long journey.

We bumped our way over miles of track so thick with grass and undergrowth that there was only the hint of a tunnel through the trees. Tall grass and small bushes scraped the underbelly of the Toyota and squealed as they travelled down the sides. It was hard driving and I drove tensely, my hands sweating on the wheel, body screwed up wire-taut. Beside me, Katy hung onto the handle on the dashboard, bouncing around and turning her head to smile at me. Through the side mirrors I could see the crushed grass and undergrowth rise slowly like a tired audience getting slowly to its feet. Here and there it was smeared with a mixture of grease and sump-oil from the bottom of the Cruiser, but the vehicle was built for this type of thing. The end came at last in a brief yielding of the saplings and a clearing in which stood our farmhouse.

The old house and the outbuildings were wreathed in stillness. Somehow I felt that it should have had a cheerful curl of smoke coming from the chimney, or the dog running out to bark. Even the hollow bang of the Toyota's door, when I got out and closed it, was out of place and unreal.

I studied the doorway that stood like an exclamation mark in the face of the building. And knew that I was home. Katy came and stood beside me and put her arm around me, then turning herself towards me and with her head on my chest she burst into tears.

'God, Jimmy, its so beautiful.'

We finally went forward together. Up onto the verandah and I pushed open the door. Everything was as we had left it. The crockery and pots and pans, even the canned provisions we had to leave behind, were still in the cupboards. Diefer's chain was looped over one of the railings on the verandah, but his body and bones had disappeared. The Coleman tilly lanterns were hanging in their place. I opened the kerosene fridge and green dust fell out on the floor. All the stuff that we had left in it when we were forced to leave so hurriedly was a mass of dry garbage, covered in a grey-green furry mould.

I walked back out to the verandah and lit a cigarette, letting the smoke roll around my dry mouth. Sitting up on one of the rails, I put my arm round Katy.

'Well this is it, princess,' I said. 'This is what I call home.'

The sun was down on the horizon by the time Katy and I finished packing our supplies into the house.

'What do we do now?' she asked me.

'We get some wood in, love, for the fire.'

There was no shortage of wood. Fallen dry branches were strewn on the ground under the trees, and there was driftwood on the sand spits of the tidal fed lagoon.

I got the big cast-iron range in the kitchen alight and we lit up the tilly lamps. Then I went round and did a few running repairs on the insect screens, so we wouldn't get eaten alive by the mosquitoes at night.

That night I was having a nightmare and woke when Katy put her arms around me.

'Jimmy! Jimmy, turn over. You've been dreaming.'

I twisted and automatically reached out and held her and we drifted off to sleep again.

At sunrise I awoke clear-headed and clear-eyed. Katy was a mound of bed clothing and a tousle of dark hair, so I slipped quietly out of bed and dressed quickly, shaved and drank a few mouthfuls of cool water out of the refrigerator, which I was pleased to see was working.

Outside, I lit my first cigarette for the day and looked around. I walked over to the Toyota and did a check to see if the big Zeiss binoculars were there. Satisfied, I kicked the engine into life and headed through the curvy looms of the bush, making good time and letting the Landcruiser sing its differential song on the run down to the overgrown gate, which I tugged back across the opening. As I stood there briefly, the only sound was the occasional buzzing of a fly.

There was smoke coming from the chimney when I got back. And when I walked inside Katy was working on getting us some breakfast.

Katy fitted in well in the strange environment, and there was only one time I saw her completely at a loss.

I was outside when I heard her hysterical scream from inside the house.

'Jiiiiimy!'

I ran inside and saw Katy, naked, crouched like a wild woman on the kitchen table.

'There's a snake in here!'

At the same instant I saw a long writhing streak fly across the kitchen floor. The snake seemed to bounce off the cupboard doors, then flashed around and streaked back towards me. Katy screamed again and I had to scramble out of its way. It was a king brown, one of the deadliest. The huge snake hit the closed screen door with a wallop, then whirled around and disappeared into one of the cupboards with a crashing of bottling jars that were in there.

Katy was terrified. Her dark hair was all awry and ringlets were sticking to her sweaty neck.

'Where is it now?' she gasped.

I pointed to the open door of the cupboard.

'Which end?'

'I don't know,' I said, 'they're interconnected.'

'What will it do now, Jimmy?'

'Well, snakes are as frightened of us as we are of them. It's hiding from us.'

'What sort is it? Is it dangerous?'

'Bloody oath. It's a fuckin' king brown, and those bastards can get pretty aggressive.'

'Can't you shoot it?'

'I can't very well shoot it in the cupboard, Katy.'

'Well what are you going to do then?' she said, half sobbing.

'Look, it won't get you up there, so just sit and take it easy.'

There was a big pot of boiling water simmering lazily on the cooking range. I looked at it then turned to the cupboard. Another of the doors wasn't completely closed, and I leant out and gingerly opened it a bit wider with a broom handle.

I couldn't see the snake and nothing happened, so I opened the door right up and poked the broom into the clutter at the bottom of the cupboard. There was a furious slithering noise as the angry snake burst out of the cupboard with a clatter of bottles and utensils and flashed across the floor, disappearing into another open cupboard.

I cautiously peered into the snake's new hiding place.

'Can you see it?' Katy whispered as if the snake would hear her.

'Yep,' I said, 'I think I can.'

'Oh God . . . what are you going to do?'

'I'll get that water off the stove and throw it in on the bastard.'

'Will that kill it?'

'It'd fuckin' kill you and me. 'Course it will.'

I went over to the stove, picked up the big aluminium boiler with a couple of oven gloves and moved over slowly toward the snake's new lair.

When I looked into the dark cupboard I could just make out some of the coils in there. I steadied myself, took a deep breath, then hurled the water in and jumped back to avoid any back splash, not to mention the fuckin' snake.

All hell broke loose. The king brown came bursting

out in a great writhing knot, coiling and contorting, a twisting brown killer about eight feet long convulsing around the kitchen floor, flashing jaws agape. Katy screamed and grabbed the broom that I'd rested against the table and swiped down at it with all her might. The snake skidded across the floor and Katy gave another scream. I raced into the bedroom up the short hall, grabbed the shotgun from the top of the cupboard and rushed back.

The snake was contorting but not so rapidly now. I opened the screen door and pushed the ring along the arm of the return so it wouldn't close.

'Give me the broom,' I said to Katy.

With the shotgun in my right hand and the broom in my left I pushed and skidded the snake over near the door. It seemed to get a new lease of life and went into convulsions that sent it tumbling out onto the verandah. I dropped the broom and shouldered the gun.

Blam! The report of the gun just about deafened us inside the kitchen. But the charge hit the snake, picking it up and shredding it in places as it went toppling over the edge of the verandah.

I walked down the steps and it was moving in a figure of eight pattern, but slowly. I put another shot into it that blew it into several pieces. Slowly the movements stopped. I got a shovel and around the back dug a hole and buried the snake.

When I went back inside Katy hung onto me for ten minutes before her shaking started to subside.

We stood facing out the door watching a side of bacon that we had killed, salted, cured and smoked

277

nearly a week ago. It was hanging from one of the rafters out on the verandah and gently swinging in the breeze.

'How soon before that's ready to eat?' Katy asked.

'It's good enough now.'

'Are you hungry? Because I am.'

'Yeah why not, I'll bring it in for you.'

While Katy laid out bacon strips in the frying pan, I watched her easy movements. Sitting in an old easy chair with my feet up on an overturned fruit box, I watched my cigarette smoke spin upwards towards the ceiling in the still air. The bacon crackled and curled, releasing its mouth-watering aroma.

'How many eggs do you want?'

'Two.'

She cracked the eggs into the pan as the bacon soaked out its grease on a brown paper bag. There was something soul-pleasing about sitting here quietly in the middle of nowhere. No phone, no TV, no newspapers. It must be how the pioneers felt, I thought. No wonder they fell in love with the open spaces. I tried to think what it would be like in the cities at this moment . . . and a shudder ran through me. My thoughts were broken by Katy.

'Coffee's coming,' she said, placing the plates on the table. 'In my next life I'm going to be a chicken,' she called to me. 'My whole life here revolves around eggs.'

We had been to Booraloola a couple of months ago and brought back six chooks and a rooster. Katy had practically done all the work on the coop, made nesting boxes for the broody hens and a special coop for the two chooks with chickens so the hawks and goannas wouldn't get them.

Katy came back with the coffee. She was loosening up after the experience with the snake. And falling in love with the bush.

26

WE HAD BEEN AT UTOPIA, AS I NAMED IT, FOR NEARLY A year now. Katy had never come with me when I went out to hunt fresh meat, but when I mentioned another trip she said she wanted to come along this time.

We left early the next morning. The Toyota was a good vehicle for slugging around up here and we bounced along through the bush until we came to a broad expanse of sand with a trickle of water flowing along it. I shifted gear, and we crawled over it without too much difficulty.

When we reached the other side we bumped up onto dry ground. Katy clutched at my knee for balance as we leant first to the left, then to the right, and she smiled up at me in a sort of apology for hanging on so tight. I didn't mind. She was looking remarkably well since we had come up here. As I changed up again with the gearshift I couldn't help noticing her hands, one gripping the seat between her legs, the other on my knee. They were brown, fingers long slim and ringless. I smiled back at her.

'This is as far as we go,' I told her.

We pulled off to the right, by the foot of a small rocky hill, and got out. I grabbed the Winchester from behind the seat.

There was a small clearing in front, and to the left there was thick stuff going to the river. A couple of times I had been lucky and found buffalo there. I took Katy's hand and helped her as we clambered up through the rocks. Soon we could see an area of grass-land that stretched down to a bend in the river. Dense jungle thickets separated the water from the grass. I lifted up the binoculars that were hanging round my neck, but they weren't really necessary. Immediately to our front three grey blobs grazed at the far side of a track that ran through the clearing. The glasses enlarged two cows and a nice-sized yearling. I handed the glasses to Katy.

'Want to take a look?'

'Gee, it feels like we could almost touch them,' she said and handed the glasses back towards me.

'Hang onto them, I've got the scope.'

I looked at the yearling . . . about 150 yards . . . no wind . . . and leant forward against the rock, adjusted the sling around my arm and brought the gun tight against my shoulder. I worked the bolt and a round snicked into the breech, too loud really. Katy sat watching, but she had placed her hands over her ears, and out among the grass the yearling raised its head. I inched the barrel up onto target, steadied and squeezed the trigger. Before the sound of the report was over the three animals were up and running towards the bush. But only the two cows made it. The yearling's evasive action had only been reflex.

I slung the rifle over my shoulder, wiped my hands down the seat of my jeans and Katy and I started back to the Landcruiser. We could drive around the rocks and out onto the grassland for the pick-up. Noise didn't matter now we had our fresh meat.

When we got to the kill, Katy preferred to wait around the vehicle while I took the best cuts. It was a shame that so much had to be left but we had no way of keeping large amounts of meat. It was gut-busting work but I finally had the meat loaded into a big plastic Esky. We had hardly cleared the area before the crows descended in a black cloud to feast. When it got dark the dingoes would be about.

They are a magnificent animal, buffalo, and the meat from a yearling is as good as the beef you will buy anywhere. And yet up here they are classified by the government as vermin. To be shot on sight.

We had just finished the evening meal. I had spent the rest of the day working on a fence I was building out of cut-and-dried straight saplings and told Katy I was a bit knackered and sore.

'Just stretch out on the couch for a while,' she said, clearing the plates from the table and blowing out a couple of candles she had lit. Without looking back, she went into the kitchen and began to wash the dishes. After a while she stole glances over her shoulder at me. Shutting off the tap, she came into the room, tiptoeing across to the other chair, removed a light cover that was lying on it and covered me with it gently. Then she tiptoed up into the bedroom and came out with a cotton jacket, wrapped it around herself and slumped into the other lounge, her legs folded up underneath her, and cuddling her chin in the heel of her hand.

I wasn't asleep and I waited for my eyes to become accustomed to the dark. I wanted to watch her, to watch the movements of her breathing, to try and read her mind. I was in exile, but she understood why I chose this way of life. She understood what it meant. By being with me wasn't she too, an exile? But she was safe. The difference was I was still in the battle.

I cleared my throat.

'I'm not asleep, Katy, I've just been lying here watching you.'

'Why?'

'Because I like what I see and I love just watching you.'

She came over and lifted up my shoulders and sat down, cradling my head in her lap, arms against her breasts. My hands reached for them in the dark, squeezing and fondling. I opened her jacket and blouse, and as I did she stroked the back of my head. I felt an uncommon stirring inside me, as if something exciting were about to happen.

As I kissed and suckled her breast for a long time, like a child gaining sustenance, I felt as if milk were actually flowing from them and into me. After some time she reached down and opened my pants, caressing the hardness of my penis. Her fingers were seeking, soft and gentle. She moved downward and took me into her mouth, I could feel her soft moving flesh, as if it were apart of me, and gave a moan. The pressure inside me was building and I knew that I would let go at any moment. She must have sensed it through her lips, the tightening, the throbbing, and she intensified her efforts as if this is what she wanted. And then the release, the magic moment of pleasure-pain exploding and bursting out of me.

Outside, it began to rain, a steady downpour that put a sheen on everything. We hopped up and dashed around the place closing the windows. Then we sat down in the kitchen and had some coffee. I looked at Katy in the bright light from the Coleman. She had a radiant look about her . . . a new softness that I had never seen before.

She saw me looking at her and then, lowering her head, she started doodling in a little puddle of spilt coffee on the table.

'When you finish the fence, you're going to have to do some more building,' she said at last.

'Where?'

'The house.'

'What do you mean?'

'We're going to need another room.'

'Why.'

She burst into tears and said, 'I'm going to have our baby.'

I felt like I'd been hooked up to high-tension cables and given 10,000 volts. Utterly shocked, I had never given it a thought. And then my heart started to sing and respond.

'Are you sure?' I said in a croaky voice.

'I've missed my last two periods. Hadn't you noticed?'

I just sat there dumbfounded.

She looked up at me. 'Don't you want it?' she asked through a flood of tears.

I jumped out of the chair and lifted her to her feet and held her to me.

'Oh Katy, Katy, 'course I do,' I said as I rocked her and kissed her and felt her lips respond under mine.

She took my hand and placed it on her stomach.

'This is our child in there,' she said.

'I can't feel anything.'

'It's not big enough yet,' she said with a little push.

She took my hand and led me into the bedroom, then moved her body tightly against mine. It seemed as if she was being deliberately, aggressively, suggestive . . . as if she just had to have me right now. Her hands reached down for me, caressing. The love I had for her responded and I could feel myself hardening under her hand. Soon I was kissing her, filling her mouth with my tongue.

'Let me undress you,' she whispered, removing my shirt, unbelting me, unzipping, then rolling down my underpants, watching, caressing me, touching the smooth hardness of my erection. I simply stood there, an object to be observed, and she was acutely aware of the enjoyment I felt from her attention.

'Now you,' I said, and I helped her undress while I wondered if she would be as pleased as I was. She continued to stroke my erection. When she was naked she stepped back, side-on. Catching a glimpse of herself in the mirror, she ran her hand down her stomach. Her body was firm and slender, her stomach still flat, her bum tight and firm, and her breasts seemed to have enlarged a little but were still upturned.

'You still have the body of a teenager,' I said, reaching for her.

Then we were in bed, and the joy of her just being there with me was overwhelming. I made everything I did to her special and soft. I played with her with my tongue until she was wet and wild and moving with emotion. I reached my hands up and rolled her erect nipples between my thumb and fingers. But before I could enter her, her body beat me to it and responded with a kind of massive seizure of pleasure, an orgasm that seemed to draw its essence from the very pit of her being, a gale wind now repeating itself when I finally entered her, feeling her wetness and warmth envelop me, drawing me up inside of her. She wrapped her arms and legs around me, as if she wanted me there forever.

Later I watched her. Her eyes appeared to be seeing something on the ceiling, following the shadows left by the lantern, but I sensed that she was looking inside herself.

'Do you really see me as a young girl?' she asked.

My concentration was distracted and I smiled.

'You *are* a young girl,' I said.

'I'm twenty-three.'

'Now you're talking about time, Katy. I'm talking about what my eyes see, and my hands touch.'

I reached over gently and placed the flat of my hand on her stomach.

'And inside?'

'Very young and very beautiful.'

'Would you please say that again?'

'Very young and very beautiful.'

'Thank you.'

She kissed my cheek, and a tear ran out of her eye.

'Do you mean that?'

I hesitated, then ignored the question.

'I'm thirty-nine, Katy,' I said with a sigh and a certain amount of regret. 'Age is an enigma.'

286

'An enigma?'

'A mystery, a puzzle, I feel young and old at the same time.' I hesitated then and looked at her. 'Once, thirty seemed old to me,' I continued. 'Now time seems to have lost its meaning. I feel sometimes I'll never grow up.'

'Why? Where does the energy come from?'

'Maybe it's anger, the search for exoneration, revenge.'

'Revenge?' As she looked at me her eyes widened a little.

'Or maybe it's the sense of impending death.'

At the mention of death, she swallowed hard, gasped, and I felt a shiver run through her.

I shouldn't have bloody well said that, I thought, and closed my eyes against the glare of the lamp. My eyelids fluttered and she leant over me and kissed them, as if the act might still them.

'Don't ever leave me, Jimmy,' she said suddenly.

I felt the panic in her voice. And her words . . . I had heard those same words before . . . many years ago in a house in Roslyn Street, Kings Cross . . . that terrible repetitive sense of impending loss. Her voice startled me and I rose up in the bed.

I leant over her and held her.

'I'm yours, Katy. There's nothing I wouldn't do for you.'

'Thank you,' she said and kissed me softly. 'Please don't talk like that again.'

I hugged her and held her to me. God I loved this girl. Then we rolled apart and looked up at the ceiling.

Outside the rain drummed on the roof of the old house. Katy seemed to be full of love, as if nothing would satisfy her. She sat up in bed and rolled over, looking down at me.

'I just want you to want me.'

Then she was back in my arms, breathing into my face as if she was trying to draw some essence from me, nuzzling my neck, holding my head between her hands, kissing my face, my eyes, my nose, my cheek. I moved her away with a strong tight gesture and looked at her.

'You're very beautiful, Katy,' I said, feeling a new understanding growing between us.

'Can I get you something?' she asked me.

'No,' I said, 'but I know what you want.'

She watched me as I caressed her breasts, the nipples hardening once more. She was proud of her body and she arched forward, enjoying the pleasure I was creating in her boobs. They were large, full, and well-formed. As she became more aroused with my growing passion, she reached down for me, then kneeling she squeezed my erection between her breasts. Then she lay down beside me, pulled me over on top of her and drew me inside her again. I felt her body billow like a sail to a fresh wind, alive and vibrant, but she moved slowly with a languor that told me she didn't want our lovemaking to end.

'I wish I could say what you mean to me, Jimmy,'

And I marvelled at the calm, unhurried progression of our mutual response, like the sputtering of the fuse on a stick of gelignite, then the explosion, powerful, absorbing, the pulsating stillness of heated tempered steel, long burning and bright, the climax of a burst of light lingering hotly. It was a strange sensation of joy non-ending.

We dozed off for a minute and when I stirred again I was still inside her, only I was soft now, sleeping. Gently I disengaged, then held her in my arms until she grew drowsy. The lamp had run out of fuel and the filament had a dull red glow like an ember in the coals of a dying fire.

We woke up in the darkness and held each other again, long, endlessly, until the light filtered through the drawn canvas blinds. With our passion ground down, the explosions ended, Katy sat up and propped the pillows behind us and we half-reclined while I lit and smoked a cigarette.

'Will they ever let us go back?' she asked.

I knew what she meant and I turned and watched her after this question, but her eyes were deliberately closed, fearful perhaps that they would reveal the fierceness of the new living attachment between us, growing inside her.

'They?' I said, 'never, Katy, not without a fight.'

She knew what I meant and became silent. I lit another cigarette and in the quiet of the room I could hear the tobacco burning and see the light change as the glow reddened.

I placed my hand on her stomach.

'Is there any movement?'

'It's too little yet, Jimmy,' she said with a quiet giggle.

We became silent again. I took another puff on my cigarette. Suddenly she sat up and turned to me to press a point, sensing that maybe it was the right moment.

'Jimmy, no matter what happens I want a piece of your life. Don't shut me out.'

'It's not as simple as it sounds, Katy.'

'There's been a lot of violence in your life and you seem to thrive on it. And I know there'll probably be more. But we're going to have a baby, so before you do anything will you please try to think of that?'

Her words came out in a rush, as if they had been pressed against her brain for too long and needed this release. I knew now that she had been waiting for this moment to tell me.

'I had no right to involve you in the first place, Katy.'

'That's bullshit, Jimmy. I involved myself. It was my commitment, not yours. Please don't shut me out.'

We made love again and finally slept until bright sunlight was coming through the edges of the windows. Katy got up and lifted the blinds and a clear, clean light blazed through the room. I went and had a shower and dressed quickly. Without waiting for coffee, I went outside to work on the fence. When I went back inside an hour later Katy was asleep on the crumpled sheets and she slept till late afternoon.

I walked in and stripped off and had another shower. Then went into the bedroom and lay down carefully beside her. She gave a little jump . . . then reached out with her hand and pulled me close beside her.

'Did I frighten you?' I asked.

'I don't frighten easily,' she replied with mock bravado. 'You'll have to do better than that to scare me.' We both laughed and hugged each other.

'I missed you today,' I said.

'Really?'

'Really.'

She seemed less tight, almost playful, as if she had just received some good news. Lying there together in the big bed I watched her, watched the transition, the humour in her face fading as I reached out for her. The pressure of my fingers triggered her own response and she reached down for me. She was lying propped against my chest and her head was rising and falling to the rhythm of my breathing. Her hands began to move gently over my skin, pausing to play with my nipples, then downward over my belly. I could feel the change in her heartbeat, a swiftness as she reached down and took hold of my penis, and I felt her stir beside me. Under her soft gentle touch my penis stiffened, and she gave a little Mmmmm sound of satisfaction, like a child who has reached the final phase of constructing a sand castle.

'You must let me be part of your life Jimmy,' she said in low tones.

'You are part of my life.'

'It's not enough. Not enough for me. I want more.'

In the context of her present activity, the idea of it sounded hilarious and I started to laugh. Katy caught the humour of it too. My erection was large and powerful, throbbing now.

'I couldn't ask for anything more than that,' she said, giving it a squeeze and caressing the tip of it with her tongue.

'I want participation,' she said. 'If you don't let me into your life, then what is it?'

I wondered if she could feel that she was creating an ultimatum. But I let it lie for a moment, watching her reaction to my silence.

'I love you, Jimmy. You've changed my life. I want to give, to be giving. I'd do anything for you.' Then she looked down at my erection and sensed my discomfort.

'And I want that. Yoooooou.'

She lifted herself, moved her body over me and directed my hard penis into herself, feeling its fullness inside her, moving her body as if she were seeking the very core of herself. I felt it too, a wrenching, soul-engulfing, explosion of pleasure sucking me in. I could feel the beginning of my release and she sensed it too, strengthening her efforts till I came into her and she threw her head back. She looked down at me, watching as the tension in my body subsided, then she held me tightly until I felt her body soften and relax.

'If only the end of it would last longer,' she said.

'Christ, love, I don't think anyone could stand coming for half an hour straight. You'd go fuckin' crazy.'

'I am part of you aren't I?'

'Yes you are, Katy, you really are.'

She lay there on top of me for a while and we both became silent.

In the morning over breakfast, I told her we couldn't stay here. 'Not now that you're going to have a baby.'

'Why, why can't we?'

292

'Christ almighty, love, we're in the fuckin' middle of nowhere . . . What if you have problems . . . shit, you know what I mean.'

'Well plenty of other women have had babies in the bush.'

'Yeah with the fuckin' Flying Doctors assisting them. How in the name of Christ could a plane land here?'

'What? Have we got to go straight away?'

'No, I'm not saying that . . . what I am saying is that we better start making plans to move out, and where we're going.'

'Well, there must be hospitals around here somewhere.'

'Sure, Katherine if we head north, and Mount bloody Isa if we go south. Both of 'em are two days away.'

She was silent for a while then said . . .

'I suppose you're right, but we're not going yet.'

When we reached Mount Isa on our way to Brisbane it was nearly two months later, and Katy's pregnancy was starting to show.

It had been a pretty hard ride for her on the way down, so we booked into a motel and I insisted that she go and see a doctor.

The doctor checked her out with me standing guard. He gave her a clean bill of health but said that she might be a bit anaemic and gave her a script for some iron tablets.

The one thing we did do in the motel was to luxuriate under the shower. There was no scarcity of hot water here and as we took full advantage of it. I felt that Katy was glad to be back in civilisation again. She certainly had some fun around the shops.

I rang Paolo from the motel and told him the news. He asked me to stay put for a few days and he would arrange for a place to live when we came down.

By the time Paolo finally got back to me we had spent five days in Mount Isa. Then we winged our way south and back to Brisbane.

27

AS THE PLANE BANKED AROUND ON ITS APPROACH TO Eagle Farm and I looked down and saw the city again, I felt a chill of apprehension. But I pushed it aside, and by the time the wheels gave a whump as they hit the tarmac it was gone.

We were making our way towards the exit when big Rocco came over, smiling, holding out that big hand of his.

'Good to see you Rocco, you remember Katy?'

'Yeah, think I do, how's it goin' Katy? They tell me you gonna have a bambino.'

Katy just blushed and squeezed my arm.

Forty-five minutes later we were in the new home Paolo had organised for us at Taringa. As we were lifting the bags from the car Rocco spoke to me quietly.

'Boss wants to see you as soon as you can make it, okay?'

'Not a problem, Rocco.'

It was a nice house, done out in nice furnishings fitted with security alarms, and pretty spacious. I couldn't help thinking what I would have to do to return this favour.

Katy walked through and inspected each room and fussed about. I got the bags into the main bedroom and then told her I'd better go down and see Paolo to thank him and what not.

'How long will you be?'

'As quick as I can, love.'

When I got to the club I didn't bother with the desk, just walked in and made my way out the back to the offices.

Paolo rose from his desk, smiling easily, holding out his hands. I could hear the tiny slapping sound the tassels of his casuals made as he crossed the carpet. 'Good to see you again, Jimmy,' he said, and the handshake he gave me was firm. He put his arm around my shoulders and guided me back to the twin chairs under the windows.

I wanted to ask him what had happened to Mandy . . . if it was her day off, or she was sick or something. A girl I had never seen before was out in the other office. But I thought it might be a mistake to show too much interest.

'Well what are you going to do now?' he asked me.

'I haven't forgotten that other matter, Paolo, I still want the bastards.'

'I was hoping in a way that you might put it on the back burner for a while.'

'What! Have you made the peace with them again?'

'No, Jimmy, it's anything but that. There's been a fair bit happening while you've been away. We've come under a lot of pressure. There's a new Commissioner and we can't get near him for love or money. He's got the whole damn Force jumping through hoops, but I've been told that he won't last long. The Premier wants to bring his own boy in to run the show. Now that's a different kettle of fish.'

'Well what do you want me to do?'

'Nothing, not a bloody thing. Sit tight, go fishing, but for Christ's sake don't do anything.'

'Look, Paolo, I can appreciate what you're on about but Vitelli and fuckin' Fingers are down in bloody NSW, not up here.'

'Yes and that's the point of the whole matter. Both states are making plenty of noise about organised crime. They've got an inter-state task force working with the Federal Police on these matters, and I can tell you now they're doing plenty of overtime. People are going down all over the place. So just take my advice and do nothing. The way it is at the moment, you can take it from me those guys in Sydney won't be doing too much either.'

I had always respected Paolo's advice, so I intended to heed it. I thanked him for the house and asked whose it was.

'Well it's mine. I was living in it before I moved to St Lucia.'

'What about rent, mate?'

'We'll work something out.'

On the way home I thought about the things Paolo had said. All I needed now was a swarm of fuckin' cops breathing down my neck. But fate moves in funny ways, as it was to show me two nights later.

Katy and I were out on the town, having dinner at the Jet Club in the Valley. We were minding our own business when I felt a tap on my shoulder and looked around. The guy looked familiar but I couldn't place him for a second.

'Remember me, Mr Diamond?'

Just then he was joined by another guy and you could smell it in the air. Police.

'You look like someone I've met but I don't remember,' I said.

'I'm Detective Senior Sergeant Murphy and this,' motioning towards his partner, 'is Detective Senior Constable John Simmonds. I wonder if we could have a little chat.'

'Christ's sake, I'm having bloody dinner.'

'Well let's put it this way then shall we, we can have our talk here or we can go down the station. What's it to be?'

'Just let me talk to my girl for a minute, okay?'

'Sure,' said Murphy, 'we'll wait over there won't we, John,' and they moved over to the cocktail bar.

'I'd better talk to them, love,' I said to Katy.

'Jesus, they're not going to arrest you are they?'

'No they'd have done that already if they were going to. The sooner I talk to them the sooner they'll be gone.'

'Be careful, Jimmy,' was all she said as I pushed my chair back.

I walked over to the bar and the barmaid looked at me in that inquiring way they have.

'Scotch and soda,' I told her. 'Make it a double thanks.'

My drink arrived and I walked down to the end of the bar where Murphy and Simmonds were sitting.

'Ah, here's Mr Diamond, John,' said Murphy, emphasising the Mister.

'Look, what's the problem? I've got no idea what you want.'

'The problem is, Mr Diamond, or can I call you Jimmy?'

'Sure,' I said, 'Jimmy's fine.'

'Right then, the problem is, Jimmy my boy, that you're a bit of a mystery man. And I hate mysteries, don't you John?'

His offsider nodded his head and had another mouthful of beer.

'You see, Jimmy, I've been doing a bit of digging around since you've been noticed back in town, and it's come to my attention that you were a pretty active boy in Sydney a few years back, weren't you?'

'Shit, it's news to me. What do you mean by active?'

'Don't get too bloody cute. You were Margo Colenzo's lover . . . now that's a fact isn't it?'

'So? What's that got to do with right here and now?'

'Well there were some people who quietly vanished after she was found dead, weren't there?'

'Look, Margo was murdered, you know that and I know that, but people disappearing . . . what bloody people?'

'Well it just doesn't end there. A little bird has whispered in our ear that you could be right for quite a few things, and not just down in Sydney. Ever heard of a bloke called Charlie Davenport?'

'No. Who's Charlie Davenport?'

'You wouldn't know where he was?'

'I just asked you. Who's Charlie Davenport?'

He ordered another round and even ordered me one.

'You went to Vietnam didn't you, Jimmy?'

'Yeah that's right.'

'You received a decoration over there too, we hear?'

'Yep. So did a lot of other blokes.'

'Now tell me, did you ever do training in the Special Operations Group?'

'I can't confirm or deny that, you should know the rules on that. It's classified.'

'Oh he's sharp this boy, isn't he John?'

'Yeah, if you ask me he'd be right for the bloody lot,' Simmonds said.

'Let's go back to that day you came and saw me up at Roma Street. Who was it that told you to come in and see me?'

'I don't remember.'

'Well, what bastard got hold of the boss and told me to pull the plug on my inquiries?'

'Search me. Did you ask the boss?'

'This boy's cute all right, John, but we'll be seeing more of you. Oh! and by the way, we know you're living in your Italian mate's old home. We'll be keeping a good watch on it from now on. We could even turn up with a search warrant.'

'You'll find fuck-all,' I said

'Yeah, I reckon you'd be too clever to have anything in the place. Righto, Jimmy, we'll be in touch. You'd better get back to your lady friend. Sorry about your dinner.'

They put their glasses down, stood up and walked out.

I went back and apologised to Katy, and we left shortly after.

I could tell that Katy was worried and in her state I didn't want to alarm her, so when we got home we sat down and talked it out.

'Aren't you worried?' she asked.

'Not a bit. If they knew anything do you think I'd be sitting here with you now? A little bird told them this, and a little bird told them that. Do you think they can go into a courtroom and tell a judge and jury what a little bird told them?'

'I suppose not.'

' 'Course the bastards can't. The little birds would be those fuckin' canaries down in Sydney. They can't get up and give evidence.'

'Well how did they know we'd be in the Jet Club tonight?'

'Most likely they've got a watch on the house. They saw me leave and the Ghost Squad followed me. That's my guess.'

'Do you think they'll come back here?'

'They could, but if you're worried about them trying to set me up, forget it. I'd let them in with a warrant, but only after I'd made some phone calls and had a couple of senior coppers here, plus a lawyer and the press. Murphy's been round a long time and he knows I'd do that, so what'd be the purpose?'

'So everything will be okay then?'

'Yeah, I'll make a couple of calls tomorrow and get this straightened out.'

The first call I made in the morning was to Percy, from a phone box.

'How's it going, Jimmy?' he said. 'Where have you been hiding yourself?'

'Right up north Perce, in my favourite place.'

'To what do I owe the pleasure of this call then, old son? You must want something.'

301

'Yeah, payback time, Perce. I'm in Brisbane, Katy's going to have a baby and we came down so she can get proper medical attention. But I've got that fuckin' Jack Murphy breathin' down my neck again.'

'Yeah there's a big flap on at the moment. It'll all come to nothing. They'll pinch a few, but it'll fizzle out again. It's all politics, son.'

'Yeah, well be that as it may. I'm not running for fuckin' office. I want this cunt off my back.'

'Don't get your knickers in a twist. I'm just laying out how it is. I'll get someone to have a word, so go have some fun. And listen.'

'What?'

'Keep your fuckin' nose clean.'

'Yeah right, Percy, thanks.'

I hung up and rang Paolo, telling him I was on my way down.

When we were alone in his office, I told him what had happened the night before. But when I told him about the little birds and my suspicions he agreed with me.

'There's no honour, any more, Jimmy. The same thing is happening over in the States. Big money is talking now. It's politics.'

'Well what are you going to do about it?'

'We're going to be patient, Jimmy. Wasn't it you that told me to forgive your enemies but never forget their names? Well in this case we'll keep doing just that.'

'And when the time is right . . . ?' I turned my finger and thumb into a gun shape and said, 'Pow.'

'That's it,' Paolo said. 'When the time is right . . . '

Thoughts went through my mind all the rest of the

day. I stuck pretty close to home, and that night Katy and I were in bed by ten-thirty.

When I woke, I was surprised to find it was still dark outside. I looked at my watch and it said twelve-fifteen. I'd slept for less than two hours. I got up quietly, wandered over to the window and pulled back the drapes. There wasn't a movement out in the street, no other cars about. The place looked utterly deserted.

What had awakened me were the thoughts racing through my mind. I spent the rest of the night going over what Paolo had said to me and weighed it up with the information Percy had given me. Something had me puzzled. Murphy had stressed the name Charlie Davenport a couple of times. Those canaries in Sydney wouldn't even know about Charlie Davenport.

There was a nigger in the woodpile somewhere, and I just had to find out where.

At first light I walked down to the phone box on the corner and called Jacko's mother in Petersham. I apologised about the hour, but she told me she'd been up for a while anyway. As soon as I had Jacko's number I thanked her and hung up.

'Jacko? Jimmy here, mate. How's it going, old son.'

'Christ, did you shit the bed or something? It's not even six o'clock yet.'

'Nah, I want you to check something out for me. Can do?'

'Yeah sure, what is it?'

I gave him the number of the place in Lowery Street and told him I wanted him to check it out.

'Just what sort of a number do you want me to do on this joint?' he asked.

'Can you get me some photos of who comes and goes from there? Car numbers, the lot. And listen, Jacko, don't come undone mate, but I need the information like yesterday.'

'Sure. I'll get right on it. Hey, when are we going to get together again?'

'As soon as you get me that info, come on up. But book into a fuckin' pub or motel, don't be seen around here. Got the message?'

'Loud and clear, old son. See ya in a few days.'

Things were coming to me now in a clearer light. While I'd been searching my brain last night for answers, one of the things that kept popping into my head was my visit to Frangiani's place at Lowery Street. The place had been deserted but nothing had been removed. And the absence of the security guy was another puzzle. Frangiani must have been warned . . . Sure he could have stacked the deck against me, but to get rid of me on his own premises would have been a bit dodgy, even for him. He wouldn't have wanted a gun battle on his doorstep. That's why he tried to take me out after I had left the place.

I had a sour taste in my mouth and a chill in my heart. As I was walking back to the house the episode at Frenchs Forest came back vividly. They were waiting there for me all right. But no one expected me to survive that. Whichever way I put it, I knew which way the finger pointed.

Back at the house I went into the bedroom and looked down at Katy, who was still asleep. I had a terrible feeling in my gut and knew she was in danger.

I didn't breathe a word of my suspicions when Katy got up, but put on a happy face for her, made her some breakfast and sat around reading the paper. Still, I wasn't going to leave her side for a second.

It was the door bell ringing at nine-fifty that had me on my feet. I opened the door and it was Murphy. His partner was sitting in the car out on the street.

'Look,' Murphy said, 'I'm not supposed to be here but I want to talk to you. And it's off the record.'

'What's the deal . . . you armed? Carrying a fuckin' wire?'

'Jesus, I've only got my service gun here, Jimmy.' He opened his coat and showed me.

'Go and give it to your offsider, and if you're wired you'd better get rid of that too. Because when I let you in here I'm going to pat you down. That's the only deal you've got, *capisce*?'

Murphy looked at me in a strange way.

'Shit, I'm trying to do you a fuckin' favour if you only knew it.'

'Just get rid of the fuckin' gun, and any other bloody thing you might have. Then we talk.'

He walked down the steps and handed his revolver to his partner. The car drove off and Murphy came back to the door.

'I've told Simmo to come back in an hour, in case you're worried about the car being seen outside.'

'You still get the pat-down.'

'Yeah well, let's get it over with, shall we?'

I let him in and ran my hands over him, feeling for a listening device, another gun, even down round his ankles in case he was carrying one there. When I was satisfied he was clean I told him we'd talk outside.

He followed me through to the back and we pulled up a couple of chairs under the pagoda next to the swimming pool.

'Righto. You've got the floor . . . what do I call you? I'm not calling you Mr Murphy, and Detective Senior Sergeant sounds bloody ridiculous.'

'Just call me Jack, that'll do.'

'Okay, Jack. What's this all about?'

'Why is it I get the feeling that you're dirty, but we're working for the same side?'

'You've got me, Jack, why?'

'Well a funny thing happened early this morning. I told you I wasn't supposed to be here and I'm fuckin' well not. You see I received a phone call not from his nibs, but from the fuckin' executive building from the Minister's office, telling me in no uncertain terms that I was to drop anything and everything on you like a hot potato. What could I say, only yes Minister, no Minister. But it pissed me off, I can tell you. I was going to ring the Super to get confirmation, but he turns up in my fuckin' office not five minutes later and he's got a geezer with him from the fuckin' Federal Branch Internal Security Office and they want your bloody file. So I had to give it to them.'

'It's all news to me, Jack,' I said.

'Look, I asked you once before . . . who do you know? But I won't ask that again. What I want to know is who the bloody hell are you because you can take it from me you don't even exist.'

'Okay, Jack, seeing we're talking truth here get this one thing between us right and there might be a bonus in it for you. When you talked to me down at the Jet Club you kept bringing up a guy's name called Davenport. Now what's the real story? Where and who did that come from?'

Just then Katy poked her head out the door.

'Would you like a drink or something, sweetheart?' she asked.

I looked at Murphy and he nodded.

'Bring us out a couple of beers love.'

We sat talking about nothing much till Katy had deposited the beers on the table. I gave her a kiss on the cheek and she went back inside.

'Where were we?' Murphy said. 'Oh yeah, Davenport . . . well he was a star witness against the Bellari Family here. He had the goods on them, and we had the goods on him. So he offered us a deal, not me personally but the guys at the time. Part of that deal was they get him out of Brisbane. He was given a couple of witness protection blokes and they took him up north, but one night he just disappeared, and he's never been seen since. The feeling was that one of the guys on the program must have been bent, but it didn't check out. There was a couple of other cunts up there who were pally with him, Frank and Barbara Todd, and they apparently committed suicide in very suspicious circumstances. But getting back to you . . . We received a call saying that you were in Brisbane, where you were living, and a lot more. So when I said a little bird told us I wasn't bullshitting.'

307

I sat there and thought for a while. The ominous feeling I had persisted.

'Why have you come here now?' I asked.

'Because I get the feeling we're working on the same side. ASIO perhaps, or ASIS. What the fuck gives? I've been warned off before but never like this, and I'm getting an ulcer worrying about it.'

'Well, Jack, I know fuck-all about what you've been talking about. All I can say is that I'm not right for any of it.'

'You've got to be bullshitting.'

'No, Jack, but I'll tell you this much. If you can find out who the little bird is that's squawking all this shit, and it confirms certain suspicions, then I'll give you something that'll give you nightmares for the rest of your fuckin' life. Deal?'

'No shit now?'

'No shit, Jack, just between you and me. Incoming calls to the cops are taped, aren't they?'

'Jesus, I can't admit that.'

'Why? You're not wired and there's only you and me here.'

'Well not all of them officially, but yes they are. Why? What have you got in mind?'

'Can you get a copy of this little bird's call and let me hear it?'

'Christ, it'd be my fuckin' job if I got caught.'

'You're looking for answers, Jack, and so am I, so what's it to be?'

'Look I'll give it a go, but don't depend on it, okay? Just supposing I get a copy, how do I reach you?'

'Give me your home number , and I'll call you.'

308

He didn't seem to be too keen on it but he relented in the end and scribbled it on the back of one of his cards.

'You don't come here any more, Jack. I call you.'

'Yeah, I can understand that.'

Katy came out then and told us there was someone at the door.

It was Murphy's mate.

'Tell him we've got a call on the radio,' Simmonds said.

'I'm on my way now John,' Murphy called out, then he turned to me and said, 'See you around'.

Katy was all questions after they'd gone and I put aside any fears that she had.

'Well what happens now?' she asked.

I looked at her and smiled.

'Sweetheart, sometimes it takes a rat to smell another rat.'

28

I GOT A CALL FROM JACKO THREE DAYS LATER. HE WAS staying at the Travel Lodge and said he had what I wanted. I didn't want to leave Katy by herself and told him that I'd meet him at twelve in the Queen Street Mall.

Katy and I were having a club sandwich and some cappuccino when I spotted Jacko. He was doing what I had been doing most of that morning—making sure he didn't have a tail.

'How's it going mate? G'day Kate,' he said after he'd pulled up a chair.

He reached inside his denim jacket and pulled out a manilla envelope.

'Feast your eyes on that lot . . . the fuckin' camera and lens cost me 600 bucks.'

I opened up the envelope and slid its contents onto the table. There were a dozen or so photos and the clarity was really good. And yep, there he was. Joseph Fingers Frangiani him-fuckin'-self. The rest of the people in the photos I had never seen before.

'Now what's the story, Jacko?'

'Well that prick lives there,' he said, pointing to Frangiani, 'no doubt about it. There's also three birds that shack up there.' He passed me their photos. 'And the rest of these cunts just fuckin' come and go.'

310

'Christ, Jacko, you're a real bloody gem, son.'

I studied the photos while Katy and Jacko gossiped. Then Katy leant back and showed Jacko her rounded tummy.

'That's junior,' she said.

Jacko punched me on the arm and yelled.

'You randy old bastard, congratulations son, good on yer Kate. Shit, you blokes must have played up while ya was away. Christ, ya gonna be a fuckin' daddy.'

We talked between ourselves for a while and then I told Jacko to head back down to Sydney, that we'd follow him tomorrow.

Jacko was about to put up an argument but I assured him there was a very good reason for it.

That night I rang Paolo and told him that we'd be away for a few days, that we were going down the coast. He asked if we wanted to use his place but I declined, telling him we'd already booked one.

We packed our bags and caught a cab to Coolangatta Airport, where I headed for the public phones and had a long and serious talk with Percy. And then we caught the flight to Sydney.

On the way down I explained to Katy that we were going to be met in Sydney and that we would be going to a house that Percy was organising. I didn't tell her any lies.

'This house, love, it's called a "safe house". Now while we're down here I have a few things to do, things that can give us a happy future. But you won't be able to come along. And the fact that you're pregnant has nothing to do with it. I'm not shutting you out. Just making sure that you and the baby will be safe.'

'Why did you tell Paolo we were going down the coast?'

'Because there's a few things that just don't add up, love, and I've got a nasty taste in my mouth over it. So I'm not trusting anyone at this point.'

'What about this Percy, can we trust him?'

'Yes we sure can sweetheart, we sure as hell can.'

Percy met us at the airport and drove us out to Bondi. He pulled into a garage fitted with an electric opening and closing device operated from the car.

'Now this is the only entrance,' he told us once we were out of the car. 'There are no outside stairs. The floor above this garage has a couple of our people in it. There's always someone there. You'll be on the top floor. You see that over there.' He pointed to a closed-circuit TV camera. 'Well there's a monitor in both places and you can see who comes in and who goes out. The door is operated by punch-code only. Right, well we better go up. By the way, this garage is wired for sound. Let us up Colleen,' he said into the box.

The door in front of us gave a buzz like a trapped bumble bee and sprang open an inch, then slid back smoothly. We hopped in a lift and up we went. It was a nice apartment, with sun streaming through the windows and a good view of the sea.

Percy took us through the place room by room and then we assembled in the dining room.

'Now the phone there serves a few purposes. If you did get into trouble up here, and it would want to be a bloody big if, that's what that button is for.' He pointed to a clear red button just below the handpiece. 'But for Christ sake don't touch it unless it's a dire bloody emergency, because all bloody hell will break loose if you do. If you need to know anything just press one, that rings downstairs and they can fill you in. Now I suppose I better tell you this before smarty pants here'—and he indicated me with a nod of his head—'finds one of the bugs. This whole place is wired for sound, but you can take my word for it that it's been turned off. You will have privacy, I give you my word on that. Now I better introduce you to Colleen.'

He picked up the phone and dialled one.

'Could you pop up here for a minute, Colleen please?'

I heard the lift hum, then the door opened and a woman walked in. She was around thirty-five, tall and a little on the heavy side. The look on her face said *Don't fuck with me*—and to back it up she had a .38 Smith and Wesson in an open leather holster at her hip.

But her demeanour changed when she smiled and walked towards us, holding out her hand.

'Hi,' she said, 'I'm Colleen. Once you get settled in you'll be fine.'

We all said our hellos, and then Colleen put her arm around Katy and offered to show her around.

'I've already done that,' Percy said.

'Well we'll just go and have another look, won't we, and I'll show you what you haven't seen?' And she led Katy up the hall.

'Now look, Jimmy, you'll be right here. I know you're doing this for Katy, but whatever you get up to

313

I don't want to know about. If you go off on a tangent on some half-arsed scheme and it comes unstuck, well there's a limit to what I can do. Get the message?'

'Sure Perce, and thanks for this. I just want to know Katy's safe and out of reach.'

'She'll be safe and sound here, mate. I think you can see that.'

'Sure. How long can we stay here, mate?'

'Shit. Don't worry about that. Unless we get some KGB bloke wanting to defect, and the chances of that are practically zero, stay as long as you like.'

Twenty minutes later they were gone and we were alone.

'Well, love, what do you think?'

'It's nice isn't it? How long will we be staying here?'

'Depends on how long it takes me to get things sorted out.'

'Can't we go out at all?'

'Sure we can,' I said, and took her into my arms. 'We can go shopping or walk and stroll on the beach. It's just that if I'm out I want you somewhere safe, where someone will be looking after you.'

'Who's going to look after you?' she said, then kissed my neck.

'I give you my word nothing is going to happen to me.'

I lifted up her lovely face and looked deep into her eyes. 'Believe me Katy I'm on top of it, love. Nothing is going to happen to me.' And I kissed her.

We put our stuff away and then I rang Colleen to tell her we were popping out to get a few things.

'Okay,' she said, 'Don't forget to take the buzzer with you.'

So, armed with the buzzer and dressed like a couple of tourists, complete with hats, sunglasses and zinc cream, we strolled down Campbell Parade to go shopping.

That night I rang Murphy in Brisbane.

'Did you get a copy of the tape?' I asked him.

'Yeah but I certainly stuck my neck out if I didn't . . . '

'Look, forget all the whys and the fuckin' wherefores. Have you got it with you?'

'Yes it's right here.'

'Right, well play it for me over the phone.'

'Hang on a minute.'

I heard background noises, a click and a voice and another click. Then Murphy said 'You there?'

'I'm all ears.'

There was a hiss and a beeping sound and then the voice came on the line. I went cold inside. There was some attempt to conceal it, but I knew the structure and the phrasing of that voice as well as I knew my own.

I yelled down the phone to tell Murphy that I'd heard enough.

'You recognise it?' he said.

'Never heard it in my life.' I lied. And hung up.

I rang Jacko and told him we had to talk.

'Where do you want to meet, son?'

'The bar of the Bondi pub in two hours.'

'See ya there then, mate.'

It was 9.30 when Jacko showed up. We had a couple of beers, then walked down to some benches

315

near the beach. There was not a person within a hundred yards of us and the noise of the traffic on Campbell Parade, plus the surf rolling in, would have stuffed up any directional microphone.

'What's gives, mate?' Jacko asked.

I lit a cigarette. 'I want you to make me a bomb,' I said. 'You were the whiz kid of the demolition squad.'

'How big do you want it?'

'Big enough to penetrate a solid floor and take out the person sitting above. Can you do it?'

'What sort of floor is it?'

'Three inches of reinforced concrete.'

'Not a problem, but I'd hate to be the cunt sittin' on top of it.'

'That's the point, Jacko. I do hate the cunt that's sitting on top of it.'

'What sort of ignition do you want to use?'

'This is where it gets a bit tricky. I want a radio-controlled detonator so I can ring. When I'm sure he's on his own I can talk to him and send the signal down the line. Then whammo!'

'You want to blow this cunt up from a fair distance away while you're here.'

'You've got it, son. Nothing wrong with your logic.'

'Am I allowed to know where this joint is?'

'It's in Brisbane . . . the Italian Club in the Valley.'

'Christ! That could be a bit dicey.'

'Not if you do it right. It's easy to get around the back, there's room underneath for you to work without being seen. The place closes around 3 a.m. You'd have all the time in the world.'

'No problem of being challenged?'

'Jesus, Jacko, there's always the unlikely in any situation, you should know that. But taking all things into account it should be a cakewalk.'

'When do you want it done?'

'Yesterday. I'm prepared to pay for it.'

'You can stick that, Jimmy. This one's on the house. I never did like those Dagoes anyway.'

'Right, well how do you want to play this?'

I took out a plan of the club, showing the position of the offices and the one I wanted to demolish. A separate drawing of the windows at the back of the club showed the same office, so there could be no mistake. Jacko said that it didn't really matter, that the office would disintegrate anyway with the charge he had in mind.

'Well I'll get hold of the stuff tomorrow,' Jacko said once we'd gone through all the detail. 'And I'll leave you the transmitter set on a frequency. All I've got to do is set the detonator to that frequency and it's show time in Brissie. But for Christ's sake don't go pressing anything till you get a ring from me.'

'I get the picture.'

'Right, well I'd better get cracking, Jimmy. I'll get the trannie over to you tomorrow. We can meet here.'

'Right mate, watch your arse.'

29

I'D JUST STEPPED OUT OF THE LIFT. IT HAD BEEN THREE days since I'd last seen Jacko and I was expecting a call. I plonked the things that I'd bought down in the kitchen and walked out into the lounge when I heard Katy's voice from the bedroom. She was sitting on the edge of the bed, talking into the telephone. She looked up at me as I walked in.

'Here he is now,' she said.

She looked up at me with an anxious little frown, and held the receiver out to me, the palm of her hand covering the mouthpiece.

'Who is it?' I asked.

'Percy.'

'For Christ's sake! What does he want? I don't want to talk to him.'

'Jimmy, please. He says it's important.' Katy's hand was shaking.

'Is that what he says?' In spite of myself, I was curious to know why he was calling and grabbed the receiver.

'Yeah, what is it, Perce?'

'I've got a bit of a proposition for you, Jimmy, that you might like, but there's someone here who wants to talk to you, you remember John McCreedy don't you?'

'Hi Jimmy!' McCreedy came on. 'How would you like to get together for a talk tomorrow about a mutual friend, I think you know who I'm talking about . . . Gino?'

'I thought we had a deal, McCreedy. Have you forgotten our last conversation already?'

'Hey look! Take it easy. This is something that can benefit us both. Will it hurt to listen to what I've got to say? Come on, be reasonable.'

He had a point there.

'At this juncture it's talk only, John,' I told him. 'No yes or no, just talk.'

'Right, okay then, I'll send a car for you and we'll talk over lunch, my treat.'

'You're all heart, John. Is Percy still there?'

'Sure I'll put him on.'

'What can I do for you?' Percy asked.

'Look, Perce, I appreciate what you've done and are doing, but try real hard not to organise my life too much will you, mate?'

'Come on, Jimmy, you're a big boy now. You know the score. Anyway I think you'll go for what John has in mind. See you then.'

I handed the phone back to Katy. She shook her head. 'That man gives me the creeps.'

'Me too.' I smiled and kissed her lightly on the lips. 'I love you. You know that, don't you?'

'And I love you too . . . '

'That's all that matters.'

I woke up to the sound of the phone buzzing and with a gritty feeling in my mouth and removed something from my tongue. It was a little coil of hair.

I looked at my watch. It was 3.15.

Extricating myself from the sprawl of Katy's limbs, and being careful not to wake her, I went into the lounge and picked up the phone.

It was Jacko.

'Just returning your early morning call, Jimmy. Took me two nights. But the job's right . . . it's show-time whenever you say go. Bye son.'

I went into the kitchen and made myself a cup of coffee. All this time I thought about Paolo. It had been his voice on the tape that Murphy had played for me. He was the one who had sent the helicopter. He was the one who had given Vitelli the news and the okay to whack me. Vitelli and Frangiani knew nothing about Charley fuckin' Davenport or the Todds. Only Paolo did. Only he knew where Carmel was. I had given Carmel his number. It was he who had been in cahoots with Rissi. He told me about the place in Frenchs Forest, hoping that I'd cop it there, but I had been lucky. It was Paolo who had given me the location of the farm at Oak Flats, and there was a bonus in that for him. If I got them, then they were out of the way, but if they got me so much the better. He was the author of Carmel's terrible end, afraid she might know of events he was trying to bury. And if he buried Carmel and me then he was home free. He gave me Frangiani's whereabouts, with a dozen people around him, knowing I'd have a go, hoping that I wouldn't make it. Carmel and I were the only living witnesses to what had gone on in the past. With us gone there would be nobody who knew what he had sanctioned and ordered. With this new task force thing, the push to stamp out organised crime, he wanted no loose ends.

Well you treacherous bastard, I thought, two can play at this game. The numbers work for me too. With you and those two other rats out of the fuckin' way, I'm on a home run. No one will know of my past either, and I waited in anticipation for tomorrow night.

It was 10.50 when the phone buzzed to tell me that there was a car downstairs for me. I kissed Katy and told her that I wouldn't be long. Colleen was in the garage and she said she'd keep an eye on Katy.

Both Percy and McCreedy were in the car. I slipped into the back and we glided away into the traffic.

'Fancy some seafood for lunch?' Percy asked, looking at me in the rear-vision mirror. 'We'll go over to Doyle's at Watsons Bay.'

'What, the joint where I met you and Fingers?'

'No, there's an upmarket one across the road. Better everything.'

Percy chose a table as far away from the general service area as he could, and I was halfway through my Sydney rock lobster, and had drunk a glass of wine when Percy turned to me.

'How'd you like a straight shot at Vitelli?'

'Is that all there is to it? What's the bottom line here, Percy. Let's have the whole enchilada, eh. What's my percentage and what's in it for you?'

'Guns,' said McCreedy.

'Guns, I don't need any fuckin' guns.'

'That's what it's all about, Jimmy,' Percy broke in.

'Look will some bastard make some fuckin' sense here or are you two guys on some sort of a fuckin' trip?'

'Well it's a pretty sensitive area we're dealing in,' McCreedy said.

'When do you guys deal with anything that's not fuckin' sensitive? I'm starting to get the picture now. It's fuckin' politics again, isn't it?'

'Jimmy,' McCreedy said, 'the whole world is insane. Back in the sixties and seventies we were in a war where we could've beaten the piss out of Charlie anytime we wanted to, but the goddamn pansies in the government wouldn't let us. They wanted to tell us how to fight the war. It was insane. They tried to rewrite the rules of war. But there are no rules, not in the field. In the bush, soldiers do what they have to. And that's what we're doing here. Doing what we have to.'

'Well, where's this leading too?' I asked.

'Okay,' McCreedy said. 'Let me give you the scenario. We want you to shotgun a planeload of guns, pick up a return cargo, and while this is being done you'll get a free crack at Vitelli.'

'Here we go with the fuckin' guns again,' I said. 'Just where are these bloody guns going to?'

'Goroka!'

'Where's fuckin' Goroka?'

'New Guinea.'

'Christ!' I said. 'Let's have the deal from the top, Percy. This is starting to look real shitty to me . . . like you guys are in strife and I've got the axe over my head, so we'll use good old Jimmy. If something goes wrong we'll deny all fuckin' knowledge, but we'll chuck in Vitelli as bait, that should whet his appetite. Am I somewhere near the truth, Perce?'

'Well it's a sort of a joint venture between us and the Australian Desk here with John. There's a fair bit of strife in PNG at the moment. I won't go into the politics, it's too complicated. But to cover it quickly. In Moresby there's the Raskal gangs. Up in the Highlands there's the tribal factions. Along with them there's the OPM freedom fighters, not to mention the Bougainville Rebel Movement. The BRM aren't that active at the moment, but they've got a fair following. Now these movements want guns, and all they can get over there is the odd .303 left over from the war. The guns are for these movements. That's what we want you to deliver. At the same time as you'll be delivering the guns Vitelli will be in receipt of a drug shipment for himself. He's just arranged a new source of hard drug supplies, on top of half a ton or so of New Guinea gold. He got into the country last month, and that's where you'll get your shot at him.'

'These guns you want taken in. Am I allowed to know what they are, or is that fuckin' classified?'

McCreedy took a sheet of paper from his pocket and handed it over without a word.

I ran my eye down the page. The list included semi-automatic AK47s, SLRs, M16s, RPGs and surface-to-ground missiles, stingers and RP7s.

'Jesus Christ, Percy! You could fight a fuckin' war with this stuff.'

'You're not wrong, old son.'

'Are you guys playing with a full deck? You sure you want to do this? . . . Christ almighty, those guys up there are Stone Age fuckin' Neanderthals.'

'It's politics, and there's a percentage in it.'

'These missiles . . . What the fuck do they want them for?'

'Helicopters,' said McCreedy.

'Come on, Percy . . . What is this, mate—a fuckin' re-run of Fire Base Gloria? Or are you two planning your own private Bay of Pigs?'

McCreedy gave a short laugh, then leant back.

'It's the Australian Iriquois helicopters on loan to the PNG forces,' he said. 'They hate them up there in the Highlands. And they're really pissed off in the Solomons, claiming that their air space is being violated all the time.'

'Fuckin' politics! I knew it, Perce . . . Australia loans them the helicopters, then supplies the guns to shoot 'em down. Re-supply and re-arm, every bastard making a fuckin' quid, and nobody gives a shit. Jesus! What a bloody fiasco. Play the ends against the middle, eradicate as many as possible and everybody comes out looking squeaky clean. And whatever interests in mining and timber the fat cats have got their greedy little fingers into stays safe.'

'Look, okay Jimmy, you know the fuckin' score, so what? I'll let you into a little secret, though. You're better off with us than with those Cosa Nostra pricks who'd like to see you in a safe place right out of the way. It's got me fucked why you ever got tangled up with those cunts in the first place.'

Percy was right. I had no right to preach.

'What do I have to bring back, Percy?'

They looked at each other for a moment.

'If I don't know I don't go,' I said.

'A shipment of drugs.'

'What! You blokes have got to be having a fuckin' lend of me.'

'We're deadly serious,' McCreedy said, emphasising the deadly. 'Look, for professional soldiers there is no such thing as a goddamn international border. You ought to know this. We cross them when we have to, do the business, get the hell home and then deny everything. That's what I mean when I said the world's insane. It goes back years. When the government here and our own goddamned Congress sliced off our funds, we improvised. We used confiscated drugs as substitute currency. Opium, heroin, morphine base, hash. . . we used it as currency to keep our insurgents motivated. Used it to keep people like you motivated too.'

'I see,' I said.

'I don't think you do,' McCreedy replied. 'Intelligence operates in a different fashion from normal military operations. It is a dirty field, one which quickly kills off the incompetents. Good intelligence men quickly learn that there is no morality, no such thing as right and wrong. Only what works. It's the same as you've been doing yourself for years. So if you locate an individual working for the opposition, as Vitelli is in this case, you excise that individual. Excise. As in surgery.'

'Where are these drugs?'

325

'Vitelli will have them with him.'

'What sort of drugs?'

'The worst kind. Heroin, cocaine and probably crack.'

'So we've got to cart this shit back with us too?'

'Jesus, Jimmy, drugs of this nature don't come in pallet loads. It'll only be a case of some description.'

'What protection can I expect if this thing turns sour?'

'None. You know the rules, mate. But if you kick a goal you'll get all you need.'

'Why the sudden interest in Vitelli?'

They looked at each other before Percy replied.

'He's proving to be quite an embarrassment with certain dealings we're having over there. In fact, he's standing between success and failure, exerting pressure on people high up in the PNG government. While Vitelli is around we aren't. It's long Jimmy and, yes, it is political. Get the picture?'

'You know I hate fuckin' politics, Perce.'

'Look, mate, don't look at it like that. Just look at it from the angle that you'll have the opportunity to remove Vitelli with extreme prejudice.'

'Jesus! I can shoot the fuckin' bastard right here in Sydney.'

'Course you can, but there's a risk factor there. Our way removes that threat.'

'What's in it for me besides Vitelli?'

'Joint protection, peace of mind and $20,000,' said McCreedy.

'How do you know that Vitelli's going to be at this particular air strip at that particular time?'

'The Federal drug boys got a tip, then gave us the wink. We'll substitute our guy for the one who's supposed to bring Vitelli back home. It's perfect. We're even going to use their plane. Only we can kill two birds with one stone by making an arms delivery at the same time.'

'How's this thing set up?'

'Right. You'll be flown over there. Vitelli will be on the strip and you take him out of the play. Go to the other plane and you'll be flown back.'

'Christ! Vitelli's going to have a fuckin' bodyguard.'

'That bit is up to you, mate,' Percy said.

'When is this show to hit the road?' I asked.

'In two days.'

'Well the next thing is I don't know what Vitelli even looks like. He's come into the arena down here after my time.'

McCreedy's hand went to his pocket again and he passed me a photograph.

I was looking at a hatchet-faced guy with hair that looked like he was long over due at the barber. I tried to think back to his brother, see if there was a likeness, but I couldn't recall.

'Mind if I keep this?' I asked McCreedy.

He just lifted his arm up and pursed his lips in a be-my-guest gesture.

'Do I get to think this out?' I asked.

'Sure,' Percy said. 'I'll order another drink.'

'What's the bottom line, Perce, if I say no deal?'

'We're taking pretty good care of your lady, mate, and there's been a lot of strings pulled high up, to give you immunity. You know what I'm talking about. We could cut those strings, Jimmy. You know how these

327

things go. *Quid pro quo* . . . However . . . that decision is yours.'

He had me by the balls and he knew it.

'Okay, then let me ask you this. So far the bit I've been given sounds pretty easy. Where does it start to get a little hairy?'

'Well the hairy bit, as you put it, will be the return. The strip you're going to land on is right out of the way, so the factions can unload the guns without coming into contact with government troops. That's why Vitelli and company use it. It's the return plane that poses the problem. Vitelli arranged his own refuelling and we can't do it at that spot. So you and Peter Logan have to get to another strip.'

'Peter Logan?'

'Your pilot.'

'Well why can't he shoot Vitelli?'

'Because he's just a fuckin' pilot,' McCreedy said. 'Flying's his speciality, this other stuff is yours.'

'Where's this other strip?'

'About forty-five miles away.'

'How do we get to it—slog through the fuckin' jungle?'

'We've got a driver and a vehicle available. It's a combi bus. You'll look like tourists.'

'Who's the driver?'

'A local. He knows the whole place like the back of his hand.'

'And the other airfield—is it easy access?'

There was silence for a moment.

'Its guarded by PNG troops,' Percy said at last. 'Our plane will be there . . . all you've got to do is get to it.'

'What, after a fire fight with a company of regulars?'

'The plane will be there for as long as it takes.'

'What sort of plane?'

'727 Cargo.'

'Is it one of ours?'

'No it's one of ours,' said McCreedy, 'Pan Am.'

'Right, like all good business, Percy. The money up front.'

Percy turned to McCreedy, 'Didn't I tell you he'd see it our way?'

I was in a frame of mind to take Percy by the throat and choke the bastard. But the point he had made was so very true . . . I didn't have much of a choice. And I was already starting to put the deal together in my head. Old habits die hard.

They dropped me back at Bondi at three.

The night was warm and clear. I stood for a while gazing up at a bright field of stars, then slid one of the windows back and the air smelled of salt, fresh and clean. The lights were out in the lounge but the television was on, with the sound turned down, throwing flickering shadows against the window frame. Katy was downstairs with Colleen and her sidekick, Arthur.

I looked at my watch—9.05. I went over dialled Murphy's home number.

'Hey!' he said, 'What was the idea of just hanging up the other night? I thought we had a deal.'

'Just shut up and listen, Jack.'

'What?'

'Just shut the fuck up and listen . . .' I paused for a

moment. All I could hear was his breathing. 'I'm going to give you a number, so write it down, it's in Sydney. I want you to keep it and remember that I rang you from down here. You got all that so far?'

'Yeah, I'm following you.'

'Then I want you to ring me back in fifteen minutes. Okay?'

'Yep, what's the number?'

I gave him the number of the phone box down on the corner, I then buzzed downstairs and told them I was just slipping out for a breath of air.

The pay phone jangled and I picked up the receiver.

'That you, Jimmy?' Murphy asked.

'It's me,' I said, 'Now, I've got some information for you, Jack. Are you interested?'

'Yeah, what is it?'

'A little bird told me that someone is going to take out Paolo Agostini outside the front of the Italian Club tonight. So I suggest you park yourself a bit down from the club and get a bird's eye view, if you know what I mean.'

'Shit! Yeah look, thank's for the tip. I might have read you the wrong way. What time is this supposed to happen?'

'The little bird tells me around eleven.'

'I better get going then, thanks for this, I won't forget.'

I broke the connection and thought, you won't forget all right.

It was 10.55 p.m. when I pulled the aerial out of the transmitter, turned the standby safety switch to activate and watched the lights flick from green to red.

Katy was asleep in bed. I picked up the phone and dialled the office at the Italian Club.

'Yes.' It was Paolo.

'Hi Paolo, how's it going? I was expecting Mandy to answer.' I had to make sure she wasn't there.

'Ah, Jimmy. No, she's gone home. How are things down the coast?'

'Up to shit, you dirty bastard.'

There was a silence and I could hear a slight hiss on the line.

'Why do you speak like that to me?' Paolo said in a raised voice.

'Because you, you fuckin' cockroach, have been running with the hares and hunting with the fucking hounds. The game's up, Paolo.'

He seemed to quieten down at my outburst.

'What are you accusing me of, Jimmy?'

'Madness, Paolo. And fuckin' treachery. I've always been loyal to you, and you have betrayed that loyalty. I always knew that you were excitable, but I put your actions down to enthusiasm to protect the Family. Not to insanity and treachery. Or to greed. You have disgraced the family name. Belittled the loyalty and friendship I gave you. You have killed and maimed others for nothing other than personal gain, not to protect the Family. You have acted against me like a criminal, not a soldier. You murdered Carmel who would have only treated you as a friend. She would have died before she betrayed you. You have made me feel dirty and ashamed to have even known you. There'll be no more killing for you, Paolo. It's all over.'

'Hey! just a minute, who . . . ?' But I wouldn't let him finish.

'The faith I had in our friendship wouldn't let me see that it was you. You've been behind the whole fuckin' thing, Paolo. I woke up when Jack Murphy asked me about Davenport and the fuckin' Todds. Only you knew about that, you fuckin' bastard. And I heard your stinking voice on a police tape. You tried to conceal it but it was your voice. When I mentioned Katy to you you didn't ask who she was. You told me she could be dangerous. Because you'd been told by Frangiani. And this is the icing on the cake you piece of shit. Only you knew where Carmel was. Remember, you cunt. Honour, trust, and loyalty. I piss on your brand of that, Paolo. You're dead as sure as I'm talking to you now.'

He gave a small nervous laugh.

'Who do you think you are?' he said. 'You think you can take me on? There's been a couple of mistakes, but I can get you. So what are you going to do?' and he laughed.

I picked up the transmitter and put the aerial between my mouth and the mouthpiece of the phone.

'What am I going to do? I'll tell you what I'm going to do, you arsehole. I'm going to blow you to kingdom come.'

'Don't make me laugh again, Jimmy. When?'

'Right now you fuckin' bastard.'

I pushed the button on the transmitter and it twittered like a bird with a series of high-pitched beeps. I guess Paolo heard it too because I heard a scream before I pulled the phone back from my ear and a clap of man-made thunder came to me over the phone. And I hung up.

Katy didn't do a joint any more since she had become pregnant, but I felt like one. It was good hash and I lit it up and did the joint all by myself.

I must have dozed off in the chair because I woke up out of a dream. I had the sensation of drifting through space, a blue-black darkness that had no limit. I was aware only of a tiny pinprick of light ahead of me. I was trying to reach it, swimming toward the light through this sea of nothingness. And the light was growing and becoming more brilliant as I approached. It was indescribably bright, with a bluish aura . . . the centre was pure white . . . yet it didn't dazzle or hurt my eyes. Irresistibly drawn toward it, I felt it giving out warmth and a kind of all-understanding love that surrounded and enveloped me so I became a part of it, conscious only of the ecstasy of being alone in that place, a region of perfect clarity where the only existence was in the pure geometrical image of the crystal.

When I woke, I felt as if I had died and been brought back to life against my will.

Not wanting to disturb Katy, I walked into the second bedroom at the back of the unit and gazed out. Gould Street is a lane that runs parallel with the Esplanade, just one block back. On weekend nights, this is the hub of Bondi's seedy and informal business district. It's even more crowded than the Cross. Walk up to any of the cars parked there, or the ones that cruise slowly by, and you can buy a blow job, a kilo of grass or even a .38. I pulled the drapes, and lay down on the bed, but my mind was racing. I got up again, poured two inches of Scotch into a glass and lit a cigarette. Smiling, I picked up the phone and dialled. It was 3.07 a.m.

'Yes,' Murphy, said a sleepy voice.

'Hi Jack! I'm just ringing to find out if that little whisper came true?'

'Christ almighty!' I heard him say in a low voice. 'Listen, they didn't try to get Agostini out the front. They blew the whole fuckin' back off the joint. Jesus what a mess!

'But what about Agostini?'

'What about Agostini? The blast near fuckin' vaporised him. I think the biggest part they found was a couple of fingers and a bit of his hand. It's a bloody miracle no one else was killed. There's a few people getting minor attention for cuts and things. It was just like the place was hit by a fucking guided missile or something. Jesus!'

'Well, Jack, I suppose I'll get the blame for that too, will I?'

'I think the Crown Law Office would have a pretty tough time trying to tie you in to that lot. I don't suppose you'd tell me who the little bird was.'

'Sorry, Jack.'

'No I didn't think you would. I just wish to Christ I knew who you are tied up with.'

'See ya, Jack.' And I hung up.

30

ABOUT FOUR HOURS AFTER LEAVING SYDNEY AND ONE connecting flight later, I was looking down on Cooktown. It gave me a sense of bitter satisfaction to think that, even though I was having to help out Percy and McCreedy, I was finally going to get a chance to square things up with Vitelli.

We made a smooth touchdown and rolled to a stop at the terminal. The outside conditions were hot and humid, with a light nor-easterly puffing in my face.

A car was hired in my assumed name and I drove north for about thirty-five kilometres to an old airstrip built during the Second World War. There were plenty of these strips all through the north. And most of them were still used, but not for their original purposes. They were a quick and quiet way in and out of Australia.

The plane was a Beechcraft Baron, fitted with long-range fuel tanks and powered by two turbo-prop Pratt & Whitney engines. All the passenger seats had been removed. Peter Logan introduced himself to me and informed me that whoever had customised the plane knew what they were up to. It had the capacity to carry almost 1100 pounds of cargo for 1600 miles, cruising at almost 400 knots. The flight we were making today would require two fuel stops en route. McCreedy and Percy's people had arranged fuel dumps at two strips. One was close to the tip of the Cape and the second one was on the island of Saibai out in Torres Strait.

As we taxied to the end of the strip, conditions were good, with the nor-easterly dropping. Peter let go the brakes, opened the taps on the twin turbos, and we hurtled down the strip until I felt the plane lift of the ground.

We levelled out at 30,000 feet, and Peter set our course.

When we crossed the coast at the north-western tip of Cape York Peninsular some time later, I remembered Percy's words before leaving.

'You'll have fuck-all to worry about being detected on that course. The Federal and Queensland boys have a station on Thursday Island with a skeleton Customs presence. Most of the time they're out chasing the boongs who try to smuggle dope out in their boats. You can fly overhead and not be molested.'

We were flying now on automatic pilot.

'This is about my tenth trip over here,' Peter said to me in a Southern drawl. 'You just sit back and take it easy there, old buddy. We've a ways to go yet.'

Far below us the water sparkled. From up here it looked green and flat, with the darker reef areas standing out through the emerald water. Two or three boats were working the area but Christ knew what they were doing. Either trawling, or carting Vietnamese or drugs to the mainland. I wondered how Katy was doing alone . . .

Peter put the Baron into a steep turning bank as we came in over Goroka, then levelled the plane out and made a bumpy touchdown on the Highlands strip. There was no crosswind, or any wind for that matter, and the mist and smoke hovered motionless in the still air over the villages and dense jungle.

We taxied over to a large shed that I supposed was once used as a hanger or storage depot and stepped down from the aircraft. It was hot and sticky and my shirt clung to my back. Peter pointed to a vehicle sitting at the other end of the building.

'There's our ride out of here,' he said. 'I'll go over and check it out.' Then he pointed to an area on the far side of the strip. 'Your party will arrive from that direction.'

Not long after I watched a black Mercedes approach. It would have been an expensive car a couple of years ago, but as it came closer I noticed that it was dirty, rusted, scratched, and had several large dents in the body work. The front bumper was bent and a crack ran through the laminated windscreen from top to bottom.

I was standing in front of the plane and Peter was nowhere in sight when the Merc pulled up just a few feet away.

The driver's door opened and a guy climbed out.

'Hey you! . . . You fuckin' Palmer?' He threw his head back a little and pointed at me with his chin.

I looked at him for a moment, then let my eyes wander over his passenger. It was Vitelli all right, sitting there looking at us through the cracked windscreen. I turned away from the car and the driver bellowed.

'Hey! . . . Hey you! I'm fuckin talkin' to you. Are you fuckin' Palmer?'

I spun round dragging out the .357 Ruger.

337

'No.' I said, 'I'm the fuckin' undertaker.' And I shot him twice in the centre of the chest before he could say another word.

He collapsed back over the car, then slid down the grille and flopped on his stomach. His face was turned toward me and his eyes were still open. He gave a twitch and was then still.

I ran to the open driver's door of the Mercedes. Vitelli was making inarticulate sounds of fear as he tried to scramble over and get in behind the wheel. He was halfway across the console and auto change lever, as I bent down and aimed the Ruger at him. He froze in that position, holding his hands straight out, palms facing me as if to ward off evil.

'Have a guess who I am, Vitelli?' I snarled at him.

'I don't know who you are. Are you the law?' His voice trembled with fright.

'No you fuckin' bastard. I'm the bloke you and that treacherous Agostini have been trying to whack.'

His eyes looked at me in total disbelief and his mouth dropped open. It was the best target in the world and I shot him straight through his gaping mouth. The round exited through the back of his head, spraying brain and bone and blood over the passenger-side window. The power of the magnum round hurled him back and as his head sagged down it smeared the gore down the glass and the door. Wiping the Ruger, I put it into his right hand and let it fall back into his lap. I then opened the rear door of the car with the cloth still in my hand and took an aluminium case off the back seat. As I sprinted over to the combi bus the driver, who looked part-Indian, brought the engine to life.

I clambered my way in through the sliding door, pulled it shut and sat down on the seat behind him.

Peter turned in the front passenger seat.

'That was pretty slick, my man,' he said. 'Yeah, real slick.'

The driver's name was Chappy, and my first guess was right. He was part-Indian and spoke with a slight accent.

'They tell me you know where we're going,' I said to him.

'Crikey, I am making deliveries to this certain aerodrome all the time. You have not to worry about me knowing where I am going.'

We drove northwards through the wet heat. After an hour and a half the track made a long curving loop to the left and joined a small road that we could just crawl over, with the combi lurching from side to side like a trawler in a big swell.

'This fuckin' thing'll crack up if we get much more of this,' I said to Chappy.

'Ah, goodness me, don't you be worrying about the vehicle. It has been greatly reinforced to cope with such obstacles.'

Progress was slow and the track was still degenerating, its surface covered with rocks and craters. Once, during the heat of the late afternoon, Chappy took his eyes of the track for a second too long while talking to Peter and nearly plunged off the road into a deep ravine. Shaken, he stopped the van and we climbed out for a spell and wiped the invisible shit out of our pants.

It was dusk when we got to a town that Chappy said was about six miles from the airfield. As we drove through the narrow street we had to pull out wide to pass an army patrol that stood grouped around a truck. But the soldiers barely spared us a glance. In New Guinea I thought we probably did look innocuous, white combi bus, native driver, and white tourists on their way to hotel, airport or whathaveyou. Peter climbed over into the back with me and then, following instructions, I pulled two black holdalls and a small leather briefcase from a compartment under the seat.

'You will be finding all you will be needing in there,' Chappy said over his shoulder.

The bags contained spare clothes and lightweight waterproof overalls, folded and vacuumed in polythene packs. On the chest and shoulders of the outfits was the embroidered badge carrying the Pan Am insignia. And weapons. In the briefcase were two passports, a set of miniature high-powered glasses, a wad of local currency and two small transceiver sets.

Peter and I changed into the gear and took a transceiver each in case the worst came to the worst.

We turned onto the airport road, and distant orange lights marked the terminal building. As we drew nearer, a few light aircraft came into sight, parked neatly along the perimeter fence, and then two jets and a C34 Transport, floating in individual pools of light, surrounded by fuel tankers and maintenance crews.

I took out the mini-binoculars. 'Pull in here for a minute, Chappy, and make out like you're checking the tyres.'

We stopped, and Chappy got out. Two other minibuses and a car passed by. I opened the sliding door and focused on the jets. The first was a Philippines Air, and as I watched a tractor pulled the steps away. The second plane was partly hidden by the first, but there was no mistaking the insignia on the high tailplane.

'Pan Am 727.' I said. 'Christ, Peter, I don't believe it! Percy and your bloke actually got something right.'

'Ah! John's a pretty smooth operator. He always comes through,' Peter said. 'He's been in the field himself.'

I dropped the glasses back into my pocket. 'Okay, drive on slowly, Chappy. And let me tell you what's going to happen.' I took a brown envelope out of the small briefcase. 'That 727's a cargo plane and it'll have a loadmaster organising things inside. You've got to bullshit your way through the air freight gate, you've been here before so that shouldn't be too hard, and take this envelope to that man. Tell him to give it to the captain immediately. Okay?'

We were halfway along the perimeter fence when the road started to veer away. There were no other vehicles in sight. Whatever was happening to keep this airfield under military guard in the cause of national security was beyond me because there was nothing happening here as far as I could see.

I reached up, wound a handle set in the roof and a section slid back.

'Pull into the fence, Chappy, so the building over there shields us from the terminal.'

The cyclone wire scraped the side of the VW abrasively and pushed the sliding door off the runners. 'Go,' I said to Peter. And he disappeared through the top of the combi. His weight bent the roof and there was a percussive sound as he leapt and the metal popped back into place.

I tapped Chappy on the shoulder. 'Good luck. If you can't get in, drive straight back this way and we'll see you. Don't stop, leave the side door open and go slow and we'll get back aboard. If everything works out then flash the lights as you're leaving.' Picking up the aluminium case I had taken from the Mercedes I put it up on the roof. Then throwing the Ingram GP30 silenced machine pistol over my shoulder by the strap, I climbed onto the roof of the combi and threw the case over the fence to Peter. Then with another pop of the roof I was over the fence. The combi pulled away.

We crouched in the grass watching the two planes and the terminal buildings. The engines on the Philippines Air rose to a crescendo and dropped again. Slowly the nose swung round till it was pointing straight at us like a hungry shark. I watched the plane move out. When I turned my attention back to the terminal, Chappy's vw combi was moving slowly along the various embarkation points. Then it turned towards the 727 and I watched its lights progressing in the semi-darkness. It stopped halfway into the pool of light around the plane and Chappy got out. He walked quickly towards the plane and started to climb the steps that normally led to the first-class section. A man in uniform appeared to stop him and Chappy waved the envelope. After a moment of hand-waving and pointing to the front of the plane they both climbed towards the cabin. The hydraulic table that lifted crates and pallets was backing off, and a big gull-winged door began to slowly close over the loading bay's square black mouth.

One by one the engines worked themselves into a fury. Minutes passed. Then Chappy came down the steps. He got back into the combi bus and it began to move, describing a large circle which would eventually have him heading back towards the terminal. As he approached the blockhouse we were using as cover, the headlights flashed on and off twice, while out on the runway the Philippines Air plane lifted off, leaving waves of noise behind it which rolled in every direction. The combi stopped at the army checkpoint and then passed through.

Peter and I ran forward and seconds later we approached the plane from the runway side, keeping it between us and the terminal. We walked behind the nose wheel and out beside the steps. The tractors were pulling away and the noise was frightening. We couldn't have spoken even if we'd wanted to. A white-shirted crew member met us at the top of the stairs and we ducked through the bulkhead door and on to the flight deck. There was barely room to stand. Dials covered the walls and part of the ceiling. Three men turned as we entered and I saw a .45 automatic trained on my midsection. I handed another envelope across to the captain, then unslung and parked the GP30 machine pistol on the floor as a gesture of goodwill. The captain quickly flicked through the papers, glancing up to check the photos. He seemed satisfied, and the other two with him relaxed.

'Welcome aboard Pan Am Cargo. I'm Captain Gillford, the man with the gun is Flight Officer Larry

Martin, and there's our engineer Gerry Bradley.' The flight officer put the gun away and offered his hand, with an apology for the security.

'There's no hosties on this run I'm afraid,' said the captain. 'But you don't know how goddamned lucky you guys are. We've been grounded for the last twenty-four hours waiting for that lot to arrive.' He said pointed down the fuselage at the cargo. 'Your number came in on the end of our flight instructions. Where to?—Darwin, Townsville—take your pick.'

Peter looked over at me, 'Townsville sounds great, what do you think?'

'Sounds good to me,' I said.

'You'll find a couple of swing seats just outside the door. Strap yourselves in. I've been flying since Korea but this is the first time I've had to do a cover job for the Intelligence Agency.'

I turned to go, but Peter grabbed my arm and stopped me.

'We'd better move quick,' he said and pointed out the window.

Streaming down the perimeter road into the orange light of the terminal was a small convoy of military vehicles. Even as we watched, two of them peeled off onto the road to the freight gate.

'Shit!' I said. 'They've found fuckin' Vitelli and the driver.'

'Are those steps away?' the captain shouted. He got an affirmative answer. 'Then let's get the hell out of here.'

I had never imagined that a big jet was so manoeuvrable. On normal flights they bank gently, taxi slowly, descend evenly. And between the passengers and the void outside there is a thick layer of comforting insulation, with in-flight magazines, sweet-smelling hostesses and the deep reassuring voice of the captain. There was none of that here. We sat on the foldaway seats, looking back down the dimly lit interior of the fuselage half-full of crates and cartons. The window I was looking out showed the port wing and a revolving pattern of lights and yellow lines. On the flight deck the radio crackled into life.

'Air Traffic Control calling Pan Am Cargo GZ 388. Your clearance for take-off is withdrawn. Return immediately to your stand. Repeat . . .' Then the engine noise drowned out the voice and someone on the flight deck slammed the bulkhead door. The plane shuddered, then leapt forward. Outside the window I watched frail necklaces of moisture wind-chased across the perspex. Beyond that were the glow-worm headlights of trucks racing over the grass. The vehicles came nearer and nearer, approaching at alarming speed. They were already over the inner runway and on a side collision course but they looked incapable of inflicting harm. The nose angled up, and after just thirty-five seconds the 727 swept into the sky, as lively as an eagle in the hot outback air. I closed my eyes and began a silent prayer to the great god Boeing. We climbed steeply on and up, and as the wheels came up a slight vibration ran through my body.

Behind and below, the airport lights flickered into obscurity and the trucks that were so real and dangerous drove away towards toytown.

I walked into the lounge just as Katy was coming out of the bathroom. The scent of her preceded her presence. It was a smell of gardenias.

'Hello sweetheart,' she said. 'I've missed you.'

'Good to see you again too, love. How's it been?'

I opened my arms in an invitation to her.

She walked over to me and we hugged and kissed. After a while Katy turned her head and gazed through the big window out across the ocean.

The night dark and mild, and the sound of the surf was gentle as the tide moved further out. I could hear faint music playing, probably from downstairs. Katy's hand reached down and covered mine.

'You're lovely, Katy.'

'It's nice when you say that.' And she squeezed my hand.

'I mean it.'

'I know,' she said.

Then she turned into my arms and kissed me softly on the lips. Our tongues touched. The feel of her made me shiver and I felt my loins react, the blood surging.

Her bathrobe had opened and I moved my head down and sucked her nipple in some vague memory of my infancy. I felt the security of it, the warmth of her flesh, and the comfort of her caress on the back of my head. She cradled my head in her arms and moved my mouth to her other breast. When she reached up under the back of my shirt, I felt an exquisite lightness as her fingers moved over my skin.

I straightened up and kissed her.

'You are beautiful,' I whispered.

346

She moved her hand down and caressed my erection.

God, the scent of her filled me with joy like I'd never known. She led me into the bedroom. I ripped the clothes from my body and she guided me inside her and I was enveloped by her. It is paradise, I thought, as I sensed all the hurts of my life being sucked out of me.

31

THREE WEEKS AFTER I'D RETURNED FROM PNG I WAS sitting in a rental car in Darlinghurst Road, Kings Cross. It was late and traffic was heading back down the hill.

Across the street an old fortune teller was folding up her card table and putting her Tarot packs away. The girls looking for business had just called it a night. People still walked along the street and window-shopped or bought takeaways.

I was watching a set of stairs that led up into shadow alongside the entrance to a club where a spruiker usually stood inviting pedestrians to come in and see 'lots of lovely ladies'. 'The best show 'n town.' The lovely ladies were tired ex-hookers with stretch marks and sagging tits who looked at you with lifeless eyes dulled with overdoses of narcotics and ampheta-mines while they ground their arses out of time to music that had a strangled sound.

The club was closed. It was owned by Frangiani and I had learnt from Jacko, who had done a fortnight's surveillance on the bastard, that he arrived and went up those stairs of a Sunday evening around 1.30 a.m.

A car came up the street and parked three cars ahead of me, practically opposite the club. A man

348

wearing a double-breasted dinner suit and the driver got out and crossed the street. Frangiani looked just what he was, a fat ponce. The driver was carrying a bag.

They walked into the doorway and up the flight of stairs. I gave them a few minutes before I left the car and made my way up the entrance stairs. There was a door at the top fitted with a Yale lock. I put my ear against the door but I couldn't detect any sound at all.

I used one of my funny keys and gingerly opened the door a fraction. Inside it was dark and gloomy. When I stepped through the door and closed it softly behind me I found myself in a large room next to the strip club. Light was filtering in from the street, past some old drapes.

Taking the Browning out of my belt, I thumbed the hammer back with a gloved hand. Ahead of me was a dark draughty corridor that smelt of cooking oil from the takeaway downstairs.

I made my way along the corridor, past a room with a bed with a heap of soiled linen and blankets on it, plus a toilet, basin and mirror in one corner. Probably where that fat toad Frangiani auditioned the sheilas he put to work. The room stank and made my flesh crawl.

The passage to my right had an orange glow as light from the street spilled through a dirty skylight. I looked down to the left, and at the end, light made a bright line under a door and I heard laughter.

I moved quietly along the corridor, hugging the wall, not trusting the timbers in the old building. Outside the door I paused. It wasn't closed, just pushed back with about a half-inch gap. I gave the silencer on the

Browning a gentle exploratory twist, shoved the door open with a bang and leant against the side of the frame.

'Don't even fuckin' blink.'

Frangiani looked up and his mouth dropped open. There was a light hanging down low over the desk and his partner had his arse propped against the end of the desk. His hand made a sudden move and I shot him immediately. He crashed sideways off his perch, knocking over a chair before he hit the floor, gave a spasm and was still.

I turned the gun back on Frangiani. His head was turning from side to side in shock and a cigarette that had been in his mouth was smouldering on the table in front of him, sending twisting blue spirals of smoke up into the light.

'Put your fuckin' hands up on the table, where I can see 'em, Joey.'

He put his hands on the edge of the desk and they were trembling.

'Push em right forward, and turn them palms up.'

He leant forward till his guts pushed against the edge of the desk and his arms stretched out.

'I told you a long time back, you cocksucker, that if you fucked with me I'd come for you.'

'What you want me to say? What you want me to do?' His accented voice was shaking. 'I can a pay you to let me go.'

'You haven't got enough money for that, Joey.'

'Yes, yes, take it. There's the whole week's takings in there. He nodded his head at the bag.

'Heard from your stinking boss lately, Joe?'

He bent his arms at the elbows and entwined his fingers, then placed them under his chin.

'Gino's a dead, so is Paolo. Please Jimmy, don't a shoot me. What must I do?'

'Pray, you bastard.' I pressed the trigger on the Browning and held it down. The shots ripped him back into the cushions of his chair, then he slumped forward over the desk. I shot him again through the top of the head and dropped the gun on the table.

I picked the bag up and opened it. Bundles of notes were jammed together. I closed it and walked out of the room, pulling the door closed behind me.

I was halfway down the hall when I started to feel really cold and damp. An icy sweat jumped onto my face, the hall felt stuffy too . . . the air felt all used up. I was finding it difficult to breathe. I tried to get some air into my lungs. On the third or fourth breath I began to feel dizzy. There was a kind of clicking sensation in the lower part of my throat and I had a strong erratic pulse. Then came the first twinge of nausea.

As I leant against the side of the wall a trembling started in me. Thinking it would pass, I continued to breathe as deeply as I could, holding each breath and then releasing it till I realised it wasn't doing any good. Feeling I was going to throw up, I dropped the bag and turned against the wall, holding myself there in a stooped position, my hands flat against the surface. The pulse in my throat suddenly grew frenzied, clicking wildly like a Geiger counter. I felt a pain in my chest, an acute tearing pain, as if someone had forced their hand down my gullet and was trying to rip my lungs out. I sank down on my knees and then rolled over on my side, hugging my knees to my chin. I couldn't breathe. I'm going to choke to death, I thought. Then the feelings started to relax, the worst of the pain had passed and I was able to breathe normally again, though I still felt sick. I climbed slowly to my feet, unsteadily.

My shirt was soaking wet as I bent and picked up the bag. I bumped off the walls moving down the hall till I came to the room with the bed in it. I walked over to the sink, closing my eyes for a moment as waves of nausea swept over me. Kneeling in front of the toilet I pushed a finger to the back of my throat, trying to make myself throw up, tasting gun-oil and the rubber of the glove. I began to gag, coughing and dry-retching, each spasm more violent and painful than the last, but I couldn't vomit. It felt as if there were some obstruction in my throat.

Then I must have blacked out.

The next thing I remember is staring down into a swirling vortex of bright blue water. I wasn't sure if I'd been sick, and I didn't remember pressing the button to flush the toilet. I felt a kind of relief, more a numbness, and clammy all over. My head ached. I stood up and moved to the wash basin, turned on the tap and scooped up some water to rinse my face.

My reflection in the mirror was ghostly pale under a beaded gloss of sweat. I took out my handkerchief and wiped my face, then took a deep breath.

I picked up the bag, weaved my way to the door and stepped out onto the landing. Hanging onto the rail, I made my way down to the bottom, a step at a time. I rested there with my head down.

There was no-one on the street. I stepped off the kerb and nearly lost my balance, stumbled a few paces, then finally made it to the car. Reeling and rolling like a drunk, I got in and lay my head against the back of the seat. Too sick to even move. But I had to get out of here. My watch said 2.40 a.m. and I couldn't believe it. I must have passed out up there for longer than I realised.

I started the car and slowly moved out onto to the road.

After about two miles I couldn't go any further, and had to stop. There was a phone box further on, just a little way down the slope, and I let the car coast against the gutter till I was outside it.

I dragged myself out from behind the wheel and, hanging onto the car, somehow managed to get into the phone booth. Leaning back against the door, I rang Percy and through spasms of nausea and chest cramp managed to tell him where I was.

Then I slid down onto the floor and blacked out.

I woke up looking at the ceiling, so white and clean, felt pressure on my hand and slowly turned my head. Katy was sitting there, holding my hand. I tried to squeeze back but the effort was too much and I blacked out again.

Next time I came to, daylight was streaming through the window. I felt dry, so dry it was hard to swallow. I tried to speak but only a croak came out. I saw Katy's face looking down at me. She was asking me what I wanted but her words sounded tinny and far away.

Then a doctor was leaning over me . . .
'Can you hear me?' and he's feeling my neck.
I tried to speak again but just croaked.
'He needs some fluid, not too much.'

As moisture trickled down my throat I felt like a plant in the desert when it suddenly rains. I made a sound for more and the moisture started again. Then I felt the prick of a needle in my arm and the room seemed to get brighter. I was so tired I closed my eyes once again and welcomed the darkness . . .

Ten days later I walked out of St Vincents with Katy on my arm. I had suffered what the doctors called a coronary thrombosis. In my language, a heart attack. I'd been placed on medication.

In a cab we went back to the safe house.

'What happened to the bag I had?' I asked Katy when we were sitting in the lounge room.

'Percy brought it over. It's in the bedroom. Where did all the money come from?'

'I found it.'

32

A MONTH LATER WE WERE STILL AT THE SAFE HOUSE, AT Percy's insistence.

'You want to really make sure things have cooled down,' he said, 'before you start moving Katy around.'

He wasn't wrong.

A few days later I'd just left the garage entrance to go for a walk, and paused for a moment to wave to Katy.

At first I didn't notice the sound of the car accelerating up the road behind me. My mind was full of thoughts of our future . . . of mine and Katy's and the baby's. Only the screamed warning from Katy up above me, followed by a squeal of tyres, shocked me out of my reverie. For most people, it would already have been too late.

Without wasting time trying to see what was happening behind me, I hurled myself away and down from the sound. Old training never dies within you. Then I rolled again, and even as I did so heard the repeated crack of an automatic and felt bullets thudding into the ground where I had been just a moment before.

Hurriedly I picked myself up, again without looking round, and dived over the fence into the front garden of the nearest house. The fence splintered behind me and I hit the ground with a thud that knocked most of the wind out of me, but I was unharmed.

While I lay there, my brain tried to catch up with what had happened.

'Go go go . . . !' I heard a man shouting.

I raised my head above the fence in time to see the Fairlane, and Rocco's familiar features along with those of Albert Riccano. They took off at breakneck speed just as Arthur burst out of the garage entrance of the safe house. He had a Colt revolver in his hand and loosed off two rounds after the car.

'Thanks Artie, I think you might have saved my arse.'

He gave me a pat on the shoulder. 'It's my job.'

A sizeable crowd was beginning to gather, and someone must have phoned the coppers. A siren in the distance was getting louder as it got nearer.

'Get inside quick, Jimmy,' Arthur said. 'I'll take care of this.'

A while after the cops had departed, Arthur came up in the lift.

'You've got to stay in, under wraps for a while, till Percy gives you the okay. That's the message.'

I just sat in the lounge, with my arm around Katy's waist, and said nothing.

It took a week to get a line on Rocco. Each day he took his boat out from Pittwater, and also went to a nearby tavern, accompanied by a guy I didn't know.

I got hold of a boat, set things up, then put my plan into action.

Rocco and his offsider walked into the tavern. They used a small private side bar that was serviced through a hatch from the main bar. Rocco might have been capable of letting loose from a moving car, but he wouldn't be into any gunplay with witnesses so close, and I decided to use this to my full advantage.

Walking into the bar, I sat three feet away from Rocco. He had his back to me, talking to his mate. The barmaid came through and I quietly ordered a stubby of Tooheys. I took a few mouthfuls and sat toying with the bottle.

'How's it going, Rocco ? I asked.

Rocco spun around on the bar stool.

'What the fuck do you want ?' Hatred flared in his eyes as they flicked over me, looking for a weapon.

I sat there before him, alone and unarmed.

'I've got a proposition for you,' I said.

Rocco just stared at me and waited.

'You may find this hard to believe,' I continued, 'but . . . '

'I find you sittin' here hard to believe,' Rocco said. Then he smiled. It was the most malevolent smile I had ever seen.

I nodded my head in wonder, breath escaping from my nose.

'I suppose you do,' I said. And nodded again. 'But what I've to say is important to us both, and time is pretty short.' Then the words tumbled out of me. 'This square-up shit has to stop, Rocco. Otherwise . . . '

Rocco's eyebrows moved up his large forehead in surprise.

'Otherwise what?' he said.

'Otherwise I'll take you out, Rocco, and any cunt that wants to back you. But I'll start with you. You get the message?'

Rocco squinted at me until his eyes were just slits. Then he tilted back his big head, threw open his mouth and laughed. He wiped the smile and laughter from his broad face with a meaty hand.

'Tell me somethin', you bastard. Why should I do this for you? Who the fuck are you to try and scare me?' He spread his two fanlike hands and gave an inquisitive shrug.

'Well,' I replied, a weak smile working at the corner of my mouth, 'since I'm the one who took out Paolo, I thought you might understand.' I clamped my jaw tightly to stifle a tremor I could feel starting, and rotated the dark bottle in my fingers.

Rocco's massive face shifted slowly, melting to a smoking glower. He shot his big hands toward me, aiming for my neck and shoulders.

I focused on Rocco's hands, dodged them, struck him with the narrow end of the bottle, quick thrusts that drove deep into the flesh under his left ear, into the carotid artery, into his larynx. I finished by trying to drive the neck of the bottle into and past the man's cavernous nostrils.

Stunned, Rocco locked his sausage-like fingers around my shirt as he fell.

Sensing the oncoming grasp, I jumped up, pushed off with the balls of my feet, and moved to Rocco's left. In a blur I streaked out of the bar, tearing away from the stunned man and leaving part of my shirt in the angry bastard's grasp. Pausing only long enough to topple over two stools on my way to the door, I raced flat-out down the littered side lane, ignoring the shouts and clamour behind me, pushing my knees up high, driving my legs and lungs to maximum performance.

The fears I had were adrenalin-charged but genuine. Rocco's and his mate's shouts pursued me in earnest. The four blocks from the tavern to the marina passed me in a nightmare of motion and noise. Reaching my tied-up boat, I gasped, tried to slow my breathing while I released the line. The key turned in the ignition and the powerful outboard coughed into life. With no regard for my wake, I shot out into the channel, then idled down. Within seconds, Rocco and his companion ran onto the dock, lurching towards his boat. I waited until Rocco's hooded eyes focused on me, then waved to the angry giant and pushed the throttles full forward, clearing the dock area.

Leaning into the bone-jarring crunch as the boat hit the choppy swell, I pointed the bows out through the channel towards the open sea, and relaxed a bit and smiled. I had accomplished my first goal.

I stripped away the blue awning and pulled on a brightly coloured print shirt, a flimsy straw hat and wraparound dark glasses.

Opening the throttle to its maximum, I leant into the impact of the veed hull on the green swells. The afternoon sun spread a shadowless glare on the sea, obscuring the distant shoreline. The streamlined craft fell into stride, with the crests of blue-green foam lunging, then crashing down on the hard surface of the water. Gauging myself about ten minutes short of Rocco's range, I softened my focus, slowed my respiration rate and shrugged the tension from my tightened shoulders. The crash and jar of the small boat's banging thrust grew faint.

I lashed the wheel with nylon occy straps and moved to the items concealed beneath a heavy green tarpaulin. Flipping back the lid of an old battered weapons box with a deliberately slow hand, I removed the gleaming Omark Hipower rifle, checked its action, and stowed it beneath the boat's dash. Next I lifted out the thirteen-shot GP13 Browning automatic, checked the magazine, and stared at the projectiles. They were tipped with soft lead, the nose of each cut with tiny crosses. The combination of calibre, powder load and filing created a projectile that left the muzzle at a little less than 800 feet per second, mushrooming within yards to an irregularly shaped, flattened disc that quickly reached the size of a ten cent coin. The shells were simple and devastating. Upon impact with human tissue they did not merely penetrate; they removed a jagged swathe of flesh and bone and followed up with a mind-numbing shock wave. Pinpoint accuracy was not a requirement. All that was needed to disable an opponent was to strike any point on his body. The projectile would do the rest.

I placed the Browning on the seat cushion and laid a flotation jacket on top of it. Then I put two magazines for it in my side pocket. Continuing to monitor my course, I avoided concentrating on the specifics of the forthcoming conflict. My combat plan was solidly formulated where possible, but the rest would have to be improvised in the field. I knew only too well that the martial skills I had learnt with the Special

Operations Group had atrophied, that my physical edge had blurred and then softened. The cumulative effects of inactivity and too many injuries were something I could not counteract, but I tried to avoid a too-frank examination of my waning abilities.

In a strange parallel to my physical limitations, I was plagued with emotional weaknesses as well. Negative emotions flooded me momentarily. The possibility . . . no the probability . . . of the death of Katy stood out starkly in my mind.

Mine was a life of debt and obligation to friends. Or it used to be, I thought. For me friendship required loyalty proportionate to the strength of the bond. Where did poor Carmel rank now in the ordering of my priorities? With the time that had elapsed since her death, the pain it caused had healed over with emotional scar tissue that both protected against additional injury and prevented full repair. My trips to her resting spot, to her remembered shrine, had grown more infrequent, my thoughts of her less and less. But the hate I had for those who had caused her demise had expanded.

I looked upon the possibility of my own death. It was a less stressful fantasy. In truth, I had faced that probability on too many occasions. On this day, when it was most likely to finally occur, I was not overly concerned. I knew that in the throes of combat, fear would grip me and would then pass, leaving me essentially unchanged. But if death should take me this time, I was prepared. I was ready for nonexistence, a mindless, dreamless sleep that possessed neither fear nor pain. And I was prepared for an afterlife, that is if there was one . . . or if I found one. I smiled at the prospect of confronting the Eternal

One. I wondered if I would falter at that moment and meekly ask for forgiveness, or if I would retain my sense of outrage and present the deity with a list of grievances. The Eternal One might be as incompetent and unscrupulous a manager as those who falsely represent his name here on Earth. Or perhaps he would be a kind and understanding old fellow who had little control over the passage of human events.

My thoughts were fanciful and I laughed out loud. Death would come. Or it wouldn't. I only hoped that the Eternal One understood how I felt over the butchering of the two girls at Port Douglas. But I had to accept the turn of the greasy playing card, or the roll of the weighted dice. It was not my game, not my table. But there would come a day, a time, when it would be my game and my table. And when that time arrived there would be hell to pay.

I throttled down to stalling speed as I scanned the sea behind me through the binoculars.

Rocco's boat was a large one, better than thirty-five feet and with a wide beam. Dark wisps of oil-laden smoke rose from the its wake, attesting to a lack of maintenance. As I watched I noticed that Rocco's partner had me in a reciprocal focus through a pair of wide-angled binoculars. I waved at the man slowly, my arm describing a lazy arc, and throttled the launch forward towards their cruiser. I read the lettering on the side through my lenses. *Disco Volante*. Flying Saucer.

My boat was a different colour since I'd peeled off the blue weather canopy, and my appearance wasn't consistent with the one I'd shown in Rocco's domain. I dropped my binoculars and wheeled the boat towards the bobbing

362

cruiser. As the distance shortened, I was able to distinguish the men on board more clearly. Rocco was at the controls on the flying bridge and was wearing a dark pair of shorts and a yellow shirt. His hair was flecked with patches of dingy grey, his moustache drooped downward to his chin, and his stomach extended over the waistband of his shorts. He wore a pair of tinted glasses and a neglected cigarette dangled from his full lips. When he issued instructions to the others, the cigarette jiggled ash onto his waiting abdomen. Tucked into the waistband of his shorts was a large automatic pistol.

I guided the boat toward the cruiser, positioning the Browning within inches of my grasp. And I sat motionless at the control panel, dropping my arms loosely to my sides. As I came closer Rocco must have seen the gun on the seat and yelled out . . .

'It's him! . . . Take him, Freddie.'

The tall, muscular partner rotated the short snout of the AR-15 a few degrees toward me. His right hand reached forward and his finger went into the trigger guard.

I stood fully erect in the cockpit, fully extended both arms in front of me, hands curled around the grip of the Browning. Thumbs locked securely down, forearms parallel and directed towards Freddie, I pulled the trigger. The impact, accompanied by a deep resonant roar of the heavy powder load, drove him and his weapon brutally backward and over the cruiser's rail in a red profusion of plasma and tissue. Squinting into the sudden recoil, I brought both hands down again, forearms locked rigid, veins bulging, and turned my aim back to the flying bridge . . . to Rocco.

Rocco recovered quickly, drawing across his pendulous belly with his right hand to pull the large-calibre automatic from his waistband. Simultaneously a man in a peaked cap who must have been below deck appeared beside him and raised a pump shotgun. I shifted aim and fired again. The shotgun-wielding man was struck in the right shoulder and the flattened lead projectile obliterated the joint and a substantial portion of his upper arm. The second projectile, milli-seconds behind the first, impacted squarely into his chest and left elbow. The limb below vanished. And so did he.

The rapid series of explosions literally deafened me, but I could see the open mouth of Rocco as he got off a shot that went wild, then threw his craft away from me as he loosed off three more shots that all smacked into my boat. I tested the controls but found no functional damage. As I worked, the ringing in my bruised ears diminished and I could hear again the throb of the powerful Johnson outboard, the thunk and slosh of water, and in the distance the scream of an angry gull.

I opened the throttle and took off after Rocco. As I drew closer he realised he couldn't out pace me and loosed off a couple of rounds, then brought the boat to a stop. He examined the automatic and I knew then that he held an empty gun in his hand. As he flew down the ladder of the flying bridge for more ammunition I considered sitting back and using the Omark, but there was no guarantee that he would show himself. And if he had a rifle below . . . then I would make a much better target. Accelerating forward quickly, I cut the motor and glided in, pulled up on the starboard side and peeked over the deck. Rocco was still below. I threw a quick knot over the rail and scrambled over the side.

I heard the gun drop from my belt, heard it hit the deck and then slip over the side.

'Shit!' I said between clenched teeth and made a dash up the side of the wheelhouse just as Rocco was coming up on deck. I dropped down behind an upraised deck cover but he saw me and two shots rang out. One of them spat sharp, flying splinters of deck wood into my right forearm. I jerked the arm back and hugged the deck, rolled onto my back and extracted a long shard of wood from the belly of my forearm muscle. The wound bled freely and the muscle quivered with an erratic rhythm.

I rolled onto my stomach and slipped head-first down the forward ladder. Jumping up I sprinted through the passageway below deck amid a splattering of impacting bullets. I slammed the sliding door that gave access from the cabin and secured it with an ornamental brass latch. Then I drew the blinds on the front bulkhead and port and starboard portholes, for the small advantage of darkness. The only weapon I had was a combat knife in a scabbard on my belt.

The wound in my arm continued to flow with blood and I grimaced as I flexed the injured tissue. A piece of wood was still in there, embedded deeply. It was painful, but my hand and arm were still functional. I removed the knife from the rear of my belt and hefted it in my weakened right hand. Dissatisfied with the feel, I switched the blade to my left hand and flattened myself against the bulkhead beside the cabin door, listening for Rocco's approach.

I saw the brass handle on the door start to move and I could hear Rocco straining. Then the brass fitting was wrenched out of the wall and the door crashed halfway back, jammed in a broken runner. Rocco must have realised that I wasn't armed because I wasn't firing back, but he paused, probably finding it difficult to focus in the curtained gloom. I held my breath as the big man's body engulfed the doorway. He stooped his basketball of a head to enter the compartment and led with his right arm and the pistol as he turned sideways to squeeze through the opening. With as much speed and power as I could muster, I swung down with the combat knife in a desperate straight-armed overhead smash that drove the sharpened blade deep into the wide wrist.

A primordial bellow burst from Rocco's large mouth, the automatic thudded to the carpeted deck, and his convulsive response flipped the hunting knife from my grip. He screamed a wordless challenge that deafened me. Then he hopped forward, pivoted, and sought to embrace me with his huge deadly arms. White flecked spittle formed in the corners of his mouth and flew from his lips. Bellowing, he lowered his broad head and shoulders and charged. His enraged rush crushed the breath from my chest, lifted me off my feet, and smashed me against the forward bulkhead. A window shattered.

I clawed at the skin of his rubbery neck and drove my knuckled thumb into his exposed mastoid. Breathless and fearing that the next few seconds would bring my own death, I struck at the small hollow with a looping inward stroke and felt the crunch of fractured mastoid bone. Rocco sagged, loosened his grip, and dropped to one knee.

A stabbing pain shot white lights behind my eyes as the expansion of my chest caused broken ribs beneath my left arm to puncture neighbouring tissue. The pain angered and enraged me beyond my terror, and I smashed my knee into the stunned face of the kneeling monster. Rocco's nose flattened, cartilage ground audibly like a wooden matchbox being crushed, and he rocked back. I drew a second searing breath and drove my knee forward once more, using both hands to steady the bloody mass of Rocco's pumpkin-sized head. Instinctively, Rocco leaned into the thrust, grabbed my swinging leg with both arms, and rolled to the side. His weight pulled me to the carpet, wrenching my knee out of its socket and forcing the knobby end of the bone to roll painfully.

A scream of pain whistled out of my mouth. Rocco's strength was still brutal. With a panic born of pain I crabbed backward on my elbows, dragging my damaged leg. Filling his lungs with frothy air, Rocco crawled forward, a bloody grin fixed on his pulped face.

My intellect reeled. I had delivered three killing blows in rapid order, and yet the man crawled steadily forward, his smile demented and flashing gold from a capped tooth. As I scrabbled further backwards I reached with both hands to my dislocated knee. I snapped the joint flat, forcing the bone to roll again over swollen and screaming tissues. Behind my eyes, bright lights flashed in kaleidoscopic fury and my body jerked with excruciating pain. Fingers of agony travelled bone-deep and upward, exploding in my skull. I threw my head back, my hands stood rigid before my face, my fingers clawed the chilled air, and a primal scream exploded out of my very soul.

Mindless of the pain, mindless of everything except the death of my tormentor, I flung myself forward, driving stiffened fingers into Rocco's half-closed eyes. Ocular fluid splashed wetly onto my wrist and I twisted my rigid digits in the gory sockets.

Rocco turned and roared with a bellow that shook the cabin as he stood fully upright and sightlessly clawed the air.

I stepped in, ducked under the windmilling arms and drove a stiffened and arched hand deep into Rocco's solar plexus, the follow-through reaching up and in to crush the man's aorta. Rocco retched and gasped, but still he remained erect. Windmilling blindly, his meaty left hand closed on my right wrist and held tight.

In amazement and desperation, I hacked at the locked hand with repeated knife-edged blows, backing constantly to evade the other groping arm. I ignored the protests of my anguished knee and tortured lungs as I dragged the sightless man in my wake, slashing repeatedly at the iron claw that paralysed my right hand.

Reaching the passageway to the front deck I was trapped. Knowing the man would surely kill me if both arms were again allowed to seize hold of my body, I aimed a kick with my injured leg at the crotch of the gory-headed giant. Lacking balance and follow-through, the blow glanced from Rocco's groin but achieved a limited effect. His grip relaxed momentarily and I fell backwards, scrambled crab-like past him through the main passageway onto the deck.

Undaunted, Rocco pursued the sound of my exertions with groping hands. Yellow fluid dripped from his destroyed eyes and blood flowed from his mangled nose, as he followed me up the stairs onto the open rear deck. I danced from the claw-like paws and circled. My efforts demanded oxygen and I drew a rattled breath. Rocco turned and sought me. Sighting a rigged heavy deep-sea fishing rod in its holder, I grabbed it and whipped it through the charged air. Weights and hooks whistled noisily and as the line wrapped around Rocco's head I jerked backward with all my weight, as if setting the hook in a surfacing marlin. Rocco roared in anguish, pawing the air for his unseen tormentor. I jerked again, setting the hooks deeper. The thick line snapped.

I cast aside the stiff rod, took two long strides into Rocco's range and leapt into the air. Bringing both palms powerfully together upon Rocco's ears, I burst his eardrums, then launched my right hand into his gory face. This is known as the collapsing fist in martial circles and was a killing blow that broke the bridge of the nose with the first impact of curled knuckles, then followed through as the fist collapsed and the heel of the palm drove the fractured bones deep into the skull and brain tissue. Seized by a blood passion of my own, I envisioned my hand emerging at the rear of Rocco's skull as I delivered the strike.

Rocco staggered back two steps but retained his stance.

Incredulous at the man's ability to withstand such an attack, I stepped forward again and hacked Rocco's larynx with the edge of my hand. His source of oxygen cut off, he reeled, windmilling his arms, fighting for balance, looking for any hold that would deliver me to him.

Fear banished, rationality swept aside, hatred burning in my mind and heart, I ducked the massive arms. I grasped Rocco's waistband and a fold of skin below the gargantuan neck and lifted the full weight of Rocco from the deck. Screaming against the strain of the impossible lift, I dropped to one knee, letting the giant's improbable weight smash the small of the spine at its weakest point. The dead weight of his body flattened me and I lay gasping for shallow breaths. Pain started in my chest, my vision shot with red hues, and my damaged knee and splintered ribs were in agony. When at last I rolled the slippery carcass off me and onto the deck, I crawled to my hands and knees and retched, then flopped over onto my back, gasping for air and waiting for my thudding heart to subside.

I unclipped the two stainless guard wires, dragged a length of chain over and wrapped it around Rocco's neck, and secured it with a short piece of rope. Then tugging and rolling, I managed to get him to the side and finally pushed him over. The extra chain rattled over the side as it followed him into the deep water.

Clambering over the side, I fell into the tethered boat, screaming as my broken ribs and injured knee sent pain racing through me. I turned the starter with trembling fingers, freed the mooring rope after three attempts, and edged the throttle forward.

As I poured on the power I was thrown back against the moulded rubber seat cushions. Intense pain seized my ribcage and blurred my vision. I raised a hand to wipe the offending cloud from my eyes, then remembered the blood from the defeated monster and rinsed myself with a hand that I kept dipping into the rushing sea.

Two suns lit the harsh blue sky and images swum before me. I eased the throttle back, the craft slowed, and I steered a course for shore.

I felt the gentle swirl of sun-warmed waters above and around me. The tropical sea bathed me sensually. I opened my eyes. Drifting green strands rose bent and twisted in the deep water eddies of the current. The white sand beneath my feet was fine, my buoyed weight not denting the dimpled surface. The sea floor was unmarked, freshly vacuumed by the currents, vacant to the limits of my sight.

A constricting pressure tightened my chest, forcing crystal bubbles from my lips. They floated obliquely up from me, trailing markers in the currents. I looked at my chest and saw a large, flat white snake slithering against my skin, drawing itself ever tighter against my lungs. My hand rose in submerged slowness to arrest its actions but was gently pushed aside by unseen fingers. Oh well, I thought, I really don't mind. The snake continued its winding constrictions, biting me sharply in the side. I started at the pain, but the waters soothed me and I lowered my hands and did not interfere.

The stark sandscape in front of me blossomed. The plant life was dense, lush, and overcrowded with twisting and spreading greenery. The sky was obliterated by a ceiling of living green and the sounds of the rainforest penetrated my ears. Brightly striped lizards flitted in stop-and-go fits of motion and repose. A small clearing in the bush materialised, the bare ground blackened by fire. Percy walked towards me and I tried to hail him, but burbled sounds and oblong bubbles escaped uselessly from my lips.

I wanted to embrace him with forgiveness, to speak to him, but the waters impeded my efforts. I tried to think of some bodily gesture I could offer, some movement or posture that would tell Percy that I, too, understood the power of fear. But while I sought vainly for the means to ease my friend's discomfort, Percy's face blurred in the shifting currents.

A large, furred spider in the centre of a three-dimensional web robbed me of the power to concentrate, fascinating me with its movements. The spider tramped up and down the fine threads of the web on its ciliated legs, repairing a tear here, spinning a new design there. The web extended in all directions, touched all people, and threatened all lives.

The spider crept down a trembling thread, approaching me, its mandibles working as if it were tasting me prior to biting me. I attempted to flee but found my legs mired in the fine undersea sand. As the beast drew closer and placed its furred leg on my arm, it grew human eyes in its rounded head. Eyes that ballooned outward, filling the warm waters with a new shape. It was Rocco, his empty eye sockets staring and huge jaws snapping. I struck out with an arm and severed the monstrous head from the bloated body, only to find a new head with larger jaws snapping goldly in the dim aquatic light. The sharp teeth sank into the flesh of my shoulder and twisted violently, tearing muscle and sending reddened clouds billowing into the currents. I opened my mouth to scream and choked as the warm, salty taste blocked all sound. The destroyed eyes of the monster smiled in evil satisfaction and shook me again.

The great white snake seized me and wrapped its coarse coils tighter, ever tighter. I opened my eyes. I was tied to crossed saplings in a small bamboo clearing. The trees were Vietnamese. Below my knees, tongues of yellow flame licked upward lovingly, but each caress brought searing pain. Surrounding the fire and saplings, a weaving line of nude figures danced, shuffling to the rhythm of unheard drummers. The figures crouched as they hopped and shuffled from right to left. Before each of them was a mask. The glow from the flames painted the masks and the smudged and dirty nakedness of the bodies in red shadows and bright planes of orange. The masks were caricatures of the men I had killed.

The tempo of the dance increased and the dancers whirled demonically. With a great shout they halted, faced the centre of the clearing, and lowered the cartoon-like faces. Behind the masks were the faces of Margo, and Rosalie, Carmel and Katy, Percy and McCreedy. The faces were older and harder than I ever knew them. In silence, each dancer raised a finger and pointed it at me. The flames grew higher and burned at my knees. The silent accusations filled me with dread. I began to shiver uncontrollably with some unknown fear, then the surrounding circle dispersed and the obscenely naked body of Lucifer, the Devil himself, appeared in their midst. He was clapping his hands, hopping from one cloven foot to the other.

'They're mine, they're mine,' he sang. 'They're all mine!'

My eyes popped open, and I stared into a closely shaven, bespectacled face.

'I sure hope you're a doctor,' I croaked hoarsely. My body was on fire with fever. The face frowned in puzzlement, then nodded.

'Yes that's right,' it said. 'Don't you remember Mr Grainger and your wife bringing you in?'

'Thanks,' I whispered, and plunged down into a dark abyss of dreamless sleep.

It was a full month before my injuries were almost healed.

33

THEY BROUGHT ME A CUP OF COFFEE, BUT MORE THAN AN hour passed before a girl with the best pair of legs I had ever seen finally appeared and asked me to follow her. Trust Percy, I thought.

As I walked along the corridor and up some stairs, the girl's legs twinkling in front of me, I felt completely calm and I wondered how I was going to be able to give Percy a more objective account of what had happened than the one he had already been given. And there was no sense going off half-cocked in this matter, because I knew who was behind it.

I was shown into the large well-lit office where Percy rose to meet me with a smile.

'Sit down, Jimmy. I'm sorry, mate, to have kept you waiting, but there were one or two points I had to straighten out with the bloody coppers. Several of the neighbours phoned the police after the shooting a month back and I wanted to wait for a report from one of my blokes who's been away.'

I returned Percy's smile and sat down without saying a word.

'How can I put this in the right way, Jimmy?'

'Just say it like it is, Perce.'

'Do you want me to get you onto the witness protection program?'

'What! Work with the coppers? Christ, Percy, they're a fuckin' sight worse than these bastards who are trying to bury me.'

'With this task force thing in your corner you might come out squeaky clean.'

'And I might come out fuckin' dead, too. Jesus, Perce! You're not that blind that you can't see that there has to be coppers behind every racket so the fuckin' thing can stay operational.'

'These guys on the task force are bloody well hand-picked.'

'The cunts are bloody well hand-picked to go to the Police Academy in the first place. And it doesn't make a bit of difference, Perce. Some of them will be got at.'

'They're not all bent, Jimmy.'

'Oh so true, Percy, but let me put a little scenario together for you. There's a guy and he wants to get away from the Mob, from crime, from whatever. He lands in some hot water, or there's a fuckin' contract hanging over his head. The coppers approach him with an offer . . . Put him on witness protection. Now the coppers baby-sitting him are maybe hand-picked. But behind the scenes is where the real action's going on, mate. It's the bent ones who are supplying the other side with information and whereabouts, names used, right down to the fuckin' time the bloke has a crap. The force is too big for anything to be completely hidden. There's always someone who knows.'

'Well what about the Feds? Would you be willing to play ball with them?'

'I wouldn't be any better off than I am now, Percy. I'd always be hiding.'

'Look, you've done a couple of things for us and we're not ungrateful. What do you want? Name a price. We won't be ungenerous.'

'You're doing enough as it is, mate. Just keep covering me while you can. And keep Katy safe, that's my price.'

Percy sat and thought for a while, then changed the subject.

'There's one aspect of your story, Jimmy, that's causing me some bewilderment.'

'And what's that?'

'Well you and I can cut the bullshit. You told Arthur you didn't see who blazed away at you. But he tells me that when he came out of the garage entrance he saw your head above the fence looking at the car. Now come on. I'm being a fairy fucking godmother to you and Katy, don't you think you owe me something better than the cock and bull story you gave Arthur?'

I looked at Percy and I felt a bit guilty. He'd gone out on a limb for me and I don't know what I would have done for Katy if he hadn't.

'Yeah you're right Perce, and I'm sorry. I guess old habits do die hard.'

'You saw them. Didn't you?'

I nodded.

'Now tell me. Who the fuck was it?'

Talking to Percy and his people was different from talking to the police, so I decided for the first time in my life to trust someone in authority.

'It was Albert Riccano and Rocco.'

'What! . . . Rocco Giorgetti? The late Paolo Agostini's enforcer?'

'That's him.'

'Yeah . . . well you've tidied that end up now haven't you? Christ, do you know how fuckin' lucky you are to be alive? Whoever it was you asked to ring me . . . if they hadn't you'd be history, brother. How do you feel about all this, Jimmy, I mean what would you do if you could do it?'

'Well, Percy, between you and me I've had a fuckin' gutful. I was wrong about Agostini, the same as I've been wrong about a lot of things I've done. We've both been there and done it, Perce, so I'm not about to start saying who's right or wrong. Any fool can criticise and condemn, and you'll find that most fools do. I just want some peace, mate, that's what it boils down to. To be able to live without a fuckin' gun under the pillow and Katy to be able to walk down the street without me worrying that someone's going to put the arm on her. I want my kid to grow up in a natural way, not jumping from one place to the next.'

'You were crazy to get mixed up in all this from the word go.'

'Yeah I suppose so, but hindsight's always been 20–20, hasn't it?' I gazed through the window out over the Botanic Gardens.

'You might be able to achieve what you want, but you'll have to clean up your own mess. I can't be seen to be involved. In fact I don't even want to know. But in the meantime you and Katy stay where you are. But remember, there are limits to what I can do. So whatever you have in mind, old son, use the bloody scone.'

I stood up and we shook hands.

'By the way,' he said, as I was about to open the door, 'as a professional matter of interest, that Agostini thing . . . Radio transmitter over the phone?'

'Do you really want me to answer that, Percy?'

'Yeah. I thought that was it. Go on, get outa here, and remember use the head.'

'I always do, Percy.'

'You never change, Jimmy do ya?'

As I walked out and closed the door, I knew exactly what he meant, once a loser, always a loser.

Over the next week I put Jacko on the tail of Albert Riccano. He'd come down from Brisbane after the club explosion and Jacko finally got a make on him and where he was living. But the place he was in was too secure for a front-on assault.

'Can we get access to his car? Does it get locked away at night?'

'No, it's in the parking bay under the building. But there's a lot of tenants, mate, and if we took him out there it'd mean some poor innocent bastard getting killed as well.'

'Can we put a package under it? I know you'll say piece of piss, but what sort of fuckin' security is there? Can we do it and get away clean?'

'You mean blow it away from the units?'

'That's exactly what I mean.'

'No problem. I haven't seen any bastard downstairs at night. And the entrance to the garage is on the side.

379

I've strolled down a couple of times but never seen any bastard that you'd call security.'

'Righto then mate, let's get down to business. Where does he usually go of a daytime?'

'Out to that joint at Frenchs Forest. You're not going to do any good out there, the place is a fuckin' fortress.'

'Don't I know it.'

Jacko dropped me off in the quiet street and drove away. I looked into a shop window and leant forward, placing my forehead against the plate glass. It was an antique shop and the display window was gloomy. The bits and pieces took on odd shapes in the dim light. Mute objects, I thought, just like me, hiding in shadows. Survivors.

The window was good cover as I waited like a patient animal, knowing that I would get my kill in time. I wanted Albert Riccano. And I wanted to get him myself. Jacko had volunteered to take him out, but I wanted to be the one who pushed the button on him.

I slipped my hand inside the pocket of my jacket to reassure myself for the third time that the radio detonator was in place. And I let my fingers run over it. It was the size of a small transistor radio and looked just as innocent, but the power it would unleash was lethal.

As the grey Falcon moved past me and neared the end of the street 200 yards away, I pulled the detonator out, pulled out the aerial, flicked the switch to ARM, and pressed the button.

People in the homes and units in the tree-lined street knew instinctively that it was a bomb blast that had intruded on the morning tranquillity. It was hardly a car backfiring. Shop windows were shattered and the pervasive odour that washed along the street had a different stench to the usual pall of pollutants associated with suburban traffic. I had watched the blast and actually saw the twisted wreckage of the Falcon as it appeared to float in the cloud of smoky afterblast.

There were faces now at windows, and spectators came out into the street, contemplating the wreckage with fascination. I strolled down and joined them. A hubcap had been blown like a discus, embedding itself in the trunk of a tree. A wheel lay on a doorstep before a wrought-iron gate at the entrance to one of the houses. And a trail of upholstery stuffing lay white like snow on the black surface of the road.

Police sirens wailed and we were all pushed back behind a hastily rigged barrier. A bomb squad vehicle arrived and experienced eyes, familiar with the impartial ruthlessness of explosives, picked knowingly among the rubbish, seeking pieces of a human being. A foot, the polished shoe still carefully laced, lay on a patch of grass a few yards from the car's mangled remains. A ringed hand rested eerily on a piece of deformed chrome ornament. Patches of red were materialising alongside the main wreckage.

One of the plain-clothed officials, a tall man with a craggy face, tamped down an involuntary retch.

'This is the worst scene I've ever examined,' he said to another cop.

The first detail he was conscious of was Albert Riccano's mangled torso, jammed in the front seat against the remains of the dashboard. But it was the sight of the head that made him want to vomit. It was cleanly severed at the neck and lying like a tossed basketball on what might have once been the car's back seat. Its eyes were open, and not at all dull as one might have expected of dead eyes. The face was ivory smooth, the flesh dark, and the mouth was set in a broad sardonic smile, showing even white teeth.

'Christ almighty!' I heard the craggy-faced copper say. He turned away several times, reassuring himself that he had conquered the urge to vomit. But he kept looking back at the face, compelled to absorb the horror of it. He looked as though he had no idea what to do. Officially, he was paralysed.

The roof of the car had been torn away and was sticking up at the back like an opened sardine can, making the macabre scene easily visible.

More sirens screeched as extra marked and unmarked police cars swarmed into the area. Wooden barriers were erected, blocking both ends of the street and police began to re-route traffic. An ambulance appeared and was quickly let through the cordon. Two paramedics stepped out, walked over and closely surveyed the scene. They hesitated, went back to the ambulance and reappeared wearing surgical gloves.

Another vehicle was allowed through the barricade and three uniformed police with braid on their caps talked quietly with the plain-clothes police as they clustered around the main area of the wreckage. The paramedics went back to the ambulance and two uniformed coppers followed them, carrying a stretcher. Behind them came two more uniformed blokes with transparent plastic bags.

'Looks like a single corpse, male Caucasian,' I heard one of the new arrivals say. He was obviously CIB, a take-charge type from his bearing, and looked like he was the acknowledged leader of the group.

'Be careful,' he said to the paramedics, 'we may be able to lift some prints.'

Another vehicle was let through and a hydraulic cutter was used to cut metal away until they had made an area big enough to remove the remains.

When the cop with the cutter moved back the paramedics moved in, poking their arms into the larger opening and gently removing the torso. Part of it seemed to disintegrate in their hands as they deftly edged it into a large plastic bag. Securing the end with a length of tape, they placed it on the waiting stretcher. Leaning over the back portion of the wreckage, one of the ambulance men lifted the head out by the hair.

'Oh my God!' someone said behind me.

A uniformed cop with a plastic bag was searching the area for other remains, like a garbage picker gathering rubbish after a country show. He picked up the severed hand, then found the foot, as well as unrecognisable parts, and put them quickly in the bag.

One of the senior cops looked over and swept his arm towards us while speaking to a plain-clothes guy. The next minute we were all told this was a crime scene and would we all please return to our homes and places of business.

I turned and walked up the street, thinking that Riccano wouldn't be hurting too many people now.

'Give my regards to Paolo and Rocco when you see them in Hell, Albert,' I said under my breath as I flagged a cab down.

34

AS I LAY BACK LETTING THE SUN WASH OVER ME THROUGH the windows of the lounge, I tried to imagine that I was lazing in the tropical sun.

'Good morning!' Katy's lips brushed mine. 'You were up early.'

Her shadow blocked out the sun. I stirred and sat up.

'The sun. Do you mind, love . . . it comes ninety-three million miles to get to me and you've got to stand in the last three bloody feet of it.'

I was trying hard to fit into a new way of life. I had promised myself that a change had to be made.

Of course there had been the other Jimmy Diamonds—what I liked to believe were earlier vintages. There was the man who had been mixed up with the Mob and the one who had done some contract work for two intelligence agencies which hid their might behind fancy modern offices with fancy names. I couldn't say anything about any of them without incriminating myself. Then there had been the times when Jimmy Diamond told himself that honour mattered most, that he was protecting people. He had been a patriot and killed in the name of Queen and Country.

Most recently, however, I had faced up to the fact that all I had been was a paid assassin. Men had died because of me. A lovely girl who had stayed by my side had suffered and died because of me. I had become sick of death, disgusted with killing. My most recent exploit had been the last straw. I had come back from it sickened. Oh, I had carried out the hit with the usual efficiency. I was very good at the job. But it was over and I had changed. The memories had to fade, the nightmares to lessen. I was trying to find peace of mind.

Percy had given me guarantees that I would be left alone. Now there was Katy and the baby and me.

I lay back and closed my eyes, determined not to allow these thoughts worry me.

Katy was still there standing behind me.

'How can you lie there and fall asleep so soon after getting out of bed?' she asked with a mock disgust.

I opened one eye. 'Since when has a bed been a place merely for sleeping?'

'Sex maniac!'

I yawned. 'You always were a good judge of character, Katy.'

The sun was warm and soporific and there was a slight throbbing in my head. I sat up and rubbed my forehead. I felt no desire to move, far less talk.

'Coffee?' Katy asked as she moved towards the kitchen.

'Oh God!' I moaned with irritation.

'Hangover, love?' Katy asked in a cool voice.

'Last night,' I explained. 'Had a few with Percy. We got carried away over old times.'

It was a small lie. We'd had more than a few, and got pissed as rats.

'Like some breakfast?' she called from the kitchen.

'Shit no. Couldn't face it.'

Three days later Katy got sick and began to bleed.

I raced her into the hospital.

Waiting out there in the corridor, unwelcome thoughts rushing through my mind. What's happening? What are they fuckin' well doing? The smell of antiseptics and medication floats down the corridor as a door is opened.

The doctor walking toward me is dressed in green coveralls and green overshoes. 'I'm sorry,' he tells me as he shakes his head. 'I'm sorry we couldn't save the baby.' I feel like lashing out, but I shove my hands in my pocket, walk out the front of the hospital and light a cigarette. My nerves are screaming. What about Katy? What's she going to feel like? Knowing her as I do she will probably blame herself. She needs me now, needs me like she's never done before.

I walk back to the ward. The doctor is still there, talking to one of the nurses. He comes over to me and puts his hand on my shoulder.

'Would you like to be with your wife?'

Wife . . . the word puzzles me for a moment. I had never thought of Katy as a wife.

'Yes . . . yes I do want to be with her.'

The doctor steers me along the corridor and takes me to a door. There's a number on the door—19—and I wonder if I'll ever forget it. It brands itself on my brain.

Then I'm sitting beside the bed. Katy is still under the anaesthetic.

The doctor leans over me.

'We had to do a caesarean section to remove the baby,' he says quietly, 'but she'll be okay.'

'What was the baby?' I ask.

'A girl.' And he pats my shoulder and leaves me alone with Katy.

Despite the trauma she's just gone through, Katy still has that look of energy on her face. I bend over, kiss her on her soft lips and squeeze her hand gently. And whisper into her ear. 'I love you, Katy, I really do. We'll make it, love, you just get better. We can have more babies. Please don't blame yourself, it's not your fault. I love you.'

Katy spent ten days in the hospital, and then I was allowed to take her back to the safe house, where we spent another eight weeks. We both had to put the death of our baby behind us in such a way that we never got over it, just learned to live with it.

We'd been to the movies one night and when we got back home Katy flopped down on the lounge and threw her purse across the room and started to sob.

'I just wish we could get out of here and go away again like we did before. I don't care any more if they get us, but I can't stand this place any more.'

She buried her face in her hands, then threw her head back and the tears ran down her face. I knelt down in front of her and pulled her to me and her head slumped down on my shoulder. Her body was racked with sobs of emotion and pent-up feelings. It was the first time I had ever seen her so distraught. After the death of the baby she was quiet, though I sensed the pain within her, but I'd never seen her like this. She hung onto me with a fierceness.

'Please don't cry love,' I kept saying to her, 'please stop crying.'

I could feel my emotion starting to crack too, but I stood up and took a deep breath, went over to the sideboard and poured us both a stiff drink.

'Here, love, drink this.'

She took the drink from me and gulped it in little jerks, then handed the glass back to me. I picked up my own drink and took it down in one swallow, feeling the warmth of it spread through my stomach. When I turned back to Katy she had become a little more composed and was wiping her eyes with the back of her sleeve. I gave her my hankie and she looked up, trying hard to smile.

I made us another drink and sat down beside her, putting my free arm around her. We were silent for a while.

'Do you know what's really hurting me?' she said at last.

I turned to her. 'What love?'

'Well, since I've come out of hospital, you haven't touched me, I feel like I'm unclean or something.' And she burst into a body-wrenching fit of weeping, wringing her hands, then beating one closed fist onto the arm of the lounge.

I felt ashamed but I didn't know what to say as I grabbed her and pulled her to me. It was true, I hadn't touched her, but not because I didn't want to. I'd left her alone out of respect.

'God, Katy, that's not how it is, love. I just didn't think you'd want to . . . I thought you'd like some peace of mind. I'm sorry I was wrong. I'm sorry I hurt you. Please forgive me.'

Lifting her face up to mine I kissed her eyes, her cheeks, and gave her a long lingering kiss on her lips. I kissed her tears.

'You are my life, Jimmy.' Then a shiver began inside her and she clung to me with all the strength in her body.

When she became calm she kept looking at the clock on the wall. She must have lost track of time . . . have been outside herself.

'I couldn't go on living without you,' she whispered.

'Is it that strong, Katy?'

'It's beyond all words, Jimmy.'

I patted her and smoothed her hair. Then leant back and turned my eyes to the ceiling. Thinking . . . I wanted a change, but the die was cast. Let it be, then. Better to go down fighting than die like a dog hiding . . . showing them that we're scared . . . fuck 'em! . . . I'm not afraid of any one of the cunts. . . . let 'em come . . . there's still enough in me to give them a fuckin' run for their money . . . Stuff it. Katy's right. I'm sick of it here too.

'What are you thinking about?' she whispered.

When I spoke, my voice had a harsh ring to it. The words seemed ejaculated, as if they had been accumulating under pressure.

'I'm thinking about my own futility,' I said. 'And those bastards who seek to destroy me. But I will fool them. I will cling to life and I will have my revenge if they come. I will taste their blood and it will be as sweet as wine. I'll drink it. And the ground they stand on will run with it. And you and I will get drunk on it.'

My words frightened her . . . their tone and the power as she envisaged the literal embodiment of the image that I had contrived. But then her face took on a new look, one of strength.

'What does it matter, Jimmy? What does any of it matter as long as we're together?'

I thought that my inner rage had intimidated her but it hadn't.

'I promise that whatever you do, I will do with you. Come what may.' More than a promise, it was a vow.

I stood up and paced over to the window.

'It'll be like fighting fuckin' Goliath . . .' I said.

'But David won, Jimmy.'

'At least he had a weapon, a slingshot that he knew would beat his foe. All I've got is this,' I said, tapping my forehead. 'And you.'

'Me?' she said. 'Am I a weapon?'

'Everything I touch becomes a fuckin' weapon, Katy.'

'I'd die for you, Jimmy.'

I walked over and took her by the shoulders and shook her gently.

'Die?' I said softly. 'You won't die, Katy.'

I held her to me and kissed her softly and tenderly, then picked her up and carried her into the bedroom. I undressed her and threw my own clothes off. Then we were lying on the bed, her head nestled in the crook of my arm. She was playing with my nipples, then she reached down and fondled my penis. She looked downward and watched it grow, fill out with its mysterious movement of blood. I reached my hand down and rubbed my finger into her softly. Then I let my lips brush the soft skin of her belly. I moved downward further, my lips touching her pubic hairs. She suddenly moved too, until we were head to toe, and took hold of my hard organ, caressed it, kissed the head and ran her lips along its length. We became a madness of love. I kissed the soft wet lips of her vagina, and titillated her clitoris with my tongue. We revelled in the animality of what we were doing, the volatile chemistry of it. Then I was over the top of her. She looked up into my eyes and pulled my head down to hers, kissing me, her tongue darting into my mouth. She was quivering in expectation as the head of my penis entered her. A sob began in the back of her throat, then turned into a low moaning as my hardness entered her, filled her, and her heartbeat accelerated, the joy of it captured on her face and suffusing her body, her soul, her every nerve end alert to my maleness. Her head went back, her mouth opened . . . We were floating on a rushing river, she gave a cry and a surge of ecstasy raced through her as I continued to plunge inside of her. Then when the repetitive crash of the waves became too much for us Katy gave a gurgled scream and clawed at my back. Something exploded within me and I filled her with all the longing that had been denied release these past long weeks.

We were quite proud of the fact that we had prepared our minds for our departure. That's why we stood there looking at what had occurred. It was 3.30 in the morning and we were fully packed, our bags were piled in front of the lift.

I poured us a couple of drinks and we stood by the window watching the lights outside flickering. The moon on the ocean was like a luminescent carpet at our feet.

'Do you think we'll make it, Jimmy?'

'We'll give it our best shot, love.'

Katy wanted to go back up to the old house up north. Come what may. And I felt the way that she did. If the worst came to the worst, as she put it, wouldn't it be better to be somewhere we liked rather than in the bloody city? Up there we were free. We ran around naked, alive, part of the bush and the jungle. We had each other and she kept saying that's all that mattered.

35

'OH JIMMY, PULL UP! I WANT TO TAKE SOME PICTURES,'
Katy yelled.

We were eight miles north of Wauchope in the
Northern Territory and on each side of the road, towering above us, were the legendary Devil's Marbles, a
massive heap of boulders, smooth and round as if they
had been individually polished. Some of them weighed
many tons, but they seemed to be balanced so precari-
ously that a puff of wind could dislodge them, sending
them down to pulverise you. Yet they have been like
this for centuries. Below and in amongst them there
were natural caverns and grottoes. Hovering over the
whole place is an aura of great antiquity, hinting at the
convulsions that must have taken place millions of
years ago, spewing these balls of granite up from the
very bowels of the earth.

We had left Sydney a month earlier and were heading back to our retreat. Katy was on top of the world
again, taking snapshots and getting them processed
wherever possible.

At the turn-off to Singleton Station we had to stop
the Toyota for a bunch of wild goats. I was tempted to
shoot the patriarch, a long-haired billy with a broken
ankle that had set wrongly to form a sort of club foot.

But as I reached up behind me for the rifle, Katy placed her hand on my arm.

'Don't, Jimmy. He looks so proud watching over the rest of them.'

Head erect, jaw jutting out, he just stood there and waited till his herd had crossed the road. When the last of them disappeared into the thin scrub he limped disdainfully across to join them, not even giving us a glance.

A mile or two further on we came to Bonney Well, a watering point for stock and any other thing that needs it. The windmill bore was pumping water into a long trough at which cattle and birds were drinking together companionably. We got out and walked over to the original well. Shored up with timber and topped with a stone support, the structure seems as solid as when it was built in the days of the Overland Telegraph line over a hundred years ago.

It was getting late now as we headed for Tennant Creek, fifty miles away. We travelled on, singing songs and watching out for cattle on the road, and we know we are not far away as we pass Cabbage Gum Bore, only ten miles out. This is the underground basin that supplies reticulated water to the town.

At last on the horizon appear the lights of Tennant Creek, surmounted by a huge neon cross placed on a strategic hill. We have travelled three hundred miles today. And we both know that four hundred and seventy miles further on is home, our hideaway. Our home.

After a good night's rest at the Desert Camp Caravan Park, we left, just after sunrise. And an hour or so later we left the main track and drove a few miles over a bumpy dirt road to look at the buildings of the old telegraph station. They have stood the test of time. Part of the stone barracks and other outbuildings are in ruins. The well is dry. The cattle and goats have long since scattered. The gardens have dried up and disappeared without trace. But the main residence and post office is in perfect condition, except for the roof from which someone has stripped sections of galvanised iron for their own use. A scarred hillside nearby shows where the builders quarried stone for cutting into big rough blocks to build the station walls nearly a century ago. Bats flit to and fro through the rooms as we walk inside and disturb them, but otherwise the place is ready for re-occupation, with only a minimum of work needed beforehand.

But as we stand there inside, it lies empty . . . lifeless.

In thousands of miles of outback travelling I have never failed to take along a spare fan belt, and I've never needed one . . . until this trip.

I stopped to let Katy take some pictures of a most unusual sight that she found quite funny. Rearing up on the right hand side of the road was a gnarled rock which, in silhouette, bears a striking resemblance to Winston Churchill. An improvised cigar in the form of a stout log of mulga completes the picture. For over twenty years this rock has been known to users of the highway as 'Churchill's Head'. It is also a magnet for vandals and there are initials and slogans painted on it everywhere Ban the Bomb. We want Gough. Bruce loves Judy. Keep the country clean. Trash the poms.

These name writers and vandals are the scourge of the Track. They have defaced dozens of memorials all over the north. As we drive along you can see the evidence everywhere, names and addresses chipped into stone cairns, inscriptions obliterated, signposts shot to pieces or turned the wrong way. We came across the sign post to Central Mount Stuart that had been taken from its rightful place and moved fifty miles up the Track where it stood pointing to some inconspicuous little hill. I pride myself on having a reasonable sense of humour, and I've been involved with the odd practical joke, but it's hard to fathom the reason why anyone would deliberately want to get someone lost in this inhospitable terrain.

We got the first warning sign when the red lamp in the dashboard started to flash. I pulled over to the side of the road and as we stopped we could hear the water in the radiator hissing and boiling away. The nearest help is about thirty miles away at Elliott. After examining the stripped and broken fan belt and refilling the radiator we settled down in the shade of the Toyota, waiting for someone to come along. The heat is stupefying. It is an unwritten rule in the outback, which we hadn't overlooked, always take plenty of water with you.

The first vehicle to come along was a tourist bus, going in the opposite direction. They couldn't help us with a fan belt but give us a few cold bottles of soft drink out of their fridge and promise to report where we are when they reached Renner Springs.

But our problems were solved in next to no time when a PMG Landcruiser came along carrying more spare parts than a local garage. We soon had a new fan belt in place with the linesmen telling us that they would radio Renner Springs that we were now okay.

The scenery of Central Australia is harsh, arid, with a grandeur that in comparison, for me anyway, pales the soft colours of a Victorian or Tasmanian countryside into insipidity. This strange and ancient landscape draws me back time and time again. Already tourism has changed The Alice. I only hope that's where it ends.

We push on through what is known as the 'Mulga Mile' because of the number of vehicles that have skidded off it in the mulga. As we drive through the long drought that has dried out most of the country, mulga and spinifex make rare green patches on the expanse of bare red earth. And as we push on, here and there, surprisingly, are pleasant glades carpeted with daisies, set among the belts of open plain and low stony hills. There is no surface water at all to be seen as we travel through this expanse, but the sight of rabbits and an occasional kangaroo show us that there must be wells or soaks somewhere.

Though arid, this country is far from being desert. Only an inch or two of rain is needed in the hills to turn the creek beds into foaming brown torrents and carpet the red ground with a variety of herbage.

An old utility loaded with Abos flagged us down and put the bite on us for some petrol. They offered to pay for it with an eight-foot spotted perenti lizard, which one of the old gins described as 'bloody good tucker, boss'. They told us they were going to the Santa Teresa Mission. We gave them some petrol and a packet of tobacco and papers, but declined the offer of the lizard. I suppose it's a tribute to progress that most of them now own motor vehicles, but somehow the silly bastards never quite seem to grasp that unless the petrol tank has something in it the engine won't go. They're always running out of fuel.

Wrecks of cars and stripped vehicles dotted the side of the road as we made our way north. Crashes are common along this highway, many of them fatal, and the reasons are not hard to find. Some come to grief when they collide with a huge bullock, but even more dangerous is the soporific effect of the road itself. Mile follows mile in everlasting sameness. It stretches ahead, often as straight as an arrow, with a surface so perfect it is an incitement to speed. After a few hours you find your head nodding, or your eyes closing momentarily, and it's time to pull up and have a quick snooze or wipe your face with a wet towel. Otherwise you find yourself trying to negotiate an all-too-rare bend only to find your reflexes are welded in place and not responding properly.

It seemed to take for ever but, finally, pandanus, thicker scrub and greener vegetation beside the track told us we were getting closer to home. Then we were through the last patch of thick bush and Katy squealed with delight when she saw the old gate come into sight.

'We're here! . . . Look there's the gate.'

Nothing had changed and everything was as we had left it. That is, except the chooks. Jesus, they'd shat all over the verandah and the railing. They were roosting in the lower branches of the trees. And a mother hen with a brood of chickens came out from under the house. So much for me worrying about the hawks and snakes.

They came running from everywhere as we got out of the Toyota, the old ones at first, and then the rest of them. We'd originally had one rooster, now there were a dozen of the buggers.

'Look at all my chooks,' Katy said in complete wonderment.

'Yeah,' I said, 'and a bloody few of 'em will be going into the pot too.'

It took a long while to unload all the supplies, but when they were all in we sat down and had a cool drink.

'I can't get over this,' Katy said, waving a couple of pieces of paper in the air.

It was Percy's parting gift to us—a ninety-nine year lease on 3,000 acres, and we were sitting smack bang in the middle of them. Not only that, but he had supplied us with one of the latest digital radios, including a phone link. Once I got a decent aerial up we could talk to any part of the country.

We had our evening meal on the cool of the verandah and in the last blue light of day, as the sun started to set, we both felt it was good to be home.

36

IN THE TOP END THERE ARE ONLY TWO SEASONS, THE 'Wet' and the 'Dry'. The Wet lasts from October to early April and is characterised by monsoons and torrential rain. It was our second Wet since we'd been back when the trouble started.

We'd been up to Darwin for a week getting supplies and had reached the top of the road at Bushmans Peak, about fifty miles from home. I changed down to third and took the Landcruiser down on compression and some brake, swung left following the road and felt like a banking pilot as I looked down on the true waste of the land that runs along the eastern side of the Territory. The road was covered in puddles that sprayed up the sides of the vehicle in brown geysers.

The road straightened and we dipped down on to the valley floor. Saplings bowed and prayed as we rolled past them on the narrow track. Then we were out of the hills and into the flat country. I slowed down to thirty as we approached our turn-off.

When I turned onto our track I slammed on the brakes and turned the wheel as I negotiated a soft patch of grass and sand. The tyres sank, spun, came free, and we rolled on through the thick bush. The speedometer wobbled undecidedly between five and ten miles an hour.

The Toyota sank again. I fed petrol to the engine, changed down and straightened the wheel. The Cruiser slewed like a crab and climbed out of the soft ruts of its own making. There was not even a track any more, just a narrow corridor of red earth that looked pretty greasy. I pulled up and switched off and told Katy I'd go forward on foot and check it out.

I climbed out just as a bunch of parrots went screeching overhead, and walked along in the baking heat which quivered in front of me like a fevered dream.

'What's it look like?' Katy yelled.

I lifted my head and blinked the sweat out of my eyes.

'Pretty shitty, but we'll have a go,' I yelled back.

I had just about reached the Toyota when I heard the sound of a helicopter as it growled out of the north. It passed half a mile west of us and began to sweep back. As I hopped in behind the wheel, started the engine and moved ahead along the track, it started to rain again.

Crash! The right-hand rear window of the Toyota exploded in a shower of glass. Twoong twoong. Two holes appeared in the front of the bonnet. And then we heard the chopper overhead. I swung the wheel left and ploughed a new tunnel through the scrub, dodging between the big timber till the going got too soft and we slithered to a stop under the trees. The chopper was forced to climb. I grabbed the rifle and webbing and opened the door.

'Get out!' I yelled. 'Quick!'

'Jimmy!' Katy stood with her hands to her ears as the roar of the helicopter's engine thundered directly overhead. The trees trembled and leaves showered to the ground.

She was becoming hysterical.

'Jimmy, for God's sake, it's no good any more. They've got us!'

'Bullshit! Get the money out of the front.' I had to shout to make myself heard. I fired two rounds up through the trees, hoping to score a hit on the underside of the chopper. Something worked because it veered away and climbed out of sight. The rain started to come down heavier and streamed down Katy's face.

The chopper kept making passes over the tops of the trees.

I grabbed Katy's hand and dragged her over behind a solid tree. 'Wait here, and don't move away.'

Running back to the Toyota, I opened the rear door. The chopper was back overhead again. Good, I thought, stay there you bastard.

I was moving all the time, crouching under the tumult just overhead and wondered when they'd open up again and feel a bullet strike me.

I flung myself into the back of the Landcruiser, hands ripping things aside frantically, trying to get at the tool box. I threw the tow rope over the front and shoved the groceries out of the way. Finally I managed to open the box and grab a cold chisel, but I couldn't find the fuckin' hammer. I grabbed a tyre lever. Fuck 'em, I thought. Then I was on my back, slithering like a snake on the mud under the Toyota's tail, feeling a stone grind into one shoulderblade and the clammy touch of the wet earth.

Katy was calling but I paid her no attention. The narrow chipped blade of the chisel was hard up against the underside of the petrol tank. I swept the tyre lever up hard, with a short blow. The tank boomed. A dent appeared. Mud spattered onto my face. I set the chisel into the dent, tensed myself, swept the lever up once more. A slight cut appeared this time. A teardrop of petrol appeared and fell lightly onto my chest.

Once more I grabbed the tyre lever. One of the edges had a burr on it and it cut into my hand, stinging. I swung my arm again with the lever. The tank reverberated again but the chisel had gone right through, the force of the blow crushing my fingers up against the tank. Petrol gushed out and I rolled away from it, crawling out from under the vehicle and scampering on all fours like a chimpanzee, bending my head awkwardly to look for the thundering danger overhead. If anything, the helicopter was lower than ever. I could just make out its dark hugeness through the thrashing foliage.

I darted back around to the back of the Toyota and grabbed the gallon tin of lawnmower fuel and, undoing the lid, let it run and merge with the spreading pool that was widening under the vehicle. Then I trailed it back to the big tree, like a liquid fuse.

I danced out of the way as it spread and soaked into the earth. Now . . . I took the matches and held four together.

'Get ready to run!' I bellowed at Katy.

I didn't wait for her nod. The matches flared and I shoved them into the petrol trail.

We made six scrambling paces away from the tree and I looked up above the Toyota at the leafy cover. For a moment I thought the matches hadn't done the job.

Then, whooooomp! The leaves were gone. It was as though a hand had swiped a cloth across a slate. And for just a moment I saw the dark rain-glistening belly of the helicopter no more than twenty feet above the vehicle. I made out the letters HVF 701 printed on its underside as a pointed yellow finger reached up and touched the helicopter. The paint smoked, popped, and turned a dirty colour. Then a giant hand seemed to lift it up in the air in the rushing cloud of oily petrol smoke that rushed straight up and engulfed it.

Shouldering the webbing and rifle again, I grabbed Katy's free hand and pulled her along in a slithering gait. Panting, grinning my delight. 'Run!' I yelled and pointed towards the south-west with the arm that held the rifle.

Impelled by the danger behind us, we laboured over the rain-slippery track, through clutching scrub, over treacherous rock strewn ground . . . until we somehow reached the base of a nearby hill. We scrambled our way up, looking down on the smouldering fire of the Toyota, the streamer of black smoke that tore away towards the south-west, and the helicopter fluttering beyond it like a wind-driven butterfly.

Breath sawed in and out of our lungs. The rain coursed down our faces. I tried to grin at Katy to give her some confidence. I felt elemental, all powerful.

'Those fuckin' bastards have got enough to do without watching us.' There was a great ache in my chest as though a balloon was being inflated inside it. 'Come on Katy,' I gasped, 'we've got some fuckin' walking to do.'

Neither of us moved. 'For Christ's sake, let's go,' I said, but I buckled over and put my hands on my knees.

Katy's hair clung to her face.

'You never used to talk like that to me.'

I just swung my drooping head from side to side.

'We've got no time for manners, love.'

'You've changed, Jimmy, you're not the same.' Her eyes glowed at me out of her pale face. 'You're going mad looking after this money and me.'

I straightened. 'Have I?' I saw her distantly, as though I was looking at her through the wrong end of a spyglass. The world spun and threatened to throw me off. But I took a deep breath and hung on.

'Look Katy.' It was my voice talking, although I heard it from a distance. 'I know a place, we've got to go on.' I tried to smile at her. 'We've got to get out of this rain. It's not a hell of a lot further. Do it for me please love. We can win this. It will work.'

'It can't work, we'll never win.' She looked like a little girl. 'I've always known we couldn't win. But I'll do it for you.'

'Why?'

'You know bloody why.'

I went to her and put my arms around her. 'Katy, I . . .'

'Jimmy.'

406

We clung together like that for a moment.

'All right, boss,' Katy said at last. 'Let's go. Which way?'

I pointed nor-east and we began to walk.

Two hours later the helicopter found us again just as we entered a thin belt of trees that led to good cover. It swooped down from the north behind us, the noise of its arrival lost in the wind until it was almost overhead. The grass at our feet writhed under the downdraft of the rotor blades. Rain-spray was flung like shining tears, and our sodden clothing crawled about on our skin.

Katy dropped the bag with our money in it and we stood together, craning our necks at the huge smudged dragonfly hovering above us.

'So that's it, Jimmy!' Katy put her arms around me. She had to shout to make herself heard.

'No I won't just give in.' Rain ran down my face and dripped off my chin. And the wet collar on my shirt was fluttering like a pulse.

'Jimmy, no, damn you!' Katy held my arm with both hands, keeping me back. 'I've done all the crazy things you wanted me to do. But let it end here, together, they've got us and it's over.' She peered at me through the rain, smiling hesitantly, shouting above the over-head tumult as though I was a difficult child. 'Listen carefully, Jimmy. You can't win any more!'

I cut her off. 'I'm not fuckin' finished yet, Katy, and neither are you. So come on.'

'Hell!' Katy dropped her hands. 'Should I be proud of you, Jimmy?'

Although I was buggered I smiled at her. 'If you reckon I'm worth it.'

'I think you are,' she sniffed. 'But we're both fucking crazy.'

We got in under thicker foliage and slogged our way forward. At the foot of a sharp short rise I pushed Katy down between some huge stones and told her to stay put. Then I scrambled my way up to the top. There was a rocky outcropping and I made my way across to it, but I was spotted from the air.

Falling forward among the rocks, I slithered into a spot that would offer me some cover.

'You bastard!' I said as I swung the .308 up at the approaching chopper.

The lens of the scope settled on the bubble of the perspex canopy, then the chopper turned side-on to give the guy with the rifle a shot. The scope was in line with the shining disc of the tail rotor, quartered exactly by the cross-hairs, and I squeezed off a shot.

I heard the vicious clang and the helicopter immediately moved out of its steady pattern, rising straight up towards the clouds with an irregular, weaving motion. The engine howled. I must have hit the gyros. The machine spun, dipped, rose again. Then it seemed to go into a continual spin and fell into the trees about a quarter of a mile away. The explosion when it hit sent a shock wave hurling pieces of timber and helicopter straight up in the air. After the bright orange flash came a thick black pall of smoke that rose straight up and then drifted away. I ran back down the hill to Katy.

'Got the bastard,' I said.

We sat down on the ground, absolutely stuffed. I put my arm around her, lifted her chin and kissed her rain-sodden face. Then I lifted my knees and let my head fall on them. When I glanced up at Katy, she had her head back letting the rain fall onto her face and into her open mouth.

I nudged her with my elbow. 'You know what?'

'What?'

'I feel horny.'

'You're impossible. You are kidding me, aren't you?'

'You're not wrong.' I said, panting, and we both started to laugh.

It was slow going, but we finally made it back to the house. Inside, we stripped off our wet gear and towelled each other dry. Then sat naked out on the verandah watching the monsoon rain cascade down.

I went inside and brought out two beers.

'How many people were in that helicopter?'

'I saw three,' I said.

'Well, shouldn't we radio somebody?'

'Radio who?'

'The police or someone.'

'The fuckin' police! Listen Katy, as far as I am concerned we never even saw a bloody helicopter.'

'Well how are we going to explain it?'

'Explain it! . . . Explain it to who? Are you on the bloody wacky baccy again? We never saw a fucking helicopter. Okay?'

'What about the bodies?'

'Well what about them?'

'You don't think any of them could still be alive?'

'Love . . . as remote as that is, if one of them was alive they wouldn't be in any condition to do anything, believe me.'

'When you said you knew a place where no-one would find us, did you just say it to make me feel better, to go on?'

'I wasn't bullshitting. It's the truth.'

'How far away is it?'

I pointed out across the lagoon, 'You see that line of hills over there?'

'Yes how far away are they?'

'About seven miles.'

'And that's where it is?'

'Yeah, we found it one day when we were out walking. It was pure chance. I followed a couple of rock wallabies, found the trail, and bingo.'

'When you say we, was it you and Carmel?'

I nodded.

Katy said nothing and I knew she thought she'd touched a raw nerve.

'I'm going to take us there,' I said. And she reached out and squeezed my hand.

Two days later, we slogged it out to the main road and hitchhiked into Borroloola. There was talk of a missing plane, but I took no part in the gossip. I rang Percy, gave him the details of what had happened and asked him for a few things that I could not obtain through regular channels. He told me that he'd get the stuff to me by road transport in the next few days.

I rang Darwin and ordered a diesel generator and all

the gear that we'd need to electrify the house. Then we booked into the motel that night, and in the morning caught the bus up to Darwin. We had to get another vehicle, and we finally settled on a Nissan Patrol.

Over the next two weeks Katy and I worked with a vengeance. And when we had finished our tasks we were satisfied that the security of the place was improved tenfold.

When this work was over I decided to make a second retreat. That night I told Katy I'd take her to the hiding spot the next day.

She got pretty excited about the whole idea, and we set out early before the heat set in. The going was not that difficult. The path we took led us away from the tidal creek and soon we found ourselves in drier country, though it was green enough because of the rain. Narrow outcrops of red and orange stone came up out of the ground, some of them rearing above the trees. In the dry sandy run-offs we saw the tracks of kangaroo and buffalo. After ninety minutes we reached the gently sloping face of a large hill and started to climb. By nine we had scaled a ridge of reddish orange rock and could see the tidal creek winding through the scrub below. We stopped for a drink and a breather. An hour later we were on top of a spur that jutted out from an escarpment.

At first sight, it appeared that the slope led directly to the foot of a rock face, but if you travelled further along it, the incline slowly lessened and eventually levelled out completely. After that the bush became thick with moist tangled vegetation, some of it above head height. What we were walking through was a giant

411

overhang. But to anyone watching from a distance, the rock face gave the impression that it rose up straight and true. The rock behind us was sheer and the roof was in deep shadow as we walked along a cavern that stretched into the rocky hillside. Fifty yards further on we heard the first sound of the water. The dripping foliage closed quietly behind us, while in front of us lay a scene that was almost unreal.

The ground dropped away sharply to a large emerald waterhole which caught and enhanced the colours of the rich greenery that surrounded it. The waterhole, forming the floor of a small abscess in the mountainous rocky hill, was cut off from the outer world except by the path we had just used. It was only in the late afternoon that the sinking sun could shine through the rocky, horizontal slit that formed the entrance. Only then did its rays illuminate the large waterhole and the single cascade of silver water that fed it, twisting and glinting as it fell from the black rock one hundred feet above. Here the wind played strange tricks, the entrance acting as a venturi with swirling gusts carrying white jewelled droplets from the waterfall.

It would be impossible to know of the existence of this place from the outside. The escarpment top overhung it, the flat red plain on the far side of the hills was too distant, and an aircraft would never travel close enough to spot it . . . even assuming it was at the right height in the right place at the right time.

Relieved, we started down to the waterhole. We had worked hard these last weeks and we were beginning to feel the strain. The cooler air chilled us a little as we began our descent, its moisture dampening our clothes.

The place was certainly eerie. Puffballs and orange fungoid growths squelched obscenely underfoot, and the high walls of the cavern were covered in places with multi-coloured moss. Up on the roof dark rows of bats hung upside down from the rock, but the air circulated too freely for any smell except the clean coolness of the water. Katy and I stood there beside the pool, looking at ourselves in the mirror surface, mesmerised. Then we dumped the supplies we had carried in and put them aside. If the worst came to the worst, once we were inside this place no one would find us. It would seem that we had just vanished off the face of the earth.

Sitting on the verandah back at the house, we had our feet up on the rail and Katy and I were blowing a joint.

'Wonder how Jacko's doing?' Katy said to me out of the blue.

Jacko . . . my mind took in a picture of him and flashed back to 1967. He and I had first met in Vietnam. We were in the same battalion, but different companies, and had both been through the Special Operations Group training school, but at different times. We decided that when we had our R&R we would take it in Bangkok, but our trip there was just about Jacko's last.

As with much of the violence in life, the affair had started as nothing, a matter from which all concerned could have walked away unscathed. The Flying Goose was a clipjoint in the heart of Bangkok's red-light district. The street outside catered for every type of perversion the Oriental mind could dream up.

Perfumed joss hung heavy in the humid air and beggars squatted close to the buildings on either side, their disfigurements displayed to the best advantage, for pity's sake. Their faces half-obscured by their conical hats, vendors tended the flickering fires of their cooking carts, and skewered satay crackled in the flames, ready to dip into bubbling bowls of peanut and chilli sauce. Young boys touted their sisters or their brothers or themselves. Girls, some of whom were boys, sat on high stools, their cheongsams split to the waist and nothing remarkable showing in the way of underwear. It was all there to be seen, to be believed. Dope to smoke, eat or mainline. Things to do or have done. Until the small hours the bicycle rickshaws and taxis brought the punters in. Many were sailors who had dreamt of this night for scores of nights in a narrow, rolling bunk. Then there were the blokes like us here on R&R. Australian and American soldiers looking for fun. All of them determined to get the best or the worst out of the city's infamous night-life. And sometimes there were embassy people, for a stroll around the quarter was as much a part of Bangkok as a walk along Bondi beach or Kings Cross was in Sydney.

When we first encountered it, Jacko and I found the nocturnal activity of the red-light area as strange as having a shit in bed. No one troubled us, we were obviously not locals, so we were treated as a source of money and were offered everything. But in this part of town, rarely an hour went by without some absurd, tragic or ugly incident that shed a little light on the myriad facets of the human psyche.

The singer was just finishing her routine as Jacko

414

came out of the dunny. A heavy smell of perfume, alcohol, incense and cigarette smoke hung in the air. Jacko had just made his way around the edge of the tiny dance floor to where we were sitting. Prior to this two girls from the chorus line had joined us. They didn't start work till 12.30. Mei and Suki were both pretty and nicely put together. Jacko kept slipping his hand into the warmth between Mei's legs in the darkness under the table, and she opened her legs to allow him better access, chatting and laughing as if nothing out of the ordinary was happening while her natural juices welled.

But as it happened, Jacko never did get back to the table. A babble of raised voices came from his left, and a man leapt to his feet into the passageway. He was well-dressed, with a dark Oriental face, Cambodian or Vietnamese. Beer had spilt all down the front of his suit and more was slopping from the glass in his hand. Jacko cannoned right into him and the man fell over backwards, landing comically on the floor. A howl of laughter went up and Jacko reached down and proffered a hand, but the man knocked it violently out of the way and scrambled to his feet. His face had gone blue-white in the low lighting of the club and the hubbub of conversation died away. A group of American soldiers on the other side of the floor turned to face the action.

'Is that guy mad, or is he . . .?'

'Sock it to him, baby!'

'Ten bucks says the kid goes through the ceiling!'

The man pushed aside the waitress who was trying ineffectually to wipe his suit, and came right out in English.

415

'You stupid young bastard. Why the hell you don't watch where you're going?'

Jacko knew there was going to be trouble. Over the man's shoulder he glanced at me quickly, looking for reassurance that I would watch his back. I shot him a wink and a slight nod of my head.

Then all the SOG training he had received jumped into his actions. His feet slid apart to a distance of about twenty inches, toes turned slightly towards each other, knees bent. In unarmed combat it was called the position of the horse. His weight was all on the big muscles at the back of his thighs.

'It was you who fuckin' run into me, mate,' Jacko said.

The man broke into a swift discourse in his native tongue, then threw his glass on the floor. There was a hush over the room. Jacko kept his eyes on the other man's face and waited.

The signal, when it came, was a tensing of the neck. Jacko sensed the blow coming and turned from the waist. His left hand, open-palmed, deflected the man's forearm into empty space. At the same time, Jacko countered, his blow starting with the elbow of his right arm in line with his sternum. His fist snapped forward a maximum of six inches, and when his arm straightened the flat surface of his knuckles flicked upwards, making an angle of forty-five degrees between the top of his forearm and the base of his thumb. The blow was too quick for the eye to follow, and looked too simple to hurt. It was part of the infighting technique we had been taught. The power of the blow was designed to expend itself half an inch behind the struck

416

surface and, properly delivered, carried a poundage equal to one and a half times the body weight of the user.

There was a hell of a crunch of splintering bone and the man's nose simply disappeared under a gush of blood. His high scream blew droplets of blood over three tables, and then, clutching his face, he fell to the floor like a dead man.

The silence seemed to last for ever. The Americans were frozen in their seats. One of them exhaled softly, and the sound carried.

'Je . . . sus!'

Jacko felt my arm pushing him towards the exit. He realised that after the blow he'd just been standing there, and made a conscious effort to pull himself together. Behind us an uproar of sound welled up the stairs in pursuit. Once in the street we both ran into the maze of alleys and made for the taxi stand on the corner of the next block. Before we got there we both stopped, leaning forward with our hands on our knees, panting.

'We'd better get back to the pub, Jimmy.'

I nodded slowly. 'Christ what a mess.'

The man had come forward under his own momentum, and moved into the blow. One of the basic precepts drummed into us from the word go was to immobilise your adversary at the first opportunity. Sometimes there was never a second chance.

The radio later that morning offered the news that a visiting businessman from Singapore had been struck down during a club brawl the night before. He had choked in his own blood before help could be summoned. A local youth was said to be helping police with their inquiries. We heard no more about it.

'I don't think we've got to worry too much about Jacko,' I said to Katy. 'He can take care of himself all right.'

37

IN THE DARKNESS OF THE NIGHT I NUDGED KATY, SLEEPING at my side on the cave floor.

'Katy hey! Come on, wake up!'

'Huh?' She moved restlessly. Then full consciousness came and she jerked upright.

'Jimmy, what's the matter?'

The tiny fire winked, and Katy's eyes were pockets of shadow.

'I've got to go out again and see what's going on.'

'Okay, wait till I get up.'

She got up, and her legs were so stiff that she over-balanced and nearly fell.

'I've got to go to the toilet,' she said, then ducked through the cave's small shrub-whisked entrance and groped her way outside.

It was quite cool inside this cavern, and I was trying to build the fire up when she came back in.

'You all right?' I asked her.

'I'm all right,' she said and knelt down next to me.

'Not much wood here,' I said.

'There's a limit to the amount of dry wood I could find in here . . . Any other complaints, you put them in writing to the management, I just work here.'

In the last darkness before dawn I lay crouched in a

cairn of rocks that I'd created and camouflaged. It had a commanding view of the flat land between the cavern and the house. I was warm and very nearly dry. The light rain spilled off a simple but effective overhead shelter above the rocks.

Curled within a nest of boulders like a great cat waiting to pounce, I purred like a tiger and felt like one as I thought of the coming dawn. I had found them yesterday afternoon when the light was too bad for a shot, and then they had disappeared into a jumble of boulders. Now I was camped virtually above them, about 300 yards away, hidden beneath the cover of some scrubby trees high on top of the escarpment. I lay scanning the surrounding flats below me through a pair of powerful Litton night and day field glasses.

We first heard the crash of the gate when they came, and we were out of the house and away before they got a chance to open up for a kill shot. They saw the direction in which we were headed and sent a couple of rounds after us that passed harmlessly overhead.

There would be no trouble in the morning, I knew. The two guys would have to find us. I didn't have to do anything, just sit tight and let them come. There would be plenty of opportunity for those few last simple shots.

I smiled out into the night, waiting for pre-dawn light. Lying down in amongst the rocks I heard the hum, croak and chatter of the nocturnal insects replaced by the screech and buzz of the daytime wildlife.

From my position on top of the overhang, I had a commanding view of the valley floor and the drama being played out on it. It was like watching toy soldiers being moved around a game board . . . except that these were no toys and the penalty for a wrong move was death.

'Here they come,' I said softly as they emerged out of the boulders. Determined not to give my position away, I stayed still. Seconds became minutes. A fly walked along my neck. A wasp buzzed in my face. But I didn't move. It was hot in the rocks now and I was sweating. It ran into my eyes. I gradually passed an arm over them and brought the power scope up and had another look . . . Shit! there's three of them. Urgency overtook me. It was imperative that I do something while I can see them all. Keep them together.

They seemed like dolls from this distance. Three dolls dressed in dirty clothes. Two of them carried rifles, the other a hand gun, as they seemed to meander idly towards me. With the scope trained on them I could see their lips working, but couldn't hear their voices.

One of them pointed up in my direction. I watched the dolls getting bigger as they threaded their way towards me.

The scope picked up rear movement and a fourth doll appeared—not from out of the boulders, but standing on top of one with a pair of binoculars and a rifle slung over his shoulder. Dressed neatly compared to the rest, he was slim, booted and ruggedly clad.

It's not too late, I thought, as I brought the scope back onto the three out front. The sound of the shots would be washed away for a moment in the stiff breeze that was blowing into my face. I lined up on the tail ender. Take him out first. The high-powered Omark coughed, the big sausage-sized silencer muting the bark of the rifle, and the tail ender became rag, then just dropped. The one in front of him turned, feeling the danger and the whiplash crack of the 7.62 mm round. I flicked the trigger and a fraction of a second later the shot was followed by the buckling of his body. As he toppled, the leader of the three crouched down behind a bush, then crabbed it across to another, but I could see him. And then he opened up and there was a sudden thunderous racket as he fired up the rocky hill in an indiscriminate fashion. I lined him up and touched the trigger for the third time. The bullet took him above the right eye and he sagged down onto the ground in a crumpled heap.

The fourth one had come down off the rock and was firing up towards the top of the rocky outcrop fifty yards away from me. I could hear the rounds ricocheting with a tweee sound.

I lined up on him just as he flicked back the bolt of his rifle . . . I watched the empty brass cartridge case as it made an arc through the air. The bolt was coming forward again with a neat, unhurried precision. It was a longer distance than the other three and I fired off a quick burst. Four bullets hit him in a line up his body, shattering a kneecap, a hip, penetrating the stomach and piercing one lung. He let the rifle drop quite idly and then followed it in a long sprawl, hitting the ground and seeming to bounce before becoming still. Then his good leg started to move.

I collected myself, stood up slowly and made my

way down the path. The first three were dead, but the last was still hanging on. In great pain. I rolled him over with my boot and he screamed.

I aimed the Omark down between his eyes and he looked up past it at me.

'Who gave the orders this time?' I asked him.

'Go fuck yourself,' he rasped, with blood dribbling out of his mouth. Air was whistling through the hole in his chest and lung. The shirt around the wound was bloodsoaked, and the torn edges lifted up like the petals of a valve when the air pushed out through the puncture.

I placed my boot on the smashed knee and applied a little pressure. His scream rose into the air, then was cut off as blood in his throat turned it into a gurgle.

I repeated the question.

'The boss sent us,' he gasped out.

'What fuckin' boss? Vitelli and Agostini are dead.'

Then he blurted it out in gasps and moans. The real villain behind the scenes. The guy you can't get near. Protected by rank. The powerbroker behind the throne who achieves all with the privilege of rank and station. Beyond reproach. Virtually untouchable. I shot his henchman.

As I looked round the horizon, my eyes slitted against the startling brightness. I saw the long, curved skyline where blue and white struck up an uneasy empathy. I saw my own and Katy's future offering little more than desolation and death unless I did something about it. To do that I was going to need help, but I was confident that I could arrange it.

I slung the Omark round my neck and stooped to

423

pick up the dead man's legs. Our saurian friends would dine well again.

Later that evening I sat on the verandah of the house, deep in thought. What was the motivation that had started all this? All I succeeded in doing was collecting fuel for my own self-pity. All those years ago I had a choice of action, but here I was lamenting the loss of something that was never mine. Love and understanding, listening to others, hearing their views..My whole fuckin' life was corrupt.

I lit a cigarette and thought about the name I had heard that morning.

It's not just me, I thought, the whole fuckin' system is corrupt. Our government ministers come to office knowing they have a job expectancy of four years if they're lucky, so they set about collecting as many hand-outs as possible in the time allowed.

Perhaps that was why I was never able to see what was wrong. I was out of time. I had become an anachronism, alienated by my own bitterness. I was playing by the rules that were set down twenty years ago, but nobody else was. Times and people had changed and I was standing still. I had reached a stage where I could no longer judge people as individuals. I was anti-social. I despised so many people just because they were people, and judged everybody by their worst performance.

Motives, I thought. What about motives? I don't even understand my own and I suddenly realised that most of the ones I had known in the past were for the wrong reason.

It isn't easy to live with so many regrets.

In the morning I decided to go for a walk. I'd hardly slept and I was angry as I plunged through the light scrub at the back of the house. Leaves slashed at me in my haste to be alone and a small branch hooked my shirt sleeve, which tore as I wrenched it loose. Splashing ankle-deep through an area of bogged marshy ground, I scrambled over an old dilapidated fence.

I flushed a pheasant in some long grass in a small clearing, rearing back as it rocketed out in a cackle of indignation, watching its short-winged bumblebee flight with blurred concentration. Heading forward, I entered a stand of tall light vegetation where the shade was flecked and dappled with sunlight. It was a hall of airy palm trees on the edge of a narrow stream where water rushed busily away, and in its garden-party shade I lay slumped, with my head and shoulders against the bole of one of the palms. And I started to rethink my position.

I don't know how long I stayed there before Katy's voice broke me out of my reverie. But I had the answers I was looking for.

'What are you doing here all alone?' Katy asked when she finally found me.

'I needed to rethink my position, love. I have to get away from here for a while, and so do you.'

'What are we going to do?'

'Do you get seasick?'

'Well I haven't been yet, but I've only been on a Manly ferry.'

'How would you like to go sailing? Not forever, just

for a cruise around the coast? It's pretty sheltered inside the reefs.'

'What do you know about boats?'

'Jesus, love, I spent most of my early life on my foster dad's trawlers. I know enough.'

My mind went back to those days with old Dad. Thirty to forty miles off the coast the Pacific was blue-green, opaque, and secretive. The breeze moist and warm.

Frantic gulls worked the rippling wake from the nets, wafting spread-winged and white-bellied, watching for the snapping leap of an escaping prawn. Dipping and diving, splashing down, complaining loudly at their unsuccessful efforts, they fled quickly and quietly when rewarded with a flicking morsel. Their cries gave harmony and balance to the muffled thrumming of the *Winona*'s diesels while the chop-slosh of the deep-vee hull provided rhythm to the swirl of life and death.

The *Winona*, sixty-four feet of steel and petroleum-based science, rode blue and salt-scoured black upon the open sea. She was like a leviathan wading heavy-legged, dipping eight degrees to port, eight degrees to starboard, eight degrees to port.

We groped our way through the glare and drone, moving with an economy of motion common to those who exist in grudging compromise with the bounty, famine, peace and violence of deep-water living.

Old Dad would kick the brake lever on the winch and the bright green nets, weighted by chains and heavy wooden sleds, would drop to the surface of the murky sea with a splash. Hundreds of metres of wire cable were then played out before old Dad put the brake on the winch. The heavy sleds would dive below the foaming surface and slow the trawler down with their descent. Both nets would spread wide and, fishing from both sides, the *Winona* would resume her stiff-legged gait. Yes, I remembered it well.

'We wouldn't sink or anything?' Katy asked.

I really couldn't blame her for asking.

'We'll be right as rain, love.'

'Where are you going to get the boat from?'

'It's Percy's pride and joy.'

'Where is it?'

'Cairns.'

'You sure he'll let you use it?'

'Stake my life on it.'

She jumped up and gave a little jig.

'Yeah, why not?' she said. 'When are we going?'

'Right now,' I replied, 'but you've got a bit of driving to do on the way. We've got to take the Land Rover that those bastards arrived in and get rid of it.'

'How?'

'Park it on the side of the road. It'll be stripped in less than twenty-four hours.'

Four hours later we were on the highway and headed for the Three-Ways.

38

WE STOOD ON THE DOCK OF THE MARLIN MARINA IN
Cairns, casting our eyes over Percy's boat.

Skedaddle, he'd named it, and her lines were an
interesting blend of traditional and modern. From
what I could see and my past knowledge of boats I was
certain she'd been designed as a genuine cruising sail-
boat. With a powerful diesel motor, she would be well
mannered, comfortable and fast. Boasting the traditional aft cockpit, raked bow, and sleek low profile
ending in a straight-cut stern, she made a lovely picture
with her royal blue hull, white cabin top, wooden deck
and stainless fittings, wheel and instruments. She was
enough to win the heart and respect of anybody who
fancied himself a sailor and loved the sea. I spent a few
extra minutes walking around the dock, unwilling to
rush those first few minutes of pleasurable impact the
boat had on me.

Moments later, Katy and I stepped aboard and carried out a thorough examination. It was a great boat,
thirty-six feet and with a beam of eleven and a half. The
inside accommodation was a joy to behold . . . a large
U-shaped aft galley with overhead glass and dish racks,
a navigation centre with a swing-away seat, five berths,
a carpeted main saloon with a fold-away drop-leaf

table and a full headroom shower with a seat. I checked the gauges and noted the 300 gallons of fresh water and 400 gallons of diesel fuel.

With Katy in tow, I looked at the carefully stowed sails, all proofed against mildew, examined the ventilators and chain locker, then returned to the deck and quickly checked the halyards and sheets, the winch and the guard rails, the anchor and chain and the rubber dingy stowed across the hatch roof. I opened the engine cover and looked at the massive diesel . . . a little larger than necessary but capable of giving a good seventeen knots.

'Jimmy, do you think we can sail this?' Katy swung her arms to encompass the boat.

I nodded. 'Yep, no worries, she's a real lady. Want to get going?' I went below and got the charts out and put the local one on the chart table.

Ten minutes later, running on the diesel, we had passed the first light marker. The wind was a gentle sailing breeze from the nor-west and the surface was choppy, with hardly any swell. We had three days on our own before Percy and his wife Amy were to join us for a week.

Once we had passed the last light marker the wind freshened and swung away from the starboard beam towards the stern. I switched off the diesel and gave Katy running instructions as we got the sails set. We were streaking through the water now, on a broad reach . . . almost running before the wind. She responded like a dog freed from a chain.

Katy was having a ball, standing up at the bow, looking out over the water.

A little after six we realised that we weren't just hungry, but ravenous. Leaving Katy at work in the galley, I returned to the deck, automatically checking the position of the sails as I cleared the hatch, then set the auto-pilot. I checked the radar. There were two vessels on the scope, both well astern and slightly to starboard. After I set the radar on the five-mile collision setting, there was nothing left to do. So we sat in the saloon and enjoyed a dinner of steak and eggs.

There was a full moon and the night was warm. Around ten we noticed an inlet on the port side. We dropped the sails and running on the diesel, with the alarm set on the depth finder, we made our way in and anchored for the night.

We made love out on the open deck and the moon and stars bore witness. Then we lay in a couple of deckchairs and drank some wine and talked quietly to each other.

I explained what I hoped to achieve for both of us, and that the whole thing hinged on Percy.

Three glorious days and nights later it was time to pick up Perce and his wife. We had arranged to meet them at Port Douglas not at Cairns, where Percy was well known. I didn't want it known that we were getting our heads together.

That night, anchored on the sheltered side of Green Island, with the girls sharing a drink in the salon, Percy and I sat out on deck with a couple of beers.

'William Passini and Fredrick Branco are the bastards who did the dirty work up at Port Douglas for Rissi. I've got an address and it's been kept under wraps. If you want them they're yours. I've got all the details inside.'

'Are they connected? Or just freelance?'

'Passini was Agostini's contact in Sydney. We've got pictures of them together, but the rest is just conjecture.'

'You're sure it's them?'

'There's no shadow of doubt whatsoever.'

Percy reached into his back pocket, pulled out some folded pages of paper and flicked them onto the table in front of me.

'I thought you might like to read that before you do anything.'

I opened the pages up and under the glow of the deck light my blood went cold.

TO AIC GRAINGER YOUR EYES ONLY.
FROM AGENT J.C. BRADLEY.
SUBJECT HOMICIDE. *Fowler, Donna Maree; and Abbot, Marianne.*

At 0848 hours the undersigned received notification from Communications Division to investigate the remains of two females at Port Douglas, Qld.

The undersigned, in company with Agent Morris Walker, arrived at the scene at 0918 hours. Which is situated at Lot 3 Park St, Port Douglas. Upon our arrival the residence, and the evidence, had been secured by Agent G.Graham.

Our investigation supplemented the findings of Agent G.Graham, and revealed the following: Retrieved from the boot of a Ford Falcon Reg. No. PMU 166, which was located behind the residence at Lot 3 Park St, were six large green plastic garbage bags containing two dismembered female human corpses. The entire vehicle was examined but revealed no other evidence. Fingerprints found under examination have been forwarded to your department for investigation.

Mrs Miranda Close of Lot 7 Park St, a residence that shares the street in common with Lot 3, then volunteered to Agent Walker the following data. Mrs Close states that a day or so earlier, she was not certain, she observed a white male, twenty-five to thirty years of age, with shoulder-length, light blond hair, as he exited the rear of the house at Lot 3 Park St and placed large and apparently heavy dark green garbage bags in the boot of the above-mentioned vehicle. She further describes the subject as tall, very muscular, like a body-builder, and having a deep tan. She recalls no facial hair or other characteristics and describes the subject's clothing as shorts and a tank top. She was unable to recall any jewellery or other distinguishing marks but was able to assist fellow Agents in assembling a likeness of the subject with the Identi-Kit. That likeness is attached to this report and has been circulated to no other division as per your instructions.

Upon arrival, the undersigned, in company with Agent Walker, forced open the door of the garage at the residence at Lot 3 Park Street. This action was undertaken without a Queensland State search warrant, or a Federal warrant to locate and assist persons in need of assistance. Examination of the interior of the garage and residence verified that the homicide and subsequent dismembering took place at that location.

Reconstruction of the crime scene suggests the following:

Entry to the house was gained without visible means of force by person or persons unknown. The deceased women, Donna Fowler and Marianne Abbot, were taken from the front bedroom in the house. There are indications that both victims were bound and secured in this bedroom. The evidence then suggests that the victim, Marianne Abbot, either gained her release or was released intentionally from her restraints and that her assailant(s) then pursued her through the home, inflicting numerous knife wounds on her face, hands, arms, legs, and torso. An abundance of blood found throughout the home indicates that the struggle was prolonged. It is the opinion of the undersigned and fellow Agents that the attack was deliberately carried out to inflict maximum horror.

Investigation further strongly supports the conclusion that the victim, Marianne Abbot, was then killed in the kitchen of the residence with a fatal wound to the throat. Our reconstruction suggests that the assailant(s) then returned to the front bedroom where the second victim, Donna Fowler, was killed by knife wounds and then dragged to the kitchen.

The reconstruction suggests that the attacker(s) then carried both victims to the attached garage, entry to which is gained through the laundry door, and systematically dismembered each corpse with the use of an electric carving knife, and hatchet. The dismembered bodies were then placed in six plastic garbage bags, and placed in the Ford Falcon Sedan. Evidence in the form of collected blood and hair taken from the bath

*strongly supports the conclusion that the suspect(s)
then showered in the bathroom.*

*In addition to the abundant physical signs of the
attack and dismemberment (see photos attached), all
telephone communication to the residence had been
tampered with, and there is strong evidence to support
the theory that the internal wiring had been attached
to another device at one time or another.*

*Numerous prints and partial prints were recovered
at the scene and are currently under analysis by your
department.*

Respectfully,
A. Bradley. Senior Agent ASIS.

I slowly folded the documents and looked out over
the water, then handed them to Percy.

'Jesus, what a pair of fuckin' animals. That Identi-
Kit likeness, was it one of the two you mentioned?'

'Yes, Passini. We took a picture with a zoom lens
and showed it to Mrs Close with five others we took
at random. She picked him first go.'

'There's got to be something done about the bastard
holding all this together, Perce. I always knew that
Bellari and Agostini were looked after by someone up
high. But you never ask these things. It's not real
healthy if you know what I mean.'

'There's been a whisper for some time about a government minister being mixed up with the bloody Ities.
But that's all it's been, just a whisper. But Christ
almighty, nobody thought he'd be that high up. How
do you propose to turn him around?'

'That's where you come into it, Perce.' I said.

434

And for the next three-quarters of an hour I discussed the whole thing with him.

'Christ! If you can pull this off you've got him and the rest of them by the balls good and proper. What happens if he won't come to the party?'

'I'll kill him, Percy, as sure as we're sitting on this boat.'

'You'll want a lot of cover if you do. There's not a damn thing I could do to look out for your arse, the whole fuckin' system'll come down on you. Fuck me I can see it now . . . Special Branch, Interpol. We'd be pulled into it too. If you dug a hole, mate, it wouldn't be deep enough.'

'Well that's the way it goes, Perce. Now what about all the other stuff I asked about?'

'Consider it done. But if you take him out of the play you're on your own. And by the way . . . if you did and they caught up with you, which let me tell you they would, there'd be no trial you know. You'd never be allowed to reach court. So bear that in mind before you pull the trigger on this bastard.'

'I'll keep it in mind, Percy.'

'When do you want to start?'

'End of the week, Perce, soon as you finish your leave. A few more days won't matter, and Katy and I can use the peace and quiet, so let's enjoy it while we can.'

Percy jumped up with a whoop. 'Right,' he said. 'Let's have a party.' He went downstairs and popped a tape in the player, turned the lights down in the saloon, and we all danced. It was the first dance Katy and I had ever had together.

39

THE SCENT OF SOME UNSEEN FLOWERS PERVADED THE cool night air. It smelled not unlike apples. Easing myself into a more comfortable position on the car seat, I resumed my observation. I gripped the sill of the car door, my heart pounding. A Statesman sedan had just pulled into the drive and a gate swung closed behind it. The gate was new. It hadn't been here before when I was almost trapped in the place. The car pulled up beside a Commodore and an obscured figure moved to the front door.

I craned my neck and squinted through half-lidded eyes. The door to the old mansion opened and a cone of light illuminated the figure. The man entered and the door closed. At once I got out of the car and quietly closed the door, hands clenched, as anger and loathing swept through me. The back-light had revealed the figure to be a blond man with shoulder-length hair. Passini!

Pulse racing, I crossed the street.

I'd been patient because time, the very concept of acknowledging one's past and future, no longer had any meaning. I was a free agent, free to do what I wanted in my own time. Yes I was free, liberated by absolute desolation, emancipated from the flimsy prison of civilisation and its rules. I'd learned enough and watched for enough days to have killed Passini and his mate many times, but instead I had waited, unaffected by the passage of time, watched and waited for the bodybuilder Passini, patient in anticipation of what was to come.

I walked down the street in darkness, willing my pace to remain casual and unhurried. One block before the wall I turned west, continuing until I reached the corner of the stone wall. I skirted the wall's grey bulk until I reached the darkest segment and vaulted up, grasped the jagged edge of the stone two feet above my head, pulling up with my arms while digging between the stones with my toes, and then lay flat. Shards of broken glass embedded in the wall jabbed me, but I avoided injury by distributing my weight evenly over the surface. I listened intently for two minutes, measuring the time with my own respiration and pulse, an old piece of training from SOG days. All I heard was the distant passing of traffic and the mournful cry of a mopoke.

I suspended my weight from my hands, lowered my dark-clothed body over the inner side of the wall, dropped noiselessly to the lawn and crouched. The large house lay about fifty yards away. My eyes picked out a thick-trunked tree fifteen yards ahead. Catlike, I moved forward through the darkness, stepped inside the darker shadow of the tree, and froze. I strained the upper limits of my hearing, struggling to hear sounds muffled by the passage of street traffic. The sound from the cars retreated, fading into the distance.

Suddenly I heard a new sound, felt it transmitted

through the ground. I crouched lower, my leg muscles bunched.

I heard the quickening drumming of hard pads running over turf. It was the unmistakable rhythm of a dog, and the heavy, drum-pounding thud of its paws told me it was a big bastard. The thudding approach stopped . . . the night was silent, and I knew the animal was scenting me. I looked to the wall, then abandoned thoughts of retreat. The hard-padded drumming resumed with greater speed.

In the time-slowed and adrenalin-charged workings of my mind, I noted other data. There were no sounds of human accompaniment. That was good. However, the animal searched for me without yelping or barking. It made no sound of challenge or warning. Either it had been surgically silenced or trained to seek violators of its territory without giving a warning. And that was bad. Very bad. The animal would be trained to attack and kill without so much as a growl.

The animal was suddenly backlit by the glow from the house. Thirty yards away, running hard with its nose to the ground, was a thick-bodied Rottweiler.

We'd had some training in handling dogs at Special Operations. There was a move . . . but I'd only seen it done once with success. And once without. I jumped from the shelter of the tree and the shadow in a low crouch, left arm extended parallel to the ground.

The big dog laid its ears flat back, bunched its muscled shoulders and leapt.

I followed the animal's leap, raising my left forearm to shoulder height. The dog stretched its powerful neck in mid-flight to seize my arm. White-tipped razors slashed through the leather of the jacket. I whipped my free hand through the darkness while simultaneously lifting higher with my left. The Rottweiler was momentarily suspended, lifted full off the ground, its neck extended while iron jaws ripped at my left forearm. I drove the edge of my rigid right hand across and under the slavering jaws and snapped the dog's spinal cord. It was dead before its heavy body touched the turf.

Grabbing the once powerful forelegs, I dragged the ninety-pound animal into the darker shadow of the tree. My own pulse and rasping breath deafening me. I knelt beside the sleek corpse of the dog and examined my forearm and fought the urge to cry out and stamp my feet, to yield to the intensity of the pain. Instead, I clenched and unclenched my hand, working it until it functioned properly. I slipped out of my leather jacket, wrapped the bite in cloth that I tore from my shirt, replaced the jacket and dismissed the pain. Then I left the sanctuary of the tree. Ghostlike visions of mutilated limbs protruding from blood-slicked plastic bags clouded my eyes and mind. I worked the hand again and moved forward through the deep shadows.

I crossed to the silent house. The dark blue Statesman and a Commodore still rested on the front drive. I melted into the shadows cast by the lights from within the house and slid soundlessly around the huge old home's perimeter. I tried each door and each ground-floor window, but the doors were locked and double-bolted and the windows were fitted with key latches and could not be opened from the outside without breaking glass. I declined that course of action and began a second tracing of the perimeter.

439

Slipping through the dense tangle of shrubbery at the rear of the house, I tripped and stumbled. I caught my balance and listened, but I heard no sound. Blessing my luck, I began a search of the shrubs, seeking an ambush position from which to strike when the occupants emerged. Prior to moving, I looked below my feet, hunting for whatever had tripped me. It was a garden hose, coiled loosely in the cover of the shrubs. I traced the hose through the dense vegetation. Several feet from the tap, a rectangular window lay hidden at ground level. I squirmed on my stomach and elbows through the brush, took out my knife and pried at the wooden window frame. Long strips of crumbling putty came away in my fingers. I exposed the corner of the pane, then worked it back and forth. More dried putty broke free and the pane tilted forward. I laid it gently on the moist earth and reached into the opening. My blind fingers found the catch and rotated it. I pushed with the heel of my hand and the ancient, neglected window opened inward, screeching as the warped wood was forced past the frame. Again I froze and listened. I could hear faint, muffled music and nothing else.

Taking a slow, deep breath, I lowered my feet through the opening and slid down the foundation wall. My feet touched the floor and I released my grip, pivoting to face the cellar.

Diffused light from a crack beneath a door enabled me to examine the room. Earthen floor, stone and mortar walls, and the smell of must and age. Above me were cobwebbed joists and a crazed tangle of electrical wiring. Finding no other exits, I approached the door which was secured by an ancient lever latch. I lifted the lever and when the door swung noiselessly inward I slid into the light and scrutinised the tiny landing. The music was no longer audible. I eased onto the far side of the first stair riser and began a painstakingly slow climb. Lowering my weight to each board in small increments, I discovered the lower limits of squeaks and creaks and avoided them by shifting my stance. At last I opened the connecting door to the first floor.

Gun in hand, I stepped full into the light. The room was empty and its silence played on my nerves. I searched the kitchen, turning corners in combat fashion, crouching. Successive empty rooms yawned at me, mocking my deadly intent.

I looked through the window. Both cars remained as before.

Thick carpet muffled my footfalls as I mounted a darkened stairway. Flattened against the wall, I crept down the hallway, forcing myself to breathe. Each empty room increased the odds that the next would reveal my quarry, but the vacant rooms seemed to laugh at me. I wiped the perspiration from my hands, changing the gun over in the process, and climbed to the top floor.

I dominated the rising charge of adrenalin and conquered the desire to move more quickly. My body quivered under the accumulation of unspent energy as I maintained my steady, thorough progress, searching every conceivable space in which a man could hide. I found nothing.

Exercising feline patience, I retraced my steps and searched every room again. Nothing. I descended to

the second floor. Nothing again . . . Not even the
sound of music. I straightened, took a breath and felt
my nostrils flare as I tried to scent something that
would aid me in my search. I retraced my path, hearing only the swishing passage of traffic on the distant
street. I smiled then as a thought hit me and I
descended the stairway that led to the cellar. My eyes
noted the unexpected cleanliness of the steps. Dust
abounded in every corner of the cellar, but the centres
of the risers were dust-free. Standing on the narrow
landing, the music touched my ears once again. The
sound was faint, very faint. I slid on quiet feet through
the doorway and stood on the earthen floor of the
small room. The music was soft and muted, but louder
than in any other part of the house. I closed the
planked door, refastened the catch and closed my eyes,
waiting until they adjusted to the darkened room.

Opening my eyes, I began an inch-by-inch examination of the cellar. There were unpainted shelves on the
far wall, and standing in front of them I could hear the
muffled music well enough to discern both the artist
and the work. It was Frank Sinatra singing 'My Way'.

I examined the shelving, applying gentle pressure at
the sides and corners. Where the dried wood abutted
the stone wall in the far corner, I tugged, and the shelving swung out from the wall a fraction of an inch.

My pulse thundered and a red mist passed over my
eyes as I saw again the coloured photographs of the
dismembered bodies Percy had shown me. I grabbed
the shelving's corner and yanked. The entire assembly
swung out on a well-oiled hinge and I faced a darkened passage through a stone-and-mortar arch. It was

442

about three paces long, ending with a metal door. Finding no indication of an upper lock or a bolt, I carefully tried the knob and it rotated freely in my hand. Without pause or thought, I abruptly pushed the door open. I went through the door at speed, low crouch diminishing the size of my body, turning with the gun in both hands. Fully inside, I halted. Two men stood before me, as though paralysed. As their shock receded, neither moved.

Putting the gun in my right hand I reached into my jacket and took out some long flat plastic zip-up ties.

'Tie that bastard up,' I said to Branco, indicating Passini with the gun.

Neither spoke a word and when Passini was tied hand and foot and lying on the floor, I levelled the gun on Branco.

'Now you! Get on the fuckin' floor.' He complied without so much as a murmur. And with the gun pressed into the side of his head I tied him up.

I looked down at Passini.

'Remember Port Douglas you fuckin' rat?' And kicked him in the balls as hard as I could. He screamed, and before the sound had died away I kicked Branco as well.

On the table they had been working at was a pile of white powder, tins of powdered glucose and a box of small plastic envelopes. In an open cupboard there were hundreds of throw-away hypodermic syringes sealed in plastic packets.

I found a glass beaker and using it as a scoop I picked up some of the powder.

'What is this shit?' I asked one and all.

'Heroin,' gasped Pascoe. 'Take it, take the lot.'

I ignored them, but Branco was trying to look over his shoulder to see what I was doing.

In the corner was an old zinc tub and a tap. There was about an inch of the powder on the bottom of the beaker and I added water and stirred it round with a long metal spoon. Going to the cupboard I took out two syringes and sucked up the deadly mixture till both of the hypos were nearly full.

Then going over to Branco I pushed him over on his belly with my foot and, finding a good vein in his arm, poked the needle into it. He gave a scream of understanding and tried to move, but I knelt on him and held him down. Pulling back on the plunger, I waited half a second and was rewarded with a show of blood. Then I pushed the plunger home.

He went into convulsions almost immediately, bumping around like a decapitated chook. Froth spewed from his mouth, his knees came up, jerked, and then kicked out straight. He went rigid for a moment, then his body shook uncontrollably for a while. Suddenly he went still.

Picking up the other needle I approached Passini. He started to scream and tried to ward me off by turning on his back and kicking out with his bound legs. But it did him no good.

'Think of those two girls, you fuckin' animal,' I said to him as I shot the lethal load into his vein.

I removed the flat plastic ties from them and put them back in my pocket, then placed their hands around the hypos and let them drop to the floor. I took the beaker over to the tub and rinsed it thoroughly, leaving it in the bottom of the tub.

I checked Branco and Passini for any signs of life, but there were none, and walked out of the room leaving the metal door open and the shelving as it was. Outside, pain and tiredness washed over me, draining away my last reserves of strength. A small rivulet of blood trickled slowly down my arm and to the earth. I looked down but saw nothing, my mind strangely detached and remote. It was always the same. Always the blood and the earth. Never changing. Would never change. The sense of purpose that had kept me going, that had helped me to endure, had begun to wane. With sudden clarity, I knew I'd been too many years on the long hard road, and that this was the time to get off it for good. Soldiers of my kind don't just fade away. They die messily.

40

IT WAS DAYLIGHT. WE'D ONLY RETURNED FROM SYDNEY the evening before. I woke up with Katy trying to lift my arm over her so she could push her back up against me and come closer.

'What's up, love?'

'Hold me, Jimmy, just hold me.'

I hugged her and she turned around in bed so we were facing each other. Holding her face between her hands, I kissed her gently on the lips. They tasted faintly of the wine we had drunk last night. She opened her mouth and slipped her tongue through my teeth, then leant on one elbow and looked down at me, her eyes wide open, earnestly searching my face.

'Do you still love me, Jimmy?'

'What sort of a question is that? For Christ's sake, you know I do.'

'Just teasing,' she said.

Sitting up in bed she began to tug at the hem of her nightgown, which had bunched up beneath her. As she worked the gown over her head, I watched how her breasts, caught in the gathered folds of the material, were drawn upward for a moment before they dropped loosely into view. I reached for her.

A vine blew against the window, scratched, and tapped out a brief halting rhythm.

'What's that noise?' Katy asked and moved closer.

'Nothing, it's just the wind.'

She felt for my hand, pulled it to her breasts, and I trailed my fingers lightly back and forth across her nipples. I put one and then the other into my mouth, sucking them until they rose in little crusted erections. She began to moan softly and, taking charge of my hand again, guided it down across the slope of her belly.

I slid my tongue into her ear and rubbed my finger into her down between her legs.

'Oh God!' I heard her sharp intake of breath. Her knees fell open and she strained upward with her pelvis.

I took my hand away.

'You've shaved your hair,' I said.

'Do you like it.'

In answer I put my hand back and twiddled her clitoris with my finger. She squirmed and gave a moan under my hand then reached down and stroked my erection.

I tried to get up but she held me down.

'Just lie still. Let me . . .'

She threw a leg over mine, crawled over on top of me, straddled both my legs. Then standing on her knees, kneeling over me, she began to ease herself down. Making little noises.

I slid my fingers into the sticky cleft of her buttocks and pulled her down on top of me.

'Oh yes!' she said, throwing her head back and moaning.

447

I reached up and ran my hands over her face, her ears, the corners of her mouth.

She began to move, rising up and down above me slowly at first, almost gently.

Then she found her pace and settled into a steady rhythm, our hands resting lightly on each other's shoulders.

But something kept turning inside my head, whirling around, each revolution coinciding with the measured slap of our bodies' coming together. We're moving now as one, gathering speed.

Then I begin to hear . . . cutting through everything . . . the faint squeak of unaligned metal parts. Foreign at this time of day, but I had heard it before.

'Listen!' I whispered. 'Katy listen!' I pulled her down by her shoulders and held her still.

'What is it?'

'That noise . . . did you hear it?'

'No.'

'But it was loud. You must have. It sounded like it came from the verandah.'

'It's nothing.' She began to move again. 'Don't pay any attention to it.'

But I couldn't help myself. That sound was driving everything else out of my mind. Katy tried to cover my mouth with hers. Her tongue flailed wetly about my ears. I pushed her over and rolled on top of her.

'What are you doing?' she moaned.

I felt myself growing soft inside her. 'It's no good, Katy. I'm sorry but I have to check it out.'

And there was the noise again.

'I can hear it now,' she whispered, clinging to me.

'It's the hinge on the screen door or something.'

'That's what it is . . . of course.' I tried to sound convinced, not wanting to frighten her. 'But I'm not going to lie here and listen to it. It's driving me crazy. I won't be long.'

'Don't go Jimmy,' she pleaded.

'I'll be right back, promise.'

The house was quiet again as I pulled on my jeans and a sweatshirt. Perhaps Katy was right. It was just the screen door in the breeze. But it didn't sound like that to me.

When an angry buzzing started I knew we had trouble. It was part of the alarm system I'd installed. Katy and I immediately went through the routine that we had discussed and practised in the past.

Picking up the rifle, I went out onto the verandah behind the lattice work we had erected. It was covered in a leafy vine.

I saw the intruder then. He had entered the fence and was sneaking along the western bank of the tidal lagoon, rifle in his hand, crouched down low and trying to keep in the cover of the knee-high grass on that side of the bank.

'Just hold it!' I yelled out. 'Right there!'

He stopped, came erect and fired a shot that smacked into the wall about three feet away from me. Then he dropped down on his knees into the grass. I took quick aim and returned his fire. The heavy .308 round bellowed and he jerked back, dropped the gun, straightened, then knelt as though in supplication. His body then arched, hands clawing upward at his neck, head thrown back. When the kneeling man's hands came away from his throat, blood spurted out in a pulsing stream.

He fell on his side, his legs scythed and he rolled onto his back. The water just out from the bank gave a swirl and a V-shaped ripple headed towards the bank. The man on the bank stretched his arms to the heaven he would probably be denied, and jerked spasmodically. A section of the bank gave way, then more collapsed and the dying man was gone in a fountain of spray, thrashing and a great swirl of water.

I heard a noise to my left and swung round, but the gun was kicked up and out of my hands before I could pump another round into the chamber.

He was a big man, not tall but heavy, slightly bald, and his tiny pig-red eyes gleamed at me as he took a pace forward, brandishing a wicked-looking knife in his right hand.

I jumped down the steps to get away from him, my eyes desperately searching around for some sort of weapon. Pig eyes came down the steps, grinning at me, slashing the knife through the air. I backed away with the verandah at my back and as I was doing this my foot kicked Diefer's discarded chain, which clinked with the dullness of rusty metal. One-handed, I bent and snatched it up, coming erect as the man lunged at me.

The glinting tip of the knife headed for my throat with almost casual accuracy. I flung myself to one side and with my right hand whipped the chain around in a blind arc. Then I lost my footing and fell, still holding the chain.

My face struck the ground and the powdery dust

flew up and made my eyes smart. There was a violent jerk on my arm as the chain burned through my fingers, but I tightened my grip automatically, reaching out with the other and locking it around my wrist. But as suddenly, the tension slackened. I scrambled to my feet, jumping backwards, seeing pig eyes through blurred and streaming eyes. The chain was wound tightly around his throat and his face was purpling, his free hand clawing at the coiled links while the other waved the knife about almost lazily now.

I fought him like a heavy fish, heaving him backwards to keep the chain tight, staggering past the end of the house, slipping, stumbling, moving in a strange tug of war towards the lagoon. My vision improved as my tears washed them clear of the dust. And I noticed a broken branch hovering before me. It was about six feet off the ground. I heaved my hands up and over it, heard the chain rattle on it, then flung myself forward and down, gripping the chain with both hands, feeling the sudden huge drag upon it, hearing the feet of the hanging man as he scrambled to find his footing.

The noise stopped eventually and there was a new and strange silence. I remained kneeling, unwound the chain from around my wrist and saw the deep indentations in the skin where the links had bitten in. When I let go, the chain was flicked away by the weight on the other end. There was the sodden thump of the body falling.

Heart pumping, gasping for breath, I turned on wooden legs and looked down on the face of the man I had just killed, at the gaping mouth from which a thick bluish tongue protruded like the labellum of the orchids that grew in the bush here. He stank. His sphincter muscle had relaxed at the moment of death. I bent down with a loathing reluctance, grabbed the heavy booted feet, and dragged the body over to the edge of the lagoon. When it toppled in, it plunged deep, surfaced almost immediately and floated back towards the bank. Then a saurian head lifted and a gaping mouth lined with wicked teeth clamped around the body and dragged it under in a swirl of muddy water.

When I finally reached the verandah Katy was standing there, tears streaming down her face, trembling, holding onto the rifle that had been kicked out of my grasp.

I worked the rifle away from her and threw it onto the bunk, then held her in my arms, making soothing sounds until her fears abated.

It was the start of another day, and I spent it in a dope-induced state.

We didn't have to cultivate grass around here; it grew in the bush like every other thing. We had found an unusually large plant that was loaded with heads. And because it was a fair distance from the house I had lopped the branches off, carted them back to the shed and hung them there upside down to dry. I'd been told that this intensifies its strength.

It was dry and smooth and potent and it seemed to take me into some sort of a fantasy time warp. As I sat in the Nissan out in the yard I was so stoned I thought it was moving. My brain felt like it was an electric motor and it kept purring, while my hands felt like they would fry people at the very touch. Usually when

I had been on the dope there was a small area of my brain that remained undisturbed and was able to view what was going on around me with some clarity. But not with this stuff. Not today. My mind had been consumed by a solitary and crazy idea that my body was only an inch thick, and if I turned side-on no one would be able to shoot me. I saw the barrel of a gun pointing at me and then the barrel drooped and melted away like a piece of hot chocolate. A warm wind blew through the window of the car and I felt myself float up and away through the side of the vehicle. I felt muddled and thought I was shrinking.

We had a squat, galvanised thousand-gallon tank that we used for a swimming pool and I walked over to it and shed my clothes. Katy came over, kissed me, and it felt like I was being sucked completely inside her. She took off her gear and we got in the tank. The water was warm and I looked for crocodiles. I hung in the water, my hand grasping the rolled top edge of the tank, dizzy, weightless, joyless. There was a pretty girl next to me. It's Katy, then her face turned flat like a magazine cover. I reached out and ran my hand over her. She giggled and I became a little more aware, but my body was made out of rubber and I could stretch myself. I reached down and felt her sex beneath the water, slippery. When I tried to kiss her it felt like I was slobbering. I put my head under the water, nuzzled up to her pubic area, and she spread her legs, but I couldn't keep my grip and my tongue licked water instead of her. The sun dazzled me and I felt like I was wallowing in acid, my skin on fire. I reached down and couldn't find my cock, it had dissolved in the water, then I found out I had my hand on Katy. I reached down with my other hand to find myself but my cock felt like it was tied on and would fall off if I didn't leave it alone. I climbed out of the tank and went and lay on the bunk on the verandah. I seemed to be floating and held onto the bunk so I wouldn't rise any higher, then I just let go and watched myself float away across the paddock and into the lagoon.

I'm in Hell looking at the devil and he smiles at me, reaches out his hand and beckons me by crooking his finger. Flames are flickering around me. I claw myself up and away from the heat and the burn and find myself in a dark room, sitting in the corner with my knees up, my arms wrapped around them. I'm rocking and I'm cold. I lifted up an arm and rubbed my hand over my face, but there's nothing there, it's gone, not even an expression. My mind switches on with a 'click', loud in the room, and I feel the electrical current running to it. Slowly wheels start to turn and I look at a computer screen, words and letters flash down in a running stream . . . ah . . . my mind sorting out thoughts and ideas. Death is the price of life, a ticket to heaven. From earth to glory, forever and ever. The two bastards in the lagoon, it's only the flesh that the crocodiles have got. The two of them would now visit the Lord and dwell in the house of tomorrow. And sooner or later, all their friends will join them. I see the Devil and he's laughing at me. 'Don't worry,' he says. 'Your soul is restored. Your future lies where it began.' The channel changes, there's an evangelist looking at me with dark eyes, yelling 'No no! Get close to God, son, and he'll let you in on some of his secrets. No one dies, they just get recycled. With God all things are possible.' His eyes glow and the picture fades. I hear the evangelist and the Devil murmuring and laughing in low tones. I'm shaking. I'm sweating. I wake up.

I shook my head and rose from the bunk. It was close to sunset. My body ached. I'm not a winner, I thought, just a survivor. The sun rises, the sun sets. Life goes on. Shit! I thought it was no time to start doubting my own invincibility.

Each day is a time for optimism. Way back I'd learned, don't get mad, get even. I had an idea. But I bet it would blow Katy's mind . . . where is Katy? . . . Safe asleep on the bed.

The sun melted like a red flame in the west and Jacko and I were sitting in a rental car, parked in the shopping centre at Frenchs Forest. The moon was just coming into view when the white LTD drove by us, gliding up the street.

'Go!' I nudged Jacko. He fired up, put the car into gear and followed the LTD to the golf club.

A week of patient surveillance had gone into this operation and we wanted it to come off without any hitches.

In the parking lot two men got out of the LTD and walked over to the club entrance. The driver remained sitting behind the wheel.

We were parked two rows behind .

'Now!' I said to Jacko, who edged the car forward until we were parked beside the LTD. The driver was listening to music, right arm hanging out the window with a cigarette stuck between his fingers. He gave us a casual glance as we pulled in and then turned away, tapping the hand with the cigarette in it in time to the music.

I hopped out of the car, drew the gun and shoved it through the open window of the LTD.

'If you move you die,' I said.

The cigarette dropped from his fingers and he was about to say something when Jacko opened the left-hand rear door, jumped in and put his gun to the back of the driver's head.

'Now get out real slow, mate, and get into our car,' Jacko said, tapping him with the barrel of his gun.

'Righto, righto, what's this all about?'

'Move!' I said, opening the door and stepping back with the gun levelled on him. He nervously stepped from the car. 'Get in the back!' I said as Jacko came round and opened the rear door for him. As the guy was bending to climb in, Jacko's hand whipped forward and stuck the dart he was holding in the side of the driver's neck. He gave a startled sound and his hand flew up to his neck as if he'd been stung by a bee. Then his eyes rolled and we had to grab him quickly before he collapsed outside the car. We bundled him in, Jacko binding his hands behind him and gagging him.

Jacko took a bag out of the rental and passed it to me, then climbed into the front passenger seat of our car. I slid into the left hand rear seat of the LTD and put the bag on the floor. The music was still on and I listened.

It was an hour and a half before the other two made their way out of the club and strolled back towards the LTD, sharing a private joke. As they neared the car we both moved together, Jacko one side and me on the other. They weren't expecting any trouble and when they saw us with silenced guns in our hands their mouths dropped open.

'Both of ya, get into the front of the LTD or we'll fuckin' kill ya where you stand.'

'You! In and drive!' Jacko said, pushing the leaner of the two forward and sliding into the back seat behind him.

'Now you, fatso!' I said to the guy on my side. 'Get in alongside fuckin' cockroach!' He was pretty nervous, but he swivelled his head around as I hopped in the back of his car.

'Do you know who I am?' he asked in a polished tone.

'We know who you fuckin' well are and you can take the fuckin' plum out of your mouth. You're not talking to the television now you cunt. Get it?' I pushed the end of the silencer into his cheek, forcing his head back around to the front.

'Lets go!' Jacko said to Alfio Fanucchi, the guy behind the wheel. 'You don't have to die, but pull any shit and I'll kill ya.'

'Yeah sure . . . righto,' he said as he started the car.

We drove quietly out of the parking lot and turned onto the main road.

'Where to?' asked Fanucchi.

'Straight ahead,' said Jacko. 'I'll tell ya when to turn.'

We drove on mainly in silence, with Jacko giving occasional instructions. After an hour or so we passed the last street lamp and Jacko told Fanucchi to turn off at the next left-hander.

Fanucchi and fatso shot a look at each other, then Fanucchi got a bit cocky.

'You pair of pricks know you're fuckin' dead, don't ya?' he said. 'You've got no idea what you're dealin' with here.'

Jacko leant forward and gave him an open hander alongside the head that rocked him.

'Just shut up and fuckin' drive.'

We made the turn-off and seesawed down a dirt road full of ruts and corrugations. A mile further on we pulled up in front of a cyclone fence with chained double gates.

'Look familiar, you bastard?' I asked fatso with a poke of the gun. 'Now have you got the fuckin' keys or do we ram the gate with this pretty car of yours?'

'Here,' he said and fished out a set of keys, sorting among them in the light from the dash. 'This one.'

'Not me, you. You get out real slow and you open the fuckin' thing and I'll be right up your arse.'

He opened the door and I got out quickly, walking behind him to the gate. Jacko sat with the Woodsman hard up against Fanucchi's head.

With the gate open we climbed back in and bumped our way over to the concrete apron in front of a large warehouse.

'Out!' I said, hopping out quickly. The two in front followed and Jacko brought up the rear, carrying the bag.

I ordered fatso to unlock the small door built into the large roller door and then asked him where the light switch was located.

'Just around to the left,' he stammered.

458

Taking him by the scruff of the neck, I pushed him through the door. 'Get 'em on!' He fumbled his way a short distance and I heard the switches click. The place flooded with light.

We shut the door and walked through the warehouse to the office section at the far end, where I pulled up a couple of chairs.

'Sit!' I said to the pair, indicating the chairs with my gun. Fatso sat straight down but Fanucchi thought it was time for heroics. As he made a wild lunge for the gun, Jacko sidestepped and swung the Woodsman up and back at full force. The heavy blow caught Fanucchi flush across his Adam's apple. I heard the trachea in his throat crunch. Gagging, he clutched at his throat and fell to his knees, as if the something that kept him erect had snapped. Blood gushed out of his mouth, spilling over his hands.

'Good God!' fatso said. I thought he was going to be sick as he looked down at his partner choking to death in a pool of blood at his feet.

'Dear me Sir fuckin' Peter,' I said. 'Does that upset you? Well you've ordered a lot fuckin' worse than that to be done.'

Jacko moved behind his chair. 'Put ya bloody arms back here.' He dragged them around and taped them to the chair, then taped his ankles to the legs.

'Now that we're all comfortable,' I said, 'we'll get this show on the road. I lifted the bag onto the table, unzipped it deliberately slowly, and took out a black square box about the same size as a walkie-talkie. Holding it up I said, 'Know what this is, Sir Peter?'

'I have absolutely no idea,' he stuttered.

'Let me give you a demo then.'

I walked over and placing one of the electrodes against the metal frame of the desk, then lifting the other one and pushed the button on the side of the box. There was a fierce crackling sound and a miniature lightening bolt, blue-white and bright, sizzled against the steel.

Sir Peter's head reeled back as he jumped with fright.

'It's called a taser, Sir Peter, and it's a nasty fuckin' thing, a bit like a cattle prod but with ten times more wallop. It can cause your body a great deal of pain, and convulsions, but will not do lasting damage. Unless of course you get too many of them.' I gave another demonstration and he flinched. 'Then it can affect the mind.'

I put the taser on the table and pulled out a telescopic tripod, passed it to Jacko and asked him to set it up. Then I pulled out a video camera and passed that to Jacko. He screwed it onto the tripod and gave me a nod.

Then we picked up the chair with Sir Peter in and carried it behind the desk. Jacko went to the camera made a few adjustments.

'Come and see what you think?'

It was good. The frame showed Sir Peter sitting behind the table as if he were in his office in the State Building. And there was not a sign that he was trussed up.

'Now you fuckin' bastard, you like giving TV interviews so you're going to give us one. And every time you get it wrong we stop the camera and you get a

taste of the old taser there.' I gave it a friendly pat.
'Got it? Good.'

Jacko moved over behind the camera and looked
through the view finder.

'Smile,' he said.

'Now, Sir Peter, what is . . . or I should say was your
connection to Gino Vitelli, Joseph Frangiani, Paolo
Agostini and Alfio Fannuchi?'

'If you think I'm going to . . .'

I wasn't going to play with this bastard, I just
walked up, pushed the taser on his hand and hit the
button.

'Aaaaaaaaaaah!' he screamed.

'Right, let's start again,' I said, and repeated the
question.

'You don't know what you're getting yourselves into.'

I put the taser on the side of his neck and gave a short
blast. After he recovered we repeated the question . . .

'They were business associates of mine.'

'What line of business was that?'

'What?'

'You heard me. What line of business was that?' I
showed him the taser.

'Importing.'

'And what is it that you imported?'

'You don't expect me to answer . . .'

'Jacko, we've gotta show this poofter that we're not
going to be here all fuckin' night.'

We walked around the table, twisted the chair and
Jacko took a folding knife from his pocket and
grabbed a handful of material in the front of Sir Peter's
pants . . .

'What . . . what are you doing?' he yelled in a strangled voice.

Jacko just kept cutting away at trousers and underpants till Sir Peter's genitals were exposed. I walked over and put the taser straight down and pressed the button. He jumped in the chair and his convulsion nearly tipped it over. We then faced the chair back to the table.

When he had recovered I returned to the camera.

'What did you import with Gino Vitelli, Joseph Frangiani, Paolo Agostini and Alfio Fannuchi?'

'Cocaine and heroin,' he said, the bluster and fight completely gone from him.

From then on it was just a formality of question and answer.

An hour later the tape was finished. Jacko rewound it and we had a look at it on replay. It looked genuine and sounded pretty good.

I sat on the corner of the table and lit a cigarette.

'You're a lucky man, Sir Peter, yep, a real, real lucky man. You see, you get to live.'

He slumped down in the chair and sat there, trembling.

'You can relax, you're safe. But I'll tell you how this thing works. That tape is going to be edited by a person of authority who hates your guts. You don't know who it is, and you won't know who it is. But when it's edited it'll have his voice asking the questions, and yours giving the answers. You follow that?'

He nodded his head.

'Do you fuckin' understand that?' I yelled at him.

'Yes. Yes I understand.'

'Right then, that tape will then be placed in a secure and very safe place. Now I know now what you're thinking. You're thinking that you'll be able to send people after me when you're safe and sound and force me to divulge the location of the tape. But don't get your hopes up too fuckin' high. I won't know where it is, either. Nor will my associate here. We don't want to know. But if anything happens to me, or to my lady or associate here, that tape will become public knowledge. You'll be arrested and the whole fuckin' show will come crashing down. Now you, you cunt, are going to make damn sure that the wolves are called off. Because if I should slip in the shower and break my neck, or if a snake bites me and I die, you are in deep shit, you bastard. You get the message?'

'Yes, I understand.'

'Well seeing as how you've got that, let me give you something else to worry about. Should your connections ever find who blew the fuckin' whistle on them, what do you think would happen?'

Jacko gave a whistling sound. 'Oooooh nasty!' he said.

'Well what do you think would happen?' and I casually picked up the taser.

'My life wouldn't be worth a plugged nickel.'

'Funny you should say that, Sir Peter. That's what we thought too. Isn't it, mate?' I asked Jacko.

'Yep, that's what we thought.'

'So you better pray, you lump of shit, pray that nothing happens. You better get to work damn quick and put a stopper on these fuckin' raids at my joint. You hear me, you prick?'

'Yes, yes I do . . . You're Jimmy Diamond aren't you?' he said in a cringing voice.

'You'd better believe it you dirty fuckin' mongrel. And you better start praying that Katy and I remain around for a fuckin' long time. Cut the bastard loose,' I said to Jacko.

'Nasty bastard, isn't he?' Jacko said to Sir Peter when he bent down to cut the tape around his ankles. Then he looked up. 'Phew! . . . do you know this dirty bastard has pissed and shit himself?'

'I . . . I couldn't help it.' Sir Peter said in an apologetic tone. 'It happened when you put that thing on me.'

'Well that's the best part of you gone then, you cunt,' I said.

We dragged the body of his offsider out into the warehouse and put him between some drums of dry-cleaning fluid. Then we up ended anything of a volatile nature, opened up the taps on the gas stove in the kitchen, and Jacko set a radio-controlled lighter fuse in some screwed up paper. We escorted Sir Peter back out, and told him to lie down on the back seat of his car. Jacko was right. Christ, he stank. We drove away from the warehouse and back through the gate. I slipped out and, using a handkerchief, I closed the gates, replaced the chain and snapped the padlock in place.

When Jacko hit the button we were just about on the main road. The night lit up behind us and a second later we heard the explosion.

41

I WAS HALFWAY ACROSS THE MARBLE FLOOR TO THE security desk when the lift doors opened and Percy's girl Friday, Pam, appeared.

'Would you like to come up, Jimmy?'

I ignored the 'Hey! . . . Hey you!' from the guards behind the desk and walked straight over.

One of the guards came scrambling out from behind the desk but Pam poked her head out.

'It's all right, George, he's expected.' The security guy mumbled something about . . . 'It'd be nice to be informed . . .' but the closing doors cut off the rest.

'Absolutely bloody priceless, Jimmy,' were Percy's words to me as he gave me a pat on the back.

'You've only got yourself to thank, Percy. We couldn't have done it without the surveillance gear and all your help.'

'You're wrong you know. Our ticket doesn't give us the authority to pull an operation within Australian territory. We're restricted, just like our cousins in the CIA. That's why we freelance. Jesus! I'd give a million bucks to be sitting in the Premier's office watching that confession.'

'Hey!' I yelled at him. 'We had a deal.'

'We've still got a deal, no sweat.' Percy smiled. 'Just kidding. That tape is priceless. Do you realise we can do more with it locked away than if it was made public. His knowing that it exists is far better than him getting nailed and fighting it out in the courtroom. No, Jimmy, it's a gem. Feel like a drink?'

'Never thought you'd ask, Perce.'

He buzzed the intercom and asked Pam to bring us something stronger than tea and coffee. The door opened and she wheeled in a mini bar, then left the room.

'Well you've got your insurance now, mate.'

He opened a draw in his desk, dragged out a file and handed me a photograph. It was Vitelli sitting under a beach umbrella having a drink with Sir Peter.

'That's what started the whole ball rolling. It was shot with a long-range lens in Hong Kong. The US DEA boys were trying to put a link into the chain and they had a meet with Vitelli, then they put a watch on him. When they got a make on Sir Peter, they handed it on to us. Pretty, isn't it?'

He took out another photo and handed it across. 'Try this one.'

It was Sir Peter again, but I didn't know the guy with him.

'Who's this other bloke?'

'Carlos Boronetti. A real shithouse, that one. He's into everything and anything. Strange breeding too. His mother was Irish and his father was Italian Spanish.'

I looked at the photo again. Black hair, the look of

the Devil on his face. Somewhere back in his ancestry a Spaniard must have crawled ashore on the Irish coast after the Armada sank and raped the first girl he saw.

'Nasty looking prick. Where does he hang his hat?'

'Right here in Sydney now. Frequent trips to Bangkok, and Manila. He's Sir Peter's right-hand man.'

Percy handed me the next five photos with a smile. 'You'll love these.'

I didn't need any introduction to the bloke in them. It was me, caught in five different poses, stark bollocky naked with Penny, the bird in the Beverley Hills brothel.

'Funny Perce, real fuckin' funny.'

I tossed all the photos back to him and he put the first two back in the folder. The last five, he tapped together neatly like a dealer with a deck of cards. Then he smiled, walked over and put them through a shredder.

'Feel better now? Where did you learn that finger thing?' he asked with a laugh.

'Your sister taught me, Percy.' I said.

An hour later we were sitting at a corner table in the bar of the Regent.

'Well what are you going to do now, old son?'

'I'm going home, Perce. I've had a gutful, mate. I'm sick of the city, I'm sick of the killing, and I'm sick of waking up at night after bad dreams. I'm going home to raise some kids, vegetables and livestock. I want to make things grow instead of cutting them down. Do you realise how long I've lived with this shit? My head's so full of it, Percy, that I sometimes wonder if there's room up there to store anything else.

'I want to sit on my verandah of an evening and watch the sun go down without having to load up a fuckin' gun and listen for the noises.'

'Katy tells me you've turned the place into a fortress.'

'Yeah, and I'll tell you another thing, mate. Give it time and all that will be coming out too. I'm not going to live like a prisoner in my own home.'

'When do you plan on going back?'

'Just as soon as Katy and I take care of a couple of things.'

'Not to-fuckin'-night you're not. We're stayin' on the piss. I've already spoken to Katy. She told me to pour you through the door when we've had enough. Shit I'm hungry. Let's do things in style in the main restaurant.'

'Sounds okay to me, son. You're in the chair, it's on you.'

When we were having coffee after our meal, Percy got serious with me.

'If you had your life over again, what would you change?'

'You wouldn't believe me if I told you, Perce.'

'Try me.'

'Well it goes back a long time. You know the aversion I have towards the clergy?'

He nodded his head and drew on his cigarette. 'Go on.'

'There was this priest, he was forever trying to get me to change my ways. He believed in all the religious

468

poppycock and was a very genuine man. I should have listened to him. I should at least have heard him out, or tried to persuade him to my views, but I wouldn't even listen. Do you know what I did?'

Percy gave me a blank look.

'I burnt his fuckin' church down. To the ground. I still have this picture in my mind of the priest wading ankle-deep through the ashes, weeping. He was trying to help me in the only way he knew. And I caused him pain.'

'Well, mate, you've got it all in front of you now. You can relax. But, Jesus, think of Sir Peter, he'll be praying all right. If something did happen to you naturally . . . I mean no time for you would be *a good time to die*, as far as he's concerned.'

And we both laughed.

I got back to the safe house late that night, pissed as a rat and happy. The light in the bedroom came on and Katy walked out, pulling on a robe.

We had some kind of a talk, but I couldn't keep my hands off her.

'To bed with you, wicked woman,' I said, trying to lace my drunken voice with princely authority.

We slipped under the sheet and pressed our bodies together. She reached down for me and her hand started to work.

'Wicked am I?' she whispered with kisses against my ear. 'What are you going to do, get your belt and give me a thrashing?'

She rolled over to her side of the bed, put her arms over her head and thrust her boobs up at me. 'Your slave girl is ready, oh master, to be tormented. Be cruel to me, I can take it. I really love it when you beat me.' Then she giggled.

I dragged her back to me, holding her to me tightly. And passed out in a drunken haze.

I awoke early that morning, made myself a cup of coffee and tried to imagine a life without the woman I loved . . . a life still in the game but with no-one to go home to. It was not enough. The game had lost its magic. But my obsession had destroyed itself only after I had succeeded in destroying others. I picked up the hand gun that was lying on the table and I turned the weapon, touched the barrel to a spot behind my ear. No man should be forced to live with failure, not if he owned his own life. No man should be compelled to . . . .

The force of an idea struck me as I was taking up the pressure on the trigger. Even now I was still playing the game! In the game men solved problems with violence, with bullets and death. Other human beings confronted life, faced and survived their failures.

Stunned with wonder at my own prolonged blindness, I lowered the pistol. I sat, strangely calm, and challenged the validity of the game. I weighed the crimes and punishments I'd seen, the penalties and rewards. I recalled the men who'd died, opponents as well as comrades, men I'd held at their deaths. It was all a horrible waste. In that moment of harsh truth, I revolted at ever having to do another deed like the ones I had done for so long. I would never again take a human life. And I vowed that never again would I commit the life of another to achieve my own success.

470

I acknowledged the ultimate value of my new insight, embracing it with the grip of a drowning man. Life, all life, was a beauty to be seen, a taste to be savoured.

I stripped the magazine from the gun, ejected the shell in the chamber and tossed the lot into the corner of the room . . . out of my hand and out of my life. Never, never ever again.

Out at the airport, Percy gave me his hand.

'Keep in touch, Jimmy, and take care of Katy.'

Percy looked much as he always did, making few noticeable concessions to the fact that he was seeing us off. Jet engines whined and moaned out on the tarmac, and in front of the building an incessant conveyor belt of taxis and private cars poured human fodder to the check-ins.

Katy was wearing a light pink dress and a pair of high-heeled sandals. She walked up to Percy and kissed him lightly on the mouth. 'Thanks for everything, we wouldn't be here now except for you.' She kissed him on the cheek.

I shook Percy's hand again, then we embraced and I turned to Katy. 'Come on Mrs Diamond, we've got a plane to catch.'

Yes, good old Percy had acted as best man. And Pam had been matron of honour. We were now Mr and Mrs Diamond.

'He really does think the world of you,' Katy said as we walked into the departure lounge. 'He told me about Vietnam . . . how you saved his life.'

'Yeah I know the story, love. But remember he's saved ours now. So the slate is clean . . . squared off.'

As we sat in the plane and it rolled away from the terminal, I ran my hand lightly over Katy's hair and wondered what things would be like a year from today. Emotional crises had never been my strong point. It always seemed better to sidestep them and make a judgment later, in the cold light of day. All my training, everything I'd ever learned, dictated that no rational decisions could ever be made in anger or in love. Love, I thought, that's what it's come to. The word seemed strange but comfortable in my mind.

Slowly I reached out and took Katy's hand, and for a long moment we just looked at each other.

'It's over now isn't it,' Katy asked. 'We're free?'

I squeezed her hand and smiled. 'Yes, love, we're free.'

From the window I saw the city dwindle beneath us. My ears popped as the plane continued to climb. Sun streamed into the cabin and bathed it in golden light, then disappeared momentarily as the plane banked. A smiling hostie pushing a trolley was taking orders. I looked out the window again and already I could see real land sprawling below, vast, green, and empty.

Every journey in life begins with a single step, the one we were taking now promised a journey of peace and happiness, and a life we'd only once been able to dream about.

I said the way was far too steep,
No further could I climb.
And stayed to weep for those summit heights
I felt could not be mine.
When lo! A stranger, far beneath,

Afraid to even start.
I dried my tears and took her hand,
And murmured, 'Take fresh heart!'
And I did find in helping thus,
My own steps firmer grew.
Nor did the way seem near so steep,
Since now that we were two.